We Are the Stories We Tell

We Are the Stories We Tell

THE BEST SHORT STORIES BY NORTH AMERICAN WOMEN SINCE 1945

Edited by Wendy Martin

PANTHEON BOOKS
NEW YORK

All rights reserved under International and Pan-American
Copyright Conventions. Published in the United States by
Pantheon Books, a division of Random House, Inc., New
York, and simultaneously in Canada by Random House of
Canada Limited, Toronto.

Permissions acknowledgments can be found on page 335.

Library of Congress Cataloging-in-Publication Data
We are the stories we tell : the best short stories by North
American women since 1945 / edited by Wendy Martin.
p.   cm.

1. Short stories, American—Women authors. 2. American
fiction—20th century. 3. Short stories, Canadian—Women
authors.
4. Canadian fiction—20th century. I. Martin, Wendy, 1940–
PS647.W6W4   1990
813'.01089287—dc20   89-39587

Book Design by Jan Melchior
Manufactured in the United States of America

To my daughter,
Laurel Martin Harris

Contents

Acknowledgments

I would like to thank Cynthia Andrzejczyk, Deborah Dietrich, Susan Imbarrato, Susan Porter, and Jo Ann Springer for their support. These students at the Claremont Graduate School collaborated in every phase of this project, and I am grateful for their generous and enthusiastic participation. Barbara Yokono also helped with the research, typing, and proofreading of the manuscript, and I appreciate her help as well.

I would also like to thank Helena Franklin, my editor at Pantheon, for her literary vision and editorial acumen. Without her, this volume would not have been possible.

We Are the Stories We Tell

Introduction

From its earliest beginnings, North American culture has been multi-ethnic and multi-racial, but only recently has there been a concerted effort to acknowledge this fact. Our official literary traditions, like our official cultural histories, have for the most part emphasized our European antecedents. Nevertheless, historians and scholars are remapping the literary territory to include a much broader range of materials, from Native American chants to the journals of early explorers, from Afro-American folktales to poems by early Chinese immigrants. In the past, the literary canon has been not only white but also largely masculine. Now, works by previously ignored women writers like the eighteenth-century Jane Turell, Milcah Martha Moore, Martha Brewster, and Ann Eliza Bleecker are becoming part of that canon, alongside works by such contemporaneous black authors as Jupiter Hammon, Prince Hall, and Gustavus Vassa.

The stories in this volume are important strands in the variegated fabric of fiction from Canada and the United States, written by women of African, Hispanic, Asian, Native American, and Jewish antecedents, as well as by women of other European ancestry. Articulating female experience in all its complexity, they give voice to what has been silenced, repressed, and excluded in women's lives. Insisting on the importance of remembering our personal and collective pasts, these narratives draw on memories, folk stories, legends, and dreams. At the same time, many suggest emancipatory strategies, opening up new lives and new worlds. They explore the diverse terrain of women's experience as it is and as it could be, often depicting struggle and risk-taking as being among the essential features of that landscape.

This collection is possible because of the radical shift in our views of issues of race, class, and gender that has taken place in the past several decades. These changing social values have had a dramatic impact on our expectations about who writes and what kind of literature is published. In the past, writing women were anomalous creatures, in the New World as well as in the Old. Very few women entered what was essentially a male literary preserve. Anne Bradstreet, a Puritan poet whose family emigrated to Massachusetts, makes it abundantly clear in the preface to her volume of poems *The Tenth Muse Lately Sprung Up in America* (1650) that women writers were not welcome:

> *I am obnoxious to each carping tongue*
> *Who says my hand a needle better fits.*
> *A Poets pen all scorn I should thus wrong,*
> *For such despite they cast on female wits:*
> *If what I do prove well, it won't advance,*
> *They'l say it's stoln, or else it was by chance.*

Most writing by American women from the time of the European settlement to the end of the Revolution took private forms—spiritual meditations, diaries, letters; increasingly, this work is being included in anthologies and literary histories. In general, it was not acceptable for women to express themselves publicly, in literature or otherwise; the example of Anne Hutchinson, a seventeenth-century midwife who was branded a heretic and exiled from the Massachusetts Bay Colony for holding meetings to read and discuss the Bible, made that abundantly clear. In the late eighteenth century, women writers of fiction wrote under double jeopardy. Not only did they have to contend with gender bias, they also had to answer their many critics who thought fiction encouraged female license (and apparently licentiousness). Puritans denounced fiction as "Satan's breeding ground," and women who wrote in this genre were accused of corrupting the community.

In spite of this hostile climate, eighteenth-century novelists like Susanna Haswell Rowson, who wrote the best-selling *Charlotte Temple*, and Hannah Webster Foster, author of *The Coquette*, had a wide readership. In the nineteenth century, E.D.E.N. Southworth, Lydia Sigourney, Louisa May Alcott, and Harriet Beecher Stowe are but a few of the authors who used the form of the sentimental novel to gain acceptance for their politics as well as their craft. While the primary plots of these enormously popular novels often centered on such themes as the seduction and abandonment of imprudent women or the punishment of female assertion, the subtexts contained other messages that encouraged women to think for themselves.

At the end of the nineteenth century and the beginning of the twentieth, extraordinary women writers like Sarah Orne Jewett, Edith Wharton, Mary Wilkins Freeman, Kate Chopin, and Willa Cather emerged. As the twentieth century progressed, such authors as Ellen Glasgow, Katherine Anne Porter, Gertrude Stein, Dorothy Parker, Lillian Hellman, Meridel le Sueur, Flannery O'Connor, and Eudora Welty began to build on these earlier female traditions. Although the Anglo-American literary tradition still dominated, black women writers like Zora Neale Hurston and Nella Larsen were introducing new subject matter and styles. But it was not until after 1945—essentially the end of World War II—that women from a wide range of backgrounds successfully entered the literary marketplace. Women from every class, race, and ethnic group had worked together in the war effort, proving that they could function effectively in the masculine sphere, and this successful collective enterprise changed the way many of these women thought about themselves.

The rapid urbanization of the postwar period—58.6 percent of the population was urban in 1945 and 73.5 percent in 1970—along with more educational opportunities for both women and men also brought increasing numbers of women into public life. During the 1950s, a period of enforced domesticity for many women, concern for individual political rights was not eclipsed. Civil-rights battles fought in the South culminated in the Civil Rights Act of 1964 and were followed in the 1960s by widespread demonstrations against the Vietnam War and, in the early 1970s, against the bombing of Cambodia. This period of exceptional social and political ferment was the catalyst for an emerging awareness about issues of race and class.

The feminist movement of the 1970s and 1980s was an extension of the civil-rights movement of the 1950s and 1960s, and it had an equally dramatic effect on American social thought. Along with race and class, gender came to be viewed as a socially constructed category that often enforced hierarchical power relationships. The feminist movement had a remarkable impact on women, as did advances in birth control.

Not surprisingly, then, there have been dramatic changes in subject matter and the way it is treated in late-twentieth-century women's writing. The stories in this collection have been selected in an effort to reflect this, to do justice to the shifts in and the variety of both women's lives and their fictional themes and styles since 1945. These stories testify to diverse cultural perspectives and individual points of view, and portray different social classes and geographical areas. Their protagonists are urban and rural, rich and poor, young and old, experimental and traditional in their way of life. The stories cover all the phases of female experience, from childhood and adolescence to adulthood and old age, and depict landmark experiences such as marriage, childbirth, and death.

The writers in this collection cross boundaries, challenge limits, and explore new possibilities. They celebrate enduring values like love, affection, and desire, and they also confront controversial and often previously taboo issues like racism, rape, abortion, sexual harassment, lesbianism, and family violence. Courtship, marriage, and other erotic relationships emerge here in their full complexity, stripped of sentimental veneer. So does parenting. The stories are written from all sorts of points of view—even from a masculine one.

Ranging from oracular, legendary, and metafictional tales to colloquial ones laced with vernacular and dialect, the works included here are all a pleasure to read and all represent the highest levels of literary craft. This book's subtitle calls them "the best" of their era because they are clearly *among* the best, not because they are superior to the many fine stories which could not be included: literature by its very nature makes such pat rankings meaningless. In order to convey a sense of the evolution of styles and subject matter, the selections have been arranged in chronological order, based on the original date of publication when available; otherwise, on the date of first publication in a collection of the author's stories. Maxine Hong Kingston's "On Discovery," which was a self-contained unit in *China Men*, is here, with the author's consent, published as a separate story for the first time. Mary McCarthy's *The Blackguard* is overtly autobiographical, although all the rest are fiction. And I have included three of Sandra Cisneros's linked stories from *The House on Mango Street* because one story alone would not convey the rich and complex texture of her work.

To articulate experience, to give language to otherwise inchoate perceptions, is always empowering and liberating. To write the truth about all sorts of experience is both the fruit and the wellspring of freedom and knowledge. Mary Gordon has observed that "working-class people, among whom I grew up, are cut off from particular kinds of language that give them power." The authors of these stories have claimed the power to name, define, and judge experiences for themselves, and to help their readers to do likewise. Surely one of the most effective—and most pleasurable—ways to understand the issues facing us today is to make an empathic leap of understanding through fiction; as the stories in this collection make abundantly clear, it is only through knowing one another that we can know ourselves. Thus, these stories can teach us much about women's lives, American lives, and life in general.

The United States has been described as a melting pot, when "crucible" might be a more evocative word, suggesting the inter-action of difference and unity and an aesthetic that is change-oriented, eclectic, and multifaceted. It implies a process that is often characterized by lively confusion and creates unpredictable but ro-bust cultural alloys. The writers in this collection honor this process with all its inherent instabilities, variations, and discontinuities, along with its extraordinary vigor.

We Are the Stories We Tell

Mary McCarthy

THE
BLACKGUARD

~~~

Were he living today, my Protestant grandfather would be displeased to hear that the fate of his soul had once been the occasion of intense theological anxiety with the Ladies of the Sacred Heart. While his mortal part, all unaware, went about its eighteen holes of golf, its rubber of bridge before dinner at the club, his immortal part lay in jeopardy with us, the nuns and pupils of a strict convent school set on a wooded hill quite near a piece of worthless real estate he had bought under the impression that the city was expanding in a northerly direction. A sermon delivered at the convent by an enthusiastic

Jesuit had disclosed to us his danger. Up to this point, the disparity in religion between my grandfather and myself had given me no serious concern, but had seemed to me merely a variant expression of our disparity in age. The death of my parents, while it had drawn us together in many senses, including the legal one (for I became his ward), had at the same time left the gulf of a generation between us, and my grandfather's Protestantism presented itself as a natural part of the grand, granite scenery on the other side. But the Jesuit's sermon destroyed this ordered view in a single thunderclap of doctrine.

As the priest would have it, this honest and upright man, a great favorite with the Mother Superior, was condemned to eternal torment by the accident of having been baptized. Had he been a Mohammedan, a Jew, a pagan, or the child of civilized unbelievers, a place in Limbo would have been assured him; Cicero and Aristotle and Cyrus the Persian might have been his companions, and the harmless souls of unbaptized children might have frolicked about his feet. But if the Jesuit were right, all baptized Protestants went straight to Hell. A good life did not count in their favor. The baptismal rite, by conferring on them God's grace, made them also liable to His organizational displeasure. That is, baptism turned them Catholic whether they liked it or not, and their persistence in the Protestant ritual was a kind of asseverated apostasy. Thus my poor grandfather, sixty years behind in his Easter duty, actually reduced his prospects of salvation every time he sat down in the Presbyterian church.

The Mother Superior's sweet frown acknowledged me, an hour after the sermon, as I curtsied, all agitation, in her office doorway. Plainly, she had been expecting me. She recognized my mission; her eyes bowed to me as if I were bereaved. Touched and thrilled by her powers of divination, by her firm sense of my character, I went in. It did not occur to me that Madame MacIllvra, an able administrator, must have been resignedly ticking off the names of the Protestant pupils and parents all during the concluding parts of the morning's service. Certainly she had a faint air, when the conversation began, of depreciating the sermon: doctrinally, perhaps, correct, it had been wanting in delicacy; the fiery Jesuit, a missionary celebrity, had lived too long among the Eskimos. This disengaged attitude encouraged me to hope. Surely this lady, the highest authority I knew, could act as mediatrix between my grand-father and God; she, a plump, middle-aged Madonna, might con-trive to make God see my grandfather as a special case, outside the brutal rule of thumb laid down by the Jesuit. It was she, after all, in the convent, from whom all exemptions flowed, who created arbitrary holidays (called *congés* by the order's French tradition); it was she who permitted us to get forbidden books from the librarian and occasionally to receive letters unread by the convent censor. (As a rule, all slang expressions, violations of syntax, errors of spelling, as well as improper sentiments, were blacked out of our friends' communications, so unless we moved in a circle of young Addisons or Burkes, the letters we longed for came to us as frag-ments, from which the original text could only be conjectured.) To my twelve-year-old mind, it appeared probable that Madame MacIllvra, the Mother Superior, had the power to give my grand-father *congé*, and I threw myself on her sympathies.

It was the unjust and paradoxical nature of the Jesuit's edict that affected me. I rebelled, as Augustine and Kierkegaard had done, against the whimsicality of God. How could it be that my grand-father, the most virtuous person I knew, whose name was a byword among his friends and colleagues for a kind of rigid and fantastic probity—how could it be that this man should be lost, while I, the object of his admonition, the despair of his example—I, who yielded to every impulse, lied, boasted, betrayed—should, by virtue of regular attendance at the sacraments and the habit of easy penitence, be saved?

Madame MacIllvra's full white brow wrinkled; her childlike blue eyes clouded. Like many headmistresses, she loved a good cry, and she clasped me to her quivering and quite feminine bosom. She understood; she, too, momentarily rebelled. She and my grand-father had, as a matter of fact, established a very amiable relation, in which both took pleasure. The masculine line and firmness of his character made an esthetic appeal to her, and the billowy softness and depth of the Mother Superior struck him favorably, but, above all, it was their difference in religion that salted their conversations.

Each of them enjoyed, whenever they met in her straight, black-and-white little office, a sense of broadness, of enlightenment, of transcendent superiority to petty animosities. My grandfather would remember that he wrote a check every Christmas for two Sisters of Charity who visited his office; Madame MacIllvra would perhaps recall her graduate studies and Hume. They had long, liberal talks which had the tone of *performances*; virtuoso feats of magnanimity were achieved on both sides. Afterward, they spoke of each other in nearly identical terms: "A very fine woman," "A very fine man."

All this (and possibly the suspicion that her verdict might be repeated at home) made Madame MacIllvra's answer slow. "Perhaps God," she murmured at last, "in His infinite mercy . . ." Yet this formulation satisfied neither of us. God's infinite mercy we believed in, but its manifestations were problematical. Sacred history showed us that it was more likely to fall on the Good Thief or the Woman Taken in Adultery than on persons of daily virtue and regular habits, like my grandfather. Our Catholic thoughts journeyed and met in a glance of alarmed recognition. Madame MacIllvra's eyelids fluttered at the blank statement of my look. A moment of silence followed, during which her lips moved ever so slightly, whether in prayer or in repetition of some half-forgotten formula, I could not tell. There were, of course, she continued smoothly, other loopholes. If he had been improperly baptized . . . a careless clergyman . . . I considered this suggestion and shook my head. My grandfather was not the kind of man who, even as an infant, would have been guilty of a slovenly baptism.

It was a measure of Madame MacIllvra's intelligence, or of her knowledge of the world, that she did not, even then, when my grandfather's soul hung, as it were, pleadingly between us, suggest the obvious, the orthodox solution. It would have been ridiculous for me to try to convert my grandfather. Indeed, as it turned out later, I might have dropped him into the pit with my innocent traps (the religious books left open beside his cigar cutter, or "Grandpa, won't you take me to Mass this Sunday? I am so tired of going alone"). "Pray for him, my dear," said Madame MacIllvra, sighing, "and I will speak to Madame Barclay. The point may be open to interpretation. She may remember something in the Fathers of the Church. . . ."

A few days later, Madame MacIllvra summoned me to her office. Not only Madame Barclay, the learned prefect of studies, but the librarian and even the convent chaplain had been called in. Books had been taken down from the highest shelves; the telephone calls had been made. The Benedictine view, it seemed, differed sharply from the Dominican, but a key passage in Saint Athanasius seemed to point to my grandfather's safety. The unbeliever, according to this generous authority, was not to be damned unless he rejected the true Church with sufficient knowledge and full consent of the will. Madame MacIllvra handed me the book, and I read the passage over. Clearly, he was saved. Sufficient knowledge he had not. The Church was foreign to him; he knew it only distantly, only by repute, like the heathen Hiawatha, who had heard strange stories of missionaries, white men in black robes who bore a Cross. Flinging my arms about Madame MacIllvra, I blessed for the first time the insularity of my grandfather's character, the long-jawed, shut face it turned toward ideas and customs not its own. I resolved to dismantle at once the little altar in my bedroom at home, to leave off grace before meals, elaborate fasting, and all ostentatious practices of devotion, lest the light of my example shine upon him too powerfully and burn him with sufficient knowledge to a crisp.

Since I was a five-day boarder, this project had no time to grow stale, and the next Sunday, at home, my grandfather remarked on the change in me, which my feeling for the dramatic had made far from unobtrusive. "I hope," he said in a rather stern and ironical voice, "that you aren't using the *irreligious* atmosphere of this house as an excuse for backsliding. There will be time enough when you are older to change your beliefs if you want to." The unfairness of this rebuke delighted me. It put me solidly in the tradition of the saints and martyrs; Our Lord had known something like it, and so had Elsie Dinsmore at the piano. Nevertheless, I felt quite angry and slammed the door of my room behind me as I went in to sulk. I almost wished that my grandfather would die at once, so that God could furnish him with the explanation of my behavior—

certainly he would have to wait till the next life to get it; in this one he would only have seen in it an invasion of his personal liberties.

As though to reward me for my silence, the following Wednesday brought the happiest moment of my life. In order to understand my happiness, which might otherwise seem perverse, the reader must yield himself to the spiritual atmosphere of the convent. If he imagines that the life we led behind those walls was bare, thin, cold, austere, sectarian, he will have to revise his views; our days were a tumult of emotion. In the first place, we ate, studied, and slept in that atmosphere of intrigue, rivalry, scandal, favoritism, tyranny, and revolt that is common to all girls' boarding schools and that makes "real" life afterward seem a long and improbable armistice, a cessation of the true anguish of activity. But above the tinkling of this girlish operetta, with its clink-clink of changing friendships, its plot of smuggled letters, notes passed from desk to desk, secrets, there sounded in the Sacred Heart Convent heavier, more solemn strains, notes of a great religious drama, which was also passion and caprice, in which salvation was the issue and God's rather sultan-like and elusive favor besought, resisted, despaired of, connived for, importuned. It was the paradoxical element in Catholic doctrine that lent this drama its suspense. The Divine Despot we courted could not be bought, like a piece of merchandise, by long hours at the prie-dieu, faithful attendance at the sacraments, obedience, reverence toward one's superiors. These solicitations helped, but it might well turn out that the worst girl in the school, whose pretty, haughty face wore rouge and a calm, closed look that advertised even to us younger ones some secret knowledge of men, was in the dark of her heart another Mary of Egypt, the strumpet-saint in our midst. Such notions furnished a strange counterpoint to discipline; surely the Mother Superior never could have expelled a girl without recalling, with a shade of perplexity, the profligate youth of Saint Augustine and of Saint Ignatius of Loyola.

This dark-horse doctrine of salvation, with all its wordly wisdom and riddling charm, was deep in the idiom of the convent. The merest lay sister could have sustained with spiritual poise her end of a conversation on the purification through sin with Mr. Auden,

Herr Kafka, or *Gospodin* Dostoevski; and Madame MacIllvra, while she would have held it bad taste to bow down, like Father Zossima, before the murder in Dmitri Karamazov's heart, would certainly have had him in for a series of long, interesting talks in her office.

Like all truly intellectual women, these ladies were romantic desperados. They despised organizational heretics of the stamp of Luther and Calvin, but the great atheists and sinners were the heroes of the costume picture they taught as a subject called history. Marlowe, Baudelaire—above all, Byron—glowed like terrible stars above their literature courses. Little girls of ten were reciting "The Prisoner of Chillon" and hearing stories of Claire Clairmont, Caroline Lamb, the Segatti, and the swim across the Hellespont. Even M. Voltaire enjoyed a left-handed popularity. The nuns spoke of him with horror and admiration mingled: "A great mind, an unconquerable spirit—and what fearful use they were put to." In Rousseau, an unbuttoned, middle-class figure, they had no interest whatever.

These infatuations, shared by the pupils, were brought into line with official Catholic opinion by a variety of stratagems. The more highly educated nuns spoke of the polarity of good and evil—did not the knowledge of evil presuppose the knowledge of God, were not the satanic poets the black apostles of the Redeemer? A simple young nun, on the other hand, who played baseball and taught arithmetic to the sixth and seventh grades, used to tell her pupils that she personally was convinced that Lord Byron in his last hours must have made an act of contrition.

It was not, therefore, unusual that a line from the works of this dissipated author should have been waiting for us on the blackboard of the eighth-grade rhetoric classroom when we filed in that Wednesday morning which remains still memorable to me. "*Zoe mou, sas agapo*": the words of Byron's last assurance to the Maid of Athens stood there in Madame Barclay's French-looking script, speaking to us of the transiency of the passions. To me, as it happened, it spoke a twice-told tale. I had read the poem before, alone in my grandfather's library; indeed, I knew it by heart, and I rather resented the infringement on my private rights in it, the democratization of the poem which was about to take place. Soon, Madame Barclay's pointer was rapping from word to word: "My . . . life . . . I . . . love . . . you," she sharply translated. When the pointer started back for its second trip, I retreated into hauteur and began drawing a picture of the girl who sat next to me. Suddenly the pointer cracked across my writing tablet.

"You're just like Lord Byron, brilliant but unsound."

I heard the pointer being set down and the drawing being torn crisply twice across, but I could not look up. Trembling with excitement and a kind of holy terror, I sank back in my seat. Up to this moment, I had believed shallowly, with Napoleon, that the day of one's First Communion was the happiest day of one's life; now, in the glory of this sentence, I felt that petit-bourgeois notion give a sudden movement inside me and quite distinctly die. Throughout the rest of the class, I sat motionless, simulating meekness, while my classmates shot me glances of wonder, awe, and congratulation, as though I had suddenly been struck by a remarkable disease, or been canonized, or transfigured. Madame Barclay's pronouncement, which I kept repeating to myself under my breath, had for us girls a kind of final and majestic certainty. She was the severest and most taciturn of our teachers. Her dark brows met in the middle; her skin was a pure olive; her upper lip had a faint mustache; she was the iron and authority of the convent. She tolerated no infractions, overlooked nothing, was utterly and obdurately fair, had no favorites; but her rather pointed face had the marks of suffering, as though her famous discipline had scored it as harshly as one of our papers. She had a bitter and sarcastic wit, and had studied at the Sorbonne. Before this day, I had once or twice dared to say to myself that Madame Barclay liked me. Her dark, quite handsome eyes would sometimes move in my direction as her lips prepared an aphorism or a satiric gibe. Yet hardly had I estimated the look, weighed and measured it to store it away in my memory book of requited affections, when a stinging penalty would recall me from my dream and I could no longer be sure. Now, however, there was no doubt left. The reproof was a declaration of love as plain as the sentence on the blackboard, which shimmered slightly before my eyes. My happiness was a confused exaltation in which the fact that I was Lord Byron and the fact that

I was loved by Madame Barclay, the most puzzling nun in the convent, blended in a Don Juanesque triumph.

In the refectory that noon, publicity was not wanting to enrich this moment. Insatiable, I could hardly wait for the weekend, to take Madame Barclay's words as though they had been a prize. With the generosity of affluence, I spoke to myself of sharing this happiness, this honor, with my grandfather. Surely, *this* would make up to him for any worry or difficulty I had caused him. At the same time, it would have the practical effect of explaining me a little to him. Phrases about my prototype rang in my head: "that unfortunate genius," "that turbulent soul," "that gifted and erratic nature."

My grandfather turned dark red when he heard the news. His forehead grew knotty with veins; he swore; he looked strange and young; it was the first time I had ever seen him angry. Argument and explanation were useless. For my grandfather, history had interposed no distance between Lord Byron and himself. Though the incestuous poet had died forty years before my grandfather was born, the romantic perspective was lacking. That insularity of my grandfather's that kept him intimate with morals and denied the reality of the exotic made him judge the poet as he judged himself or one of his neighbors—that is, on the merit of his actions. He was on the telephone at once, asking the Mother Superior in a thundering, courtroom voice what right one of her sisters had to associate his innocent granddaughter with that degenerate blackguard, Byron. On Monday, Madame Barclay, with tight-drawn lips, told her class that she had a correction to make: Mary McCarthy did not resemble Lord Byron in any particular; she was neither brilliant, loose-living, nor unsound.

The interviews between my grandfather and Madame MacIllvra came to an end. To that remarkable marriage of minds the impediment had at last been discovered. But from this time on, Madame Barclay's marks of favor to me grew steadily more distinct, while the look of suffering tightened on her face, till some said she had cancer (a theory supported by the yellowness of her skin) and some said she was being poisoned by an antipathy to the Mother Superior.

Eudora Welty

No Place for You, My Love

∿∿

They were strangers to each other, both fairly well strangers to the place, now seated side by side at luncheon—a party combined in a free-and-easy way when the friends he and she were with recognized each other across Galatoire's. The time was a Sunday in summer—those hours of afternoon that seem Time Out in New Orleans.

The moment he saw her little blunt, fair face, he thought that here was a woman who was having an affair. It was one of those odd meetings when such an impact is felt that it has to be translated at once into some sort of speculation.

With a married man, most likely, he supposed, slipping quickly into a groove—he was long married—and feeling more conventional, then, in his curiosity as she sat there, leaning her cheek on her hand, looking no further before her than the flowers on the table, and wearing that hat.

He did not like her hat, any more than he liked tropical flowers. It was the wrong hat for her, thought this Eastern businessman who had no interest whatever in women's clothes and no eye for them; he thought the unaccustomed thing crossly.

It must stick out all over me, she thought, so people think they can love me or hate me just by looking at me. How did it leave us—the old, safe, slow way people used to know of learning how one another feels, and the privilege that went with it of shying away if it seemed best? People in love like me, I suppose, give away the short cuts to everybody's secrets.

Something, though, he decided, had been settled about her predicament—for the time being, anyway; the parties to it were all still alive, no doubt. Nevertheless, her predicament was the only one he felt so sure of here, like the only recognizable shadow in that restaurant, where mirrors and fans were busy agitating the light, as the very local talk drawled across and agitated the peace. The shadow lay between her fingers, between her little square hand and her cheek, like something always best carried about the person. Then suddenly, as she took her hand down, the secret fact was still there—it lighted her. It was a bold and full light, shot up under the brim of that hat, as close to them all as the flowers in the center of the table.

Did he dream of making her disloyal to that hopelessness that he saw very well she'd been cultivating down here? He knew very well that he did not. What they amounted to was two Northerners keeping each other company. She glanced up at the big gold clock on the wall and smiled. He didn't smile back. She had that naïve face that he associated, for no good reason, with the Middle West—because it said "Show me," perhaps. It was a serious, now-watch-out-everybody face, which orphaned her entirely in the company of these Southerners. He guessed her age, as he could not guess theirs: thirty-two. He himself was further along.

Of all human moods, deliberate imperviousness may be the most quickly communicated—it may be the most successful, most fatal signal of all. And two people can indulge in imperviousness as well as in anything else. "You're not very hungry either," he said.

The blades of fan shadows came down over their two heads, as he saw inadvertently in the mirror, with himself smiling at her now like a villain. His remark sounded dominant and rude enough for everybody present to listen back a moment; it even sounded like an answer to a question she might have just asked him. The other women glanced at him. The Southern look—Southern mask—of life-is-a-dream irony, which could turn to pure challenge at the drop of a hat, he could wish well away. He liked naïveté better.

"I find the heat down here depressing," she said, with the heart of Ohio in her voice.

"Well—I'm in somewhat of a temper about it, too," he said.

They looked with grateful dignity at each other.

"I have a car here, just down the street," he said to her as the luncheon party was rising to leave, all the others wanting to get back to their houses and sleep. "If it's all right with—Have you ever driven down south of here?"

Out on Bourbon Street, in the bath of July, she asked at his shoulder, "South of New Orleans? I didn't know there was any south to *here*. Does it just go on and on?" She laughed, and adjusted the exasperating hat to her head in a different way. It was more than frivolous, it was conspicuous, with some sort of glitter or flitter tied in a band around the straw and hanging down.

"That's what I'm going to show you."

"Oh—you've been there?"

"No!"

His voice rang out over the uneven, narrow sidewalk and dropped back from the walls. The flaked-off, colored houses were spotted like the hides of beasts faded and shy, and were hot as a wall of growth that seemed to breathe flower-like down onto them as they walked to the car parked there.

"It's just that it couldn't be any worse—we'll see."

"All right, then," she said. "We will."

So, their actions reduced to amiability, they settled into the car—a faded-red Ford convertible with a rather threadbare canvas top, which had been standing in the sun for all those lunch hours.

"It's rented," he explained. "I asked to have the top put down, and was told I'd lost my mind."

"It's out of this world. *Degrading* heat," she said and added, "Doesn't matter."

The stranger in New Orleans always sets out to leave it as though following the clue in a maze. They were threading through the narrow and one-way streets, past the pale-violet bloom of tired squares, the brown steeples and statues, the balcony with the live and probably famous black monkey dipping along the railing as over a ballroom floor, past the grillework and the lattice-work to all the iron swans painted flesh color on the front steps of bungalows outlying.

Driving, he spread his new map and put his finger down on it. At the intersection marked Arabi, where their road led out of the tangle and he took it, a small Negro seated beneath a black umbrella astride a box chalked "Shou Shine" lifted his pink-and-black hand and waved them languidly good-by. She didn't miss it, and waved back.

Below New Orleans there was a raging of insects from both sides of the concrete highway, not quite together, like the playing of separated marching bands. The river and the levee were still on her side, waste and jungle and some occasional settlements on his— poor houses. Families bigger than housefuls thronged the yards. His nodding, driving head would veer from side to side, looking and almost lowering. As time passed and the distance from New Orleans grew, girls ever darker and younger were disposing themselves over the porches and the porch steps, with jet-black hair pulled high, and ragged palm-leaf fans rising and falling like rafts of butterflies. The children running forth were nearly always naked ones.

She watched the road. Crayfish constantly crossed in front of the wheels, looking grim and bonneted, in a great hurry.

"How the Old Woman Got Home," she murmured to herself.

He pointed, as it flew by, at a saucepan full of cut zinnias which stood waiting on the open lid of a mailbox at the roadside, with a little note tied onto the handle.

They rode mostly in silence. The sun bore down. They met

fishermen and other men bent on some local pursuits, some in sulphur-colored pants, walking and riding; met wagons, trucks, boats in trucks, autos, boats on top of autos—all coming to meet them, as though something of high moment were doing back where the car came from, and he and she were determined to miss it. There was nearly always a man lying with his shoes off in the bed of any truck otherwise empty—with the raw, red look of a man sleeping in the daytime, being jolted about as he slept. Then there was a sort of dead man's land, where nobody came. He loosened his collar and tie. By rushing through the heat at high speed, they brought themselves the effect of fans turned onto their cheeks. Clearing alternated with jungle and canebrake like something tried, tried again. Little shell roads led off on both sides; now and then a road of planks led into the yellow-green.

"Like a dance floor in there." She pointed.

He informed her, "In there's your oil, I think."

There were thousands, millions of mosquitoes and gnats—a universe of them, and on the increase.

A family of eight or nine people on foot strung along the road in the same direction the car was going, beating themselves with the wild palmettos. Heels, shoulders, knees, breasts, back of the heads, elbows, hands, were touched in turn—like some game, each playing it with himself.

He struck himself on the forehead, and increased their speed. (His wife would not be at her most charitable if he came bringing malaria home to the family.)

More and more crayfish and other shell creatures littered their path, scuttling or dragging. These little samples, little jokes of creation, persisted and sometimes perished, the more of them the deeper down the road went. Terrapins and turtles came up steadily over the horizons of the ditches.

Back there in the margins were worse—crawling hides you could not penetrate with bullets or quite believe, grins that had come down from the primeval mud.

"Wake up." Her Northern nudge was very timely on his arm. They had veered toward the side of the road. Still driving fast, he spread his map.

Like a misplaced sunrise, the light of the river flowed up; they were mounting the levee on a little shell road.

"Shall we cross here?" he asked politely.

He might have been keeping track over years and miles of how long they could keep that tiny ferry waiting. Now skidding down the levee's flank, they were the last-minute car, the last possible car that could squeeze on. Under the sparse shade of one willow tree, the small, amateurish-looking boat slapped the water, as, expertly, he wedged on board.

"Tell him we put him on hub cap!" shouted one of the numerous olive-skinned, dark-eyed young boys standing dressed up in bright shirts at the railing, hugging each other with delight that that last straw was on board. Another boy drew his affectionate initials in the dust of the door on her side.

She opened the door and stepped out, and, after only a moment's standing at bay, started up a little iron stairway. She appeared above the car, on the tiny bridge beneath the captain's window and the whistle.

From there, while the boat still delayed in what seemed a trance— as if it were too full to attempt the start—she could see the panlike deck below, separated by its rusty rim from the tilting, polished water.

The passengers walking and jostling about there appeared oddly amateurish, too—amateur travelers. They were having such a good time. They all knew each other. Beer was being passed around in cans, bets were being loudly settled and new bets made, about local and special subjects on which they all doted. One red-haired man in a burst of wildness even tried to give away his truckload of shrimp to a man on the other side of the boat—nearly all the trucks were full of shrimp—causing taunts and then protests of "They good! They good!" from the giver. The young boys leaned on each other thinking of what next, rolling their eyes absently.

A radio pricked the air behind her. Looking like a great tomcat just above her head, the captain was digesting the news of a fine stolen automobile.

At last a tremendous explosion burst—the whistle. Everything

shuddered in outline from the sound, everybody said something—
everybody else.

They started with no perceptible motion, but her hat blew off.
It went spiraling to the deck below, where he, thank heaven, sprang
out of the car and picked it up. Everybody looked frankly up at
her now, holding her hands to her head.

The little willow tree receded as its shade was taken away. The
heat was like something falling on her head. She held the hot rail
before her. It was like riding a stove. Her shoulders dropping, her
hair flying, her skirt buffeted by the sudden strong wind, she stood
there, thinking they all must see that with her entire self all she did
was wait. Her set hands, with the bag that hung from her wrist
and rocked back and forth—all three seemed objects bleaching
there, belonging to no one; she could not feel a thing in the skin
of her face; perhaps she was crying, and not knowing it. She could
look down and see him just below her, his black shadow, her hat,
and his black hair. His hair in the wind looked unreasonably long
and rippling. Little did he know that from here it had a red un-
dergleam like an animal's. When she looked up and outward, a
vortex of light drove through and over the brown waves like a star
in the water.

He did after all bring the retrieved hat up the stairs to her. She
took it back—useless—and held it to her skirt. What they were
saying below was more polite than their searchlight faces.

"Where you think he come from, that man?"

"I bet he come from Lafitte."

"Lafitte? What you bet, eh?"—all crouched in the shade of trucks,
squatting and laughing.

Now his shadow fell partly across her; the boat had jolted into
some other strand of current. Her shaded arm and shaded hand felt
pulled out from the blaze of light and water, and she hoped humbly
for more shade for her head. It had seemed so natural to climb up
and stand in the sun.

The boys had a surprise—an alligator on board. One of them
pulled it by a chain around the deck, between the cars and trucks,
like a toy—a hide that could walk. He thought, Well they had to
catch one sometime. It's Sunday afternoon. So they have him on

board now, riding him across the Mississippi River. . . . The play-fulness of it beset everybody on the ferry. The hoarseness of the boat whistle, commenting briefly, seemed part of the general appreciation.

"Who want to rassle him? Who want to, eh?" two boys cried, looking up. A boy with shrimp-colored arms capered from side to side, pretending to have been bitten.

What was there so hilarious about jaws that could bite? And what danger was there once in this repulsiveness—so that the last worldly evidence of some old heroic horror of the dragon had to be paraded in capture before the eyes of country clowns?

He noticed that she looked at the alligator without flinching at all. Her distance was set—the number of feet and inches between herself and it mattered to her.

Perhaps her measuring coolness was to him what his bodily shade was to her, while they stood pat up there riding the river, which felt like the sea and looked like the earth under them—full of the red-brown earth, charged with it. Ahead of the boat it was like an exposed vein of ore. The river seemed to swell in the vast middle with the curve of the earth. The sun rolled under them. As if in memory of the size of things, uprooted trees were drawn across their path, sawing at the air and tumbling one over the other.

When they reached the other side, they felt that they had been racing around an arena in their chariot, among lions. The whistle took and shook the stairs as they went down. The young boys, looking taller, had taken out colored combs and were combing their wet hair back in solemn pompadour above their radiant fore-heads. They had been bathing in the river themselves not long before.

The cars and trucks, then the foot passengers and the alligator, waddling like a child to school, all disembarked and wound up the weed-sprung levee.

Both respectable and merciful, their hides, she thought, forcing herself to dwell on the alligator as she looked back. Deliver us all from the naked in heart. (As she had been told.)

When they regained their paved road, he heard her give a little sigh and saw her turn her straw-colored head to look back once more. Now that she rode with her hat in her lap, her earrings were conspicuous too. A little metal ball set with small pale stones danced beside each square, faintly downy cheek.

Had she felt a wish for someone else to be riding with them? He thought it was more likely that she would wish for her husband if she had one (his wife's voice) than for the lover in whom he believed. Whatever people liked to think, situations (if not scenes) were usually three-way—there was somebody else always. The one who didn't—couldn't—understand the two made the formidable third.

He glanced down at the map flapping on the seat between them, up at his wristwatch, out at the road. Out there was the incredible brightness of four o'clock.

On this side of the river, the road ran beneath the brow of the levee and followed it. Here was a heat that ran deeper and brighter and more intense than all the rest—its nerve. The road grew one with the heat as it was one with the unseen river. Dead snakes stretched across the concrete like markers—inlaid mosaic bands, dry as feathers, which their tires licked at intervals that began to seem clocklike.

No, the heat faced them—it was ahead. They could see it waving at them, shaken in the air above the white of the road, always at a certain distance ahead, shimmering finely as a cloth, with running edges of green and gold, fire and azure.

"It's never anything like this in Syracuse," he said.

"Or in Toledo, either," she replied with dry lips.

They were driving through greater waste down here, through fewer and even more insignificant towns. There was water under everything. Even where a screen of jungle had been left to stand, splashes could be heard from under the trees. In the vast open, sometimes boats moved inch by inch through what appeared endless meadows of rubbery flowers.

Her eyes overcome with brightness and size, she felt a panic rise, as sudden as nausea. Just how far below questions and answers, concealment and revelation, they were running now—that was still a new question, with a power of its own, waiting. How dear—how costly—could this ride be?

"It looks to me like your road can't go much further," she remarked cheerfully. "Just over there, it's all water."

"Time out," he said, and with that he turned the car into a sudden road of white shells that rushed at them narrowly out of the left.

They bolted over a cattle guard, where some rayed and crested purple flowers burst out of the vines in the ditch, and rolled onto a long, narrow, green, mowed clearing: a churchyard. A paved track ran between two short rows of raised tombs, all neatly whitewashed and now brilliant as faces against the vast flushed sky.

The track was the width of the car with a few inches to spare. He passed between the tombs slowly but in the manner of a feat. Names took their places on the walls slowly at a level with the eye, names as near as the eyes of a person stopping in conversation, and as far away in origin, and in all their music and dead longing, as Spain. At intervals were set packed bouquets of zinnias, oleanders, and some kind of purple flowers, all quite fresh, in fruit jars, like nice welcomes on bureaus.

They moved on into an open plot beyond, of violent-green grass, spread before the green-and-white frame church with worked flower beds around it, flowerless poinsettias growing up to the windowsills. Beyond was a house, and left on the doorstep of the house a fresh-caught catfish the size of a baby—a fish wearing whiskers and bleeding. On a clothesline in the yard, a priest's black gown on a hanger hung airing, swaying at man's height, in a vague, trainlike, ladylike sweep along an evening breath that might otherwise have seemed imaginary from the unseen, felt river.

With the motor cut off, with the raging of the insects about them, they sat looking out at the green and white and black and red and pink as they leaned against the sides of the car.

"What is your wife like?" she asked. His right hand came up and spread—iron, wooden, manicured. She lifted her eyes to his face. He looked at her like that hand.

Then he lit a cigarette, and the portrait, and the right-hand testimonial it made, were blown away. She smiled, herself as unaffected as by some stage performance; and he was annoyed in the cemetery. They did not risk going on to her husband—if she had one.

Under the supporting posts of the priest's house, where a boat was, solid ground ended and palmettos and water hyacinths could not wait to begin; suddenly the rays of the sun, from behind the car, reached that lowness and struck the flowers. The priest came out onto the porch in his underwear, stared at the car a moment as if he wondered what time it was, then collected his robe off the line and his fish off the doorstep and returned inside. Vespers was next, for him.

After backing out between the tombs he drove on still south, in the sunset. They caught up with an old man walking in a sprightly way in their direction, all by himself, wearing a clean bright shirt printed with a pair of palm trees fanning green over his chest. It might better be a big colored woman's shirt, but she didn't have it. He flagged the car with gestures like hoops.

"You're coming to the end of the road," the old man told them. He pointed ahead, tipped his hat to the lady, and pointed again. "End of the road." They didn't understand that he meant, "Take me."

They drove on. "If we do go any further, it'll have to be by water—is that it?" he asked her, hesitating at this odd point.

"You know better than I do," she replied politely.

The road had for some time ceased to be paved; it was made of shells. It was leading into a small, sparse settlement like the others a few miles back, but with even more of the camp about it. On the lip of the clearing, directly before a green willow blaze with the sunset gone behind it, the row of houses and shacks faced out on broad, colored, moving water that stretched to reach the horizon and looked like an arm of the sea. The houses on their shaggy posts, patchily built, some with plank runways instead of steps, were flimsy and alike, and not much bigger than the boats tied up at the landing.

"Venice," she heard him announce, and he dropped the crackling map in her lap.

They coasted down the brief remainder. The end of the road— she could not remember ever seeing a road simply end—was a spoon shape, with a tree stump in the bowl to turn around by.

Around it, he stopped the car, and they stepped out, feeling put down in the midst of a sudden vast pause or subduement that was like a yawn. They made their way on foot toward the water, where at an idle-looking landing men in twos and threes stood with their backs to them.

The nearness of darkness, the still uncut trees, bright water partly under a sheet of flowers, shacks, silence, dark shapes of boats tied up, then the first sounds of people just on the other side of thin walls—all this reached them. Mounds of shells like day-old snow, pink-tinted, lay around a central shack with a beer sign on it. An old man up on the porch there sat holding an open newspaper, with a fat white goose sitting opposite him on the floor. Below, in the now shadowless and sunless open, another old man, with a colored pencil bright under his hat brim, was late mending a sail.

When she looked clear around, thinking they had a fire burning somewhere now, out of the heat had risen the full moon. Just beyond the trees, enormous, tangerine-colored, it was going solidly up. Other lights just striking into view, looking farther distant, showed moss shapes hanging, or slipped and broke matchlike on the water that so encroached upon the rim of ground they were standing on.

There was a touch at her arm—his, accidental.

"We're at the jumping-off place," he said.

She laughed, having thought his hand was a bat, while her eyes rushed downward toward a great pale drift of water hyacinths—still partly open, flushed and yet moonlit, level with her feet—through which paths of water for the boats had been hacked. She drew her hands up to her face under the brim of her hat; her own cheeks felt like the hyacinths to her, all her skin still full of too much light and sky, exposed. The harsh vesper bell was ringing.

"I believe there must be something wrong with me, that I came on this excursion to begin with," she said, as if he had already said this and she were merely in hopeful, willing, maddening agreement with him.

He took hold of her arm, and said, "Oh, come on—I see we can get something to drink here, at least."

But there was a beating, muffled sound from over the darkening water. One more boat was coming in, making its way through the tenacious, tough, dark flower traps, by the shaken light of what first appeared to be torches. He and she waited for the boat, as if on each other's patience. As if borne in on a mist of twilight or a breath, a horde of mosquitoes and gnats came singing and striking at them first. The boat bumped, men laughed. Somebody was offering somebody else some shrimp.

Then he might have cocked his dark city head down at her; she did not look up at him, only turned when he did. Now the shell mounds, like the shacks and trees, were solid purple. Lights had appeared in the not-quite-true window squares. A narrow neon sign, the lone sign, had come out in bright blush on the beer shack's roof: "Baba's Place." A light was on on the porch.

The barnlike interior was brightly lit and unpainted, looking not quite finished, with a partition dividing this room from what lay behind. One of the four cardplayers at a table in the middle of the floor was the newspaper reader; the paper was in his pants pocket. Midway along the partition was a bar, in the form of a pass-through to the other room, with a varnished, second-hand fretwork overhang. They crossed the floor and sat, alone there, on wooden stools. An eruption of humorous signs, newspaper cutouts and cartoons, razor-blade cards, and personal messages of significance to the owner or his friends decorated the overhang, framing where Baba should have been but wasn't.

Through there came a smell of garlic and cloves and red pepper, a blast of hot cloud escaped from a cauldron they could see now on a stove at the back of the other room. A massive back, presumably female, with a twist of gray hair on top, stood with a ladle akimbo. A young man joined her and with his fingers stole something out of the pot and ate it. At Baba's they were boiling shrimp.

When he got ready to wait on them, Baba strolled out to the counter, young, black-headed, and in very good humor.

"Coldest beer you've got. And food—What will you have?"

"Nothing for me, thank you," she said. "I'm not sure I could eat, after all."

"Well, I could," he said, shoving his jaw out. Baba smiled. "I want a good solid ham sandwich."

"I could have asked him for some water," she said, after he had gone.

While they sat waiting, it seemed very quiet. The bubbling of the shrimp, the distant laughing of Baba, and the slap of cards, like the beating of moths on the screens, seemed to come in fits and starts. The steady breathing they heard came from a big rough dog asleep in the corner. But it was bright. Electric lights were strung riotously over the room from a kind of spider web of old wires in the rafters. One of the written messages tacked before them read, "Joe! At the boyy!!" It looked very yellow, older than Baba's Place. Outside, the world was pure dark.

Two little boys, almost alike, almost the same size, and just cleaned up, dived into the room with a double bang of the screen door, and circled around the card game. They ran their hands into the men's pockets.

"Nickel for some pop!"

"Nickel for some pop!"

"Go 'way and let me play, you!"

They circled around and shrieked at the dog, ran under the lid of the counter and raced through the kitchen and back, and hung over the stools at the bar. One child had a live lizard on his shirt, clinging like a breast pin—like lapis lazuli.

Bringing in a strong odor of geranium talcum, some men had come in now—all in bright shirts. They drew near the counter, or stood and watched the game.

When Baba came out bringing the beer and sandwich, "Could I have some water?" she greeted him.

Baba laughed at everybody. She decided the woman back there must be Baba's mother.

Beside her, he was drinking his beer and eating his sandwich— ham, cheese, tomato, pickle, and mustard. Before he finished, one of the men who had come in beckoned from across the room. It was the old man in the palm-tree shirt.

She lifted her head to watch him leave her, and was looked at, from all over the room. As a minute passed, no cards were laid down. In a far-off way, like accepting the light from Arcturus, she accepted it that she was more beautiful or perhaps more fragile than the women they saw every day of their lives. It was just this thought coming into a woman's face, and at this hour, that seemed familiar to them.

Baba was smiling. He had set an opened, frosted brown bottle before her on the counter, and a thick sandwich, and stood looking at her. Baba made her eat some supper, for what she was.

"What the old fellow wanted," said he when he came back at last, "was to have a friend of his apologize. Seems church is just out. Seems the friend made a remark coming in just now. His pals told him there was a lady present."

"I see you bought him a beer," she said.

"Well, the old man looked like he wanted *something.*"

All at once the juke box interrupted from back in the corner, with the same old song as anywhere. The half-dozen slot machines along the wall were suddenly all run to like Maypoles, and thrown into action—taken over by further battalions of little boys.

There were three little boys to each slot machine. The local custom appeared to be that one pulled the lever for the friend he was holding up to put the nickel in, while the third covered the pictures with the flat of his hand as they fell into place, so as to surprise them all if anything happened.

The dog lay sleeping on in front of the raging juke box, his ribs working fast as a concertina's. At the side of the room a man with a cap on his white thatch was trying his best to open a side screen door, but it was stuck fast. It was he who had come in with the remark considered ribald; now he was trying to get out the other way. Moths as thick as ingots were trying to get in. The cardplayers broke into shouts of derision, then joy, then tired derision among themselves; they might have been here all afternoon—they were the only ones not cleaned up and shaved. The original pair of little boys ran in once more, with the hyphenated bang. They got nickels this time, then were brushed away from the table like mosquitoes, and they rushed under the counter and on to the cauldron behind, clinging to Baba's mother there. The evening was at the threshold.

They were quite unnoticed now. He was eating another sandwich, and she, having finished part of hers, was fanning her face with her hat. Baba had lifted the flap of the counter and come out into the room. Behind his head there was a sign lettered in orange crayon: "Shrimp Dance Sun. PM." That was tonight, still to be.

And suddenly she made a move to slide down from her stool, maybe wishing to walk out into that nowhere down the front steps to be cool a moment. But he had hold of her hand. He got down from his stool, and, patiently, reversing her hand in his own—just as she had had the look of being about to give up, faint—began moving her, leading her. They were dancing.

"I get to thinking this is what we get—what you and I deserve," she whispered, looking past his shoulder into the room. "And all the time, it's real. It's a real place—away off down here. . . ."

They danced gratefully, formally, to some song carried on in what must be the local patois, while no one paid any attention as long as they were together, and the children poured the family nickels steadily into the slot machines, walloping the handles down with regular crashes and troubling nobody with winning.

She said rapidly, as they began moving together too well, "One of those clippings was an account of a shooting right here. I guess they're proud of it. And that awful knife Baba was carrying . . . I wonder what he called me," she whispered in his ear.

"Who?"

"The one who apologized to you."

If they had ever been going to overstep themselves, it would be now as he held her closer and turned her, when she became aware that he could not help but see the bruise at her temple. It would not be six inches from his eyes. She felt it come out like an evil star. (Let it pay him back, then, for the hand he had stuck in her face when she'd tried once to be sympathetic, when she'd asked about his wife.) They danced on still as the record changed, after standing wordless and motionless, linked together in the middle of the room, for the moment between.

Then, they were like a matched team—like professional, Spanish dancers wearing masks—while the slow piece was playing.

Surely even those immune from the world, for the time being, need the touch of one another, or all is lost. Their arms encircling each other, their bodies circling the odorous, just-nailed-down floor, they were, at last, imperviousness in motion. They had found

it, and had almost missed it: they had had to dance. They were
what their separate hearts desired that day, for themselves and each
other.

They were so good together that once she looked up and half
smiled. "For whose benefit did we have to show off?"

Like people in love, they had a superstition about themselves
almost as soon as they came out on the floor, and dared not think
the words "happy" or "unhappy," which might strike them, one
or the other, like lightning.

In the thickening heat they danced on while Baba himself sang
with the mosquito-voiced singer in the chorus of *"Moi pas l'aimez
ça,"* enumerating the *ça's* with a hot shrimp between his fingers.
He was counting over the platters the old woman now set out on
the counter, each heaped with shrimp in their shells boiled to iri-
descence, like mounds of honeysuckle flowers.

The goose wandered in from the back room under the lid of the
counter and hitched itself around the floor among the table legs
and people's legs, never seeing that it was neatly avoided by two
dancers—who nevertheless vaguely thought of this goose as
learned, having earlier heard an old man read to it. The children
called it Mimi, and lured it away. The old thatched man was again
drunkenly trying to get out by the stuck side door; now he gave
it a kick, but was prevailed on to remain. The sleeping dog shuddered and snored.

It was left up to the dancers to provide nickels for the juke box;
Baba kept a drawerful for every use. They had grown fond of all
the selections by now. This was the music you heard out of the
distance at night—out of the roadside taverns you fled past, around
the late corners in cities half asleep, drifting up from the carnival
over the hill, with one odd little strain always managing to repeat
itself. This seemed a homey place.

Bathed in sweat, and feeling the false coolness that brings, they
stood finally on the porch in the lapping night air for a moment
before leaving. The first arrivals of the girls were coming up the
steps under the porch light—all flowered fronts, their black pom-
padours giving out breathlike feelers from sheer abundance. Where
they'd resprinkled it since church, the talcum shone like mica on

their downy arms. Smelling solidly of geranium, they filed across the porch with short steps and fingers joined, just timed to turn their smiles loose inside the room. He held the door open for them.

"Ready to go?" he asked her.

Going back, the ride was wordless, quiet except for the motor and the insects driving themselves against the car. The windshield was soon blinded. The headlights pulled in two other spinning storms, cones of flying things that, it seemed, might ignite at the last minute. He stopped the car and got out to clean the windshield thoroughly with his brisk, angry motions of driving. Dust lay thick and cratered on the roadside scrub. Under the now ash-white moon, the world traveled through very faint stars—very many slow stars, very high, very low.

It was a strange land, amphibious—and whether water-covered or grown with jungle or robbed entirely of water and trees, as now, it had the same loneliness. He regarded the great sweep—like steppes, like moors, like deserts (all of which were imaginary to him); but more than it was like any likeness, it was South. The vast, thin, wide-thrown, pale, unfocused star-sky, with its veils of lightning adrift, hung over this land as it hung over the open sea. Standing out in the night alone, he was struck as powerfully with recognition of the extremity of this place as if all other bearings had vanished—as if snow had suddenly started to fall.

He climbed back inside and drove. When he moved to slap furiously at his shirtsleeves, she shivered in the hot, licking night wind that their speed was making. Once the car lights picked out two people—a Negro couple, sitting on two facing chairs in the yard outside their lonely cabin—half undressed, each battling for self against the hot night, with long white rags in endless, scarflike motions.

In peopleless open places there were lakes of dust, smudge fires burning at their hearts. Cows stood in untended rings around them, motionless in the heat, in the night—their horns standing up sharp against that glow.

At length, he stopped the car again, and this time he put his arm under her shoulder and kissed her—not knowing ever whether gently or harshly. It was the loss of that distinction that told him this was now. Then their faces touched unkissing, unmoving, dark, for a length of time. The heat came inside the car and wrapped them still, and the mosquitoes had begun to coat their arms and even their eyelids.

Later, crossing a large open distance, he saw at the same time two fires. He had the feeling that they had been riding for a long time across a face—great, wide, and upturned. In its eyes and open mouth were those fires they had had glimpses of, where the cattle had drawn together: a face, a head, far down here in the South—south of South, below it. A whole giant body sprawled downward then, on and on, always, constant as a constellation or an angel. Flaming and perhaps falling, he thought.

She appeared to be sound asleep, lying back flat as a child, with her hat in her lap. He drove on with her profile beside his, behind his, for he bent forward to drive faster. The earrings she wore twinkled with their rushing motion in an almost regular beat. They might have spoken like tongues. He looked straight before him and drove on, at a speed that, for the rented, overheated, not at all new Ford car, was demoniac.

It seemed often now that a barnlike shape flashed by, roof and all outlined in lonely neon—a movie house at a crossroads. The long white flat road itself, since they had followed it to the end and turned around to come back, seemed able, this far up, to pull them home.

A thing is incredible, if ever, only after it is told—returned to the world it came out of. For their different reasons, he thought, neither of them would tell this (unless something was dragged out of them): that, strangers, they had ridden down into a strange land together and were getting safely back—by a slight margin, perhaps, but margin enough. Over the levee wall now, like an aurora borealis, the sky of New Orleans, across the river, was flickering gently. This time they crossed by bridge, high above everything, merging into a long light-stream of cars turned cityward.

For a time afterward he was lost in the streets, turning almost at random with the noisy traffic until he found his bearings. When he stopped the car at the next sign and leaned forward frowning to make it out, she sat up straight on her side. It was Arabi. He turned the car right around.

"We're all right now," he muttered, allowing himself a cigarette.

Something that must have been with them all along suddenly, then, was not. In a moment, tall as panic, it rose, cried like a human, and dropped back.

"I never got my water," she said.

She gave him the name of her hotel, he drove her there, and he said good night on the sidewalk. They shook hands.

"Forgive . . ." For, just in time, he saw she expected it of him.

And that was just what she did, forgive him. Indeed, had she waked in time from a deep sleep, she would have told him her story. She disappeared through the revolving door, with a gesture of smoothing her hair, and he thought a figure in the lobby strolled to meet her. He got back in the car and sat there.

He was not leaving for Syracuse until early in the morning. At length, he recalled the reason; his wife had recommended that he stay where he was this extra day so that she could entertain some old, unmarried college friends without him underfoot.

As he started up the car, he recognized in the smell of exhausted, body-warm air in the streets, in which the flow of drink was an inextricable part, the signal that the New Orleans evening was just beginning. In Dickie Grogan's, as he passed, the well-known Josefina at her organ was charging up and down with "*Clair de Lune.*" As he drove the little Ford safely to its garage, he remembered for the first time in years when he was young and brash, a student in New York, and the shriek and horror and unholy smother of the subway had its original meaning for him as the lilt and expectation of love.

Flannery O'Connor

A VIEW OF
THE WOODS

∽≈∾

The week before, Mary Fortune and the old man had spent every morning watching the machine that lifted out dirt and threw it in a pile. The construction was going on by the new lakeside on one of the lots that the old man had sold to somebody who was going to put up a fishing club. He and Mary Fortune drove down there every morning about ten o'clock and he parked his car, a battered mulberry-colored Cadillac, on the embankment that overlooked the spot where the work was going on. The red corrugated lake eased up to within fifty feet of the construction and was bordered on the other side by a black line of woods which appeared at both ends of the view to walk across the water and continue along the edge of the fields.

He sat on the bumper and Mary Fortune straddled the hood and they watched, sometimes for hours, while the machine systematically ate a square red hole in what had once been a cow pasture. It happened to be the only pasture that Pitts had succeeded in getting the bitterweed off and when the old man had sold it, Pitts had nearly had a stroke; and as far as Mr. Fortune was concerned, he could have gone on and had it.

"Any fool that would let a cow pasture interfere with progress is not on my books," he had said to Mary Fortune several times from his seat on the bumper, but the child did not have eyes for anything but the machine. She sat on the hood, looking down into the red pit, watching the big disembodied gullet gorge itself on the clay, then, with the sound of a deep sustained nausea and a slow mechanical revulsion, turn and spit it up. Her pale eyes behind her spectacles followed the repeated motion of it again and again and her face—a small replica of the old man's—never lost its look of complete absorption.

No one was particularly glad that Mary Fortune looked like her grandfather except the old man himself. He thought it added greatly to her attractiveness. He thought she was the smartest and the prettiest child he had ever seen and he let the rest of them know that if—IF that was—he left anything to anybody, it would be Mary Fortune he left it to. She was now nine, short and broad like himself, with his very light blue eyes, his wide prominent forehead, his steady penetrating scowl and his rich florid complexion; but she was like him on the inside too. She had, to a singular degree, his intelligence, his strong will, and his push and drive. Though there was seventy years' difference in their ages, the spiritual distance between them was slight. She was the only member of the family he had any respect for.

He didn't have any use for her mother, his third or fourth daughter (he could never remember which), though she considered that she took care of him. She considered—being careful not to say it, only to look it—that she was the one putting up with him in his old age and that she was the one he should leave the place to. She had married an idiot named Pitts and had had seven children, all likewise idiots except the youngest, Mary Fortune, who was a throwback to him. Pitts was the kind who couldn't keep his hands on a nickel and Mr. Fortune had allowed them, ten years ago, to move onto his place and farm it. What Pitts made went to Pitts but the land belonged to Fortune and he was careful to keep the fact before them. When the well had gone dry, he had not allowed Pitts to have a deep well drilled but had insisted that they pipe their water from the spring. He did not intend to pay for a drilled well himself and he knew that if he let Pitts pay for it, whenever he had occasion to say to Pitts, "It's my land you're sitting on," Pitts would be able to say to him, "Well, it's my pump that's pumping the water you're drinking."

Being there ten years, the Pittses had got to feel as if they owned the place. The daughter had been born and raised on it but the old man considered that when she married Pitts she showed that she preferred Pitts to home; and when she came back, she came back like any other tenant, though he would not allow them to pay rent for the same reason he would not allow them to drill a well. Anyone over sixty years of age is in an uneasy position unless he controls the greater interest and every now and then he gave the Pittses a practical lesson by selling off a lot. Nothing infuriated Pitts more than to see him sell off a piece of the property to an outsider, because Pitts wanted to buy it himself.

Pitts was a thin, long-jawed, irascible, sullen, sulking individual and his wife was the duty-proud kind: It's my duty to stay here and take care of Papa. Who would do it if I didn't? I do it knowing full well I'll get no reward for it. I do it because it's my duty.

The old man was not taken in by this for a minute. He knew they were waiting impatiently for the day when they could put him in a hole eight feet deep and cover him up with dirt. Then, even if he did not leave the place to them, they figured they would be able to buy it. Secretly he had made his will and left everything in trust to Mary Fortune, naming his lawyer and not Pitts as executor. When he died Mary Fortune could make the rest of them jump; and he didn't doubt for a minute that she would be able to do it.

Ten years ago they had announced that they were going to name the new baby Mark Fortune Pitts, after him, if it were a boy, and he had not delayed in telling them that if they coupled his name with the name Pitts he would put them off the place. When the baby came, a girl, and he had seen that even at the age of one day she bore his unmistakable likeness, he had relented and suggested himself that they name her Mary Fortune, after his beloved mother, who had died seventy years ago, bringing him into the world.

The Fortune place was in the country on a clay road that left the paved road fifteen miles away and he would never have been able to sell off any lots if it had not been for progress, which had always been his ally. He was not one of these old people who fight improvement, who object to everything new and cringe at every change. He wanted to see a paved highway in front of his house with plenty of new-model cars on it, he wanted to see a supermarket store across the road from him, he wanted to see a gas station, a motel, a drive-in picture show within easy distance. Progress had suddenly set all this in motion. The electric power company had built a dam on the river and flooded great areas of the surrounding country and the lake that resulted touched his land along a half-mile stretch. Every Tom, Dick and Harry, every dog and his brother, wanted a lot on the lake. There was talk of their getting a telephone line. There was talk of paving the road that ran in front of the Fortune place. There was talk of an eventual town. He thought this should be called Fortune, Georgia. He was a man of advanced vision, even if he was seventy-nine years old.

The machine that drew up the dirt had stopped the day before and today they were watching the hole being smoothed out by two huge yellow bulldozers. His property had amounted to eight hundred acres before he began selling lots. He had sold five twenty-acre lots on the back of the place and every time he sold one, Pitts's blood pressure had gone up twenty points. "The Pittses are the kind that would let a cow pasture interfere with the future," he said to Mary Fortune, "but not you and me." The fact that Mary Fortune was a Pitts too was something he ignored, in a gentlemanly fashion, as if it were an affliction the child was not responsible for. He liked to think of her as being thoroughly of his clay. He sat on the bumper and she sat on the hood with her bare feet on his shoulders. One of the bulldozers had moved under them to shave the side of the embankment they were parked on. If he had moved his feet a few inches out, the old man could have dangled them over the edge.

"If you don't watch him," Mary Fortune shouted above the noise of the machine, "he'll cut off some of your dirt!"

"Yonder's the stob," the old man yelled. "He hasn't gone beyond the stob."

"Not YET he hasn't," she roared.

The bulldozer passed beneath them and went on to the far side. "Well you watch," he said. "Keep your eyes open and if he knocks that stob, I'll stop him. The Pittses are the kind that would let a cow pasture or a mule lot or a row of beans interfere with progress," he continued. "The people like you and me with heads on their shoulders know you can't stop the marcher time for a cow. . . ."

"He's shaking the stob on the other side!" she screamed and before he could stop her, she had jumped down from the hood and was running along the edge of the embankment, her little yellow dress billowing out behind.

"Don't run so near the edge," he yelled but she had already reached the stob and was squatting down by it to see how much it had been shaken. She leaned over the embankment and shook her fist at the man on the bulldozer. He waved at her and went on about his business. More sense in her little finger than all the rest of that tribe in their heads put together, the old man said to himself, and watched with pride as she started back to him.

She had a head of thick, very fine, sand-colored hair—the exact kind he had had when he had had any—that grew straight and was cut just above her eyes and down the sides of her cheeks to the tips of her ears so that it formed a kind of door opening onto the central part of her face. Her glasses were silver-rimmed like his and she even walked the way he did, stomach forward, with a careful abrupt gait, something between a rock and a shuffle. She was walking so close to the edge of the embankment that the outside of her right foot was flush with it.

"I said don't walk so close to the edge," he called; "you fall off

there and you won't live to see the day this place gets built up."
He was always very careful to see that she avoided dangers. He
would not allow her to sit in snakey places or put her hands on
bushes that might hide hornets.

She didn't move an inch. She had a habit of his of not hearing
what she didn't want to hear and since this was a little trick he had
taught her himself, he had to admire the way she practiced it. He
foresaw that in her own old age it would serve her well. She reached
the car and climbed back onto the hood without a word and put
her feet back on his shoulders where she had had them before, as
if he were no more than a part of the automobile. Her attention
returned to the far bulldozer.

"Remember what you won't get if you don't mind," her grandfather remarked.

He was a strict disciplinarian but he had never whipped her.
There were some children, like the first six Pittses, whom he
thought should be whipped once a week on principle, but there
were other ways to control intelligent children and he had never
laid a rough hand on Mary Fortune. Furthermore, he had never
allowed her mother or her brothers and sisters so much as to slap
her. The elder Pitts was a different matter.

He was a man of a nasty temper and of ugly unreasonable re-
sentments. Time and again, Mr. Fortune's heart had pounded to
see him rise slowly from his place at the table—not the head, Mr.
Fortune sat there, but from his place at the side—and abruptly, for
no reason, with no explanation, jerk his head at Mary Fortune and
say, "Come with me," and leave the room, unfastening his belt as
he went. A look that was completely foreign to the child's face
would appear on it. The old man could not define the look but it
infuriated him. It was a look that was part terror and part respect
and part something else, something very like cooperation. This
look would appear on her face and she would get up and follow
Pitts out. They would get in his truck and drive down the road
out of earshot, where he would beat her.

Mr. Fortune knew for a fact that he beat her because he had
followed them in his car and had seen it happen. He had watched
from behind a boulder about a hundred feet away while the child

clung to a pine tree and Pitts, as methodically as if he were whacking a bush with a sling blade, beat her around the ankles with his belt. All she had done was jump up and down as if she were standing on a hot stove and make a whimpering noise like a dog that was being peppered. Pitts had kept at it for about three minutes and then he had turned, without a word, and got back in his truck and left her there, and she had slid down under the tree and taken both feet in her hands and rocked back and forth. The old man had crept forward to catch her. Her face was contorted into a puzzle of small red lumps and her nose and eyes were running. He sprang on her and sputtered, "Why didn't you hit him back? Where's your spirit? Do you think I'd a let him beat me?"

She had jumped up and started backing away from him with her jaw stuck out. "Nobody beat me," she said.

"Didn't I see it with my own eyes?" he exploded.

"Nobody is here and nobody beat me," she said. "Nobody's ever beat me in my life and if anybody did, I'd kill him. You can see for yourself nobody is here."

"Do you call me a liar or a blindman!" he shouted. "I saw him with my own two eyes and you never did a thing but let him do it, you never did a thing but hang onto that tree and dance up and down a little and blubber and if it had been me, I'd a swung my fist in his face and . . ."

"Nobody was here and nobody beat me and if anybody did I'd kill him!" she yelled and then turned and dashed off through the woods.

"And I'm a Poland china pig and black is white!" he had roared after her and he had sat down on a small rock under the tree, disgusted and furious. This was Pitt's revenge on him. It was as if it were *he* that Pitts was driving down the road to beat and it was as if *he* were the one submitting to it. He had thought at first that he could stop him by saying that if he beat her, he would put them off the place but when he had tried that, Pitts had said, "Put me off and you put her off too. Go right ahead. She's mine to whip and I'll whip her every day of the year if it suits me."

Anytime he could make Pitts feel his hand he was determined to do it and at present he had a little scheme up his sleeve that was going to be a considerable blow to Pitts. He was thinking of it with relish when he told Mary Fortune to remember what she wouldn't get if she didn't mind, and he added, without waiting for an answer, that he might be selling another lot soon and that if he did, he might give her a bonus but not if she gave him any sass. He had frequent little verbal tilts with her but this was a sport like putting a mirror up in front of a rooster and watching him fight his reflection.

"I don't want no bonus," Mary Fortune said.

"I ain't ever seen you refuse one."

"You ain't ever seen me ask for one neither," she said.

"How much have you laid by?" he asked.

"Noner yer bidnis," she said and stamped his shoulders with her feet. "Don't be buttin into my bidnis."

"I bet you got it sewed up in your mattress," he said, "just like an old nigger woman. You ought to put it in the bank. I'm going to start you an account just as soon as I complete this deal. Won't anybody be able to check on it but me and you."

The bulldozer moved under them again and drowned out the rest of what he wanted to say. He waited and when the noise had passed, he could hold it in no longer. "I'm going to sell the lot right in front of the house for a gas station," he said. "Then we won't have to go down the road to get the car filled up, just step out the front door."

The Fortune house was set back about two hundred feet from the road and it was this two hundred feet that he intended to sell. It was the part that his daughter airily called "the lawn" though it was nothing but a field of weeds.

"You mean," Mary Fortune said after a minute, "the lawn?"

"Yes mam!" he said. "I mean the lawn," and he slapped his knee.

She did not say anything and he turned and looked up at her. There in the little rectangular opening of hair was his face looking back at him, but it was a reflection not of his present expression but of the darker one that indicated his displeasure. "That's where we play," she muttered.

"Well there's plenty of other places you can play," he said, irked by this lack of enthusiasm.

"We won't be able to see the woods across the road," she said. The old man stared at her. "The woods across the road?" he repeated.

"We won't be able to see the view," she said.

"The view?" he repeated.

"The woods," she said; "we won't be able to see the woods from the porch."

"The woods from the porch?" he repeated.

Then she said, "My daddy grazes his calves on that lot."

The old man's wrath was delayed an instant by shock. Then it exploded in a roar. He jumped up and turned and slammed his fist on the hood of the car. "He can graze them somewheres else!"

"You fall off that embankment and you'll wish you hadn't," she said.

He moved from in front of the car around to the side, keeping his eye on her all the time. "Do you think I care where he grazes his calves! Do you think I'll let a calf interfere with my bidnis? Do you think I give a damn hoot where that fool grazes his calves?"

She sat, her red face darker than her hair, exactly reflecting his expression now. "He who calls his brother a fool is subject to hell fire," she said.

"Jedge not," he shouted, "lest ye be not jedged!" The tinge of his face was a shade more purple than hers. "You!" he said. "You let him beat you any time he wants to and don't do a thing but blubber a little and jump up and down!"

"He nor nobody else has ever touched me," she said, measuring off each word in a deadly flat tone. "Nobody's ever put a hand on me and if anybody did, I'd kill him."

"And black is white," the old man piped, "and night is day!"

The bulldozer passed below them. With their faces about a foot apart, each held the same expression until the noise had receded. Then the old man said, "Walk home by yourself. I refuse to ride a Jezebel!"

"And I refuse to ride with the Whore of Babylon," she said and slid off the other side of the car and started off through the pasture.

"A whore is a woman!" he roared. "That's how much you know!" But she did not deign to turn around and answer him back, and as he watched the small robust figure stalk across the yellow-dotted field toward the woods, his pride in her, as if it couldn't help itself, returned like the gentle little tide on the new lake—all except that part of it that had to do with her refusal to stand up to Pitts; that pulled back like an undertow. If he could have taught her to stand up to Pitts the way she stood up to him, she would have been a perfect child, as fearless and sturdy-minded as anyone could want; but it was her one failure of character. It was the one point on which she did not resemble him. He turned and looked away over the lake to the woods across it and told himself that in five years, instead of woods, there would be houses and stores and parking places, and that the credit for it could go largely to him.

He meant to teach the child spirit by example and since he had definitely made up his mind, he announced that noon at the dinner table that he was negotiating with a man named Tilman to sell the lot in front of the house for a gas station.

His daughter, sitting with her worn-out air at the foot of the table, let out a moan as if a dull knife were being turned slowly in her chest. "You mean the lawn!" she moaned and fell back in her chair and repeated in an almost inaudible voice, "He means the lawn."

The other six Pitts children began to bawl and pipe, "Where we play!" "Don't let him do that, Pa!" "We won't be able to see the road!" and similar idiocies. Mary Fortune did not say anything. She had a mulish reserved look as if she were planning some business of her own. Pitts had stopped eating and was staring in front of him. His plate was full but his fists sat motionless like two dark quartz stones on either side of it. His eyes began to move from child to child around the table as if he were hunting for one particular one of them. Finally they stopped on Mary Fortune sitting next to her grandfather. "You done this to us," he muttered.

"I didn't," she said but there was no assurance in her voice. It was only a quaver, the voice of a frightened child.

Pitts got up and said, "Come with me," and turned and walked out, loosening his belt as he went, and to the old man's complete despair, she slid away from the table and followed him, almost ran after him, out the door and into the truck behind him, and they drove off.

This cowardice affected Mr. Fortune as if it were his own. It made him physically sick. "He beats an innocent child," he said to his daughter, who was apparently still prostrate at the end of the table, "and not one of you lifts a hand to stop him."

"You ain't lifted yours neither," one of the boys said in an undertone and there was a general mutter from that chorus of frogs.

"I'm an old man with a heart condition," he said. "I can't stop an ox."

"She put you up to it," his daughter murmured in a languid listless tone, her head rolling back and forth on the rim of her chair. "She puts you up to everything."

"No child never put me up to nothing!" he yelled. "You're no kind of a mother! You're a disgrace! That child is an angel! A saint!" he shouted in a voice so high that it broke and he had to scurry out of the room.

The rest of the afternoon he had to lie on his bed. His heart, whenever he knew the child had been beaten, felt as if it were slightly too large for the space that was supposed to hold it. But now he was more determined than ever to see the filling station go up in front of the house, and if it gave Pitts a stroke, so much the better. If it gave him a stroke and paralyzed him, he would be served right and he would never be able to beat her again.

Mary Fortune was never angry with him for long, or seriously, and though he did not see her the rest of that day, when he woke up the next morning, she was sitting astride his chest ordering him to make haste so that they would not miss the concrete mixer.

The workmen were laying the foundation for the fishing club when they arrived and the concrete mixer was already in operation. It was about the size and color of a circus elephant; they stood and watched it churn for a half-hour or so. At eleven-thirty, the old man had an appointment with Tilman to discuss his transaction and they had to leave. He did not tell Mary Fortune where they were going but only that he had to see a man.

Tilman operated a combination country store, filling station, scrap-metal dump, used-car lot and dance hall five miles down the highway that connected with the dirt road that passed in front of the Fortune place. Since the dirt road would soon be paved, he wanted a good location on it for another such enterprise. He was an up-and-coming man—the kind, Mr. Fortune thought, who was never just in line with progress but always a little ahead of it so that he could be there to meet it when it arrived. Signs up and down the highway announced that Tilman's was only five miles away, only four, only three, only two, only one; "Watch out for Tilman's, Around this bend!" and finally, "Here it is, Friends, TILMAN's!" in dazzling red letters.

Tilman's was bordered on either side by a field of old used-car bodies, a kind of ward for incurable automobiles. He also sold outdoor ornaments, such as stone cranes and chickens, urns, jardinieres, whirligigs, and farther back from the road, so as not to depress his dance hall customers, a line of tombstones and monuments. Most of his businesses went on out-of-doors, so that his store building itself had not involved excessive expense. It was a one-room wooden structure onto which he had added, behind, a long tin hall equipped for dancing. This was divided into two sections, Colored and White, each with its private nickelodeon. He had a barbecue pit and sold barbecued sandwiches and soft drinks.

As they drove up under the shed of Tilman's place, the old man glanced at the child sitting with her feet drawn up on the seat and her chin resting on her knees. He didn't know if she would remember that it was Tilman he was going to sell the lot to or not.

"What you going in here for?" she asked suddenly, with a sniffing look as if she scented an enemy.

"Noner yer bidnis," he said. "You just sit in the car and when I come out, I'll bring you something."

"Don'tcher bring me nothing," she said darkly, "because I won't be here."

"Haw!" he said. "Now you're here, it's nothing for you to do but wait," and he got out and without paying her any further attention, he entered the dark store where Tilman was waiting for him.

When he came out in half an hour, she was not in the car. Hiding, he decided. He started walking around the store to see if she was in the back. He looked in the doors of the two sections of the dance hall and walked on around by the tombstones. Then his eye roved over the field of sinking automobiles and he realized that she could be in or behind any one of two hundred of them. He came back out in front of the store. A Negro boy, drinking a purple drink, was sitting on the ground with his back against the sweating ice cooler.

"Where did that little girl go to, boy?" he asked.

"I ain't seen nair little girl," the boy said.

The old man irritably fished in his pocket and handed him a nickel and said, "A pretty little girl in a yeller cotton dress."

"If you speakin about a stout chile look lak you," the boy said, "she gone off in a truck with a white man."

"What kind of a truck, what kind of a white man?" he yelled.

"It were a green pickup truck," the boy said smacking his lips, "and a white man she call 'daddy.' They gone thataway some time ago."

The old man, trembling, got in his car and started home. His feelings raced back and forth between fury and mortification. She had never left him before and certainly never for Pitts. Pitts had ordered her to get in the truck and she was afraid not to. But when he reached this conclusion he was more furious than ever. What was the matter with her that she couldn't stand up to Pitts? Why was there this one flaw in her character when he had trained her so well in everything else? It was an ugly mystery.

When he reached the house and climbed the front steps, there she was sitting in the swing, looking glum-faced in front of her across the field he was going to sell. Her eyes were puffy and pink-rimmed but he didn't see any red marks on her legs. He sat down in the swing beside her. He meant to make his voice severe but instead it came out crushed, as if it belonged to a suitor trying to reinstate himself.

"What did you leave me for? You ain't ever left me before," he said.

"Because I wanted to," she said, looking straight ahead.

"You never wanted to," he said. "He made you."

"I toljer I was going and I went," she said in a slow emphatic voice, not looking at him, "and now you can go on and lemme alone." There was something very final, in the sound of this, a tone that had not come up before in their disputes. She stared across the lot where there was nothing but a profusion of pink and yellow and purple weeds, and on across the red road, to the sullen line of black pine woods fringed on top with green. Behind that line was a narrow gray-blue line of more distant woods and beyond that nothing but the sky, entirely blank except for one or two threadbare clouds. She looked into this scene as if it were a person that she preferred to him.

"It's my lot, ain't it?" he asked. "Why are you so up-in-the-air about me selling my own lot?"

"Because it's the lawn," she said. Her nose and eyes began to run horribly but she held her face rigid and licked the water off as soon as it was in reach of her tongue. "We won't be able to see across the road," she said.

The old man looked across the road to assure himself again that there was nothing over there to see. "I never have seen you act in such a way before," he said in an incredulous voice. "There's not a thing over there but the woods."

"We won't be able to see 'um," she said, "and that's the *lawn* and my daddy grazes his calves on it."

At that the old man stood up. "You act more like a Pitts than a Fortune," he said. He had never made such an ugly remark to her before and he was sorry the instant he had said it. It hurt him more than it did her. He turned and went in the house and upstairs to his room.

Several times during the afternoon, he got up from his bed and looked out the window across the "lawn" to the line of woods she said they wouldn't be able to see any more. Every time he saw the same thing: woods—not a mountain, not a waterfall, not any kind of planted bush or flower, just woods. The sunlight was woven through them at that particular time of the afternoon so that every thin pine trunk stood out in all its nakedness. A pine trunk is a pine trunk, he said to himself, and anybody that wants to see one don't have to go far in this neighborhood. Every time he got up and looked out, he was reconvinced of his wisdom in selling the lot. The dissatisfaction it caused Pitts would be permanent, but he could make it up to Mary Fortune by buying her something. With grown people, a road led either to heaven or hell, but with children there were always stops along the way where their attention could be turned with a trifle.

The third time he got up to look at the woods, it was almost six o'clock and the gaunt trunks appeared to be raised in a pool of red light that gushed from the almost hidden sun setting behind them. The old man stared for some time, as if for a prolonged instant he were caught up out of the rattle of everything that led to the future and were held there in the midst of an uncomfortable mystery that he had not apprehended before. He saw it, in his hallucination, as if someone were wounded behind the woods and the trees were bathed in blood. After a few minutes this unpleasant vision was broken by the presence of Pitts's pickup truck grinding to a halt below the window. He returned to his bed and shut his eyes and against the closed lids hellish red trunks rose up in a black wood.

At the supper table nobody addressed a word to him, including Mary Fortune. He ate quickly and returned again to his room and spent the evening pointing out to himself the advantages for the future of having an establishment like Tilman's so near. They would not have to go any distance for gas. Anytime they needed a loaf of bread, all they would have to do would be step out their front door into Tilman's back door. They could sell milk to Tilman. Tilman was a likable fellow. Tilman would draw other business. The road would soon be paved. Travelers from all over the country would stop at Tilman's. If his daughter thought she was better than Tilman, it would be well to take her down a little. All men were created free and equal. When this phrase sounded in his head, his patriotic sense triumphed and he realized that it was his duty to sell the lot, that he must insure the future. He looked out the window at the moon shining over the woods across the road and listened for a while to the hum of crickets and treefrogs, and beneath their racket, he could hear the throb of the future town of Fortune.

He went to bed certain that just as usual, he would wake up in the morning looking into a little red mirror framed in a door of fine hair. She would have forgotten all about the sale and after breakfast they would drive into town and get the legal papers from the courthouse. On the way back he would stop at Tilman's and close the deal.

When he opened his eyes in the morning, he opened them on the empty ceiling. He pulled himself up and looked around the room but she was not there. He hung over the edge of the bed and looked beneath it but she was not there either. He got up and dressed and went outside. She was sitting in the swing on the front porch, exactly the way she had been yesterday, looking across the lawn into the woods. The old man was very much irritated. Every morning since she had been able to climb, he had waked up to find her either on his bed or underneath it. It was apparent that this morning she preferred the sight of the woods. He decided to ignore her behavior for the present and then bring it up later when she was over her pique. He sat down in the swing beside her but she continued to look at the woods. "I thought you and me'd go into town and have us a look at the boats in the new boat store," he said.

She didn't turn her head but she asked suspiciously, in a loud voice. "What else are you going for?"

"Nothing else," he said.

After a pause she said, "If that's all, I'll go," but she did not bother to look at him.

"Well put on your shoes," he said. "I ain't going to the city with a barefoot woman." She did not bother to laugh at this joke.

The weather was as indifferent as her disposition. The sky did not look as if it were going to rain or as if it were not going to rain. It was an unpleasant gray and the sun had not troubled to come out. All the way into town, she sat looking at her feet, which stuck out in front of her, encased in heavy brown school shoes. The old man had often sneaked up on her and found her alone in conversation with her feet and he thought she was speaking with them silently now. Every now and then her lips moved but she said nothing to him and let all his remarks pass as if she had not heard them. He decided it was going to cost him considerable to buy her good humor again and that he had better do it with a boat, since he wanted one too. She had been talking boats ever since the water backed up onto his place. They went first to the boat store. "Show us the yachts for po' folks!" he shouted jovially to the clerk as they entered.

"They're all for po' folks!" the clerk said. "You'll be po' when you finish buying one!" He was a stout youth in a yellow shirt and blue pants and he had a ready wit. They exchanged several clever remarks in rapid-fire succession. Mr. Fortune looked at Mary Fortune to see if her face had brightened. She stood staring absently over the side of an outboard motor boat at the opposite wall.

"Ain't the lady innerested in boats?" the clerk asked.

She turned and wandered back out onto the sidewalk and got in the car again. The old man looked after her with amazement. He could not believe that a child of her intelligence could be acting this way over the mere sale of a field. "I think she must be coming down with something," he said. "We'll come back again," and he returned to the car.

"Let's go get us an ice-cream cone," he suggested, looking at her with concern.

"I don't want no ice-cream cone," she said.

His actual destination was the courthouse but he did not want to make this apparent. "How'd you like to visit the ten-cent store while I tend to a little bidnis of mine?" he asked. "You can buy yourself something with a quarter I brought along."

"I ain't got nothing to do in no ten-cent store," she said. "I don't want no quarter of yours."

If a boat was of no interest, he should not have thought a quarter would be and reproved himself for that stupidity. "Well what's the matter, sister?" he asked kindly. "Don't you feel good?"

She turned and looked him straight in the face and said with a slow concentrated ferocity, "It's the lawn. My daddy grazes his calves there. We won't be able to see the woods any more."

The old man had held his fury in as long as he could. "He beats you!" he shouted. "And you worry about where he's going to graze his calves!"

"Nobody's ever beat me in my life," she said, "and if anybody did, I'd kill him."

A man seventy-nine years of age cannot let himself be run over by a child of nine. His face set in a look that was just as determined as hers. "Are you a Fortune," he said, "or are you a Pitts? Make up your mind."

Her voice was loud and positive and belligerent. "I'm Mary—Fortune—Pitts," she said.

"Well I," he shouted, "am PURE Fortune!"

There was nothing she could say to this and she showed it. For an instant she looked completely defeated, and the old man saw with a disturbing clearness that this was the Pitts look. What he saw was the Pitts look, pure and simple, and he felt personally stained by it, as if it had been found on his own face. He turned in disgust and backed the car out and drove straight to the courthouse.

The courthouse was a red and white blaze-faced building set in the center of a square from which most of the grass had been worn off. He parked in front of it and said, "Stay here," in an imperious tone and got out and slammed the car door.

It took him a half hour to get the deed and have the sale paper drawn up and when he returned to the car, she was sitting on the back seat in the corner. The expression on that part of her face that he could see was foreboding and withdrawn. The sky had darkened also and there was a hot sluggish tide in the air, the kind felt when a tornado is possible.

"We better get on before we get caught in a storm," he said and emphatically, "because I got one more place to stop at on the way home," but he might have been chauffeuring a small dead body for all the answer he got.

On the way to Tilman's he reviewed once more the many just reasons that were leading him to his present action and he could not locate a flaw in any of them. He decided that while this attitude of hers would not be permanent, he was permanently disappointed in her and that when she came around she would have to apologize; and that there would be no boat. He was coming to realize slowly that his trouble with her had always been that he had not shown enough firmness. He had been too generous. He was so occupied with these thoughts that he did not notice the signs that said how many miles to Tilman's until the last one exploded joyfully in his face: "Here it is, Friends, TILMAN's!" He pulled in under the shed.

He got out without so much as looking at Mary Fortune and entered the dark store where Tilman, leaning on the counter in front of a triple shelf of canned goods, was waiting for him.

Tilman was a man of quick action and few words. He sat habitually with his arms folded on the counter and his insignificant head weaving snake-fashion above them. He had a triangular-shaped face with the point at the bottom and the top of his skull was covered with a cap of freckles. His eyes were green and very narrow and his tongue was always exposed in his partly opened mouth. He had his checkbook handy and they got down to business at once. It did not take him long to look at the deed and sign the bill of sale. Then Mr. Fortune signed it and they grasped hands over the counter.

Mr. Fortune's sense of relief as he grasped Tilman's hand was extreme. What was done, he felt, was done and there could be no more argument, with her or with himself. He felt that he had acted on principle and that the future was assured.

Just as their hands loosened, an instant's change came over Tilman's face and he disappeared completely under the counter as if he had been snatched by the feet from below. A bottle crashed against the line of tinned goods behind where he had been. The old man whirled around. Mary Fortune was in the door, red-faced and wild-looking, with another bottle lifted to hurl. As he ducked, it broke behind him on the counter and she grabbed another from the crate. He sprang at her but she tore to the other side of the store, screaming something unintelligible and throwing everything within her reach. The old man pounced again and this time he caught her by the tail of her dress and pulled her backward out of the store. Then he got a better grip and lifted her, wheezing and whimpering but suddenly limp in his arms, the few feet to the car. He managed to get the door open and dump her inside. Then he ran around to the other side and got in himself and drove away as fast as he could.

His heart felt as if it were the size of the car and was racing forward, carrying him to some inevitable destination faster than he had ever been carried before. For the first five minutes he did not think but only sped forward as if he were being driven inside his own fury. Gradually the power of thought returned to him. Mary Fortune, rolled into a ball in the corner of the seat, was snuffling and heaving.

He had never seen a child behave in such a way in his life. Neither his own children nor anyone else's had ever displayed such temper in his presence, and he had never for an instant imagined that the child he had trained himself, the child who had been his constant companion for nine years, would embarrass him like this. The child he had never lifted a hand to!

Then he saw, with the sudden vision that sometimes comes with delayed recognition, that that had been his mistake.

She respected Pitts because, even with no just cause, he beat her; and if he—with his just cause—did not beat her now, he would have nobody to blame but himself if she turned out a hellion. He saw that the time had come, that he could no longer avoid whipping her, and as he turned off the highway onto the dirt road leading to home, he told himself that when he finished with her, she would never throw another bottle again.

He raced along the clay road until he came to the line where his own property began and then he turned off onto a side path, just wide enough for the automobile and bounced for a half a mile through the woods. He stopped the car at the exact spot where he had seen Pitts take his belt to her. It was a place where the road widened so that two cars could pass or one could turn around, an ugly red bald spot surrounded by long thin pines that appeared to be gathered there to witness anything that would take place in such a clearing. A few stones protruded from the clay.

"Get out," he said and reached across her and opened the door.

She got out without looking at him or asking what they were going to do and he got out on his side and came around the front of the car.

"Now I'm going to whip you!" he said and his voice was extra loud and hollow and had a vibrating quality that appeared to be taken up and passed through the tops of the pines. He did not want to get caught in a downpour while he was whipping her and he said, "Hurry up and get ready against that tree," and began to take off his belt.

What he had in mind to do appeared to come very slowly as if it had to penetrate a fog in her head. She did not move but gradually her confused expression began to clear. Where a few seconds before her face had been red and distorted and unorganized, it drained now of every vague line until nothing was left on it but positiveness, a look that went slowly past determination and reached certainty. "Nobody has ever beat me," she said, "and if anybody tries it, I'll kill him."

"I don't want no sass," he said and started toward her. His knees felt very unsteady, as if they might turn either backward or forward.

She moved exactly one step back and, keeping her eye on him steadily, removed her glasses and dropped them behind a small rock near the tree he had told her to get ready against. "Take off your glasses," she said.

"Don't give me orders!" he said in a high voice and slapped awkwardly at her ankles with his belt.

She was on him so quickly that he could not have recalled which blow he felt first, whether the weight of her whole solid body or the jabs of her feet or the pummeling of her fist on his chest. He flailed the belt in the air, not knowing where to hit but trying to get her off him until he could decide where to get a grip on her.

"Leggo!" he shouted. "Leggo I tell you!" But she seemed to be everywhere, coming at him from all directions at once. It was as if he were being attacked not by one child but by a pack of small demons all with stout brown school shoes and small rocklike fists. His glasses flew to the side.

"I toljer to take them off," she growled without pausing.

He caught his knee and danced on one foot and a rain of blows fell on his stomach. He felt five claws in the flesh of his upper arm where she was hanging from while her feet mechanically battered his knees and her free fist pounded him again and again in the chest. Then with horror he saw her face rise up in front of his, teeth exposed, and he roared like a bull as she bit the side of his jaw. He seemed to see his own face coming to bite him from several sides at once but he could not attend to it for he was being kicked indiscriminately, in the stomach and then in the crotch. Suddenly he threw himself on the ground and began to roll like a man on fire. She was on top of him at once, rolling with him and still kicking, and now with both fists free to batter his chest.

"I'm an old man!" he piped. "Leave me alone!" But she did not stop. She began a fresh assault on his jaw.

"Stop stop!" he wheezed. "I'm your grandfather!"

She paused, her face exactly on top of his. Pale identical eye looked into pale identical eye. "Have you had enough?" she asked.

The old man looked up into his own image. It was triumphant and hostile. "You been whipped," it said, "by me," and then it added, bearing down on each word, "and I'm PURE Pitts."

In the pause she loosened her grip and he got hold of her throat. With a sudden surge of strength, he managed to roll over and reverse their positions so that he was looking down into the face that was his own but had dared to call itself Pitts. With his hands still tight around her neck, he lifted her head and brought it down once hard against the rock that happened to be under it. Then he brought it down twice more. Then looking into the face in which the eyes, slowly rolling back, appeared to pay him not the slightest attention, he said, "There's not an ounce of Pitts in me."

He continued to stare at his conquered image until he perceived that though it was absolutely silent, there was no look of remorse on it. The eyes had rolled back down and were set in a fixed glare that did not take him in. "This ought to teach you a good lesson," he said in a voice that was edged with doubt.

He managed painfully to get up on his unsteady kicked legs and to take two steps, but the enlargement of his heart which had begun in the car was still going on. He turned his head and looked behind him for a long time at the little motionless figure with its head on the rock.

Then he fell on his back and looked up helplessly along the bare trunks into the tops of the pines and his heart expanded once more with a convulsive motion. It expanded so fast that the old man felt as if he were being pulled after it through the woods, felt as if he were running as fast as he could with the ugly pines toward the lake. He perceived that there would be a little opening there, a little place where he could escape and leave the woods behind him. He could see it in the distance already, a little opening where the white sky was reflected in the water. It grew as he ran toward it until suddenly the whole lake opened up before him, riding majestically in little corrugated folds toward his feet. He realized suddenly that he could not swim and that he had not bought the boat. On both sides of him he saw that the gaunt trees had thickened into mysterious dark files that were marching across the water and away into the distance. He looked around desperately for someone to help him but the place was deserted except for one huge yellow monster which sat to the side, as stationary as he was, gorging itself on clay.

Grace Paley

An
Interest
in Life

~~~

My husband gave me a broom one Christmas. This wasn't right. No one can tell me it was meant kindly.

"I don't want you not to have anything for Christmas while I'm away in the Army," he said. "Virginia, please look at it. It comes with this fancy dustpan. It hangs off a stick. Look at it, will you? Are you blind or crosseyed?"

"Thanks, chum," I said. I had always wanted a dustpan hooked up that way. It was a good one. My husband doesn't shop in bargain basements or January sales.

Still and all, in spite of the quality, it was a mean present to give

a woman you planned on never seeing again, a person you had
children with and got onto all the time, drunk or sober, even when
everybody had to get up early in the morning.

I asked him if he could wait and join the Army in a half hour,
as I had to get the groceries. I don't like to leave kids alone in a
three-room apartment full of gas and electricity. Fire may break
out from a nasty remark. Or the oldest decides to get even with
the youngest.

"Just this once," he said. "But you better figure out how to get
along without me."

"You're a handicapped person mentally," I said. "You should've
been institutionalized years ago." I slammed the door. I didn't want
to see him pack his underwear and ironed shirts.

I never got further than the front stoop, though, because there
was Mrs. Raftery, wringing her hands, tears in her eyes as though
she had a monopoly on all the good news.

"Mrs. Raftery!" I said, putting my arm around her. "Don't cry."
She leaned on me because I am such a horsy build. "Don't cry,
Mrs. Raftery, please!" I said.

"That's like you, Virginia. Always looking at the ugly side of
things. 'Take in the wash. It's rainin'!' That's you. You're the first
one knows it when the dumb-waiter breaks."

"Oh, come on now, that's not so. It just isn't so," I said. "I'm
the exact opposite."

"Did you see Mrs. Cullen yet?" she asked, paying no attention.

"Where?"

"Virginia!" she said, shocked. "She's passed away. The whole
house knows it. They've got her in white like a bride and you never
saw a beautiful creature like that. She must be eighty. Her husband's
proud."

"She was never more than an acquaintance; she didn't have any
children," I said.

"Well, I don't care about that. Now, Virginia, you do what I
say now, you go downstairs and you say like this—listen to me—
say, 'I hear, Mr. Cullen, your wife's passed away. I'm sorry.' Then
ask him how he is. Then you ought to go around the corner and
see her. She's in Witson & Wayde. Then you ought to go over to
the church when they carry her over."

"It's not my church," I said.

"That's no reason, Virginia. You go up like this," she said, parting from me to do a prancy dance. "Up the big front steps, into the church you go. It's beautiful in there. You can't help kneeling only for a minute. Then round to the right. Then up the other stairway. Then you come to a great oak door that's arched above you, then," she said, seizing a deep, deep breath, for all the good it would do her, "and then turn the knob slo-owly and open the door and see for yourself: Our Blessed Mother is in charge. Beautiful. Beautiful. Beautiful."

I sighed in and I groaned out, so as to melt a certain pain around my heart. A steel ring like arthritis, at my age.

"You are a groaner," Mrs. Raftery said, gawking into my mouth.

"I am not," I said. I got a whiff of her, a terrible cheap wine lush.

My husband threw a penny at the door from the inside to take my notice from Mrs. Raftery. He rattled the glass door to make sure I looked at him. He had a fat duffel bag on each shoulder. Where did he acquire so much worldly possession? What was in them? My grandma's goose feathers from across the ocean? Or all the diaper-service diapers? To this day the truth is shrouded in mystery.

"What the hell are you doing, Virginia?" he said, dumping them at my feet. "Standing out here on your hind legs telling everybody your business? The Army gives you a certain time, for God's sakes, they're not kidding." Then he said, "I beg your pardon," to Mrs. Raftery. He took hold of me with his two arms as though in love and pressed his body hard against mine so that I could feel him for the last time and suffer my loss. Then he kissed me in a mean way to nearly split my lip. Then he winked and said, "That's all for now," and skipped off into the future, duffel bags full of rags.

He left me in an embarrassing situation, nearly fainting, in front of that old widow, who can't even remember the half of it. "He's a crook," said Mrs. Raftery. "Is he leaving for good or just temporarily, Virginia?"

"Oh, he's probably deserting me," I said, and sat down on the stoop, pulling my big knees up to my chin.

"If that's the case, tell the Welfare right away," she said. "He's

a bum, leaving you just before Christmas. Tell the cops," she said.
"They'll provide the toys for the little kids gladly. And don't forget
to let the grocer in on it. He won't be so hard on you expecting
payment."

She saw that sadness was stretched worldwide across my face.
Mrs. Raftery isn't the worst person. She said, "Look around for
comfort, dear." With a nervous finger she pointed to the truckers
eating lunch on their haunches across the street, leaning on the
loading platforms. She waved her hand to include in all the men
marching up and down in search of a decent luncheonette. She
didn't leave out the six longshoremen loafing under the fish-market
marquee. "If their lungs and stomachs ain't crushed by overwork,
they disappear somewhere in the world. Don't be disappointed,
Virginia. I don't know a man living'd last you a lifetime."

Ten days later Girard asked, "Where's Daddy?"

"Ask me no questions, I'll tell you no lies." I didn't want the
children to know the facts. Present or past, a child should have a
father.

"Where *is* Daddy?" Girard asked the week after that.

"He joined the Army," I said.

"He made my bunk bed," said Phillip.

"The truth shall make ye free," I said.

Then I sat down with pencil and pad to get in control of my
resources. The facts, when I added and subtracted them, were that
my husband had left me with fourteen dollars, and the rent unpaid,
in an emergency state. He'd claimed he was sorry to do this, but
my opinion is, out of sight, out of mind. "The city won't let you
starve," he'd said. "After all, you're half the population. You're
keeping up the good work. Without you the race would die out.
Who'd pay the taxes? Who'd keep the streets clean? There wouldn't
be no Army. A man like me wouldn't have no place to go."

I sent Girard right down to Mrs. Raftery with a request about
the whereabouts of Welfare. She responded RSVP with an extra
comment in left-handed script: "Poor Girard . . . he's never the
boy my John was!"

Who asked her?

I called on Welfare right after the new year. In no time I discovered that they're rigged up to deal with liars, and if you're truthful it's disappointing to them. They may even refuse to handle your case if you're too truthful.

They asked sensible questions at first. They asked where my husband had enlisted. I didn't know. They put some letter writers and agents after him. "He's not in the United States Army," they said. "Try the Brazilian Army," I suggested.

They have no sense of kidding around. They're not the least bit lighthearted and they tried. "Oh no," they said. "That was incorrect. He is not in the Brazilian Army."

"No?" I said. "How strange! He must be in the Mexican Navy."

By law, they had to hound his brothers. They wrote to his brother who has a first-class card in the Teamsters and owns an apartment house in California. They asked his two brothers in Jersey to help me. They have large families. Rightfully they laughed. Then they wrote to Thomas, the oldest, the smart one (the one they all worked so hard for years to keep him in college until his brains could pay off). He was the one who sent ten dollars immediately, saying, "What a bastard! I'll send something time to time, Ginny, but whatever you do, don't tell the authorities." Of course I never did. Soon they began to guess they were better people than me, that I was in trouble because I deserved it, and then they liked me better.

But they never fixed my refrigerator. Every time I called I said patiently, "The milk is sour . . ." I said, "Corn beef went bad." Sitting in that beer-stinking phone booth in Felan's for the sixth time (sixty cents) with the baby on my lap and Barbie tapping at the glass door with an American flag, I cried into the secretary's hardhearted ear, "I bought real butter for the holiday, and it's rancid . . ." They said, "You'll have to get a better bid on the repair job."

While I waited indoors for a man to bid, Girard took to swinging back and forth on top of the bathroom door, just to soothe himself, giving me the laugh, dreamy, nibbling calcimine off the ceiling. On first sight Mrs. Raftery said, "Whack the monkey, he'd be better off on arsenic."

But Girard is my son and I'm the judge. It means a terrible thing for the future, though I don't know what to call it.

It was from constantly thinking of my foreknowledge on this and other subjects, it was from observing when I put my lipstick on daily, how my face was just curling up to die, that John Raftery came from Jersey to rescue me.

On Thursdays, anyway, John Raftery took the tubes to visit his mother. The whole house knew it. She was cheerful even before breakfast. She sang out loud in a girlish brogue that only came to tongue for grand occasions. Hanging out the wash, she blushed to recall what a remarkable boy her John had been. "Ask the sisters around the corner," she said to the open kitchen windows. "They'll never forget John."

That particular night after supper Mrs. Raftery said to her son, "John, how come you don't say hello to your old friend Virginia? She's had hard luck and she's gloomy."

"Is that so, Mother?" he said, and immediately climbed two flights to knock at my door.

"Oh, John," I said at the sight of him, hat in hand in a white shirt and blue-striped tie, spick-and-span, a Sunday-school man. "Hello!"

"Welcome, John!" I said. "Sit down. Come right in. How are you? You look awfully good. You do. Tell me, how've you been all this time, John?"

"How've I been?" he asked thoughtfully. To answer within reason, he described his life with Margaret, marriage, work, and children up to the present day.

I had nothing good to report. Now that he had put the subject around before my very eyes, every burnt-up day of my life smoked in shame, and I couldn't even get a clear view of the good half hours.

"Of course," he said, "you do have lovely children. Noticeable-looking, Virginia. Good looks is always something to be thankful for."

"Thankful?" I said. "I don't have to thank anything but my own foolishness for four children when I'm twenty-six years old, deserted, and poverty-struck, regardless of looks. A man can't help it, but I could have behaved better."

"Don't be so cruel on yourself, Ginny," he said. "Children come from God."

"You're still great on holy subjects, aren't you? You know damn well where children come from."

He did know. His red face reddened further. John Raftery has had that color coming out on him boy and man from keeping his rages so inward.

Still he made more sense in his conversation after that, and I poured fresh tea to tell him how my husband used to like me because I was a passionate person. That was until he took a look around and saw how in the long run this life only meant more of the same thing. He tried to turn away from me once he came to this understanding, and make me hate him. His face changed. He gave up his brand of cigarettes, which we had in common. He threw out the two pairs of socks I knitted by hand. "If there's anything I hate in this world, it's navy blue," he said. Oh, I could have dyed them. I would have done anything for him, if he were only not too sorry to ask me.

"You were a nice kid in those days," said John, referring to certain Saturday nights. "A wild, nice kid."

"Aaah," I said, disgusted. Whatever I was then, was on the way to where I am now. "I was fresh. If I had a kid like me, I'd slap her cross-eyed."

The very next Thursday John gave me a beautiful radio with a record player. "Enjoy yourself," he said. That really made Welfare speechless. We didn't own any records, but the investigator saw my burden was lightened and he scribbled a dozen pages about it in his notebook.

On the third Thursday he brought a walking doll (twenty-four inches) for Linda and Barbie with a card inscribed, "A baby doll for a couple of dolls." He had also had a couple of drinks at his mother's, and this made him want to dance. "La-la-la, let yourself go . . ."

"You gotta give a little," he sang, "live a little . . ." He said, "Virginia, may I have this dance?"

"Sssh, we finally got them asleep. Please, turn the radio down. Quiet. Deathly silence, John Raftery."

"Let me do your dishes, Virginia."

"Don't be silly, you're a guest in my house," I said. "I still regard you as a guest."

"Tell me I'm the most gorgeous thing," I said, dipping my arm to the funny bone in dish soup.

He didn't answer. "I'm having a lot of trouble at work," was all he said. Then I heard him push the chair back. He came up behind me, put his arms around my waistline, and kissed my cheek. He whirled me around and took my hands. He said, "An old friend is better than rubies." He looked me in the eye. He held my attention by trying to be honest. And he kissed me a short sweet kiss on my mouth.

"Please sit down, Virginia," he said. He kneeled before me and put his head in my lap. I was stirred by so much activity. Then he looked up at me and, as though proposing marriage for life, he offered—because he was drunk—to place his immortal soul in peril to comfort me.

First I said, "Thank you." Then I said, "No."

I was sorry for him, but he's devout, a leader of the Fathers' Club at his church, active in all the lay groups for charities, orphans, etc. I knew that if he stayed late to love with me, he would not do it lightly but would in the end pay terrible penance and ruin his long life. The responsibility would be on me.

So I said no.

And Barbie is such a light sleeper. All she has to do, I thought, is wake up and wander in and see her mother and her new friend John with his pants around his knees, wrestling on the kitchen table. A vision like that could affect a kid for life.

I said no.

Everyone in this building is so goddamn nosy. That evening I had to say no.

But John came to visit, anyway, on the fourth Thursday. This time he brought the discarded dresses of Margaret's daughters, organdy party dresses and glazed cotton for every day. He gently admired Barbara and Linda, his blue eyes rolling to back up a couple of dozen oohs and ahs.

Even Phillip, who thinks God gave him just a certain number of hellos and he better save them for the final judgment, Phillip leaned on John and said, "Why don't you bring your boy to play with me? I don't have nobody who to play with." (Phillip's a liar.

There must be at least seventy-one children in this house, pale pink to medium brown, English-talking and gibbering in Spanish, rough-and-tough boys, the Lone Ranger's bloody pals, or the exact picture of Supermouse. If a boy wanted a friend, he could pick the very one out of his neighbors.)

Also, Girard is a cold fish. He was in a lonesome despair. Sometimes he looked in the mirror and said, "How come I have such an ugly face? My nose is funny. Mostly people don't like me." He was a liar too. Girard has a face like his father's. His eyes are the color of those little blue plums in August. He looks like an advertisement in a magazine. He could be a child model and make a lot of money. He is my first child, and if he thinks he is ugly, I think I am ugly.

John said, "I can't stand to see a boy mope like that. . . . What do the sisters say in school?"

"He doesn't pay attention is all they say. You can't get much out of them."

"My middle boy was like that," said John. "Couldn't take an interest. Aaah, I wish I didn't have all that headache on the job. I'd grab Girard by the collar and make him take notice of the world. I wish I could ask him out to Jersey to play in all that space."

"Why not?" I said.

"Why, Virginia, I'm surprised you don't know why not. You know I can't take your children out to meet my children."

I felt a lot of strong arthritis in my ribs.

"My mother's the funny one, Virginia." He felt he had to continue with the subject matter. "I don't know. I guess she likes the idea of bugging Margaret. She says, 'You goin' up, John?' 'Yes, Mother,' I say. 'Behave yourself, John,' she says. 'That husband might come home and hacksaw you into hell. You're a Catholic man, John,' she says. But I figured it out. She likes to know I'm in the building. I swear, Virginia, she wishes me the best of luck."

"I do too, John," I said. We drank a last glass of beer to make sure of a peaceful sleep. "Good night, Virginia," he said, looping his muffler neatly under his chin. "Don't worry. I'll be thinking of what to do about Girard."

I got into the big bed that I share with the girls in the little room.

For once I had no trouble falling asleep. I only had to worry about Linda and Barbara and Phillip. It was a great relief to me that John had taken over the thinking about Girard.

John was sincere. That's true. He paid a lot of attention to Girard, smoking out all his sneaky sorrows. He registered him into a wild pack of cub scouts that went up to the Bronx once a week to let off steam. He gave him a Junior Erector Set. And sometimes when his family wasn't listening he prayed at great length for him.

One Sunday, Sister Veronica said in her sweet voice from another life, "He's not worse. He might even be a little better. How are *you*, Virginia?" putting her hand on mine. Everybody around here acts like they know everything.

"Just fine," I said.

"We ought to start on Phillip," John said, "if it's true Girard's improving."

"You should've been a social worker, John."

"A lot of people have noticed that about me," said John.

"Your mother was always acting so crazy about you, how come she didn't knock herself out a little to see you in college? Like we did for Thomas?"

"Now, Virginia, be fair. She's a poor old woman. My father was a weak earner. She had to have my wages, and I'll tell you, Virginia, I'm not sorry. Look at Thomas. He's still in school. Drop him in this jungle and he'd be devoured. He hasn't had a touch of real life. And here I am with a good chunk of a family, a home of my own, a name in the building trades. One thing I have to tell you, the poor old woman is sorry. I said one day (oh, in passing— years ago) that I might marry you. She stuck a knife in herself. It's a fact. Not more than an eighth of an inch. You never saw such a gory Sunday. One thing—you would have been a better daughter-in-law to her than Margaret."

"Marry me?" I said.

"Well, yes. . . . aah—I always liked you, then . . . Why do you think I'd sit in the shade of this kitchen every Thursday night? For God's sakes, the only warm thing around here is this teacup. Yes, sir, I did want to marry you, Virginia."

"No kidding, John? Really?" It was nice to know. Better late than never, to learn you were desired in youth.

I didn't tell John, but the truth is, I would never have married him. Once I met my husband with his winking looks, he was my only interest. Wild as I had been with John and others, I turned all my wildness over to him and then there was no question in my mind.

Still, face facts, if my husband didn't budge on in life, it was my fault. On me, as they say, be it. I greeted the morn with a song. I had a hello for everyone but the landlord. Ask the people on the block, come or go—even the Spanish ones, with their sad dark faces—they have to smile when they see me.

But for his own comfort, he should have done better lifewise and moneywise. I was happy, but I am now in possession of knowledge that this is wrong. Happiness isn't so bad for a woman. She gets fatter, she gets older, she could lie down, nuzzling a regiment of men and little kids, she could just die of the pleasure. But men are different, they have to own money, or they have to be famous, or everybody on the block has to look up to them from the cellar stairs.

A woman counts her children and acts snotty, like she invented life, but men *must* do well in the world. I know that men are not fooled by being happy.

"A funny guy," said John, guessing where my thoughts had gone. "What stopped him up? He was nobody's fool. He had a funny thing about him, Virginia, if you don't mind my saying so. He wasn't much distance up, but he was all set and ready to be looking down on us all."

"He was very smart, John. You don't realize that. His hobby was crossword puzzles, and I said to him real often, as did others around here, that he ought to go out on the '$64 Question.' Why not? But he laughed. You know what he said? He said, 'That proves how dumb you are if you think I'm smart.' "

"A funny guy, " said John. "Get it all off your chest," he said. "Talk it out, Virginia; it's the only way to kill the pain."

By and large, I was happy to oblige. Still I could not carry through about certain cruel remarks. It was like trying to move back into the dry mouth of a nightmare to remember that the last day I was happy was the middle of a week in March, when I told my husband I was going to have Linda. Barbara was five months old to the hour. The boys were three and four. I had to tell him. It was the last day with anything happy about it.

Later on he said, "Oh, you make me so sick, you're so goddamn big and fat, you look like a goddamn brownstone, the way you're squared off in front."

"Well, where are you going tonight?" I asked.

"How should I know?" he said. "Your big ass takes up the whole goddamn bed," he said. "There's no room for me." He bought a sleeping bag and slept on the floor.

I couldn't believe it. I would start every morning fresh. I couldn't believe that he would turn against me so, while I was still young and even his friends still liked me.

But he did, he turned absolutely against me and became no friend of mine. "All you ever think about is making babies. This place stinks like the men's room in the BMT. It's a fucking *pissoir*." He was strong on truth all through the year. "That kid eats more than the five of us put together," he said. "Stop stuffing your face, you fat dumbbell," he said to Phillip.

Then he worked on the neighbors. "Get that nosy old bag out of here," he said. "If she comes on once more with 'my son in the building trades' I'll squash her for the cat."

Then he turned on Spielvogel, the checker, his oldest friend, who only visited on holidays and never spoke to me (shy, the way some bachelors are). "That sonofabitch, don't hand me that friendship crap, all he's after is your ass. That's what I need—a little shitmaker of his using up the air in this flat."

And then there was no one else to dispose of. We were left alone fair and square, facing each other.

"Now, Virginia," he said, "I come to the end of my rope. I see a black wall ahead of me. What the hell am I supposed to do? I only got one life. Should I lie down and die? I don't know what to do any more. I'll give it to you straight, Virginia, if I stick around, you can't help it, you'll hate me . . ."

"I hate you right now," I said. "So do whatever you like."

"This place drives me nuts," he mumbled. "I don't know what to do around here. I want to get you a present. Something."

"I told you, do whatever you like. Buy me a rattrap for rats."

That's when he went down to the House Appliance Store, and he brought back a new broom and a classy dustpan. "A new broom sweeps clean," he said. "I got to get out of here," he said. "I'm going nuts." Then he began to stuff the duffel bags, and I went to the grocery store but was stopped by Mrs. Raftery, who had to tell me what she considered so beautiful—death—then he kissed and went to join some army somewhere.

I didn't tell John any of this, because I think it makes a woman look too bad to tell on how another man has treated her. He begins to see her through the other man's eyes, a sitting duck, a skinful of flaws. After all, I had come to depend on John. All my husband's friends were strangers now, though I had always said to them, "Feel welcome."

And the family men in the building looked too cunning, as though they had all personally deserted me. If they met me on the stairs, they carried the heaviest groceries up and helped bring Linda's stroller down, but they never asked me a question worth answering at all.

Besides that, Girard and Phillip taught the girls the days of the week: Monday, Tuesday, Wednesday, Johnday, Friday. They waited for him once a week, under the hallway lamp, half asleep like bugs in the sun, sitting in their little chairs with their names on in gold, a birth present from my mother-in-law. At fifteen after eight he punctually came, to read a story, pass out some kisses, and tuck them into bed.

But one night, after a long Johnday of them squealing my eardrum split, after a rainy afternoon with brother constantly raising up his hand against brother, with the girls near ready to go to court over the proper ownership of Melinda Lee, the twenty-four-inch walking doll, the doorbell rang three times. Not any of those times did John's face greet me.

I was too ashamed to call down to Mrs. Raftery, and she was too mean to knock on my door and explain.

He didn't come the following Thursday either. Girard said sadly, "He must've run away, John."

I had to give him up after two weeks' absence and no word. I didn't know how to tell the children: something about right and wrong, goodness and meanness, men and women. I had it all at my finger tips, ready to hand over. But I didn't think I ought to take mistakes and truth away from them. Who knows? They might make a truer friend in this world somewhere than I have ever made. So I just put them to bed and sat in the kitchen and cried.

In the middle of my third beer, searching in my mind for the next step, I found the decision to go on "Strike It Rich." I scrounged some paper and pencil from the toy box and I listed all my troubles, which must be done in order to qualify. The list when complete could have brought tears to the eye of God if He had a minute. At the sight of it my bitterness began to improve. All that is really necessary for survival of the fittest, it seems, is an interest in life, good, bad, or peculiar.

As always happens in these cases where you have begun to help yourself with plans, news comes from an opposite direction. The doorbell rang, two short and two long—meaning John.

My first thought was to wake the children and make them happy. "No! No!" he said. "Please don't put yourself to that trouble. Virginia, I'm dog-tired," he said. "Dog-tired. My job is a damn headache. It's too much. It's all day and it scuttles my mind at night, and in the end who does the credit go to?

"Virginia," he said, "I don't know if I can come any more. I've been wanting to tell you. I just don't know. What's it all about? Could you answer me if I asked you? I can't figure this whole thing out at all."

I started the tea steeping because his fingers when I touched them were cold. I didn't speak. I tried looking at it from his man point of view, and I thought he had to take a bus, the tubes, and a subway to see me; and then the subway, the tubes, and a bus to go back home at 1 A.M. It wouldn't be any trouble at all for him to part with us forever. I thought about my life, and I gave strongest consideration to my children. If given the choice, I decided to choose not to live without him.

"What's that?" he asked, pointing to my careful list of troubles. "Writing a letter?"

"Oh no," I said, "it's for 'Strike It Rich.' I hope to go on the program."

"Virginia, for goodness' sakes," he said, giving it a glance, "you don't have a ghost. They'd laugh you out of the studio. Those people really suffer."

"Are you sure, John?" I asked.

"No question in my mind at all," said John. "Have you ever seen that program? I mean, in addition to all of this—the little disturbances of man"—he waved a scornful hand at my list—"they *suffer*. They live in the forefront of tornadoes, their lives are washed off by floods—catastrophes of God. Oh, Virginia."

"Are you sure, John?"

"For goodness' sake . . ."

Sadly I put my list away. Still, if things got worse, I could always make use of it.

Once that was settled, I acted on an earlier decision. I pushed his cup of scalding tea aside. I wedged myself onto his lap between his hard belt buckle and the table. I put my arms around his neck and said, "How come you're so cold, John?" He has a kind face and he knew how to look astonished. He said, "Why, Virginia, I'm getting warmer." We laughed.

John became a lover to me that night.

Mrs. Raftery is sometimes silly and sick from her private source of cheap wine. She expects John often. "Honor your mother, what's the matter with you, John?" she complains. "Honor. Honor."

"Virginia dear," she says. "You never would've taken John away to Jersey like Margaret. I wish he'd've married you."

"You didn't like me much in those days."

"That's a lie," she says. I know she's a hypocrite, but no more than the rest of the world.

What is remarkable to me is that it doesn't seem to conscience John as I thought it might. It is still hard to believe that a man who sends out the Ten Commandments every year for a Christmas card can be so easy buttoning and unbuttoning.

Of course we must be very careful not to wake the children or disturb the neighbors who will enjoy another person's excitement just so far, and then the pleasure enrages them. We must be very careful for ourselves too, for when my husband comes back, realizing the babies are in school and everything easier, he won't forgive me if I've started it all up again—noisy signs of life that are so much trouble to a man.

We haven't seen him in two and a half years. Although people have suggested it, I do not want the police or Intelligence or a private eye or anyone to go after him to bring him back. I know that if he expected to stay away forever he would have written and said so. As it is, I just don't know what evening, any time, he may appear. Sometimes, stumbling over a blockbuster of a dream at midnight, I wake up to vision his soft arrival.

He comes in the door with his old key. He gives me a strict look and says, "Well, you look older, Virginia." "So do you," I say, although he hasn't changed a bit.

He settles in the kitchen because the children are asleep all over the rest of the house. I unknot his tie and offer him a cold sandwich. He raps my backside, paying attention to the bounce. I walk around him as though he were a Maypole, kissing as I go.

"I didn't like the Army much," he says. "Next time I think I might go join the Merchant Marine."

"What army?" I say.

"It's pretty much the same everywhere," he says.

"I wouldn't be a bit surprised," I say.

"I lost my cuff link, goddamnit," he says, and drops to the floor to look for it. I go down too on my knees, but I know he never had a cuff link in his life. Still I would do a lot for him.

"Got you off your feet that time," he says, laughing. "Oh yes, I did." And before I can even make myself half comfortable on that polka-dotted linoleum, he got onto me right where we were and the truth is, we were so happy, we forgot the precautions.

Paule Marshall

BROOKLYN

~~~~

A summer wind, soaring just before it died, blew the dusk and the first scattered lights of downtown Brooklyn against the shut windows of the classroom, but Professor Max Berman—B.A., 1919, M.A., 1921, New York; Docteur de l'Université, 1930, Paris—alone in the room, did not bother to open the windows to the cooling wind. The heat and airlessness of the room, the perspiration inching its way like an ant around his starched collar were discomforts he enjoyed, they obscured his larger discomfort: the anxiety which chafed his heart and tugged his left eyelid so that he seemed to be winking, roguishly, behind his glasses.

To steady his eye and ease his heart, to fill the time until his students arrived and his first class in years began, he reached for his cigarettes. As always he delayed lighting the cigarette so that his need for it would be greater and, thus, the relief and pleasure it would bring, fuller. For some time he fondled it, his fingers shaping soft, voluptuous gestures, his warped old man's hands looking strangely abandoned on the bare desk and limp as if the bones had been crushed, and so white—except for the tobacco burn on the index and third fingers—it seemed his blood no longer traveled that far.

He lit the cigarette finally and as the smoke swelled his lungs, his eyelid stilled and his lined face lifted, the plume of white hair wafting above his narrow brow; his body—short, blunt, the shoulders slightly bent as if in deference to his sixty-three years—settled back in the chair. Delicately Max Berman crossed his legs and, looking down, examined his shoes for dust. (The shoes were of a very soft, fawn-colored leather and somewhat foppishly pointed at the toe. They had been custom made in France and were his one last indulgence. He wore them in memory of his first wife, a French Jewess from Alsace-Lorraine whom he had met in Paris while lingering over his doctorate and married to avoid returning home. She had been gay, mindless and very excitable—but at night, she had also been capable of a profound stillness as she lay in bed waiting for him to turn to her, and this had always awed and delighted him. She had been a gift—and her death in a car accident had been a judgment on him for never having loved her, for never, indeed, having even allowed her to matter.) Fastidiously Max Berman unbuttoned his jacket and straightened his vest, which had a stain two decades old on the pocket. Through the smoke his veined eyes contemplated other, more pleasurable scenes. With his neatly shod foot swinging and his cigarette at a rakish tilt, he might have been an old *boulevardier* taking the sun and an absinthe before the afternoon's assignation.

A young face, the forehead shiny with earnestness, hung at the half-opened door. "Is this French Lit, fifty-four? Camus and Sartre?"

Max Berman winced at the rawness of the voice and the flat "a" in Sartre and said formally, "This is Modern French Literature, number fifty-four, yes, but there is some question as to whether we will take up Messieurs Camus and Sartre this session. They might prove hot work for a summer evening course. We will probably do Gide and Mauriac, who are considerably more temperate. But come in nonetheless. . . ."

He was the gallant, half rising to bow her to a seat. He knew that she would select the one in the front row directly opposite his desk. At the bell her pen would quiver above her blank notebook, ready to commit his first word—indeed, the clearing of his throat— to paper, and her thin buttocks would begin sidling toward the edge of her chair.

His eyelid twitched with solicitude. He wished that he could have drawn the lids over her fitful eyes and pressed a cool hand to her forehead. She reminded him of what he had been several life- times ago: a boy with a pale, plump face and harried eyes, running from the occasional taunts at his yarmulke along the shrill streets of Brownsville in Brooklyn, impeded by the heavy satchel of books which he always carried as proof of his scholarship. He had been proud of his brilliance at school and the Yeshiva, but at the same time he had been secretly troubled by it and resentful, for he could never believe that he had come by it naturally or that it belonged to him alone. Rather, it was like a heavy medal his father had hung around his neck—the chain bruising his flesh—and constantly ex- horted him to wear proudly and use well.

The girl gave him an eager and ingratiating smile and he looked away. During his thirty years of teaching, a face similar to hers had crowded his vision whenever he had looked up from a desk. Perhaps it was fitting, he thought, and lighted another cigarette from the first, that she should be present as he tried again at life, unaware that behind his rimless glasses and within his ancient suit, he had been gutted.

He thought of those who had taken the last of his substance and smiled tolerantly. "The boys of summer," he called them, his in- quisitors, who had flailed him with a single question: "Are you now or have you ever been a member of the Communist party?" Max Berman had never taken their question seriously—perhaps because he had never taken his membership in the party seriously—and he had refused to answer. What had disturbed him, though, even when the investigation was over, was the feeling that he had really been under investigation for some other offense which did matter and of which he was guilty; that behind their accusations and charges had lurked another which had not been political but personal. For had he been disloyal to the government? His denial was a short, hawking laugh. Simply, he had never ceased being religious. When his father's God had become useless and even a little embarrassing, he had sought others: his work for a time, then the party. But he had been middle-aged when he joined and his faith, which had been so full as a boy, had grown thin. He had come, by then, to distrust all pieties, so that when the purges in Russia during the thirties confirmed his distrust, he had withdrawn into a modest cynicism.

But he had been made to answer for that error. Ten years later his inquisitors had flushed him out from the small community college in upstate New York where he had taught his classes from the same neat pack of notes each semester and had led him bound by subpoena to New York and bandied his name at the hearings until he had been dismissed from his job.

He remembered looking back at the pyres of burning autumn leaves on the campus his last day and feeling that another lifetime had ended—for he had always thought of his life as divided into many small lives, each with its own beginning and end. Like a hired mute, he had been present at each dying and kept the wake and wept professionally as the bier was lowered into the ground. Because of this feeling, he told himself that his final death would be anticlimactic.

After his dismissal he had continued living in the small house he had built near the college, alone except for an occasional visit from a colleague, idle but for some tutoring in French, content with the income he received from the property his parents had left him in Brooklyn—until the visits and tutoring had tapered off and a silence had begun to choke the house, like weeds springing up around a deserted place. He had begun to wonder then if he were still alive. He would wake at night from the recurrent dream of the hearings, where he was being accused of an unstated crime, to listen for his heart, his hand fumbling among the bedclothes to press the place. During the day he would pass repeatedly in front of the mirror with the pretext that he might have forgotten to shave that morning or that something had blown into his eye. Above all, he had begun to think of his inquisitors with affection and to long for the sound of their voices. They, at least, had assured him of being alive.

As if seeking them out, he had returned to Brooklyn and to the house in Brownsville where he had lived as a boy and had boldly applied for a teaching post without mentioning the investigation. He had finally been offered the class which would begin in five minutes. It wasn't much: a six-week course in the summer evening session of a college without a rating, where classes were held in a converted factory building, a college whose campus took in the bargain department stores, the five-and-dime emporiums and neon-spangled movie houses of downtown Brooklyn.

Through the smoke from his cigarette, Max Berman's eyes—a waning blue that never seemed to focus on any one thing—drifted over the students who had gathered meanwhile. Imbuing them with his own disinterest, he believed that even before the class began, most of them were longing for its end and already anticipating the soft drinks at the soda fountain downstairs and the synthetic dramas at the nearby movie.

They made him sad. He would have liked to lead them like a Pied Piper back to the safety of their childhoods—all of them: the loud girl with the formidable calves of an athlete who reminded him, uncomfortably, of his second wife (a party member who was always shouting political heresy from some picket line and who had promptly divorced him upon discovering his irreverence); the two sallow-faced young men leaning out the window as if searching for the wind that had died; the slender young woman with crimped black hair who sat very still and apart from the others, her face turned toward the night sky as if to a friend.

Her loneliness interested him. He sensed its depth and his eye paused. He saw then that she was a Negro, a very pale mulatto with skin the color of clear, polished amber and a thin, mild face. She was somewhat older than the others in the room—a schoolteacher from the South, probably, who came north each summer to take courses toward a graduate degree. He felt a fleeting discomfort and irritation: discomfort at the thought that although he had been sinned against as a Jew he still shared in the sin against her and suffered from the same vague guilt, irritation that she recalled his own humiliations: the large ones, such as the fact that despite his brilliance he had been unable to get into a medical school as a young man because of the quota on Jews (not that he had wanted to be a doctor; that had been his father's wish) and had changed his studies from medicine to French; the small ones which had worn him thin: an eye widening imperceptibly as he gave his name, the savage glance which sought the Jewishness in his nose, his chin, in the set of his shoulders, the jokes snuffed into silence at his appearance. . . .

Tired suddenly, his eyelid pulsing, he turned and stared out the window at the gaudy constellation of neon lights. He longed for a drink, a quiet place and then sleep. And to bear him gently into sleep, to stay the terror which bound his heart then reminding him of those oleographs of Christ with the thorns binding his exposed heart—fat drops of blood from one so bloodless—to usher him into sleep, some pleasantly erotic image: a nude in a boudoir scattered with her frilled garments and warmed by her frivolous laugh, with the sun like a voyeur at the half-closed shutters. But this time instead of the usual Rubens nude with thighs like twin portals and a belly like a huge alabaster bowl into which he poured himself, he chose Gauguin's Aita Parari, her languorous form in the straight back chair, her dark, sloping breasts, her eyes like the sun under shadow.

With the image still on his inner eye, he turned to the Negro girl and appraised her through a blind of cigarette smoke. She was still gazing out at the night sky and something about her fixed stare, her hands stiffly arranged in her lap, the nerve fluttering within the curve of her throat, betrayed a vein of tension within the rock of her calm. It was as if she had fled long ago to a remote region within herself, taking with her all that was most valuable and most vulnerable about herself.

She stirred finally, her slight breasts lifting beneath her flowered summer dress as she breathed deeply—and Max Berman thought again of Gauguin's girl with the dark, sloping breasts. What would this girl with the amber-colored skin be like on a couch in a sunlit room, nude in a straight-back chair? And as the question echoed along each nerve and stilled his breathing, it seemed suddenly that life, which had scorned him for so long, held out her hand again— but still a little beyond his reach. Only the girl, he sensed, could bring him close enough to touch it. She alone was the bridge. So that even while he repeated to himself that he was being presump- tuous (for she would surely refuse him) and ridiculous (for even if she did not, what could he do—his performance would be a mere scramble and twitch), he vowed at the same time to have her. The challenge eased the tightness around his heart suddenly; it soothed the damaged muscle of his eye and as the bell rang he rose and said briskly, "Ladies and gentlemen, may I have your attention, please. My name is Max Berman. The course is Modern French Literature, number fifty-four. May I suggest that you check your program cards to see whether you are in the right place at the right time."

Her essay on Gide's *The Immoralist* lay on his desk and the note from the administration informing him, first, that his past political activities had been brought to their attention and then dismissing him at the end of the session weighed the inside pocket of his jacket. The two, her paper and the note, were linked in his mind. Her paper reminded him that the vow he had taken was still an empty one, for the term was half over and he had never once spoken to her (as if she understood his intention she was always late and disappeared as soon as the closing bell rang, leaving him trapped in a clamorous circle of students around his desk), while the note which wrecked his small attempt to start anew suddenly made that vow more urgent. It gave him the edge of desperation he needed to act finally. So that as soon as the bell rang, he returned all the papers but hers, announced that all questions would have to wait until their next meeting and, waving off the students from his desk, called above their protests, "Miss Williams, if you have a moment, I'd like to speak with you briefly about your paper."

She approached his desk like a child who has been cautioned not to talk to strangers, her fingers touching the backs of the chair as if for support, her gaze following the departing students as though she longed to accompany them.

Her slight apprehensiveness pleased him. It suggested a submissiveness which gave him, as he rose uncertainly, a feeling of certainty and command. Her hesitancy was somehow in keeping with the color of her skin. She seemed to bring not only herself but the host of black women whose bodies had been despoiled to make her. He would not only possess her but them also, he thought (not really thought, for he scarcely allowed these thoughts to form before he snuffed them out). Through their collective suffering, which she contained, his own personal suffering would be eased; he would be pardoned for whatever sin it was he had committed against life.

"I hope you weren't unduly alarmed when I didn't return your paper along with the others," he said, and had to look up as she reached the desk. She was taller close up and her eyes, which he had thought were black, were a strong, flecked brown with very small pupils which seemed to shrink now from the sight of him. "But I found it so interesting I wanted to give it to you privately."

"I didn't know what to think," she said, and her voice—he heard it for the first time for she never recited or answered in class—was low, cautious, Southern.

"It was, to say the least, refreshing. It not only showed some original and mature thinking on your part, but it also proved that you've been listening in class—and after twenty-five years and more of teaching it's encouraging to find that some students do listen. If you have a little time I'd like to tell you, more specifically, what I liked about it. . . ."

Talking easily, reassuring her with his professional tone and a deft gesture with his cigarette, he led her from the room as the next class filed in, his hand cupped at her elbow but not touching it, his manner urbane, courtly, kind. They paused on the landing at the end of the long corridor with the stairs piled in steel tiers above and plunging below them. An intimate silence swept up the stairwell in a warm gust and Max Berman said, "I'm curious. Why did you choose *The Immoralist?*"

She started suspiciously, afraid, it seemed, that her answer might expose and endanger the self she guarded so closely within.

"Well," she said finally, her glance reaching down the stairs to the door marked EXIT at the bottom, "when you said we could use anything by Gide I decided on *The Immoralist*, since it was the first book I read in the original French when I was in undergraduate school. I didn't understand it then because my French was so weak, I guess, but I always thought about it afterward for some odd reason. I was shocked by what I did understand, of course, but something else about it appealed to me, so when you made the assignment I thought I'd try reading it again. I understood it a little better this time. At least I think so. . . ."

"Your paper proves you did."

She smiled absently, intent on some other thought. Then she said cautiously, but with unexpected force, "You see, to me, the book seems to say that the only way you begin to know what you are and how much you are capable of is by daring to try something, by doing something which tests you. . . ."

"Something bold," he said.

"Yes."

"Even sinful."

She paused, questioning this, and then said reluctantly, "Yes, perhaps even sinful."

"The salutary effects of sin, you might say." He gave the little bow.

But she had not heard this; her mind had already leaped ahead. "The only trouble, at least with the character in Gide's book, is that what he finds out about himself is so terrible. He is so unhappy. . . ."

"But at least he knows, poor sinner." And his playful tone went unnoticed.

"Yes," she said with the same startling forcefulness. "And another thing, in finding out what he is, he destroys his wife. It was as if she had to die in order for a person to live and know himself. Perhaps in order for a person to live and know himself somebody else must die. Maybe there's always a balancing out. . . . In a way"—and he had to lean close now to hear her—"I believe this."

Max Berman edged back as he glimpsed something move within her abstracted gaze. It was like a strong and restless seed that had taken root in the darkness there and was straining now toward the light. He had not expected so subtle and complex a force beneath her mild exterior and he found it disturbing and dangerous, but fascinating.

"Well, it's a most interesting interpretation," he said. "I don't know if M. Gide would have agreed, but then he's not around to give his opinion. Tell me, where did you do your undergraduate work?"

"At Howard University."

"And you majored in French?"

"Yes."

"Why, if I may ask?" he said gently.

"Well, my mother was from New Orleans and could still speak a little Creole and I got interested in learning how to speak French through her, I guess. I teach it now at a junior high school in Richmond. Only the beginner courses because I don't have my master's. You know *je vais, tu vas, il va* and *Frère Jacques.* It's not very inspiring."

"You should do something about that then, my dear Miss Williams. Perhaps it's time for you, like our friend in Gide, to try something new and bold."

"I know," she said, and her pale hand sketched a vague, despairing gesture. "I thought maybe if I got my master's . . . that's why I decided to come north this summer and start taking some courses. . . ."

Max Berman quickly lighted a cigarette to still the flurry inside him, for the moment he had been awaiting had come. He flicked her paper, which he still held. "Well, you've got the makings of a master's thesis right here. If you like I will suggest some ways for you to expand it sometime. A few pointers from an old pro might help."

He had to turn from her astonished and grateful smile—it was like a child's. He said carefully, "The only problem will be to find a place where we can talk quietly. Regrettably, I don't rate an office. . . ."

"Perhaps we could use one of the empty classrooms," she said.

"That would be much too dismal a setting for a pleasant discussion."

He watched the disappointment wilt her smile and when he spoke he made certain that the same disappointment weighed his voice. "Another difficulty is that the term's half over, which gives us little or no time. But let's not give up. Perhaps we can arrange to meet and talk over a weekend. The only hitch there is that I spend weekends at my place in the country. Of course you're perfectly welcome to come up there. It's only about seventy miles from New York, in the heart of what's very appropriately called the Borsch Circuit, even though, thank God, my place is a good distance away from the borsch. That is, it's very quiet and there's never anybody around except with my permission."

She did not move, yet she seemed to start; she made no sound, yet he thought he heard a bewildered cry. And then she did a strange thing, standing there with the breath sucked into the hollow of her throat and her smile, that had opened to him with such trust, dying—her eyes, her hands faltering up begged him to declare himself.

"There's a lake near the house," he said, "so that when you get tired of talking—or better, listening to me talk—you can take a swim, if you like. I would very much enjoy that sight." And as the nerve tugged at his eyelid, he seemed to wink behind his rimless glasses.

Her sudden, blind step back was like a man groping his way through a strange room in the dark, and instinctively Max Berman reached out to break her fall. Her arms, bare to the shoulder because of the heat (he knew the feel of her skin without even touching it—it would be like a rich, fine-textured cloth which would soothe and hide him in its amber warmth), struck out once to drive him off and then fell limp at her side, and her eyes became vivid and convulsive in her numbed face. She strained toward the stairs and the exit door at the bottom, but she could not move. Nor could she speak. She did not even cry. Her eyes remained dry and dull with disbelief. Only her shoulders trembled as though she was silently weeping inside.

It was as though she had never learned the forms and expressions of anger. The outrage of a lifetime, of her history, was trapped inside her. And she stared at Max Berman with this mute, paralyzing rage. Not really at him but to his side, as if she caught sight of others behind him. And remembering how he had imagined a column of dark women trailing her to his desk, he sensed that she glimpsed a legion of old men with sere flesh and lonely eyes flanking him: "old lechers with a love on every wind. . . ."

"I'm sorry, Miss Williams," he said, and would have welcomed her insults, for he would have been able, at least, to distill from them some passion and a kind of intimacy. It would have been, in a way, like touching her. "It was only that you are a very attractive young woman and although I'm no longer young"—and he gave the tragic little laugh which sought to dismiss that fact—"I can still appreciate and even desire an attractive woman. But I was wrong. . . ." his self disgust, overwhelming him finally, choked off his voice. "And so very crude. Forgive me. I can offer no excuse for my behavior other than my approaching senility."

He could not even manage the little marionette bow this time. Quickly he shoved the paper on Gide into her lifeless hand, but it fell, the pages separating, and as he hurried past her downstairs and out the door, he heard the pages scattering like dead leaves on the steps.

She remained away until the night of the final examination, which was also the last meeting of the class. By that time Max Berman, believing that she would not return, had almost succeeded in forgetting her. He was no longer even certain of how she looked, for her face had been absorbed into the single, blurred, featureless face of all the women who had ever refused him. So that she startled him as much as a stranger would have when he entered the room that night and found her alone amid a maze of empty chairs, her face turned toward the window as on the first night and her hands serene in her lap. She turned at his footstep and it was as if she had also fórgotten all that had passed between them. She waited until he said, "I'm glad you decided to take the examination. I'm sure you won't have any difficulty with it"; then she gave him a nod that was somehow reminiscent of his little bow and turned again to the window.

He was relieved yet puzzled by her composure. It was as if during her three-week absence she had waged and won a decisive contest with herself and was ready now to act. He was wary suddenly and all during the examination he tried to discover what lay behind her strange calm, studying her bent head amid the shifting heads of the other students, her slim hand guiding the pen across the page, her legs—the long bone visible, it seemed, beneath the flesh. Desire flared and quickly died.

"Excuse me, Professor Berman, will you take up Camus and Sartre next semester, maybe?" The girl who sat in front of his desk was standing over him with her earnest smile and finished examination folder.

"That might prove somewhat difficult, since I won't be here."

"No more?"

"No."

"I mean, not even next summer?"

"I doubt it."

"Gee, I'm sorry. I mean, I enjoyed the course and everything."

He bowed his thanks and held his head down until she left. Her compliment, so piteous somehow, brought on the despair he had forced to the dim rear of his mind. He could no longer flee the thought of the exile awaiting him when the class tonight ended. He could either remain in the house in Brooklyn, where the memory of his father's face above the radiance of the Sabbath candles haunted him from the shadows, reminding him of the certainty he had lost and never found again, where the mirrors in his father's room were still shrouded with sheets, as on the day he lay dying and moaning into his beard that his only son was a bad Jew; or he could return to the house in the country, to the silence shrill with loneliness.

The cigarette he was smoking burned his fingers, rousing him, and he saw over the pile of examination folders on his desk that the room was empty except for the Negro girl. She had finished— her pen lay aslant the closed folder on her desk—but she had remained in her seat and she was smiling across the room at him— a set, artificial smile that was both cold and threatening. It utterly denuded him and he was wildly angry suddenly that she had seen him give way to despair; he wanted to remind her (he could not stay the thought; it attacked him like an assailant from a dark turn in his mind) that she was only black after all. . . . His head dropped and he almost wept with shame.

The girl stiffened as if she had seen the thought and then the tiny muscles around her mouth quickly arranged the bland smile. She came up to his desk, placed her folder on top of the others and said pleasantly, her eyes like dark, shattered glass that spared Max Berman his reflection, "I've changed my mind. I think I'd like to spend a day at your place in the country if your invitation still holds."

He thought of refusing her, for her voice held neither promise nor passion, but he could not. Her presence, even if it was only for a day, would make his return easier. And there was still the possibility of passion despite her cold manner and the deliberate smile. He thought of how long it had been since he had had someone, of how badly he needed the sleep which followed love and of awakening certain, for the first time in years, of his existence.

"Of course the invitation still holds. I'm driving up tonight."

"I won't be able to come until Sunday," she said firmly. "Is there a train then?"

"Yes, in the morning, he said, and gave her the schedule.

"You'll meet me at the station?"

"Of course. You can't miss my car. It's a very shabby but venerable Chevy."

She smiled stiffy and left, her heels awakening the silence of the empty corridor, the sound reaching back to tap like a warning finger on Max Berman's temple.

The pale sunlight slanting through the windshield lay like a cat on his knees. and the motor of his old Chevy, turning softly under him could have been the humming of its heart. A little distance from the car a log-cabin station house—the logs blackened by the seasons—stood alone against the hills, and the hills, in turn, lifted softly, still green although the summer was ending, into the vague autumn sky.

The morning mist and pale sun, the green that was still somehow new, made it seem that the season was stirring into life even as it died, and this contradiction pained Max Berman at the same time that it pleased him. For it was his own contradiction after all: his desires which remained those of a young man even as he was dying.

He had been parked for some time in the deserted station, yet his hands were still tensed on the steering wheel and his foot hovered near the accelerator. As soon as he had arrived in the station he had wanted to leave. But like the girl that night on the landing, he was too stiff with tension to move. He could only wait, his eyelid twitching with foreboding, regret, curiosity and hope.

Finally and with no warning the train charged through the fiery green, setting off a tremor underground. Max Berman imagined the girl seated at a window in the train, her hands arranged quietly in her lap and her gaze scanning the hills that were so familiar to him, and yet he could not believe that she was really there. Perhaps her plan had been to disappoint him. She might be in New York or on her way back to Richmond now, laughing at the trick she had played on him. He was convinced of this suddenly, so that even when he saw her walking toward him through the blown steam from under the train, he told himself that she was a mirage created by the steam. Only when she sat beside him in the car, bringing with her, it seemed, an essence she had distilled from the morning air and rubbed into her skin, was he certain of her reality.

"I brought my bathing suit but it's much too cold to swim," she said and gave him the deliberate smile.

He did not see it; he only heard her voice, its warm Southern lilt in the chill, its intimacy in the closed car—and an excitement swept him, cold first and then hot, as if the sun had burst in his blood.

"It's the morning air," he said. "By noon it should be like summer again."

"Is that a promise?"

"Yes."

By noon the cold morning mist had lifted above the hills and below, in the lake valley, the sunlight was a sheer gold net spread out on the grass as if to dry, draped on the trees and flung, glinting, over the lake. Max Berman felt it brush his shoulders gently as he sat by the lake waiting for the girl, who had gone up to the house to change into her swimsuit.

He had spent the morning showing her the fields and small wood near his house. During the long walk he had been careful to keep a little apart from her. He would extend a hand as they climbed a rise or when she stepped uncertainly over a rock, but he would not really touch her. He was afraid that at his touch, no matter how slight and casual, her scream would spiral into the morning calm, or worse, his touch would unleash the threatening thing he sensed behind her even smile.

He had talked of her paper and she had listened politely and occasionally even asked a question or made a comment. But all the while detached, distant, drawn within herself as she had been that first night in the classroom. And then halfway down a slope she had paused and, pointing to the canvas tops of her white sneakers, which had become wet and dark from the dew secreted in the grass, she had laughed. The sound, coming so abruptly in the midst of her tense quiet, joined her, it seemed, to the wood and wide fields, to the hills; she shared their simplicity and held within her the same strong current of life. Max Berman had felt privileged suddenly, and humble. He had stopped questioning her smile. He had told himself then that it would not matter even if she stopped and picking up a rock bludgeoned him from behind.

"There's a lake near my home, but it's not like this," the girl said, coming up behind him. "Yours is so dark and serious-looking."

He nodded and followed her gaze out to the lake, where the ripples were long, smooth welts raised by the wind, and across to the other bank, where a group of birches stepped delicately down to the lake and bending over touched the water with their branches as if testing it before they plunged.

The girl came and stood beside him now—and she was like a pale gold naiad, the spirit of the lake, her eyes reflecting its somber autumnal tone and her body as supple as the birches. She walked slowly into the water, unaware, it seemed, of the sudden passion in his gaze, or perhaps uncaring; and as she walked she held out her arms in what seemed a gesture of invocation (and Max Berman remembered his father with the fringed shawl draped on his out-stretched arms as he invoked their God each Sabbath with the same gesture); her head was bent as if she listened for a voice beneath the water's murmurous surface. When the ground gave way she still seemed to be walking and listening, her arms outstretched. The water reached her waist, her small breasts, her shoulders. She lifted her head once, breathed deeply and disappeared.

She stayed down for a long time and when her white cap finally broke the water some distance out, Max Berman felt strangely stranded and deprived. He understood suddenly the profound cleavage between them and the absurdity of his hope. The water between them became the years which separated them. Her white cap was the sign of her purity, while the silt darkening the lake was the flotsam of his failures. Above all, their color—her arms a pale, flashing gold in the sunlit water and his bled white and flaccid with the veins like angry blue penciling—marked the final barrier.

He was sad as they climbed toward the house late that afternoon and troubled. A crow cawed derisively in the bracken, heralding the dusk which would not only end their strange day but would also, he felt, unveil her smile, so that he would learn the reason for her coming. And because he was sad, he said wryly, "I think I should tell you that you've been spending the day with something of an outcast."

"Oh," she said and waited.

He told her of the dismissal, punctuating his words with the little hoarse, deprecating laugh and waving aside the pain with his cigarette. She listened, polite but neutral, and because she remained unmoved, he wanted to confess all the more. So that during dinner and afterward when they sat outside on the porch, he told her of the investigation.

"It was very funny once you saw it from the proper perspective, which I did, of course." he said. "I mean here they were accusing me of crimes I couldn't remember committing and asking me for the names of people with whom I had never associated. It was pure farce. But I made a mistake. I should have done something dramatic or something just as farcical. Bared my breast in the public market place or written a tome on my apostasy, naming names. It would have been a far different story then. Instead of my present ignominy I would have been offered a chairmanship at Yale. . . . No? Well, Brandeis then. I would have been draped in honorary degrees. . . ."

"Well, why didn't you confess?" she said impatiently.

"I've often asked myself the same interesting question, but I haven't come up with a satisfactory answer yet. I suspect, though, that I said nothing because none of it really mattered that much."

"What did matter?" she asked sharply.

He sat back, waiting for the witty answer, but none came, because just then the frame upon which his organs were strung seemed to snap and he felt his heart, his lungs, his vital parts fall in a heap within him. Her question had dealt the severing blow, for it was the same question he understood suddenly that the vague forms in his dream asked repeatedly. It had been the plaintive undercurrent to his father's dying moan, the real accusation behind the charges of his inquisitors at the hearing.

For what had mattered? He gazed through his sudden shock at the night squatting on the porch steps, at the hills asleep like gentle beasts in the darkness, at the black screen of the sky where the events of his life passed in a mute, accusing review—and he saw nothing there to which he had given himself or in which he had truly believed since the belief and dedication of his boyhood.

"Did you hear my question?" she asked, and he was glad that he sat within the shadows clinging to the porch screen and could not be seen.

"Yes, I did," he said faintly, and his eyelid twitched. "But I'm afraid it's another one of those I can't answer satisfactorily." And then he struggled for the old flippancy. "You make an excellent examiner, you know. Far better than my inquisitors."

"What will you do now?" her voice and cold smile did not spare him.

He shrugged and the motion, a slow, eloquent lifting of the shoulders, brought with it suddenly the weight and memory of his boyhood. It was the familiar gesture of the women hawkers in Belmont Market, of the men standing outside the temple on Saturday mornings, each of them reflecting his image of God in their forbidding black coats and with the black, tumbling beards in which he had always imagined he could hide as in a forest. All this had mattered, he called loudly to himself, and said aloud to the girl, "Let me see if I can answer this one at least. What *will* I do?" He paused and swung his leg so that his foot in the fastidious French shoe caught the light from the house. "Grow flowers and write my memoirs. How's that? That would be the proper way for a gentleman and scholar to retire. Or hire one of those hefty housekeepers who will bully me and when I die in my sleep draw the sheet over my face and call my lawyer. That's somewhat European, but how's that?"

When she said nothing for a long time, he added soberly. "But that's not a fair question for me any more. I leave all such considerations to the young. To you, for that matter. What will you do, my dear Miss Williams?"

It was as if she had been expecting the question and had been readying her answer all the time that he had been talking. She leaned forward eagerly and with her face and part of her body fully in the light, she said, "I will do something. I don't know what yet, but something."

Max Berman started back a little. The answer was so unlike her vague, resigned "I know" on the landing that night when he had admonished her to try something new.

He edged back into the darkness and she leaned further into the light, her eyes overwhelming her face and her mouth set in a thin, determined line. "I will do something," she said, bearing down on each word, "because for the first time in my life I feel almost brave."

He glimpsed this new bravery behind her hard gaze and sensed something vital and purposeful, precious, which she had found and guarded like a prize within her center. He wanted it. He would have liked to snatch it and run like a thief. He no longer desired her but it, and starting forward with a sudden envious cry, he caught her arm and drew her close, seeking it.

But he could not get to it. Although she did not pull away her arm, although she made no protest as his face wavered close to hers, he did not really touch her. She held herself and her prize out of his desperate reach and her smile was a knife she pressed to his throat. He saw himself for what he was in her clear, cold gaze: an old man with skin the color and texture of dough that had been kneaded by the years into tragic folds, with faded eyes adrift behind a pair of rimless glasses and the roughened flesh at his throat like a bird's wattles. And as the disgust which he read in her eyes swept

him, his hand dropped from her arm. He started to murmur, "Forgive me . . ." when suddenly she caught hold of his wrist, pulling
him close again, and he felt the strength which had borne her swiftly
through the water earlier hold him now as she said quietly and
without passion, "And do you know why, Dr. Berman, I feel
almost brave today? Because ever since I can remember my parents
were always telling me, 'Stay away from white folks. Just leave
them alone. You mind your business and they'll mind theirs. Don't
go near them.' And they made sure I didn't. My father, who was
the principal of a colored grade school in Richmond, used to drive
me to and from school every day. When I needed something from
downtown my mother would take me and if the white saleslady
asked me anything she would answer. . . .

"And my parents were also always telling me, 'Stay away from
niggers,' and that meant anybody darker than we were." She held
out her arm in the light and Max Berman saw the skin almost as
white as his but for the subtle amber shading. Staring at the arm
she said tragically, "I was so confused I never really went near
anybody. Even when I went away to college I kept to myself. I
didn't marry the man I wanted to because he was dark and I knew
my parents would disapprove. . . ." She paused, her wistful gaze
searching the darkness for the face of the man she had refused, it
seemed, and not finding it she went on sadly. "So after graduation
I returned home and started teaching and I was just as confused
and frightened and ashamed as always. When my parents died I
went on the same way. And I would have gone on like that the
rest of my life if it hadn't been for you, Dr. Berman"—and the
sarcasm leaped behind her cold smile. "In a way you did me a
favor. You let me know how you and most of the people like you—
see me."

"My dear Miss Williams, I assure you I was not attracted to you
because you were colored. . . ." And he broke off, remembering
just how acutely aware of her color he had been.

"I'm not interested in your reasons!" she said brutally. "What
matters is what it meant to me. I thought about this these last three
weeks and about my parents how wrong they had been, how frightened, and the terrible thing they had done to me . . . and I wasn't

confused any longer." Her head lifted, tremulous with her new assurance. "I can do something now! I can begin," she said with her head poised. "Look how I came all the way up here to tell you this to your face. Because how could you harm me? You're so old you're like a cup I could break in my hand." And her hand tightened on his wrist, wrenching the last of his frail life from him, it seemed. Through the quick pain he remembered her saying on the landing that night: "Maybe in order for a person to live someone else must die" and her quiet "I believe this" then. Now her sudden laugh, an infinitely cruel sound in the warm night, confirmed her belief.

Suddenly she was the one who seemed old, indeed ageless. Her touch became mortal and Max Berman saw the darkness that would end his life gathered in her eyes. But even as he sprang back, jerking his arm away, a part of him rushed forward to embrace that darkness, and his cry, wounding the night, held both ecstasy and terror.

"That's all I came for," she said, rising. "You can drive me to the station now."

They drove to the station in silence. Then, just as the girl started from the car, she turned with an ironic, pitiless smile and said, "You know, it's been a nice day, all things considered. It really turned summer again as you said it would. And even though your lake isn't anything like the one near my home, it's almost as nice."

Max Berman bowed to her for the last time, accepting with that gesture his responsibility for her rage, which went deeper than his, and for her anger, which would spur her finally to live. And not only for her, but for all those at last whom he had wronged through his indifference: his father lying in the room of shrouded mirrors, the wives he had never loved, his work which he had never believed in enough and lastly (even though he knew it was too late and he would not be spared), himself.

Too weary to move, he watched the girl cross to the train which would bear her south, her head lifted as though she carried life as lightly there as if it were a hat made of tulle. When the train departed his numbed eyes followed it until its rear light was like a single firefly in the immense night or the last flickering of his life. Then he drove back through the darkness.

Joyce Carol Oates

WHERE ARE YOU GOING, WHERE HAVE YOU BEEN?

∿

Her name was Connie. She was fifteen and she had a quick, nervous giggling habit of craning her neck to glance into mirrors or checking other people's faces to make sure her own was all right. Her mother, who noticed everything and knew everything and who hadn't much reason any longer to look at her own face, always scolded Connie about it. "Stop gawking at yourself. Who are you? You think you're so pretty?" she would say. Connie would raise her eyebrows at these familiar old complaints and look right through her mother, into a shadowy vision of herself as she was right at that moment: she knew she was pretty and that was everything. Her mother had been pretty once too, if you could believe those old snapshots in the album, but now her looks were gone and that was why she was always after Connie.

"Why don't you keep your room clean like your sister? How've you got your hair fixed—what the hell stinks? Hair spray? You don't see your sister using that junk."

Her sister June was twenty-four and still lived at home. She was a secretary in the high school Connie attended, and if that wasn't bad enough—with her in the same building—she was so plain and chunky and steady that Connie had to hear her praised all the time by her mother and her mother's sisters. June did this, June did that, she saved money and helped clean the house and cooked and Connie couldn't do a thing, her mind was all filled with trashy daydreams. Their father was away at work most of the time and when he came home he wanted supper and he read the newspaper at supper and after supper he went to bed. He didn't bother talking much to them, but around his bent head Connie's mother kept picking at her until Connie wished her mother was dead and she herself was dead and it was all over. "She makes me want to throw up sometimes," she complained to her friends. She had a high, breathless, amused voice that made everything she said sound a little forced, whether it was sincere or not.

There was one good thing: June went places with girl friends of hers, girls who were just as plain and steady as she, and so when Connie wanted to do that her mother had no objections. The father of Connie's best girl friend drove the girls the three miles to town and left them at a shopping plaza so they could walk through the stores or go to a movie, and when he came to pick them up again at eleven he never bothered to ask what they had done.

They must have been familiar sights, walking around the shopping plaza in their shorts and flat ballerina slippers that always scuffed the sidewalk, with charm bracelets jingling on their thin wrists; they would lean together to whisper and laugh secretly if someone passed who amused or interested them. Connie had long dark blond hair that drew anyone's eye to it, and she wore part of it pulled up on her head and puffed out and the rest of it she let fall down her back. She wore a pullover jersey blouse that looked one way when she was at home and another way when she was away from home. Everything about her had two sides to it, one for home and one for anywhere that was not home: her walk, which could be childlike and bobbing, or languid enough to make anyone think she was hearing music in her head; her mouth, which was pale and smirking most of the time, but bright and pink on these evenings out; her laugh, which was cynical and drawling at home—"Ha, ha, very funny"—but high-pitched and nervous anywhere else, like the jingling of the charms on her bracelet.

Sometimes they did go shopping or to a movie, but sometimes they went across the highway, ducking fast across the busy road, to a drive-in restaurant where older kids hung out. The restaurant was shaped like a big bottle, though squatter than a real bottle, and on its cap was a revolving figure of a grinning boy holding a hamburger aloft. One night in midsummer they ran across, breathless with daring, and right away someone leaned out a car window and invited them over, but it was just a boy from high school they didn't like. It made them feel good to be able to ignore him. They went up through the maze of parked and cruising cars to the bright-lit, fly-infested restaurant, their faces pleased and expectant as if they were entering a sacred building that loomed up out of the night to give them what haven and blessing they yearned for. They sat at the counter and crossed their legs at the ankles, their thin shoulders rigid with excitement, and listened to the music that made everything so good: the music was always in the background, like music at a church service; it was something to depend upon.

A boy named Eddie came in to talk with them. He sat backwards on his stool, turning himself jerkily around in semicircles and then stopping and turning back again, and after a while he asked Connie if she would like something to eat. She said she would and so she tapped her friend's arm on her way out—her friend pulled her face up into a brave, droll look—and Connie said she would meet her at eleven, across the way. "I just hate to leave her like that," Connie said earnestly, but the boy said that she wouldn't be alone for long. So they went out to his car, and on the way Connie couldn't help but let her eyes wander over the windshields and faces all around her, her face gleaming with a joy that had nothing to do with Eddie or even this place; it might have been the music. She drew her shoulders up and sucked in her breath with the pure pleasure of being alive, and just at that moment she happened to glance at a face just a few feet from hers. It was a boy with shaggy black hair, in a convertible jalopy painted gold. He stared at her and then his lips widened into a grin. Connie slit her eyes at him and turned away, but she couldn't help glancing back and there he was, still watching her. He wagged a finger and laughed and said, "Gonna get you, baby," and Connie turned away again without Eddie noticing anything.

She spent three hours with him, at the restaurant where they ate hamburgers and drank Cokes in wax cups that were always sweating, and then down an alley a mile or so away, and when he left her off at five to eleven only the movie house was still open at the plaza. Her girl friend was there, talking with a boy. When Connie came up, the two girls smiled at each other and Connie said, "How was the movie?" and the girl said, "*You* should know." They rode off with the girl's father, sleepy and pleased, and Connie couldn't help but look back at the darkened shopping plaza with its big empty parking lot and its signs that were faded and ghostly now, and over at the drive-in restaurant where cars were still circling tirelessly. She couldn't hear the music at this distance.

Next morning June asked her how the movie was and Connie said, "So-so."

She and that girl and occasionally another girl went out several times a week, and the rest of the time Connie spent around the house—it was summer vacation—getting in her mother's way and thinking, dreaming about the boys she met. But all the boys fell back and dissolved into a single face that was not even a face but an idea, a feeling, mixed up with the urgent insistent pounding of the music and the humid night air of July. Connie's mother kept dragging her back to the daylight by finding things for her to do or saying suddenly, "What's this about the Pettinger girl?"

And Connie would say nervously, "Oh, her. That dope." She always drew thick clear lines between herself and such girls, and her mother was simple and kind enough to believe it. Her mother was so simple, Connie thought, that it was maybe cruel to fool her

so much. Her mother went scuffling around the house in old bedroom slippers and complained over the telephone to one sister about
the other, then the other called up and the two of them complained
about the third one. If June's name was mentioned her mother's
tone was approving, and if Connie's name was mentioned it was
disapproving. This did not really mean she disliked Connie, and
actually Connie thought that her mother preferred her to June just
because she was prettier, but the two of them kept up a pretense
of exasperation, a sense that they were tugging and struggling over
something of little value to either of them. Sometimes, over coffee,
they were almost friends, but something would come up—some
vexation that was like a fly buzzing suddenly around their heads—
and their faces went hard with contempt.

One Sunday Connie got up at eleven—none of them bothered
with church—and washed her hair so that it could dry all day long
in the sun. Her parents and sister were going to a barbecue at an
aunt's house and Connie said no, she wasn't interested, rolling her
eyes to let her mother know just what she thought of it. "Stay
home alone then," her mother said sharply. Connie sat out back
in a lawn chair and watched them drive away, her father quiet and
bald, hunched around so that he could back the car out, her mother
with a look that was still angry and not at all softened through the
windshield, and in the back seat poor old June, all dressed up as if
she didn't know what a barbecue was, with all the running yelling
kids and the flies. Connie sat with her eyes closed in the sun,
dreaming and dazed with the warmth about her as if this were a
kind of love, the caresses of love, and her mind slipped over onto
thoughts of the boy she had been with the night before and how
nice he had been, how sweet it always was, not the way someone
like June would suppose but sweet, gentle, the way it was in movies
and promised in songs; and when she opened her eyes she hardly
knew where she was, the back yard ran off into weeds and a fence-
like line of trees and behind it the sky was perfectly blue and still.
The asbestos "ranch house" that was now three years old startled
her—it looked small. She shook her head as if to get awake.

It was too hot. She went inside the house and turned on the radio
to drown out the quiet. She sat on the edge of her bed, barefoot,

and listened for an hour and a half to a program called XYZ Sunday Jamboree, record after record of hard, fast, shrieking songs she sang along with, interspersed by exclamations from "Bobby King": "An' look here, you girls at Napoleon's—Son and Charley want you to pay real close attention to this song coming up!"

And Connie paid close attention herself, bathed in a glow of slow-pulsed joy that seemed to rise mysteriously out of the music itself and lay languidly about the airless little room, breathed in and breathed out with each gentle rise and fall of her chest.

After a while she heard a car coming up the drive. She sat up at once, startled, because it couldn't be her father so soon. The gravel kept crunching all the way in from the road—the driveway was long—and Connie ran to the window. It was a car she didn't know. It was an open jalopy, painted a bright gold that caught the sunlight opaquely. Her heart began to pound and her fingers snatched at her hair, checking it, and she whispered, "Christ. Christ," wondering how bad she looked. The car came to a stop at the side door and the horn sounded four short taps, as if this were a signal Connie knew.

She went into the kitchen and approached the door slowly, then hung out the screen door, her bare toes curling down off the step. There were two boys in the car and now she recognized the driver: he had shaggy, shabby black hair that looked crazy as a wig and he was grinning at her.

"I ain't late, am I?" he said.

"Who the hell do you think you are?" Connie said.

"Toldja I'd be out, didn't I?"

"I don't even know who you are."

She spoke sullenly, careful to show no interest or pleasure, and he spoke in a fast, bright monotone. Connie looked past him to the other boy, taking her time. He had fair brown hair, with a lock that fell onto his forehead. His sideburns gave him a fierce, embarrassed look, but so far he hadn't even bothered to glance at her. Both boys wore sunglasses. The driver's glasses were metallic and mirrored everything in miniature.

"You wanta come for a ride?" he said.

Connie smirked and let her hair fall loose over one shoulder.

"Don'tcha like my car? New paint job," he said. "Hey."

"What?"

"You're cute."

She pretended to fidget, chasing flies away from the door.

"Don'tcha believe me, or what?" he said.

"Look, I don't even know who you are," Connie said in disgust.

"Hey, Ellie's got a radio, see. Mine broke down." He lifted his friend's arm and showed her the little transistor radio the boy was holding, and now Connie began to hear the music. It was the same program that was playing inside the house.

"Bobby King?" she said.

"I listen to him all the time. I think he's great."

"He's kind of great," Connie said reluctantly.

"Listen, that guy's *great*. He knows where the action is."

Connie blushed a little, because the glasses made it impossible for her to see just what this boy was looking at. She couldn't decide if she liked him or if he was just a jerk, and so she dawdled in the doorway and wouldn't come down or go back inside. She said, "What's all that stuff painted on your car?"

"Can'tcha read it?" He opened the door very carefully, as if he were afraid it might fall off. He slid out just as carefully, planting his feet firmly on the ground, the tiny metallic world in his glasses slowing down like gelatine hardening, and in the midst of it Connie's bright green blouse. "This here is my name, to begin with," he said. ARNOLD FRIEND was written in tarlike black letters on the side, with a drawing of a round, grinning face that reminded Connie of a pumpkin, except it wore sunglasses. "I wanta introduce myself, I'm Arnold Friend and that's my real name and I'm gonna be your friend, honey, and inside the car's Ellie Oscar, he's kinda shy." Ellie brought his transistor radio up to his shoulder and balanced it there. "Now, these numbers are a secret code, honey," Arnold Friend explained. He read off the numbers 33, 19, 17 and raised his eyebrows at her to see what she thought of that, but she didn't think much of it. The left rear fender had been smashed and around it was written, on the gleaming gold background: DONE BY CRAZY WOMAN DRIVER. Connie had to laugh at that. Arnold Friend was pleased at her laughter and looked up at her. "Around the other side's a lot more—you wanta come and see them?"

"No."

"Why not?"

"Why should I?"

"Don'tcha wanta see what's on the car? Don'tcha wanta go for a ride?"

"I don't know."

"Why not?"

"I got things to do."

"Like what?"

"Things."

He laughed as if she had said something funny. He slapped his thighs. He was standing in a strange way, leaning back against the car as if he were balancing himself. He wasn't tall, only an inch or so taller than she would be if she came down to him. Connie liked the way he was dressed, which was the way all of them dressed: tight faded jeans stuffed into black, scuffed boots, a belt that pulled his waist in and showed how lean he was, and a white pullover shirt that was a little soiled and showed the hard small muscles of his arms and shoulders. He looked as if he probably did hard work, lifting and carrying things. Even his neck looked muscular. And his face was a familiar face, somehow: the jaw and chin and cheeks slightly darkened because he hadn't shaved for a day or two, and the nose long and hawklike, sniffing as if she were a treat he was going to gobble up and it was all a joke.

"Connie, you ain't telling the truth. This is your day set aside for a ride with me and you know it," he said, still laughing. The way he straightened and recovered from his fit of laughing showed that it had been all fake.

"How do you know what my name is?" she said suspiciously.

"It's Connie."

"Maybe and maybe not."

"I know my Connie," he said, wagging his finger. Now she remembered him even better, back at the restaurant, and her cheeks warmed at the thought of how she had sucked in her breath just at the moment she passed him—how she must have looked to him. And he had remembered her. "Ellie and I come out here especially for you," he said. "Ellie can sit in back. How about it?"

"Where?"

"Where what?"

"Where're we going?"

He looked at her. He took off the sunglasses and she saw how pale the skin around his eyes was, like holes that were not in shadow but instead in light. His eyes were like chips of broken glass that catch the light in an amiable way. He smiled. It was as if the idea of going for a ride somewhere, to someplace, was a new idea to him.

"Just for a ride, Connie sweetheart."

"I never said my name was Connie," she said.

"But I know what it is. I know your name and all about you, lots of things," Arnold Friend said. He had not moved yet but stood still leaning back against the side of his jalopy. "I took a special interest in you, such a pretty girl, and found out all about you—like I know your parents and sister are gone somewheres and I know where and how long they're going to be gone, and I know who you were with last night, and your best girl friend's name is Betty. Right?"

He spoke in a simple lilting voice, exactly as if he were reciting the words to a song. His smile assured her that everything was fine. In the car Ellie turned up the volume on his radio and did not bother to look around at them.

"Ellie can sit in the back seat," Arnold Friend said. He indicated his friend with a casual jerk of his chin, as if Ellie did not count and she should not bother with him.

"How'd you find out all that stuff?" Connie said.

"Listen: Betty Schultz and Tony Fitch and Jimmy Pettinger and Nancy Pettinger," he said in a chant. "Raymond Stanley and Bob Hutter—"

"Do you know all those kids?"

"I know everybody."

"Look, you're kidding. You're not from around here."

"Sure."

"But—how come we never saw you before?"

"Sure you saw me before," he said. He looked down at his boots, as if he were a little offended. "You just don't remember."

"I guess I'd remember you," Connie said.

"Yeah?" He looked up at this, beaming. He was pleased. He began to mark time with the music from Ellie's radio, tapping his fists lightly together. Connie looked away from his smile to the car, which was painted so bright it almost hurt her eyes to look at it. She looked at that name, ARNOLD FRIEND. And up at the front fender was an expression that was familiar—MAN THE FLYING SAUCERS. It was an expression kids had used the year before but didn't use this year. She looked at it for a while as if the words meant something to her that she did not yet know.

"What're you thinking about? Huh?" Arnold Friend demanded. "Not worried about your hair blowing around in the car, are you?"

"No."

"Think I maybe can't drive good?"

"How do I know?"

"You're a hard girl to handle. How come?" he said. "Don't you know I'm your friend? Didn't you see me put my sign in the air when you walked by?"

"What sign?"

"My sign." And he drew an X in the air, leaning out toward her. They were maybe ten feet apart. After his hand fell back to his side the X was still in the air, almost visible. Connie let the screen door close and stood perfectly still inside it, listening to the music from her radio and the boy's blend together. She stared at Arnold Friend. He stood there so stiffly relaxed, pretending to be relaxed, with one hand idly on the door handle as if he were keeping himself up that way and had no intention of ever moving again. She recognized most things about him, the tight jeans that showed his thighs and buttocks and the greasy leather boots and the tight shirt, and even that slippery friendly smile of his, that sleepy dreamy smile that all the boys used to get across ideas they didn't want to put into words. She recognized all this and also the singsong way he talked, slightly mocking, kidding, but serious and a little melancholy, and she recognized the way he tapped one fist against the other in homage to the perpetual music behind him. But all these things did not come together.

She said suddenly, "Hey, how old are you?"

His smiled faded. She could see then that he wasn't a kid, he was much older—thirty, maybe more. At this knowledge her heart began to pound faster.

"That's a crazy thing to ask. Can'tcha see I'm your own age?"

"Like hell you are."

"Or maybe a coupla years older. I'm eighteen."

"Eighteen?" she said doubtfully.

He grinned to reassure her and lines appeared at the corners of his mouth. His teeth were big and white. He grinned so broadly his eyes became slits and she saw how thick the lashes were, thick and black as if painted with a black tarlike material. Then, abruptly, he seemed to become embarrassed and looked over his shoulder at Ellie. "*Him*, he's crazy," he said. "Ain't he a riot? He's a nut, a real character." Ellie was still listening to the music. His sunglasses told nothing about what he was thinking. He wore a bright orange shirt unbuttoned halfway to show his chest, which was a pale, bluish chest and not muscular like Arnold Friend's. His shirt collar was turned up all around and the very tips of the collar pointed out past his chin as if they were protecting him. He was pressing the transistor radio up against his ear and sat there in a kind of daze, right in the sun.

"He's kinda strange," Connie said.

"Hey, she says you're kinda strange! Kinda strange!" Arnold Friend cried. He pounded on the car to get Ellie's attention. Ellie turned for the first time and Connie saw with shock that he wasn't a kid either—he had a fair, hairless face, cheeks reddened slightly as if the veins grew too close to the surface of his skin, the face of a forty-year-old baby. Connie felt a wave of dizziness rise in her at this sight and she stared at him as if waiting for something to change the shock of the moment, make it all right again. Ellie's lips kept shaping words, mumbling along with the words blasting in his ear.

"Maybe you two better go away," Connie said faintly.

"What? How come?" Arnold Friend cried. "We come out here to take you for a ride. It's Sunday." He had the voice of the man on the radio now. It was the same voice, Connie thought. "Don'tcha know it's Sunday all day? And honey, no matter who you were with last night, today you're with Arnold Friend and don't you forget it! Maybe you better step out here," he said, and this last was in a different voice. It was a little flatter, as if the heat was finally getting to him.

"No. I got things to do."

"Hey."

"You two better leave."

"We ain't leaving until you come with us."

"Like hell I am—"

"Connie, don't fool around with me. I mean—I mean, don't fool *around*," he said, shaking his head. He laughed incredulously. He placed his sunglasses on top of his head, carefully, as if he were indeed wearing a wig, and brought the stems down behind his ears. Connie stared at him, another wave of dizziness and fear rising in her so that for a moment he wasn't even in focus but was just a blur standing there against his gold car, and she had the idea that he had driven up the driveway all right but had come from nowhere before that and belonged nowhere and that everything about him and even about the music that was so familiar to her was only half real.

"If my father comes and sees you—"

"He ain't coming. He's at a barbecue."

"How do you know that?"

"Aunt Tillie's. Right now they're—uh—they're drinking. Sitting around," he said vaguely, squinting as if he were staring all the way to town and over to Aunt Tillie's back yard. Then the vision seemed to get clear and he nodded energetically. "Yeah. Sitting around. There's your sister in a blue dress, huh? And high heels, the poor sad bitch—nothing like you, sweetheart! And your mother's helping some fat woman with the corn, they're cleaning the corn—husking the corn—"

"What fat woman?" Connie cried.

"How do I know what fat woman, I don't know every goddamn fat woman in the world!" Arnold Friend laughed.

"Oh, that's Mrs. Hornsby. . . . Who invited her?" Connie said. She felt a little lightheaded. Her breath was coming quickly.

"She's too fat. I don't like them fat. I like them the way you are, honey," he said, smiling sleepily at her. They stared at each other for a while through the screen door. He said softly, "Now, what you're going to do is this: you're going to come out that door. You're going to sit up front with me and Ellie's going to sit in the back, the hell with Ellie, right? This isn't Ellie's date. You're my date. I'm your lover, honey."

"What? You're crazy—"

"Yes, I'm your lover. You don't know what that is but you will," he said. "I know that too. I know all about you. But look: it's real nice and you couldn't ask for nobody better than me, or more polite. I always keep my word. I'll tell you how it is, I'm always nice at first, the first time. I'll hold you so tight you won't think you have to try to get away or pretend anything because you'll know you can't. And I'll come inside you where it's all secret and you'll give in to me and you'll love me—"

"Shut up! You're crazy!" Connie said. She backed away from the door. She put her hands up against her ears as if she'd heard something terrible, something not meant for her. "People don't talk like that, you're crazy," she muttered. Her heart was almost too big now for her chest and its pumping made sweat break out all over her. She looked out to see Arnold Friend pause and then take a step toward the porch, lurching. He almost fell. But, like clever drunken man, he managed to catch his balance. He wobbled in his high boots and grabbed hold of one of the porch posts.

"Honey?" he said. "You still listening?"

"Get the hell out of here!"

"Be nice, honey. Listen."

"I'm going to call the police—"

He wobbled again and out of the side of his mouth came a fast spat curse, an aside not meant for her to hear. But even this "Christ!" sounded forced. Then he began to smile again. She watched this smile come, awkward as if he were smiling from inside a mask. His whole face was a mask, she thought wildly, tanned down to his throat but then running out as if he had plastered make-up on his face but had forgotten about his throat.

"Honey—? Listen, here's how it is. I always tell the truth and I promise you this: I ain't coming in that house after you."

"You better not! I'm going to call the police if you—if you don't—"

"Honey," he said, talking right through her voice, "honey, I'm not coming in there but you are coming out here. You know why?" She was panting. The kitchen looked like a place she had never seen before, some room she had run inside but that wasn't good enough, wasn't going to help her. The kitchen window had never had a curtain, after three years, and there were dishes in the sink for her to do—probably—and if you ran your hand across the table you'd probably feel something sticky there.

"You listening, honey? Hey?"

"—going to call the police—"

"Soon as you touch the phone I don't need to keep my promise and can come inside. You won't want that."

She rushed forward and tried to lock the door. Her fingers were shaking. "But why lock it," Arnold Friend said gently, talking right into her face. "It's just a screen door. It's just nothing." One of his boots was at a strange angle, as if his foot wasn't in it. It pointed out to the left, bent at the ankle. "I mean, anybody can break through a screen door and glass and wood and iron or anything else if he needs to, anybody at all, and specially Arnold Friend. If the place got lit up with a fire, honey, you'd come runnin' out into my arms, right into my arms an' safe at home—like you knew I was your lover and'd stopped fooling around. I don't mind a nice shy girl but I don't like no fooling around." Part of those words were spoken with a slight rhythmic lilt, and Connie somehow recognized them—the echo of a song from last year, about a girl rushing into her boy friend's arms and coming home again—

Connie stood barefoot on the linoleum floor, staring at him. "What do you want?" she whispered.

"I want you," he said.

"What?"

"Seen you that night and thought, that's the one, yes sir. I never needed to look anymore."

"But my father's coming back. He's coming to get me. I had to wash my hair first—" She spoke in a dry, rapid voice, hardly raising it for him to hear.

"No, your daddy is not coming and yes, you had to wash your hair and you washed it for me. It's nice and shining and all for me. I thank you sweetheart," he said with a mock bow, but again he almost lost his balance. He had to bend and adjust his boots. Evidently his feet did not go all the way down; the boots must have been stuffed with something so that he would seem taller. Connie stared out at him and behind him at Ellie in the car, who seemed to be looking off toward Connie's right, into nothing. This Ellie said, pulling the words out of the air one after another as if he were just discovering them, "You want me to pull out the phone?"

"Shut your mouth and keep it shut," Arnold Friend said, his face red from bending over or maybe from embarrassment because Connie had seen his boots. "This ain't none of your business."

"What—what are you doing? What do you want?" Connie said. "If I call the police they'll get you, they'll arrest you—"

"Promise was not to come in unless you touch that phone, and I'll keep that promise," he said. He resumed his erect position and tried to force his shoulders back. He sounded like a hero in a movie, declaring something important. But he spoke too loudly and it was as if he were speaking to someone behind Connie. "I ain't made plans for coming in that house where I don't belong but just for you to come out to me, the way you should. Don't you know who I am?"

"You're crazy," she whispered. She backed away from the door but did not want to go into another part of the house, as if this would give him permission to come through the door. "What do you . . . you're crazy, you. . . ."

"Huh? What're you saying, honey?"

Her eyes darted everywhere in the kitchen. She could not remember what it was, this room.

"This is how it is, honey: you come out and we'll drive away, have a nice ride. But if you don't come out we're gonna wait till your people come home and then they're all going to get it."

"You want that telephone pulled out?" Ellie said. He held the radio away from his ear and grimaced, as if without the radio the air was too much for him.

"I toldja shut up, Ellie," Arnold Friend said, "you're deaf, get a hearing aid, right? Fix yourself up. This little girl's no trouble and's gonna be nice to me, so Ellie keep to yourself, this ain't your date—right? Don't hem in on me, don't hog, don't crush, don't bird dog, don't trail me," he said in a rapid, meaningless voice, as if he were running through all the expressions he'd learned but was no longer sure which of them was in style, then rushing on to new ones, making them up with his eyes closed. "Don't crawl under my fence, don't squeeze in my chipmunk hole, don't sniff my glue, suck my popsicle, keep your own greasy fingers on yourself!" He shaded his eyes and peered in at Connie, who was backed against the kitchen table. "Don't mind him, honey, he's just a creep. He's a dope. Right? I'm the boy for you and like I said, you come out here nice like a lady and give me your hand, and nobody else gets hurt, I mean, your nice old bald-headed daddy and your mummy and your sister in her high heels. Because listen: why bring them in this?"

"Leave me alone," Connie whispered.

"Hey, you know that old woman down the road, the one with the chickens and stuff—you know her?"

"She's dead!"

"Dead? What? You know her?" Arnold Friend said.

"She's dead—"

"Don't you like her?"

"She's dead—she's—she isn't here any more—"

"But don't you like her, I mean, you got something against her? Some grudge or something?" Then his voice dipped as if he were conscious of a rudeness. He touched the sunglasses perched up on top of his head as if to make sure they were still there. "Now, you be a good girl."

"What are you going to do?"

"Just two things, or maybe three," Arnold Friend said. "But I promise it won't last long and you'll like me the way you get to like people you're close to. You will. It's all over for you here, so come on out. You don't want your people in any trouble, do you?"

She turned and bumped against a chair or something, hurting her leg, but she ran into the back room and picked up the telephone. Something roared in her ear, a tiny roaring, and she was so sick with fear that she could do nothing but listen to it—the telephone was clammy and very heavy and her fingers groped down to the dial but were too weak to touch it. She began to scream into the phone, into the roaring. She cried out, she cried for her mother, she felt her breath start jerking back and forth in her lungs as if it were something Arnold Friend was stabbing her with again and again with no tenderness. A noisy sorrowful wailing rose all about her and she was locked inside it the way she was locked inside this house.

After a while she could hear again. She was sitting on the floor with her wet back against the wall.

Arnold Friend was saying from the door, "That's a good girl. Put the phone back."

She kicked the phone away from her.

"No, honey. Pick it up. Put it back right."

She picked it up and put it back. The dial tone stopped.

"That's a good girl. Now, you come outside."

She was hollow with what had been fear but what was now just an emptiness. All that screaming had blasted it out of her. She sat, one leg cramped under her, and deep inside her brain was something like a pinpoint of light that kept going and would not let her relax. She thought, I'm not going to see my mother again. She thought, I'm not going to sleep in my bed again. Her bright green blouse was all wet.

Arnold Friend said, in a gentle-loud voice that was like a stage voice, "The place where you came from ain't there any more, and where you had in mind to go is cancelled out. This place you are now—inside your daddy's house—is nothing but a cardboard box I can knock down any time. You know that and always did know it. You hear me?"

She thought, I have got to think. I have got to know what to do.

"We'll go out to a nice field, out in the country here where it smells so nice and it's sunny," Arnold Friend said. "I'll have my arms tight around you so you won't need to try to get away and I'll show you what love is like, what it does. The hell with this house! It looks solid all right," he said. He ran a fingernail down the screen and the noise did not make Connie shiver, as it would have the day before. "Now, put your hand on your heart, honey. Feel that? That feels solid too but we know better. Be nice to me, be sweet like you can because what else is there for a girl like you but to be sweet and pretty and give in?—and get away before her people come back?"

She felt her pounding heart. Her hand seemed to enclose it. She thought for the first time in her life that it was nothing that was hers, that belonged to her, but just a pounding, living thing inside this body that wasn't really hers either.

"You don't want them to get hurt," Arnold Friend went on. "Now, get up, honey. Get up all by yourself."

She stood.

"Now, turn this way. That's right. Come over here to me.—Ellie, put that away, didn't I tell you? You dope. You miserable creepy dope," Arnold Friend said. His words were not angry but only part of an incantation. The incantation was kindly. "Now, come out through the kitchen to me, honey, and let's see a smile, try it, you're a brave, sweet little girl and now they're eating corn and hot dogs cooked to bursting over an outdoor fire, and they don't know one thing about you and never did and honey, you're better than them because not a one of them would have done this for you."

Connie felt the linoleum under her feet; it was cool. She brushed her hair back out of her eyes. Arnold Friend let go of the post tentatively and opened his arms for her, his elbows pointing in toward each other and his wrists limp, to show that this was an embarrassed embrace and a little mocking, he didn't want to make her self-conscious.

She put out her hand against the screen. She watched herself push the door slowly open as if she were back safe somewhere in the other doorway, watching this body and this head of long hair moving out into the sunlight where Arnold Friend waited.

"My sweet little blue-eyed girl," he said in a half-sung sigh that had nothing to do with her brown eyes but was taken up just the same by the vast sunlit reaches of the land behind him and on all sides of him—so much land that Connie had never seen before and did not recognize except to know that she was going to it.

Toni Cade Bambara

My Man
Bovanne

~❧~

Blind people got a hummin
jones if you notice. Which
is understandable completely
once you been around one and notice what no eyes will force you
into to see people, and you get past the first time, which seems to
come out of nowhere, and it's like you in church again with fat-
chest ladies and old gents gruntin a hum low in the throat to whatever the preacher be saying. Shakey Bee bottom lip all swole up
with Sweet Peach and me explainin how come the sweet-potato
bread was a dollar-quarter this time stead of dollar regular and he
say uh hunh he understand, then he break into this *thizzin* kind of
hum which is quiet, but fiercesome just the same, if you ain't ready

for it. Which I wasn't. But I got used to it and the onliest time I had to say somethin bout it was when he was playin checkers on the stoop one time and he commenst to hummin quite churchy seem to me. So I says, "Look here Shakey Bee, I can't beat you and Jesus too." He stop.

So that's how come I asked My Man Bovanne to dance. He ain't my man mind you, just a nice ole gent from the block that we all know cause he fixes things and the kids like him. Or used to fore Black Power got hold their minds and mess em around till they can't be civil to ole folks. So we at this benefit for my niece's cousin who's runnin for somethin with this Black party somethin or other behind her. And I press up close to dance with Bovanne who blind and I'm hummin and he hummin, chest to chest like talkin. Not jammin my breasts into the man. Wasn't bout tits. Was bout vibrations. And he dug it and asked me what color dress I had on and how my hair was fixed and how I was doin without a man, not nosy but nice-like, and who was at this affair and was the canapés dainty-stingy or healthy enough to get hold of proper. Comfy and cheery is what I'm tryin to get across. Touch talkin like the heel of the hand on the tambourine or on a drum.

But right away Joe Lee come up on us and frown for dancin so close to the man. My own son who knows what kind of warm I am about; and don't grown men all call me long distance and in the middle of the night for a little Mama comfort? But he frown. Which ain't right since Bovanne can't see and defend himself. Just a nice old man who fixes toasters and busted irons and bicycles and things and changes the lock on my door when my men friends get messy. Nice man. Which is not why they invited him. Grass roots you see. Me and Sister Taylor and the woman who does heads at Mamies and the man from the barber shop, we all there on account of we grass roots. And I ain't never been souther than Brooklyn Battery and no more country than the window box on my fire escape. And just yesterday my kids tellin me to take them countrified rags off my head and be cool. And now can't get Black enough to suit em. So everybody passin sayin My Man Bovanne. Big deal, keep steppin and don't even stop a minute to get the man a drink or one of them cute sandwiches or tell him what's goin on.

And him standin there with a smile ready case someone do speak he want to be ready. So that's how come I pull him on the dance floor and we dance squeezin past the tables and chairs and all them coats and people standin round up in each other face talkin bout this and that but got no use for this blind man who mostly fixed skates and skooters for all these folks when they was just kids. So I'm pressed up close and we touch talkin with the hum. And here come my daughter cuttin her eye at me like she do when she tell me about my "apolitical" self like I got hoof and mouf disease and there ain't no hope at all. And I don't pay her no mind and just look up in Bovanne shadow face and tell him his stomach like a drum and he laugh. Laugh real loud. And here come my youngest, Task, with a tap on my elbow like he the third grade monitor and I'm cuttin up on the line to assembly.

"I was just talkin on the drums," I explained when they hauled me into the kitchen. I figured drums was my best defense. They can get ready for drums what with all this heritage business. And Bovanne stomach just like that drum Task give me when he come back from Africa. You just touch it and it hum thizzm, thizzm. So I stuck to the drum story. "Just drummin that's all."

"Mama, what are you talkin about?"

"She had too much to drink," say Elo to Task cause she don't hardly say nuthin to me direct no more since that ugly argument about my wigs.

"Look here Mama," say Task, the gentle one. "We just tryin to pull your coat. You were makin a spectacle of yourself out there dancing like that."

"Dancin like what?"

Task run a hand over his left ear like his father for the world and his father before that.

"Like a bitch in heat," say Elo.

"Well uhh, I was goin to say like one of them sex-starved ladies gettin on in years and not too discriminating. Know what I mean?"

I don't answer cause I'll cry. Terrible thing when your own children talk to you like that. Pullin me out the party and hustlin me into some stranger's kitchen in the back of a bar just like the damn police. And ain't like I'm old old. I can still wear me some sleeveless dresses without the meat hangin off my arm. And I keep up with some thangs through my kids. Who ain't kids no more. To hear them tell it. So I don't say nuthin.

"Dancin with that tom," say Elo to Joe Lee, who leanin on the folks' freezer. "His feet can smell a cracker a mile away and go into their shuffle number post haste. And them eyes. He could be a little considerate and put on some shades. Who wants to look into them blown-out fuses that—"

"Is this what they call the generation gap?" I say.

"Generation gap," spits Elo, like I suggested castor oil and fricassee possum in the milk-shakes or somethin. "That's a white concept for a white phenomenon. There's no generation gap among Black people. We are a col—"

"Yeh, well never mind," says Joe Lee. "The point is Mama . . . well, it's pride. You embarrass yourself and us too dancin like that."

"I wasn't shame." Then nobody say nuthin. Them standin there in they pretty clothes with drinks in they hands and gangin up on me, and me in the third-degree chair and nary a olive to my name. Felt just like the police got hold to me.

"First of all," Task say, holdin up his hand and tickin off the offenses, "the dress. Now that dress is too short, Mama, and too low-cut for a woman your age. And Tamu's going to make a speech tonight to kick off the campaign and will be introducin you and expecting you to organize the council of elders—"

"Me? Didn nobody ask me nuthin. You mean Nisi? She change her name?"

"Well, Norton was supposed to tell you about it. Nisi wants to introduce you and then encourage the older folks to form a Council of the Elders to act as an advisory—"

"And you going to be standing there with your boobs out and that wig on your head and that hem up to your ass. And people'll say, 'Ain't that the horny bitch that was grindin with the blind dude?' "

"Elo, be cool a minute," say Task, gettin to the next finger. "And then there's the drinkin. Mama, you know you can't drink cause next thing you know you be laughin loud and carryin on," and he grab another finger for the loudness. "And then there's the dancin. You been tattooed on the man for four records straight and slow draggin even on the fast numbers. How you think that look for a woman your age?"

"What's my age?"

"What?"

"I'm axin you all a simple question. You keep talkin bout what's proper for a woman my age. How old am I anyhow?" And Joe Lee slams his eyes shut and squinches up his face to figure. And Task run a hand over his ear and stare into his glass like the ice cubes goin calculate for him. And Elo just starin at the top of my head like she goin rip the wig off any minute now.

"Is your hair braided up under that thing? If so, why don't you take it off? You always did do a neat cornroll."

"Uh huh," cause I'm thinkin how she couldn't undo her hair fast enough talking bout cornroll so countrified. None of which was the subject. "How old, I say?"

"Sixtee-one or—"

"You a damn lie Joe Lee Peoples."

"And that's another thing," say Task on the fingers.

"You know what you all can kiss," I say, gettin up and brushin the wrinkles out my lap.

"Oh, Mama," Elo say, puttin a hand on my shoulder like she hasn't done since she left home and the hand landin light and not sure it supposed to be there. Which hurt me to my heart. Cause this was the child in our happiness fore Mr. Peoples die. And I carried that child strapped to my chest till she was nearly two. We was close is what I'm tryin to tell you. Cause it was more me in the child than the others. And even after Task it was the girlchild I covered in the night and wept over for no reason at all less it was she was a chub-chub like me and not very pretty, but a warm child. And how did things get to this, that she can't put a sure hand on me and say Mama we love you and care about you and you entitled to enjoy yourself cause you a good woman?

"And then there's Reverend Trent," say Task, glancin from left to right like they hatchin a plot and just now lettin me in on it. "You were suppose to be talking with him tonight, Mama, about giving us his basement for campaign headquarters and—"

"Didn nobody tell me nuthin. If grass roots mean you kept in the dark I can't use it. I really can't. And Reven Trent a fool anyway the way he tore into the widow man up there on Edgecomb cause he wouldn't take in three of them foster children and the woman not even comfy in the ground yet and the man's mind messed up and—"

"Look here," say Task. "What we need is a family conference so we can get all this stuff cleared up and laid out on the table. In the meantime I think we better get back into the other room and tend to business. And in the meantime, Mama, see if you can't get to Reverend Trent and—"

"You want me to belly rub with the Reven, that it?"

"Oh damn," Elo say and go through the swingin door.

"We'll talk about all this at dinner. How's tomorrow night, Joe Lee?" While Joe Lee being self-important I'm wonderin who's doin the cookin and how come no body ax me if I'm free and do I get a corsage and things like that. Then Joe nod that it's O.K. and he go through the swingin door and just a little hubbub come through from the other room. Then Task smile his smile, lookin just like his daddy, and he leave. And it just me in this stranger's kitchen, which was a mess I wouldn't never let my kitchen look like. Poison you just to look at the pots. Then the door swing the other way and it's My Man Bovanne standin there sayin Miss Hazel but lookin at the deep fry and then at the steam table, and most surprised when I come up on him from the other direction and take him on out of there. Pass the folks pushin up towards the stage where Nisi and some other people settin and ready to talk, and folks gettin to the last of the sandwiches and the booze fore they settle down in one spot and listen serious. And I'm thinkin bout tellin Bovanne what a lovely long dress Nisi got on and the earrings and her hair piled up in a cone and the people bout to hear how we all gettin screwed and gotta form our own party and everybody there listenin and lookin. But instead I just haul the man on out of there, and Joe Lee and his wife look at me like I'm terrible, but they ain't said boo to the man yet. Cause he blind and old and don't nobody there need him since they grown up and don't need they skates fixed no more.

"Where we goin, Miss Hazel?" Him knowin all the time.

"First we gonna buy you some dark sunglasses. Then you comin with me to the supermarket so I can pick up tomorrow's dinner, which is goin to be a grand thing proper and you invited. Then we goin to my house."

"That be fine. I surely would like to rest my feet." Bein cute, but you got to let men play out they little show, blind or not. So he chat on bout how tired he is and how he appreciate me takin him in hand this way. And I'm thinkin I'll have him change the lock on my door first thing. Then I'll give the man a nice warm bath with jasmine leaves in the water and a little Epsom salt on the sponge to do his back. And then a good rubdown with rose water and olive oil. Then a cup of lemon tea with a taste in it. And a little talcum, some of that fancy stuff Nisi mother sent over last Christmas. And then a massage, a good face massage round the forehead which is the worryin part. Cause you gots to take care of the older folks. And let them know they still needed to run the mimeo machine and keep the spark plugs clean and fix the mailboxes for folks who might help us get the breakfast program goin, and the school for the little kids and the campaign and all. Cause old folks in the nation. That what Nisi was sayin and I mean to do my part.

"I imagine you are a very pretty woman, Miss Hazel."

"I surely am," I say just like the hussy my daughter always say I was.

Leslie Marmon Silko

YELLOW
WOMAN

My thigh clung to his with dampness, and I watched the sun rising up through the tamaracks and willows. The small brown water birds came to the river and hopped across the mud, leaving brown scratches in the alkali-white crust. They bathed in the river silently. I could hear the water, almost at our feet where the narrow fast channel bubbled and washed green ragged moss and fern leaves. I looked at him beside me, rolled in the red blanket on the white river sand. I cleaned the sand out of the cracks between my toes, squinting because the sun was above the willow trees. I looked at him for the last time, sleeping on the white river sand.

I felt hungry and followed the river south the way we had come the afternoon before, following our footprints that were already blurred by lizard tracks and bug trails. The horses were still lying down, and the black one whinnied when he saw me but he did not get up—maybe it was because the corral was made out of thick cedar branches and the horses had not yet felt the sun like I had. I tried to look beyond the pale red mesas to the pueblo. I knew it was there, even if I could not see it, on the sandrock hill above the river, the same river that moved past me now and had reflected the moon last night.

The horse felt warm underneath me. He shook his head and pawed the sand. The bay whinnied and leaned against the gate trying to follow, and I remembered him asleep in the red blanket beside the river. I slid off the horse and tied him close to the other horse. I walked north with the river again, and the white sand broke loose in footprints over footprints.

"Wake up."

He moved in the blanket and turned his face to me with his eyes still closed. I knelt down to touch him.

"I'm leaving."

He smiled now, eyes still closed. "You are coming with me, remember?" He sat up now with his bare dark chest and belly in the sun.

"Where?"

"To my place."

"And will I come back?"

He pulled his pants on. I walked away from him, feeling him behind me and smelling the willows.

"Yellow Woman," he said.

I turned to face him. "Who are you?" I asked.

He laughed and knelt on the low, sandy bank, washing his face in the river. "Last night you guessed my name, and you knew why I had come."

I stared past him at the shallow moving water and tried to remember the night, but I could only see the moon in the water and remember his warmth around me.

"But I only said that you were him and that I was Yellow Woman—I'm not really her—I have my own name and I come from the pueblo on the other side of the mesa. Your name is Silva and you are a stranger I met by the river yesterday afternoon."

He laughed softly. "What happened yesterday has nothing to do with what you will do today, Yellow Woman."

"I know—that's what I'm saying—the old stories about the ka'tsina spirit and Yellow Woman can't mean us."

My old grandpa liked to tell those stories best. There is one about Badger and Coyote who went hunting and were gone all day, and when the sun was going down they found a house. There was a girl living there alone, and she had light hair and eyes and she told them that they could sleep with her. Coyote wanted to be with her all night so he sent Badger into a prairie-dog hole, telling him he thought he saw something in it. As soon as Badger crawled in, Coyote blocked up the entrance with rocks and hurried back to Yellow Woman.

"Come here," he said gently.

He touched my neck and I moved close to him to feel his breathing and to hear his heart. I was wondering if Yellow Woman had known who she was—if she knew that she would become part of the stories. Maybe she'd had another name that her husband and relatives called her so that only the ka'tsina from the north and the storytellers would know her as Yellow Woman. But I didn't go on; I felt him all around me, pushing me down into the white river sand.

Yellow Woman went away with the spirit from the north and lived with him and his relatives. She was gone for a long time, but then one day she came back and she brought twin boys.

"Do you know the story?"

"What story?" He smiled and pulled me close to him as he said this. I was afraid lying there on the red blanket. All I could know was the way he felt, warm, damp, his body beside me. This is the way it happens in the stories, I was thinking, with no thought beyond the moment she meets the ka'tsina spirit and they go.

"I don't have to go. What they tell in stories was real only then, back in time immemorial, like they say."

He stood up and pointed at my clothes tangled in the blanket. "Let's go," he said.

I walked beside him, breathing hard because he walked fast, his hand around my wrist. I had stopped trying to pull away from him, because his hand felt cool and the sun was high, drying the river bed into alkali. I will see someone, eventually I will see someone, and then I will be certain that he is only a man—some man from nearby—and I will be sure that I am not Yellow Woman. Because she is from out of time past and I live now and I've been to school and there are highways and pickup trucks that Yellow Woman never saw.

It was an easy ride north on horseback. I watched the change from the cottonwood trees along the river to the junipers that brushed past us in the foothills, and finally there were only piñons, and when I looked up at the rim of the mountain plateau I could see pine trees growing on the edge. Once I stopped to look down, but the pale sandstone had disappeared and the river was gone and the dark lava hills were all around. He touched my hand, not speaking, but always singing softly a mountain song and looking into my eyes.

I felt hungry and wondered what they were doing at home now—my mother, my grandmother, my husband, and the baby. Cooking breakfast, saying, "Where did she go?—maybe kidnaped," and Al going to the tribal police with the details: "She went walking along the river."

The house was made with black lava rock and red mud. It was high above the spreading miles of arroyos and long mesas. I smelled a mountain smell of pitch and buck brush. I stood there beside the black horse, looking down on the small, dim country we had passed, and I shivered.

"Yellow Woman, come inside where it's warm."

II

He lit a fire in the stove. It was an old stove with a round belly and an enamel coffeepot on top. There was only the stove, some faded Navajo blankets, and a bedroll and cardboard box. The floor was made of smooth adobe plaster, and there was one small window facing east. He pointed at the box.

"There's some potatoes and the frying pan." He sat on the floor with his arms around his knees pulling them close to his chest and he watched me fry the potatoes, I didn't mind him watching me because he was always watching me—he had been watching me since I came upon him sitting on the river bank trimming leaves from a willow twig with his knife. We ate from the pan and he wiped the grease from his fingers on his Levis.

"Have you brought women here before?" He smiled and kept chewing, so I said, "Do you always use the same tricks?"

"What tricks?" He looked at me like he didn't understand.

"The story about being a ka'tsina from the mountains. The story about Yellow Woman."

Silva was silent; his face was calm.

"I don't believe it. Those stories couldn't happen now," I said.

He shook his head and said softly, "But someday they will talk about us, and they will say, 'Those two lived long ago when things like that happened.' "

He stood up and went out. I ate the rest of the potatoes and thought about things—about the noise the stove was making and the sound of the mountain wind outside. I remembered yesterday and the day before, and then I went outside.

I walked past the corral to the edge where the narrow trail cut through the black rim rock. I was standing in the sky with nothing around me but the wind that came down from the blue mountain peak behind me. I could see faint mountain images in the distance miles across the vast spread of mesas and valleys and plains. I wondered who was over there to feel the mountain wind on those sheer blue edges—who walks on the pine needles in those blue mountains.

"Can you see the pueblo?" Silva was standing behind me.

I shook my head. "We're too far away."

"From here I can see the world." He stepped out on the edge. "The Navajo reservation begins over there." He pointed to the east. "The Pueblo boundaries are over here." He looked below us to the south, where the narrow trail seemed to come from. "The Texans have their ranches over there, starting with that valley, the Concho Valley. The Mexicans run some cattle over there too."

"Do you ever work for them?"

"I steal from them," Silva answered. The sun was dropping behind us and shadows were filling the land below. I turned away from the edge that dropped forever into the valleys below.

"I'm cold," I said; "I'm going inside." I started wondering about this man who could speak the Pueblo language so well but who lived on a mountain and rustled cattle. I decided that this man Silva must be Navajo, because Pueblo men didn't do things like that.

"You must be a Navajo."

Silva shook his head gently. "Little Yellow Woman," he said, "you never give up, do you? I have told you who I am. The Navajo people know me, too." He knelt down and unrolled the bedroll and spread the extra blankets out on a piece of canvas. The sun was down, and the only light in the house came from outside— the dim orange light from sundown.

I stood there and waited for him to crawl under the blankets.

"What are you waiting for?" he said, and I lay down beside him. He undressed me slowly like the night before beside the river— kissing my face gently and running his hands up and down my belly and legs. He took off my pants and then he laughed.

"Why are you laughing?"

"You are breathing so hard."

I pulled away from him and turned my back to him.

He pulled me around and pinned me down with his arms and chest. "You don't understand, do you, little Yellow Woman? You will do what I want."

And again he was all around me with his skin slippery against mine, and I was afraid because I understood that his strength could hurt me. I lay underneath him and I knew that he could destroy me. But later, while he slept beside me, I touched his face and I had a feeling—the kind of feeling for him that overcame me that morning along the river. I kissed him on the forehead and he reached out for me.

When I woke up in the morning he was gone. It gave me a strange feeling because for a long time I sat there on the blankets and looked around the little house for some object of his—some proof that he had been there or maybe that he was coming back.

Only the blankets and the cardboard box remained. The .30-30 that had been leaning in the corner was gone, and so was the knife I had used the night before. He was gone, and I had my chance to go now. But first I had to eat, because I knew it would be a long walk home.

I found some dried apricots in the cardboard box, and I sat down on a rock at the edge of the plateau rim. There was no wind and the sun warmed me. I was surrounded by silence. I drowsed with apricots in my mouth, and I didn't believe that there were highways or railroads or cattle to steal.

When I woke up, I stared down at my feet in the black mountain dirt. Little black ants were swarming over the pine needles around my foot. They must have smelled the apricots. I thought about my family far below me. They would be wondering about me, because this had never happened to me before. The tribal police would file a report. But if old Grandpa weren't dead he would tell them what happened—he would laugh and say, "Stolen by a ka'tsina, a mountain spirit. She'll come home—they usually do." There are enough of them to handle things. My mother and grandmother will raise the baby like they raised me. Al will find someone else, and they will go on like before, except that there will be a story about the day I disappeared while I was walking along the river. Silva had come for me; he said he had. I did not decide to go. I just went. Moonflowers blossom in the sand hills before dawn, just as I followed him. That's what I was thinking as I wandered along the trail through the pine trees.

It was noon when I got back. When I saw the stone house I remembered that I had meant to go home. But that didn't seem important any more, maybe because there were little blue flowers growing in the meadow behind the stone house and the gray squirrels were playing in the pines next to the house. The horses were standing in the corral, and there was a beef carcass hanging on the shady side of a big pine in front of the house. Flies buzzed around the clotted blood that hung from the carcass. Silva was washing his hands in a bucket full of water. He must have heard me coming because he spoke to me without turning to face me.

"I've been waiting for you."

"I went walking in the big pine trees."

I looked into the bucket full of bloody water with brown-and-white animal hairs floating in it. Silva stood there letting his hands drip, examining me intently.

"Are you coming with me?"

"Where?" I asked him.

"To sell the meat in Marquez."

"If you're sure it's O.K."

"I wouldn't ask you if it wasn't," he answered.

He sloshed the water around in the bucket before he dumped it out and set the bucket upside down near the door. I followed him to the corral and watched him saddle the horses. Even beside the horses he looked tall, and I asked him again if he wasn't Navajo. He didn't say anything; he just shook his head and kept cinching up the saddle.

"But Navajos are tall."

"Get on the horse," he said, "and let's go."

The last thing he did before we started down the steep trail was to grab the .30–30 from the corner. He slid the rifle into the scabbard that hung from his saddle.

"Do they ever try to catch you?" I asked.

"They don't know who I am."

"Then why did you bring the rifle?"

"Because we are going to Marquez where the Mexicans live."

III

The trail leveled out on a narrow ridge that was steep on both sides like an animal spine. On one side I could see where the trail went around the rocky gray hills and disappeared into the southeast where the pale sandrock mesas stood in the distance near my home. On the other side was a trail that went west, and as I looked far into the distance I thought I saw the little town. But Silva said no, that I was looking in the wrong place, that I just thought I saw houses. After that I quit looking off into the distance; it was hot and the wildflowers were closing up their deep-yellow petals. Only the waxy cactus flowers bloomed in the bright sun, and I saw every color that a cactus blossom can be; the white ones and the red ones were still buds, but the purple and the yellow were blossoms, open full and the most beautiful of all.

Silva saw him before I did. The white man was riding a big gray horse, coming up the trail toward us. He was traveling fast and the gray horse's feet sent rocks rolling off the trail into the dry tumbleweeds. Silva motioned for me to stop and we watched the white man. He didn't see us right away, but finally his horse whinnied at our horses and he stopped. He looked at us briefly before he loped the gray horse across the three hundred yards that separated us. He stopped his horse in front of Silva, and his young fat face was shadowed by the brim of his hat. He didn't look mad, but his small, pale eyes moved from the blood-soaked gunny sacks hanging from my saddle to Silva's face and then back to my face.

"Where did you get the fresh meat?" the white man asked.

"I've been hunting," Silva said, and when he shifted his weight in the saddle the leather creaked.

"The hell you have, Indian. You've been rustling cattle. We've been looking for the thief for a long time."

The rancher was fat, and sweat began to soak through his white cowboy shirt and the wet cloth stuck to the thick rolls of belly fat. He almost seemed to be panting from the exertion of talking, and he smelled rancid, maybe because Silva scared him.

Silva turned to me and smiled. "Go back up the mountain, Yellow Woman."

The white man got angry when he heard Silva speak in a language he couldn't understand. "Don't try anything, Indian. Just keep riding to Marquez. We'll call the state police from there."

The rancher must have been unarmed because he was very frightened and if he had a gun he would have pulled it out then. I turned my horse around and the rancher yelled, "Stop!" I looked at Silva for an instant and there was something ancient and dark—something I could feel in my stomach—in his eyes, and when I glanced at his hand I saw his finger on the trigger of the .30-30 that was still in the saddle scabbard. I slapped my horse across the flank and the sacks of raw meat swung against my knees as the horse leaped up the trail. It was hard to keep my balance, and once I thought I felt the saddle slipping backward; it was because of this that I could not look back.

I didn't stop until I reached the ridge where the trail forked. The horse was breathing deep gasps and there was a dark film of sweat on its neck. I looked down in the direction I had come from, but I couldn't see the place. I waited. The wind came up and pushed warm air past me. I looked up at the sky, pale blue and full of thin clouds and fading vapor trails left by jets.

I think four shots were fired—I remembered hearing four hollow explosions that reminded me of deer hunting. There could have been more shots after that, but I couldn't have heard them because my horse was running again and the loose rocks were making too much noise as they scattered around his feet.

Horses have a hard time running downhill, but I went that way instead of uphill to the mountain because I thought it was safer. I felt better with the horse running southeast past the round gray hills that were covered with cedar trees and black lava rock. When I got to the plain in the distance I could see the dark green patches of tamaracks that grew along the river; and beyond the river I could see the beginning of the pale sandrock mesas. I stopped the horse and looked back to see if anyone was coming; then I got off the horse and turned the horse around, wondering if it would go back to its corral under the pines on the mountain. It looked back at me for a moment and then plucked a mouthful of green tumbleweeds before it trotted back up the trail with its ears pointed forward, carrying its head daintily to one side to avoid stepping on the dragging reins. When the horse disappeared over the last hill, the gunny sacks full of meat were still swinging and bouncing.

IV

I walked toward the river on a wood-hauler's road that I knew would eventually lead to the paved road. I was thinking about waiting beside the road for someone to drive by, but by the time

I got to the pavement I had decided it wasn't very far to walk if I followed the river back the way Silva and I had come.

The river water tasted good, and I sat in the shade under a cluster of silvery willows. I thought about Silva, and I felt sad at leaving him; still, there was something strange about him, and I tried to figure it out all the way back home.

I came back to the place on the river bank where he had been sitting the first time I saw him. The green willow leaves that he had trimmed from the branch were still lying there, wilted in the sand. I saw the leaves and I wanted to go back to him—to kiss him and to touch him—but the mountains were too far away now. And I told myself, because I believe it, he will come back sometime and be waiting again by the river.

I followed the path up from the river into the village. The sun was getting low, and I could smell supper cooking when I got to the screen door of my house. I could hear their voices inside—my mother was telling my grandmother how to fix the Jell-O and my husband, Al, was playing with the baby. I decided to tell them that some Navajo had kidnaped me, but I was sorry that old Grandpa wasn't alive to hear my story because it was the Yellow Woman stories he liked to tell best.

Margaret Atwood

GIVING
BIRTH

~~~

But who gives it? And to whom is it given? Certainly it doesn't feel like giving, which implies a flow, a gentle handing over, no coercion. But there is scant gentleness here, it's too strenuous, the belly like a knotted fist, squeezing, the heavy trudge of the heart, every muscle in the body tight and moving, as in a slow motion shot of a high-jump, the faceless body sailing up, turning, hanging for a moment in the air, and then—back to real time again—the plunge, the rush down, the result. Maybe the phrase was made by someone viewing the result only: in this case, the rows of babies to whom birth has occurred, lying like neat packages in their expertly wrapped blankets, pink or blue, with their labels scotch-taped to their clear plastic cots, behind the plate-glass window.

No one ever says *giving death*, although they are in some ways the same, events, not things. And *delivering*, that act the doctor is generally believed to perform: who delivers what? Is it the mother who is delivered, like a prisoner being released? Surely not; nor is the child delivered to the mother like a letter through a slot. How can you be both the sender and the receiver at once? Was someone in bondage, is someone made free? Thus language, muttering in its archaic tongues of something, yet one more thing, that needs to be renamed.

It won't be by me, though. These are the only words I have, I'm stuck with them, stuck in them. (That image of the tar sands, old tableau in the Royal Ontario Museum, second floor north, how persistent it is. Will I break free, or will I be sucked down, fossilized, a sabre-toothed tiger or lumbering brontosaurus who ventured out too far? Words ripple at my feet, black, sluggish, lethal. Let me try once more, before the sun gets me, before I starve or drown, while I can. It's only a tableau after all, it's only a metaphor. See, I can speak, I am not trapped, and you on your part can understand. So we will go ahead as if there were no problem about language.)

This story about giving birth is not about me. In order to convince you of that I should tell you what I did this morning, before I sat down at this desk—a door on top of two filing cabinets, radio to the left, calendar to the right, these devices by which I place myself in time. I got up at twenty-to-seven, and, halfway down the stairs, met my daughter, who was ascending, autonomously she thought, actually in the arms of her father. We greeted each other with hugs and smiles; we then played with the alarm clock and the hot water bottle, a ritual we go through only on the days her father has to leave the house early to drive into the city. This ritual exists to give me the illusion that I am sleeping in. When she finally decided it was time for me to get up, she began pulling my hair. I got dressed while she explored the bathroom scales and the mysterious white altar of the toilet. I took her downstairs and we had the usual struggle over her clothes. Already she is wearing miniature jeans, miniature T-shirts. After this she fed herself: orange, banana, muffin, porridge.

We then went out to the sunporch, where we recognized anew, and by their names, the dog, the cats and the birds, bluejays and goldfinches at this time of year, which is winter. She puts her fingers on my lips as I pronounce these words; she hasn't yet learned the secret of making them. I am waiting for her first word: surely it will be miraculous, something that has never yet been said. But if so, perhaps she's already said it and I, in my entrapment, my addiction to the usual, have not heard it.

In her playpen I discovered the first alarming thing of the day. It was a small naked woman, made of that soft plastic from which jiggly spiders and lizards and the other things people hang in their car windows are also made. She was given to my daughter by a friend, a woman who does props for movies, she was supposed to have been a prop but she wasn't used. The baby loved her and would crawl around the floor holding her in her mouth like a dog carrying a bone, with the head sticking out one side and the feet out the other. She seemed chewy and harmless, but the other day I noticed that the baby had managed to make a tear in the body with her new teeth. I put the woman into the cardboard box I use for toy storage.

But this morning she was back in the playpen and the feet were gone. The baby must have eaten them, and I worried about whether or not the plastic would dissolve in her stomach, whether it was toxic. Sooner or later, in the contents of her diaper, which I examine with the usual amount of maternal brooding, I knew I would find two small pink plastic feet. I removed the doll and later, while she was still singing to the dog outside the window, dropped it into the garbage. I am not up to finding tiny female arms, breasts, a head, in my daughter's disposable diapers, partially covered by undigested carrots and the husks of raisins, like the relics of some gruesome and demented murder.

Now she's having her nap and I am writing this story. From what I have said, you can see that my life (despite these occasional surprises, reminders of another world) is calm and orderly, suffused with that warm, reddish light, those well-placed blue highlights and reflecting surfaces (mirrors, plates, oblong window panes) you think of as belonging to Dutch genre paintings; and like them it is realistic in detail and slightly sentimental. Or at least it has an aura of sentiment. (Already I'm having moments of muted grief over those of my daughter's baby clothes which are too small for her to wear any more. I will be a keeper of hair, I will store things in trunks, I will weep over photos.) But above all it's solid, everything here has solidity. No more of those washes of light, those shifts, nebulous effects of cloud, Turner sunsets, vague fears, the impalpables Jeannie used to concern herself with.

I call this woman Jeannie after the song. I can't remember any more of the song, only the title. The point (for in language there are always these "points," these reflections; this is what makes it so rich and sticky, this is why so many have disappeared beneath its dark and shining surface, why you should never try to see your own reflection in it; you will lean over too far, a strand of your hair will fall in and come out gold, and, thinking it is gold all the way down, you yourself will follow, sliding into those outstretched arms, towards the mouth you think is opening to pronounce your name but instead, just before your ears fill with pure sound, will form a word you have never heard before . . .)

The point, for me, is in the hair. My own hair is not light brown, but Jeannie's was. This is one difference between us. The other point is the dreaming, for Jeannie isn't real in the same way that I am real. But by now, and I mean your time, both of us will have the same degree of reality, we will be equal: wraiths, echoes, re verberations in your own brain. At the moment though Jeannie is to me as I will some day be to you. So she is real enough.

Jeannie is on her way to the hospital, to give birth, to be delivered. She is not quibbling over these terms. She's sitting in the back seat of the car, with her eyes closed and her coat spread over her like a blanket. She is doing her breathing exercises and timing her contractions with a stopwatch. She has been up since two-thirty in the morning, when she took a bath and ate some lime Jello, and it's now almost ten. She has learned to count, during the slow breathing, in numbers (from one to ten while breathing in, from ten to one while breathing out) which she can actually see while she is silently pronouncing them. Each number is a different colour and, if she's concentrating very hard, a different typeface. They range

from plain Roman to ornamented circus numbers, red with gold
filigree and dots. This is a refinement not mentioned in any of the
numerous books she's read on the subject. Jeannie is a devotee of
handbooks. She has at least two shelves of books that cover everything from building kitchen cabinets to auto repairs to smoking
your own hams. She doesn't do many of these things, but she does
some of them, and in her suitcase, along with a washcloth, a package
of lemon lifesavers, a pair of glasses, a hot water bottle, some talcum
powder and a paper bag, is the book that suggested she take along
all of these things.

(By this time you may be thinking that I've invented Jeannie in
order to distance myself from these experiences. Nothing could be
further from the truth. I am, in fact, trying to bring myself closer
to something that time has already made distant. As for Jeannie,
my intention is simple: I am bringing her back to life.)

There are two other people in the car with Jeannie. One is a man,
whom I will call A., for convenience. A. is driving. When Jeannie
opens her eyes, at the end of every contraction, she can see the
back of his slightly balding head and his reassuring shoulders. A.
drives well and not too quickly. From time to time he asks her
how she is, and she tells him how long the contractions are lasting
and how long there is between them. When they stop for gas he
buys them each a styrofoam container of coffee. For months he has
helped her with the breathing exercises, pressing on her knee as
recommended by the book, and he will be present at the delivery.
(Perhaps it's to him that the birth will be given, in the same sense
that one gives a performance.) Together they have toured the hospital maternity ward, in company with a small group of other pairs
like them: one thin solicitous person, one slow bulbous person.
They have been shown the rooms, shared and private, the sitz-
baths, the delivery room itself, which gave the impression of being
white. The nurse was light-brown, with limber hips and elbows;
she laughed a lot as she answered questions.

"First they'll give you an enema. You know what it is? They
take a tube of water and put it up your behind. Now, the gentlemen
must put on this—and these, over your shoes. And these hats, this
one for those with long hair, this for those with short hair."

"What about those with no hair?" says A.

The nurse looks up at his head and laughs. "Oh, you still have some," she said. "If you have a question, do not be afraid to ask."

They have also seen the film made by the hospital, a full-colour film of a woman giving birth to, can it be a baby? "Not all babies will be this large at birth," the Australian nurse who introduces the movie says. Still, the audience, half of which is pregnant, doesn't look very relaxed when the lights go on. ("If you don't like the visuals," a friend of Jeannie's has told her, "you can always close your eyes.") It isn't the blood so much as the brownish-red disinfectant that bothers her. "I've decided to call this whole thing off," she says to A., smiling to show it's a joke. He gives her a hug and says, "Everything's going to be fine."

And she knows it is. Everything will be fine. But there is another woman in the car. She's sitting in the front seat, and she hasn't turned or acknowledged Jeannie in any way. She, like Jeannie, is going to the hospital. She too is pregnant. She is not going to the hospital to give birth, however, because the word, the words, are too alien to her experience, the experience she is about to have, to be used about it at all. She's wearing a cloth coat with checks in maroon and brown, and she has a kerchief tied over her hair. Jeannie has seen her before, but she knows little about her except that she is a woman who did not wish to become pregnant, who did not choose to divide herself like this, who did not choose any of these ordeals, these initiations. It would be no use telling her that everything is going to be fine. The word in English for unwanted intercourse is rape, but there is no word in the language for what is about to happen to this woman.

Jeannie has seen this woman from time to time throughout her pregnancy, always in the same coat, always with the same kerchief. Naturally, being pregnant herself has made her more aware of other pregnant women, and she has watched them, examined them covertly, every time she has seen one. But not every other pregnant woman is this woman. She did not, for instance, attend Jeannie's prenatal classes at the hospital, where the women were all young, younger than Jeannie.

"How many will be breast-feeding?" asks the Australian nurse with the hefty shoulders.

All hands but one shoot up. A modern group, the new generation, and the one lone bottle-feeder, who might have (who knows?) something wrong with her breasts, is ashamed of herself. The others look politely away from her. What they want most to discuss, it seems, are the differences between one kind of disposable diaper and another. Sometimes they lie on mats and squeeze each other's hands, simulating contractions and counting breaths. It's all very hopeful. The Australian nurse tells them not to get in and out of the bathtub by themselves. At the end of an hour they are each given a glass of apple juice.

There is only one woman in the class who has already given birth. She's there, she says, to make sure they give her a shot this time. They delayed it last time and she went through hell. The others look at her with mild disapproval. *They* are not clamouring for shots, they do not intend to go through hell. Hell comes from the wrong attitude, they feel. The books talk about *discomfort*.

"It's not discomfort, it's pain, baby," the woman says.

The others smile uneasily and the conversation slides back to disposable diapers.

Vitaminized, conscientious, well-read Jeannie, who has managed to avoid morning sickness, varicose veins, stretch marks, toxemia, and depression, who has had no aberrations of appetite, no blurrings of vision—why is she followed, then, by this other? At first it was only a glimpse now and then, at the infants' clothing section in Simpson's Basement, in the supermarket lineup, on streetcorners as she herself slid by in A.'s car: the haggard face, the bloated torso, the kerchief holding back the too-sparse hair. In any case, it was Jeannie who saw her, not the other way around. If she knew she was following Jeannie she gave no sign.

As Jeannie has come closer and closer to this day, the unknown day on which she will give birth, as time has thickened around her so that it has become something she must propel herself through, a kind of slush, wet earth underfoot, she has seen this woman more and more often, though always from a distance. Depending on the light, she has appeared by turns as a young girl of perhaps twenty to an older woman of forty or forty-five, but there was never any doubt in Jeannie's mind that it was the same woman. In fact it did not occur to her that the woman was not real in the usual sense (and perhaps she was, originally, on the first or second sighting, as the voice that causes an echo is real), until A. stopped for a red light during this drive to the hospital and the woman, who had been standing on the corner with a brown paper bag in her arms, simply opened the front door of the car and got in. A. didn't react, and Jeannie knows better than to say anything to him. She is aware that the woman is not really there: Jeannie is not crazy. She could even make the woman disappear by opening her eyes wider, by staring, but it is only the shape that would go away, not the feeling. Jeannie isn't exactly afraid of this woman. She is afraid for her.

When they reach the hospital, the woman gets out of the car and is through the door by the time A. has come around to help Jeannie out of the back seat. In the lobby she is nowhere to be seen. Jeannie goes through Admission in the usual way, unshadowed.

There has been an epidemic of babies during the night and the maternity ward is overcrowded. Jeannie waits for her room behind a dividing screen. Nearby someone is screaming, screaming and mumbling between screams in what sounds like a foreign language. Portuguese, Jeannie thinks. She tells herself that for them it is different, you're supposed to scream, you're regarded as queer if you don't scream, it's a required part of giving birth. Nevertheless she knows that the woman screaming is the other woman and she is screaming from pain. Jeannie listens to the other voice, also a woman's, comforting, reassuring her mother? A nurse?

A. arrives and they sit uneasily, listening to the screams. Finally Jeannie is sent for and she goes for her prep. *Prep school*, she thinks. She takes off her clothes—when will she see them again?—and puts on the hospital gown. She is examined, labelled around the wrist, and given an enema. She tells the nurse she can't take Demerol because she's allergic to it, and the nurse writes this down. Jeannie doesn't know whether this is true or not but she doesn't want Demerol, she has read the books. She intends to put up a struggle over her pubic hair—surely she will lose her strength if it is all shaved off—but it turns out the nurse doesn't have very strong feelings about it. She is told her contractions are not far enough along to be taken seriously, she can even have lunch. She puts on her dressing gown and rejoins A., in the freshly vacated room, eats some tomato soup and a veal cutlet, and decides to take a nap while A. goes out for supplies.

Jeannie wakes up when A. comes back. He has brought a paper, some detective novels for Jeannie, and a bottle of Scotch for himself. A. reads the paper and drinks Scotch, and Jeannie reads *Poirot's Early Cases*. There is no connection between Poirot and her labour, which is now intensifying, unless it is the egg-shape of Poirot's head and the vegetable marrows he is known to cultivate with strands of wet wool (placentae? umbilical cords?). She is glad the stories are short; she is walking around the room now, between contractions. Lunch was definitely a mistake.

"I think I have back labour," she says to A. They get out the handbook and look up the instructions for this. It's useful that everything has a name. Jeannie kneels on the bed and rests her forehead on her arms while A. rubs her back. A. pours himself another Scotch, in the hospital glass. The nurse, in pink, comes, looks, asks about the timing, and goes away again. Jeannie is beginning to sweat. She can only manage half a page or so of Poirot before she has to clamber back up on the bed again and begin breathing and running through the coloured numbers.

When the nurse comes back, she has a wheelchair. It's time to go down to the labour room, she says. Jeannie feels stupid sitting in the wheelchair. She tells herself about peasant women having babies in the fields, Indian women having them on portages with hardly a second thought. She feels effete. But the hospital wants her to ride, and considering the fact that the nurse is tiny, perhaps it's just as well. What if Jeannie were to collapse, after all? After all her courageous talk. An image of the tiny pink nurse, ant-like, trundling large Jeannie through the corridors, rolling her along like a heavy beachball.

As they go by the check-in desk a woman is wheeled past on a table, covered by a sheet. Her eyes are closed and there's a bottle feeding into her arm through a tube. Something is wrong. Jeannie looks back—she thinks it was the other woman—but the sheeted table is hidden now behind the counter.

In the dim labour room Jeannie takes off her dressing gown and is helped up onto the bed by the nurse. A. brings her suitcase,

which is not a suitcase actually but a small flight bag; the significance
of this has not been lost on Jeannie, and in fact she now has some
of the apprehensive feelings she associates with planes, including
the fear of a crash. She takes out her Lifesavers, her glasses, her
washcloth and the other things she thinks she will need. She re-
moves her contact lenses and places them in their case, reminding
A. that they must not be lost. Now she is purblind.

There is something else in her bag that she doesn't remove. It's
a talisman, given to her several years ago as a souvenir by a travelling friend of hers. It's a rounded oblong of opaque blue glass,
with four yellow and white eye shapes on it. In Turkey, her friend
has told her, they hang them on mules to protect against the Evil
Eye. Jeannie knows this talisman probably won't work for her, she
is not Turkish and she isn't a mule, but it makes her feel safer to
have it in the room with her. She had planned to hold it in her
hand during the most difficult part of labour but somehow there
is no longer any time for carrying out plans like this.

An old woman, a fat old woman dressed all in green, comes into
the room and sits beside Jeannie. She says to A., who is sitting on
the other side of Jeannie, "That is a good watch. They don't make
watches like that any more." She is referring to his gold pocket
watch, one of his few extravagances, which is on the night table.
Then she places her hand on Jeannie's belly to feel the contraction.
"This is good," she says; her accent is Swedish or German. "This,
I call a contraction. Before, it was nothing." Jeannie can no longer
remember having seen her before. "Good. Good."

"When will I have it?" Jeannie asks, when she can talk, when
she is no longer counting.

The old woman laughs. Surely that laugh, those tribal hands,
have presided over a thousand beds, a thousand kitchen tables . . .
"A long time yet," she says. "Eight, ten hours."

"But I've been *doing* this for twelve hours already," Jeannie says.

"Not hard labour," the woman says. "Not good, like this."

Jeannie settles into herself for the long wait. At the moment she
can't remember why she wanted to have a baby in the first place.
That decision was made by someone else, whose motives are now
unclear. She remembers the way women who had babies used to

smile at one another, mysteriously, as if there was something they knew that she didn't, the way they would casually exclude her from their frame of reference. What was the knowledge, the mystery, or was having a baby really no more inexplicable than having a car accident or an orgasm? (But these too were indescribable, events of the body, all of them; why should the mind distress itself trying to find a language for them?) She has sworn she will never do that to any woman without children, engage in those passwords and exclusions. She's old enough, she's been put through enough years of it to find it tiresome and cruel.

But—and this is the part of Jeannie that goes with the talisman hidden in her bag, not with the part that longs to build kitchen cabinets and smoke hams—she is, secretly, hoping for a mystery. Something more than this, something else, a vision. After all she is risking her life, though it's not too likely she will die. Still, some women do. Internal bleeding, shock, heart failure, a mistake on the part of someone, a nurse, a doctor. She deserves a vision, she deserves to be allowed to bring something back with her from this dark place into which she is now rapidly descending.

She thinks momentarily about the other woman. Her motives, too, are unclear. Why doesn't she want to have a baby? Has she been raped, does she have ten other children, is she starving? Why hasn't she had an abortion? Jeannie doesn't know, and in fact it no longer matters why. *Uncross your fingers*, Jeannie thinks to her. Her face, distorted with pain and terror, floats briefly behind Jeannie's eyes before it too drifts away.

Jeannie tries to reach down to the baby, as she has many times before, sending waves of love, colour, music, down through her arteries to it, but she finds she can no longer do this. She can no longer feel the baby as a baby, its arms and legs poking, kicking, turning. It has collected itself together, it's a hard sphere, it does not have time right now to listen to her. She's grateful for this because she isn't sure anyway how good the message would be. She no longer has control of the numbers either, she can no longer see them, although she continues mechanically to count. She realizes she has practised for the wrong thing, A. squeezing her knee was nothing, she should have practised for this, whatever it is.

"Slow down," A. says. She's on her side now, he's holding her hand. "Slow it right down."

"I can't, I can't do it, I can't do this."

"Yes you can."

"Will I sound like that?"

"Like what?" A. says. Perhaps he can't hear it: it's the other woman, in the room next door or the room next door to that. She's screaming and crying, screaming and crying. While she cries she is saying, over and over, "It hurts. It hurts."

"No, you won't," he says. So there is someone, after all.

A doctor comes in, not her own doctor. They want her to turn over on her back.

"I can't," she says. "I don't like it that way." Sounds have receded, she has trouble hearing them. She turns over and the doctor gropes with her rubber-gloved hand. Something wet and hot flows over her thighs.

"It was just ready to break," the doctor says. "All I had to do was touch it. Four centimetres," she says to A.

"Only *four?*" Jeannie says. She feels cheated; they must be wrong. The doctor says her own doctor will be called in time. Jeannie is outraged at them. They have not understood, but it's too late to say this and she slips back into the dark place, which is not hell, which is more like being inside, trying to get out. *Out*, she says or thinks. Then she is floating, the numbers are gone, if anyone told her to get up, go out of the room, stand on her head, she would do it. From minute to minute she comes up again, grabs for air.

"You're hyperventilating," A. says. "Slow it down." He is rubbing her back now, hard, and she takes his hand and shoves it viciously farther down, to the right place, which is not the right place as soon as his hand is there. She remembers a story she read once, about the Nazis tying the legs of Jewish women together during labour. She never really understood before how that could kill you.

A nurse appears with a needle. "I don't want it," Jeannie says.

"Don't be hard on yourself," the nurse says. "You don't have to go through pain like that." *What pain?* Jeannie thinks. When there is no pain she feels nothing, when there is pain, she feels nothing because there is no *she*. This, finally, is the disappearance of language. *You don't remember afterwards*, she has been told by almost everyone.

Jeannie comes out of a contraction, gropes for control. "Will it hurt the baby?" she says.

"It's a mild analgesic," the doctor says. "We wouldn't allow anything that would hurt the baby." Jeannie doesn't believe this. Nevertheless she is jabbed, and the doctor is right, it is very mild, because it doesn't seem to do a thing for Jeannie, though A. later tells her she has slept briefly between contractions.

Suddenly she sits bolt upright. She is wide awake and lucid. "You have to ring that bell right now," she says. "This baby is being born."

A. clearly doesn't believe her. "I can feel it, I can feel the head," she says. A. pushes the button for the call bell. A nurse appears and checks, and now everything is happening too soon, nobody is ready. They set off down the hall, the nurse wheeling. Jeannie feels fine. She watches the corridors, the edges of everything shadowy because she doesn't have her glasses on. She hopes A. will remember to bring them. They pass another doctor.

"Need me?" she asks.

"Oh no," the nurse answers breezily. "Natural childbirth."

Jeannie realizes that this woman must have been the anaesthetist. "What?" she says, but it's too late now, they are in the room itself, all those glossy surfaces, tubular strange apparatus like a science fiction movie, and the nurse is telling her to get onto the delivery table. No one else is in the room.

"You must be crazy," Jeannie says.

"Don't push," the nurse says.

"What do you mean?" Jeannie says. This is absurd. Why should she wait, why should the baby wait for them because they're late?

"Breathe through your mouth," the nurse says. "Pant," and Jeannie finally remembers how. When the contraction is over she uses the nurse's arm as a lever and hauls herself across onto the table.

From somewhere her own doctor materializes, in her doctor suit already, looking even more like Mary Poppins than usual, and Jeannie says, "Bet you weren't expecting to see me so soon!" The baby is being born when Jeannie said it would, though just three days ago the doctor said it would be at least another week, and this makes Jeannie feel jubilant and smug. Not that she knew, she'd believed the doctor.

She's being covered with a green tablecloth, they are taking far too long, she feels like pushing the baby out now, before they are ready. A. is there by her head, swathed in robes, hats, masks. He has forgotten her glasses. "Push now," the doctor says. Jeannie grips with her hands, grits her teeth, face, her whole body together, a snarl, a fierce smile, the baby is enormous, a stone, a boulder, her bones unlock, and, once, twice, the third time, she opens like a birdcage turning slowly inside out.

A pause; a wet kitten slithers between her legs. "Why don't you look?" says the doctor, but Jeannie still has her eyes closed. No glasses, she couldn't have seen a thing anyway. "Why don't you look?" the doctor says again.

Jeannie opens her eyes. She can see the baby, who has been wheeled up beside her and is fading already from the alarming birth purple. *A good baby*, she thinks, meaning it as the old woman did: *a good watch*, well-made, substantial. The baby isn't crying; she squints in the new light. Birth isn't something that has been given to her, nor has she taken it. It was just something that has happened so they could greet each other like this. The nurse is stringing beads for her name. When the baby is bundled and tucked beside Jeannie, she goes to sleep.

As for the vision, there wasn't one. Jeannie is conscious of no special knowledge; already she's forgetting what it was like. She's tired and very cold; she is shaking, and asks for another blanket. A. comes back to the room with her; her clothes are still there. Everything is quiet, the other woman is no longer screaming. Something has happened to her, Jeannie knows, Is she dead? Is the baby dead? Perhaps she is one of those casualties (and how can Jeannie herself be sure, yet, that she will not be among them) who will go into postpartum depression and never come out. "You see, there was nothing to be afraid of," A. says before he leaves, but he was wrong.

The next morning Jeannie wakes up when it's light. She's been warned about getting out of bed the first time without the help of a nurse, but she decides to do it anyway (peasant in the field! Indian on the portage!). She's still running on adrenalin; she's also weaker than she thought, but she wants very much to look out the window. She feels she's been inside too long, she wants to see the sun come up. Being awake this early always makes her feel a little unreal, a little insubstantial, as if she's partly transparent, partly dead.

(It was to me, after all, that the birth was given, Jeannie gave it, I am the result. What would she make of me? Would she be pleased?)

The window is two panes with a venetian blind sandwiched between them; it turns by a knob at the side. Jeannie has never seen a window like this before. She closes and opens the blind several times. Then she leaves it open and looks out.

All she can see from the window is a building. It's an old stone building, heavy and Victorian, with a copper roof oxidized to green. It's solid, hard, darkened by soot, dour, leaden. But as she looks at this building, so old and seemingly immutable, she sees that it's made of water. Water, and some tenuous jellylike substance. Light flows through it from behind (the sun is coming up), the building is so thin, so fragile, that it quivers in the slight dawn wind. Jeannie sees that if the building is this way (a touch could destroy it, a ripple of the earth, why has no one noticed, guarded it against accidents?) then the rest of the world must be like this too, the entire earth, the rocks, people, trees, everything needs to be protected, cared for, tended. The enormity of this task defeats her; she will never be up to it, and what will happen then?

Jeannie hears footsteps in the hall outside her door. She thinks it must be the other woman, in her brown and maroon checked coat, carrying her paper bag, leaving the hospital now that her job is done. She has seen Jeannie safely through, she must go now to hunt through the streets of the city for her next case. But the door opens, it's only a nurse, who is just in time to catch Jeannie as she sinks to the floor, holding onto the edge of the air-conditioning unit. The nurse scolds her for getting up too soon.

After that the baby is carried in, solid, substantial, packed together like an apple. Jeannie examines her, she is complete, and in the days that follow Jeannie herself becomes drifted over with new words, her hair slowly darkens, she ceases to be what she was and is replaced, gradually, by someone else.

Anne Tyler

HOLDING
THINGS
TOGETHER

~~~

He says that when he was ten, a family invited him to the movies and he got all dressed up in a new suit and tie and a blue striped shirt. But he didn't know how to tie the tie, and his father had died the year before and no one else in that household of women—mother, aunt, two sisters— knew how, either. They experimented most of Sunday afternoon, knotting and unknotting it until it was limp and crumpled. Finally, his aunt put it in her purse and caught a bus downtown. Standing in front of the show window at Patterson Brothers Menswear, she tied the tie so that it looked like the one on the mannequin. Then she took the bus home again and fastened the knot to his shirt with two straight pins. All through the movie he held his head at an angle, his hands hovering over his chest, protecting his long, clumsy tie as people squeezed past him to their seats.

There are a lot of questions I would like to ask about this. Couldn't he have gone to a neighbor? Didn't he have a male friend? Why wear a tie to a movie anyhow? At age *ten?*

You'd think at least he would have used a safety pin.

But I don't want to make too much of it. We've been married two years and I know by now: he doesn't like to talk about himself. In fact, I'm surprised he told me that story at all. I'm surprised he even remembered it.

He is forty years old, fifteen years my senior. A high-school principal. A large, pale, tired-looking man going bald. He always dresses formally, even for casual events—a home football game, a picnic—but generally there's something off kilter about his clothing. His lapels are spotted; his trousers are rumpled; his shirt is pricked with cigarette burns. His suit jacket always hangs lower in front, and the points of his collar curl up.

Of course, he knows how to tie a tie by now, but there are other things he's never learned. He can't fix a leaky faucet, for instance. He can't change the storm windows or put on tire chains. Is it because he lost his father so young? I was reared to believe that men take charge; I feel cheated. I do it myself, grumpily, or I call in a professional. I tell him I don't know where he'd be without me to hold things together. This always bothers him, and he walks away from me with his hands jammed into his pockets and his jacket sleeves rucked up to his elbows. Then I feel sorry; I never meant to sound so overbearing.

My car developed a shriek in the brakes and I had to take it to Exxon. This was last April, a beautiful, leafy April morning, but I was too upset to enjoy it. I can't stand to have something go wrong with my car. At the slightest symptom, I despair; I picture being stranded on the roadside, hood raised and white handkerchief fluttering, no one to stop for me but a couple of escaping convicts. Now here I was on my way to work and I heard this long, high

shriek as I braked for a stoplight. I turned right around and drove
to Exxon, where they know me. The mechanic on duty was
Victor—a red-headed man with a carrot tattooed on his forearm.
"Oh, Victor, just listen," I told him, and I had him stand out front
while I drove back and forth, stopping every few feet. The brakes
shrilled, though maybe not quite as loudly as before. I cut the motor
and stepped out of the car. "What do you think it might be?" I
asked.

He pulled at his nose. I waited. (My husband would have pres-
sured him, supplied too much information, pushed for an immediate answer, but I knew enough to let him take his time.) Finally
he said, "Just now start up?"

"Five minutes back," I told him.

"Little as *you* drive, chances are it's nothing at all."

"Yes, but what if I try to stop and can't? When it's the brakes,
I get worried, Victor."

"Well, no, just calm down. You go in and have a seat. I'll give
her a look."

I went into the office, with its two vinyl chairs and the coffee
table stacked with *Popular Mechanics*. Tins of motor oil and bottles
of windshield detergent were lined up neatly on the shelves. The
tall blond boy named Joel was thumbing through an auto-parts
catalogue. "Morning, Mrs. S.," he said. (He's fonder of me than
Victor is; I think he likes the way I look. One time he asked where
I bought my clothes, so that he could tell his wife.) He said, "Something gone wrong with the car again?"

"Victor's out checking my brakes," I told him. "Every time I
slow down, they make this squeaky sound."

"Never mind. Lots of times brakes'll do that," he said.

"Really?"

"Sure. I wouldn't give it a thought."

"Oh, Joel, I hope you're right," I said.

Then I sank onto one of the chairs, and fluffed my skirt around
my knees. I felt better already. Smaller boned. Joel was standing
in a shaft of sunlight with lazy dust specks drifting around his head,
and the chair was warm and smooth, and something gave off a
nice leathery smell. When Victor came to get me (it was nothing,

after all), I really was sorry to leave. I believe I could have sat there all morning.

My husband drives a Plymouth with a dented left fender, a smashed tail-light, and a BB scar like a little rayed sun on its right rear window. He seems determined just to use his car up—run it into the ground and walk away from it, as if it were something to be beaten into submission. Like his battered suits, or his shoes with the heels worn to lopsided slivers. What is it about him? I myself drive a Ford; I believe it's easiest to get parts for a Ford. It's five years old but it looks brand-new. Even the engine looks new; last year I had it steam-cleaned. Some people don't know you can do that, but you can.

If the weather has been dry, you can see the names of a couple of dozen high-school students written in the dust on my husband's fenders. Not to mention four-letter words, smiling faces, valentines. Inside, there are tattered files and magazines strewn across the seats, and squashed cigarette packs on the floor. The gearshift snaps in an alarming way when he goes into "Drive," and the engine tends to diesel long after he's cut the ignition. Also, his fan belt is loose; every time he makes a sharp turn you can hear a sound like a puppy's whimper. I tell him he ought to get it seen to. "You have to stay on top of these things," I tell him. "A machine is only worth the care you give it."

I feel ridiculous. I feel I'm turning into my father, a thorough, methodical man who wouldn't let me get my driver's license till I'd learned how to change a spare tire. Still, I know I'm right. "What if we're stranded somewhere?" I ask. "What if we're taking a very long trip and the car drops dead in the middle of an eight-lane highway?"

"Why, this is a *fine* car," my husband says.

He's offended, I can tell. He slumps in his seat, steering with only one wrist propped across the top of the wheel. He always drives abysmally—dashing start-ups, sudden swerves, jerky stops. At red lights, he refuses to shift to neutral. I tell him he ought to, but he says it's pointless. "Why get a car that's automatic and then spend your life shifting gears?" he asks.

"To save wear and tear on your transmission, of course."

He groans, and starts off again with a screech. I promise myself I won't say another word. But I can't resist a silent comment: as the car heads toward a curve at sixty miles an hour, I raise a hand deliberately and brace myself against the dashboard.

Last June, my old college roommate came to town and I took her out to lunch. Just the two of us; my husband doesn't like her. (He says she's brassy, loud, opinionated, but I believe he's jealous. Men imagine women are closer than they really are.) I picked her up at her sister-in-law's and drove her to Nardulli's, a little Italian restaurant I hardly ever get to go to. Bee looked wonderful. She wore tight white pants and a loose top, and ropes and ropes of branch coral. During the meal, we had all sorts of things to talk about—our jobs, our husbands, old friends—but by the time our coffee came we had more or less petered out. We drove back in near silence, the comfortable kind. Bee hummed "Star Dust" and let her arm hang loose out the window. I coasted down St. Johns Street, timing the lights perfectly.

Then on Delmore, where I had to turn left, the engine died. For no earthly reason. "Now, what . . .?" I said. I shifted gears and started up again. We rode smoothly till the stop sign on Furgan Street; then the engine died again. After that, it died every time I slowed down. Red and green warning signals flashed on the instrument panel; horns kept honking behind me. My accelerator foot started shaking. "Oh, Lord, something has gone wrong," I told Bee.

"Maybe you're out of gas," she said.

"Gas? How could it be the gas? It keeps on starting up again, doesn't it? That's ridiculous," I said.

Bee glanced at me but said nothing. I was too frantic to apologize. "Listen, I've got to get to Exxon," I said.

"There's a Texaco station just ahead."

"But Exxon is where they know my car, and it's only two more blocks."

The engine died again. "Thank God we're not out on some highway," I said, and I wiped my eyes on my sleeve. I could feel Bee's sideways stare.

Then just as we rolled into Exxon the car gave a final shudder, like a desert wanderer staggering into an oasis. I jumped out, leaving the door swinging open behind me. I ran into the garage, where Joel was standing under an elevated Volkswagen, whistling and squinting upward with his thumbs hitched through his belt loops. "Joel?" I said. "My car's developed this terrible problem."

He stopped whistling. "Why, hello, Mrs. S.," he said.

"Can't you take a look for me?"

He followed me into the sunlight. I felt better already; he was so slow and peaceful. All the while I was telling him the symptoms, he was just coolly raising the hood, poking around, humming whatever he'd been whistling. "Turn her on," he told me. I slid behind the wheel, started the engine, and stopped it when he signalled. Then I got out and went to look under the hood again. I watched his long, bony fingers, which seemed to have more texture than other people's because of the grime in the creases. He jiggled a little black wire.

"Is it the fuel pump?" I asked him. I'd had a terrible experience once with a fuel pump. (I'm learning auto parts the hard way, the same way soldiers learn geography.)

But Joel said, "Can't tell for sure. Going to bring her on inside. It won't take long."

I told Bee. She got out and we went to the office to wait. In the summer, the leathery smell was stronger than ever. I collapsed on one of the chairs, closed my eyes, and tipped my head back. "I'm sorry," I told Bee. "I just get so upset when my car doesn't work."

"You know what I would do?" said Bee. "Take a course in auto mechanics."

I opened my eyes and looked at her.

"Sure," she said. "That's what I did when our lawn started getting me down. I went over to the college and studied landscape architecture. I got up at six every morning for this course on television. I bought a machine to spread lime on the—"

"Yes," I said, "but I already have so much to—"

"Be adventurous! There aren't any *roles* anymore. Just jump in and do what you feel like."

I thought a minute.

"Bee," I said finally, "tell me the truth. Did you do that because you felt like it? Or because you saw that no one else was going to do it?"

"Hmm?" she said. But by then she had picked up one of the magazines, and was idly flipping pages. It was plain she didn't think the question was important.

After a while, Joel came in, wiping his hands on a rag. "It's the filter," he told me. "You've got to get your filter changed."

"Is that serious?"

"No, we can have her ready by five this afternoon."

Bee said, "I'll call my sister-in-law. She can come pick us up."

"But the car," I said. "I mean, after this will it be as good as ever? Will it run without stalling?"

"No reason why it shouldn't," Joel said.

He wrote my name on a printed form: Mrs. Simmons, in large, competent capitals. At the second line, his pencil paused. "Address? Phone?" he said.

"Four four four four Nelson Road. Eight four four, two two four four."

"Four must be your lucky number," he said.

"No, nine."

He looked up. Then he laughed.

"Well, you asked," I told him. Then I laughed too, ignoring Bee's blank stare. I felt young and scatterbrained, but in a pleasant way. It was wonderful to know that by five o'clock everything would be all right again.

Bee's sister-in-law came to get us in a great big lavender Cadillac, and she drove me home. Before I got out, I apologized again to Bee. "Oh, listen," she said, "forget it. But how about later, will you need a ride back to the station?"

"Oh, no. I'm sure Alfred will be home by then," I said.

"Well, if he isn't, now . . ."

"I'll call you," I promised.

But I was right. My husband was home in time to take me. Just barely, though: I had to rush him right back out the door. He seemed befuddled, out of step. He drove more sloppily than ever. "*What* did you say went wrong? Last week, your car looked fine," he said. He turned right, bouncing over the curb. He went through a yellow light that was changing to red. At Exxon, he slowed and gazed dimly out the window. "Don't leave till I make sure it's fixed," I said. (You have to tell him these things.) I hopped out and went into the garage, where Joel was spinning a tire on a turntable. He smiled when he saw me. "All set," he said. "Feel better now?"

"I certainly do," I said. Then I turned and waved to my husband, telling him he was free to go. He waved back. His sleeve looked like a used lunch bag. For some reason, it made me sad to see his dusty little car go puttering off into traffic again.

I first met my husband while I was student-teaching at his school. I didn't like teaching at all, as it turned out (now I work in a library), but I thought I should go ahead and get my certificate anyway. Just in case, was how I put it—meaning in case I never married, or was widowed young, or something like that.

Alfred when I met him was exactly the way he is now—shabby, shambling, absentminded. The only difference was that he seemed so authoritative. I heard the teachers talking about him: he was "Mr. Simmons" and he didn't like undisciplined classrooms. When he came to a room to observe, some electricity seemed to pass through the students. They acted more alert. The teacher grew crisper. Now I sit across from him at the supper table and I try and try to see him again in that shine of unquestioned assurance. I squint, giving him distance. He becomes so distraught that he drops his fork. "What's the matter?" he asks. "Have I done something wrong?"

Yet at school, the few times I've been back, I notice that the teachers still make improvements in their posture when they see him coming down the hall.

While we were courting, it never occurred to me to ask what he knew how to do. Could he change the oil? Hang a screen door? Well, of course he could; all men could. And even if he couldn't, what difference did it make? I loved him. I would go weak with love just watching his cuff button spin dizzily from one frayed thread. If he got lost while driving me to a restaurant, I was glad; I hadn't wanted to eat anyhow. I was only waiting for the moment when he would park the car in front of my apartment and take me in his arms. His hands (with their spatulate nails, their pink, uncalloused palms that should have been a warning) seemed to mold me; I curved within them and grew taller, slimmer, prettier. It was hardly the moment to ask if he knew how to replace a wall switch.

Then we married and went to live in a middle-aged house on Coker Street. It was a hard time; my parents thought Alfred was disappointing, and they more or less withdrew themselves. I felt orphaned. I started work in the library, and every evening when I came home (dead tired, feet aching) I had to fix supper, take out the garbage, vacuum, dust. On weekends, I mowed the lawn and pruned the shrubs, and then I washed the woodwork, painted rooms, varnished floors. My husband only watched, from various doorways. I don't mean to imply that he was lazy. It's just that he didn't know how to help. He would gladly take out the garbage for me but forgot to replace the trash-can lid, so dogs would tip the can over and spread the garbage everywhere. He dripped paint, stepped in the varnish, broke a window trying to open it. It turned out that he had never learned how to handle money, and had therefore been assigned one of those special bank tellers who balance checkbooks for rich, helpless widows. Also, he had a cubbyhole in his desk at home that contained nothing but unpaid parking tickets.

Well, I paid the tickets, I took over the checkbook, I drew up a yearly budget. Quizzing him on deductible expenses (my father's task, in my childhood), I felt I was becoming angular, wider shouldered. I developed my father's habit of offering forth one flat, spread hand, palm upward, inviting others to be reasonable. "Well, think, Alfred. Did you buy any stamps? Office supplies? Any books that had to do with your profession?"

"Books?" he would say. "Why, yes, I believe I did."

"How much were they? Do you have the receipts?"

"Oh, no. I must have lost them."

"Five dollars? Ten?"

"I'm not quite sure."

"Think of the titles. Maybe that will help. Fifteen dollars? Twenty? Was it under twenty-five?"

"I just don't *know*, Lucy. Please, does it matter all that much?"

At night, I began to have insomnia. I lay in bed with my hands curled tight, no matter how often I told myself to open them. I felt I was clutching all the strings of the house, keeping it together. Everything depended on me.

"When I start the motor," I told Joel, "it sounds just fine. Then I go faster and I'm waiting for that click, you know? That click that tells me the car's shifted gears? But I don't seem to hear it. And it seems to me the motor whines a little, has the wrong sound; I don't know how to explain it."

"Just hope it's not the transmission," Joel said. "That can get expensive."

We were waiting for a stoplight; he was driving. He was going to test the automatic shift for me. It was August and very hot and sunny (Joel's face was glazed with sweat and his yellow hair had a glittery look), but I didn't open my window. I liked the feeling of soaking in heat; I'd felt cold and anxious all morning. I liked the fact that Joel, waiting serenely for the light, whistled "Let It Be" and drummed his fingers on the steering wheel. My car seemed humble and obedient.

"I hope I don't have to buy a new one," I said.

"You won't," he told me.

The light changed. Joel started right off, but we were following someone—some old lady in a Studebaker who just wouldn't get up any speed. "Shoot," Joel said. He switched lanes. Now we really were travelling, and Joel had his head cocked to hear the sound of the motor. "Well?" he said. "Seems to me like she's shifting just about on schedule."

"No, wait a minute, give it a minute . . ."

I was listening too, but I couldn't hear what I heard when I was alone.

We turned off onto a smaller road, a residential street with no traffic lights. Joel stopped the car, then started again and went up to sixty, all the time keeping his head cocked. He braked and shifted to neutral; his knuckles moved beneath the skin like well-oiled machine parts. "Let's run her through again," he said.

The second run carried us to the end of the road—a surprise, a
field full of goldenrod and beer cans. He stopped the car and wiped
his upper lip with the back of his hand. "Well," he said, gazing
out at the field. Behind his eyes (which were long and blue, as clear
as windows) I imagined sheets of information, all the facts he knew
being reviewed in an orderly way. "No," he said finally, and shook
his head. "She seems O.K. to me."

You'd think I'd be relieved, but I wasn't. If something is wrong,
it can be fixed; then you know it won't go wrong again for a while.
But if nothing's been pinpointed, if it's just this nebulous feeling
of *error* in your mind . . . I sighed and gripped my purse. Joel
looked over at me. "I must be going crazy," I told him.

"Oh, no . . ."

"I seem to be taking this car so seriously. Lately, I've stopped
driving on freeways. I don't want to be too far from a service
station. I've had to give up the League of Women Voters and my
favorite supermarket. Even here in town, I only go by routes that
have service stations. Streets with nothing but houses make me
anxious."

"Shoot, this car's in *fine* shape," he told me, giving the wheel a
pat. "You don't have to feel like that."

"I'm worried pretty soon I'll just have to stay at home all day."

That made him laugh. "So what?" he said. "What's so bad about
home?"

"I'd lose my job, for one thing."

"Well, I just wish my wife would have your problem," he said.
"That's all she does all day—drive around. Drops me off at the
station and then drives here, drives there . . . spends all our money,
wears out the baby . . ."

"But she does have you to call if something goes wrong," I said.

"Where, forty miles out on the Beltway? Out at Korvettes, or
K Mart, or Two Guys? And none of what she buys is worth much.
All these skimpy sweaters, tacky plastic earrings . . . I don't be-
grudge the money, but she could save it up and buy something
good, like your tan coat—you know your tan coat?—and be a whole
lot better off. I tell her that, but think she'll listen?"

"Maybe she's lonely," I said.

"Maybe so," he said, "but I'd sure like a wife who stayed home some. And she doesn't take care of herself—she's so sloppy. She's let her hair grow long, and every time I come home I think, Well, who's this? I mean it never stops being a surprise, I never get used to it. I think, Is this *it*, is this who I'm with, this lady with the stringy hair? It's like I have amnesia. I just can't figure how it all happened."

"No one told us it would be so permanent," I said.

"Why, no," he said. "Not so as to make us believe it."

He looked over at me. His hands fell off the wheel. Outside, I could hear the locusts whirring, pointing up our silence. "Well!" I said, and Joel said, "Well! Victor will be having kittens by now." And he started up the car again, and turned around, and we drove on back to the station.

Last September, I went South to visit my parents for a week. It didn't go well, though. I'd been away too long; something had stiffened between us. I watched my younger sister teasing them at the supper table and I felt more orphaned than ever. My father stayed down in his workshop, taking things apart and putting them back together; my mother and I were so polite it was painful. I was glad when it was time to leave.

Alfred met me at the train station, carrying roses. I was so happy to see him. His crumpled clothes gave me a soothed and trustful feeling; I rested on his smell of old tobacco. "Don't let me leave you again," I told him. He smiled and laid the roses in my arms.

Driving home, he asked about my family: Were they used to the idea of our marriage yet? "Oh, sure," I told him offhandedly. What did my family have to do with us?

He parked in front of our house, with two wheels on the curb. He took my suitcase from the trunk, and we climbed the front steps, holding hands. "You notice I've mowed the grass for you," he said.

I was surprised. I looked around at the lawn—straggly, dotted with the first few leaves of fall. Plainly, something had been chewing at it. I saw the narrow, tufted rows he'd missed. "Why, Alfred!" I said.

He seemed uneasy.

"That's wonderful!" I told him.

"Yes, but—Lucy? I'm not so sure about the lawnmower."

"Lawnmower?"

"I mean, it seems to me that something's wrong with it."

"Oh, well, I'll check it later," I told him.

"It's right over there, if you want to take a look."

In the grass at the side of the house, he meant; he'd left it out. It was an electric mower, and fairly expensive—not a thing you'd leave sitting around. But I didn't tell him so. "What seems to be the trouble?" I asked.

"Well—"

He set my suitcase on the porch and went over to the mower. He turned the mower upside down without unplugging it (I winced but said nothing) and pointed to the blades. "See there?" he said.

Well, they *used* to be blades. Now they were mangled hunks of metal, notched and torn and twisted. I said, "What on earth?" I bent closer. One of the hunks of metal wasn't a blade at all, it turned out, but something flatter and wider. "Why, that's the foot guard," I said. "It's supposed to be attached to the rear of the mower."

"Evidently it came loose," Alfred said.

"Yes, but—what happened, you just went on mowing? You mowed on over your own foot guard and let the blades gnash it up?"

"I didn't realize what was going on," he said.

"But the noise must have been horrendous!"

"Well, I thought it was the . . . I don't know. I just thought it was having a little spell of some sort, caught a twig or something."

I pictured it exactly: Alfred doggedly pushing on, with terrible shrieks and clatters coming from the mower. It gave me a feeling of despair. I couldn't seem to rise above this. "Oh, Alfred," I said, "can't you do something right? Will I always have to be the one?"

He straightened up and looked at me. His face had grown white. His eyes (ordinarily a mild gray) had widened and darkened; they seemed to be all iris. "I knew you would say that, Lucy," he said.

"If you knew, then why—"

"Nothing I do will satisfy you. You always want everything perfect and you always do it yourself; or stand over me and nag and belittle, find fault with every move I make. You just have to be in control; it's always you that holds the power."

"Is that how you see it?" I said. "Do you think I choose to be this way? Do you think I *want* the power? Take it! Why won't you take it? Do you think I'd hold it if anybody else would? *Take* it!"

And I shook my hands in his face, offering all that was in them, but he merely looked at me with a stoic expression. My hands were left raised before me. I let them drop. I watched him turn to right the mower and unplug it and trundle it toward the garage: a large, sad man in a baggy suit, slumping slightly as he walked.

My car's been running well lately, though I haven't given up worrying. In fact, the last time I went to Exxon it was just to fill the gas tank. I went on a foggy October morning, the first really cold day of fall. Joel was the one on duty. He seemed grim, maybe hung over; and I had a headache from sitting up to watch the late show after Alfred had gone to bed. So all I did was nod, and Joel nodded back and went to start the pump. While the tank was filling, he stood waiting with his arms folded. I stared straight ahead, watching my breath steam the windshield. Then I paid him six dollars and twenty-four cents and put my billfold back in my purse and drove away.

Alice Munro

ROYAL
BEATINGS

~≈~

Royal Beating. That was Flo's
promise. You are going to get
one Royal Beating.

The word Royal lolled on Flo's tongue, took on trappings. Rose
had a need to picture things, to pursue absurdities, that was stronger
than the need to stay out of trouble, and instead of taking this threat
to heart she pondered: how is a beating royal? She came up with
a tree-lined avenue, a crowd of formal spectators, some white horses
and black slaves. Someone knelt, and the blood came leaping out
like banners. An occasion both savage and splendid. In real life they
didn't approach such dignity, and it was only Flo who tried to

supply the event with some high air of necessity and regret. Rose and her father soon got beyond anything presentable.

Her father was king of the royal beatings. Those Flo gave never amounted to much; they were quick cuffs and slaps dashed off while her attention remained elsewhere. You get out of my road, she would say. You mind your own business. You take that look off your face.

They lived behind a store in Hanratty, Ontario. There were four of them: Rose, her father, Flo, Rose's young half brother Brian. The store was really a house, bought by Rose's father and mother when they married and set up here in the furniture and upholstery repair business. Her mother could do upholstery. From both parents Rose should have inherited clever hands, a quick sympathy with materials, an eye for the nicest turns of mending, but she hadn't. She was clumsy, and when something broke she couldn't wait to sweep it up and throw it away.

Her mother had died. She said to Rose's father during the afternoon, "I have a feeling that is so hard to describe. It's like a boiled egg in my chest, with the shell left on." She died before night, she had a blood clot on her lung. Rose was a baby in a basket at the time, so of course could not remember any of this. She heard it from Flo, who must have heard it from her father. Flo came along soon afterward, to take over Rose in the basket, marry her father, open up the front room to make a grocery store. Rose, who had known the house only as a store, who had known only Flo for a mother, looked back on the sixteen or so months her parents spent here as an orderly, far gentler and more ceremonious time, with little touches of affluence. She had nothing to go on but some egg cups her mother had bought, with a pattern of vines and birds on them, delicately drawn as if with red ink; the pattern was beginning to wear away. No books or clothes or pictures of her mother remained. Her father must have got rid of them, or else Flo would. Flo's only story about her mother, the one about her death, was oddly grudging. Flo liked the details of a death: the things people said, the way they protested or tried to get out of bed or swore or laughed (some did those things), but when she said that Rose's mother mentioned a hard-boiled egg in her chest she made the comparison sound slightly foolish, as if her mother really was the kind of person who might think you could swallow an egg whole. Her father had a shed out behind the store, where he worked at his furniture repairing and restoring. He caned chair seats and backs, mended wickerwork, filled cracks, put legs back on, all most admirably and skillfully and cheaply. That was his pride: to startle people with such fine work, such moderate, even ridiculous charges. During the Depression people could not afford to pay more, perhaps, but he continued the practice through the war, through the years of prosperity after the war, until he died. He never discussed with Flo what he charged or what was owing. After he died she had to go out and unlock the shed and take all sorts of scraps of paper and torn envelopes from the big wicked-looking hooks that were his files. Many of these she found were not accounts or receipts at all but records of the weather, bits of information about the garden, things he had been moved to write down.

Ate new potatoes 25th June. Record.
Dark Day, 1880's, nothing supernatural. Clouds of ash from forest fires.
Aug 16, 1938. Giant thunderstorm in evng. Lightning str. Pres. Church, Turberry Twp. Will of God?
Scald strawberries to remove acid.
All things are alive. Spinoza.

Flo thought Spinoza must be some new vegetable he planned to grow, like broccoli or eggplant. He would often try some new thing. She showed the scrap of paper to Rose and asked, did she know what Spinoza was? Rose did know, or had an idea—she was in her teens by that time—but she replied that she did not. She had reached an age where she thought she could not stand to know any more, about her father, or about Flo; she pushed any discovery aside with embarrassment and dread.

There was a stove in the shed, and many rough shelves covered with cans of paint and varnish, shellac and turpentine, jars of soaking brushes and also some dark sticky bottles of cough medicine.

Why should a man who coughed constantly, whose lungs took in a whiff of gas in the War (called, in Rose's earliest childhood, not the First, but the Last, War) spend all his days breathing fumes of paint and turpentine? At the time, such questions were not asked as often as they are now. On the bench outside Flo's store several old men from the neighborhood sat gossiping, drowsing, in the warm weather, and some of these old men coughed all the time too. The fact is they were dying, slowly and discreetly, of what was called, without any particular sense of grievance, "the foundry disease." They had worked all their lives at the foundry in town, and now they sat still, with their wasted yellow faces, coughing, chuckling, drifting into aimless obscenity on the subject of women walking by, or any young girl on a bicycle.

From the shed came not only coughing, but speech, a continual muttering, reproachful or encouraging, usually just below the level at which separate words could be made out. Slowing down when her father was at a tricky piece of work, taking on a cheerful speed when he was doing something less demanding, sandpapering or painting. Now and then some words would break through and hang clear and nonsensical on the air. When he realized they were out, there would be a quick bit of cover-up coughing, a swallowing, an alert, unusual silence.

"Macaroni, pepperoni, Botticelli, beans—"

What could that mean? Rose used to repeat such things to herself. She could never ask him. The person who spoke these words and the person who spoke to her as her father were not the same, though they seemed to occupy the same space. It would be the worst sort of taste to acknowledge the person who was not supposed to be there; it would not be forgiven. Just the same, she loitered and listened.

The cloud-capped towers, she heard him say once.

"The cloud-capped towers, the gorgeous palaces."

That was like a hand clapped against Rose's chest, not to hurt, but astonish her, to take her breath away. She had to run then, she had to get away. She knew that was enough to hear, and besides, what if he caught her? It would be terrible.

This was something the same as bathroom noises. Flo had saved

up, and had a bathroom put in, but there was no place to put it
except in a corner of the kitchen. The door did not fit, the walls
were only beaverboard. The result was that even the tearing of a
piece of toilet paper, the shifting of a haunch, was audible to those
working or talking or eating in the kitchen. They were all familiar
with each other's nether voices, not only in their more explosive
moments but in their intimate sighs and growls and pleas and
statements. And they were all most prudish people. So no one ever
seemed to hear, or be listening, and no reference was made. The
person creating the noises in the bathroom was not connected with
the person who walked out.

They lived in a poor part of town. There was Hanratty and West
Hanratty, with the river flowing between them. This was West
Hanratty. In Hanratty the social structure ran from doctors and
dentists and lawyers down to foundry workers and factory workers
and draymen; in West Hanratty it ran from factory workers and
foundry workers down to large improvident families of casual boot-
leggers and prostitutes and unsuccessful thieves. Rose thought of
her own family as straddling the river, belonging nowhere, but
that was not true. West Hanratty was where the store was and they
were, on the straggling tail end of the main street. Across the road
from them was a blacksmith shop, boarded up about the time the
war started, and a house that had been another store at one time.
The Salada Tea sign had never been taken out of the front window;
it remained as a proud and interesting decoration though there was
no Salada Tea for sale inside. There was just a bit of sidewalk, too
cracked and tilted for roller-skating, though Rose longed for roller
skates and often pictured herself whizzing along in a plaid skirt,
agile and fashionable. There was one street light, a tin flower; then
the amenities gave up and there were dirt roads and boggy places,
front-yard dumps and strange-looking houses. What made the
houses strange-looking were the attempts to keep them from going
completely to ruin. With some the attempt had never been made.
These were gray and rotted and leaning over, falling into a landscape
of scrub hollows, frog ponds, cattails and nettles. Most houses,
however, had been patched up with tarpaper, a few fresh shingles,
sheets of tin, hammered-out stovepipes, even cardboard. This was,

of course, in the days before the war, days of what would later be legendary poverty, from which Rose would remember mostly low-down things—serious-looking anthills and wooden steps, and a cloudy, interesting, problematical light on the world.

There was a long truce between Flo and Rose in the beginning. Rose's nature was growing like a prickly pineapple, but slowly, and secretly, hard pride and skepticism overlapping, to make something surprising even to herself. Before she was old enough to go to school, and while Brian was still in the baby carriage, Rose stayed in the store with both of them—Flo sitting on the high stool behind the counter, Brian asleep by the window; Rose knelt or lay on the wide creaky floorboards working with crayons on pieces of brown paper too torn or irregular to be used for wrapping.

People who came to the store were mostly from the houses around. Some country people came too, on their way home from town, and a few people from Hanratty, who walked across the bridge. Some people were always on the main street, in and out of stores, as if it was their duty to be always on display and their right to be welcomed. For instance, Becky Tyde.

Becky Tyde climbed up on Flo's counter, made room for herself beside an open tin of crumbly jam-filled cookies.

"Are these any good?" she said to Flo, and boldly began to eat one. "When are you going to give us a job, Flo?"

"You could go and work in the butcher shop," said Flo innocently. "You could go and work for your brother."

"Roberta?" said Becky with a stagey sort of contempt. "You think I'd work for him?" Her brother who ran the butcher shop was named Robert but often called Roberta, because of his meek and nervous ways. Becky Tyde laughed. Her laugh was loud and noisy like an engine bearing down on you.

She was a big-headed loud-voiced dwarf, with a mascot's sexless swagger, a red velvet tam, a twisted neck that forced her to hold her head on one side, always looking up and sideways. She wore little polished high-heeled shoes, real lady's shoes. Rose watched her shoes, being scared of the rest of her, of her laugh and her neck. She knew from Flo that Becky Tyde had been sick with polio as a child, that was why her neck was twisted and why she had not grown any taller. It was hard to believe that she had started out differently, that she had ever been normal. Flo said she was not cracked, she had as much brains as anybody, but she knew she could get away with anything.

"You know I used to live out here?" Becky said, noticing Rose. "Hey! What's-your-name! Didn't I used to live out here, Flo?"

"If you did it was before my time," said Flo, as if she didn't know anything.

"That was before the neighborhood got so downhill. Excuse me saying so. My father built his house out here and he built his slaughterhouse and we had half an acre of orchard."

"Is that so?" said Flo, using her humoring voice, full of false geniality, humility even. "Then why did you ever move away?"

"I told you, it got to be such a downhill neighborhood," said Becky. She would put a whole cookie in her mouth if she felt like it, let her cheeks puff out like a frog's. She never told any more.

Flo knew anyway, and who didn't. Everyone knew the house, red brick with the veranda pulled off and the orchard, what was left of it, full of the usual outflow—car seats and washing machines and bedsprings and junk. The house would never look sinister, in spite of what had happened in it, because there was so much wreckage and confusion all around.

Becky's old father was a different kind of butcher from her brother according to Flo. A bad-tempered Englishman. And different from Becky in the matter of mouthiness. His was never open. A skinflint, a family tyrant. After Becky had polio he wouldn't let her go back to school. She was seldom seen outside the house, never outside the yard. He didn't want people gloating. That was what Becky said, at the trial. Her mother was dead by that time and her sisters married. Just Becky and Robert at home. People would stop Robert on the road and ask him, "How about your sister, Robert? Is she altogether better now?"

"Yes."

"Does she do the housework? Does she get your supper?"

"Yes."

"And is your father good to her, Robert?"

The story being that the father beat them, had beaten all his children and beaten his wife as well, beat Becky more now because of her deformity, which some people believed he had caused (they did not understand about polio). The stories persisted and got added to. The reason that Becky was kept out of sight was now supposed to be her pregnancy, and the father of the child was supposed to be her own father. Then people said it had been born, and disposed of.

"What?"

"Disposed of," Flo said. "They used to say go and get your lamb chops at Tyde's, get them nice and tender! It was all lies in all probability," she said regretfully.

Rose could be drawn back—from watching the wind shiver along the old torn awning, catch in the tear—by this tone of regret, caution, in Flo's voice. Flo telling a story—and this was not the only one, or even the most lurid one, she knew—would incline her head and let her face go soft and thoughtful, tantalizing, warning.

"I shouldn't even be telling you this stuff."

More was to follow.

Three useless young men, who hung around the livery stable, got together—or were got together, by more influential and respectable men in town—and prepared to give old man Tyde a horsewhipping, in the interests of public morality. They blacked their faces. They were provided with whips and a quart of whiskey apiece, for courage. They were: Jelly Smith, a horse-racer and a drinker; Bob Temple, a ballplayer and strongman; and Hat Nettleton, who worked on the town dray, and had his nickname from a bowler hat he wore, out of vanity as much as for the comic effect. He still worked on the dray, in fact; he had kept the name if not the hat, and could often be seen in public—almost as often as Becky Tyde—delivering sacks of coal, which blackened his face and arms. That should have brought to mind his story, but didn't. Present time and past, the shady melodramatic past of Flo's stories, were quite separate, at least for Rose. Present people could not be fitted into the past. Becky herself, town oddity and public pet, harmless and malicious, could never match the butcher's prisoner, the cripple daughter, a white streak at the window: mute, beaten, impregnated. As with the house, only a formal connection could be made.

The young men primed to do the horsewhipping showed up late, outside Tyde's house, after everybody had gone to bed. They had a gun, but they used up their ammunition firing it off in the yard. They yelled for the butcher and beat on the door; finally they broke it down. Tyde concluded they were after his money, so he put some bills in a handkerchief and sent Becky down with them, maybe thinking those men would be touched or scared by the sight of a little wry-necked girl, a dwarf. But that didn't content them. They came upstairs and dragged the butcher out from under his bed, in his nightgown. They dragged him outside and stood him in the snow. The temperature was four below zero, a fact noted later in court. They meant to hold a mock trial but they could not remember how it was done. So they began to beat him and kept beating him until he fell. They yelled at him, *Butcher's meat!* and continued beating him while his nightgown and the snow he was lying in turned red. His son Robert said in court that he had not watched the beating. Becky said that Robert had watched at first but had run away and hid. She herself had watched all the way through. She watched the men leave at last and her father make his delayed bloody progress through the snow and up the steps of the veranda. She did not go out to help him, or open the door until he got to it. Why not? she was asked in court, and she said she did not go out because she just had her nightgown on, and she did not open the door because she did not want to let the cold into the house.

Old man Tyde then appeared to have recovered his strength. He sent Robert to harness the horse, and made Becky heat water so that he could wash. He dressed and took all the money and with no explanation to his children got into the cutter and drove to Belgrave where he left the horse tied in the cold and took the early morning train to Toronto. On the train he behaved oddly, groaning and cursing as if he was drunk. He was picked up on the streets of Toronto a day later, out of his mind with fever, and was taken to a hospital, where he died. He still had all the money. The cause of death was given as pneumonia.

But the authorities got wind, Flo said. The case came to trial. The three men who did it all received long prison sentences. A farce, said Flo. Within a year they were all free, had all been pardoned, had jobs waiting for them. And why was that? It was because too many higher-ups were in on it. And it seemed as if Becky and Robert had no interest in seeing justice done. They were left well-off. They bought a house in Hanratty. Robert went into the store. Becky after her long seclusion started on a career of public sociability and display.

That was all. Flo put the lid down on the story as if she was sick of it. It reflected no good on anybody.

"Imagine," Flo said.

Flo at this time must have been in her early thirties. A young woman. She wore exactly the same clothes that a woman of fifty, or sixty, or seventy, might wear: print housedresses loose at the neck and sleeves as well as the waist; bib aprons, also of print, which she took off when she came from the kitchen into the store. This was a common costume at the time, for a poor though not absolutely poverty-stricken woman; it was also, in a way, a scornful deliberate choice. Flo scorned slacks, she scorned the outfits of people trying to be in style, she scorned lipstick and permanents. She wore her own black hair cut straight across, just long enough to push behind her ears. She was tall but fine-boned, with narrow wrists and shoulders, a small head, a pale, freckled, mobile, mon-keyish face. If she had thought it worthwhile, and had the resources, she might have had a black-and-pale, fragile, nurtured sort of pret-tiness; Rose realized that later. But she would have to have been a different person altogether; she would have to have learned to resist making faces, at herself and others.

Rose's earliest memories of Flo were of extraordinary softness and hardness. The soft hair, the long, soft, pale cheeks, soft almost invisible fuzz in front of her ears and above her mouth. The sharp-ness of her knees, hardness of her lap, flatness of her front.

When Flo sang:

> Oh the buzzin' of the bees in the cigarette trees
> And the soda-water fountain . . .

Rose thought of Flo's old life before she married her father, when she worked as a waitress in the coffee shop in Union Station, and went with her girl friends Mavis and Irene to Centre Island, and was followed by men on dark streets and knew how pay phones and elevators worked. Rose heard in her voice the reckless dangerous life of cities, the gum-chewing sharp answers.

And when she sang:

> Then slowly, slowly, she got up
> And slowly she came nigh him
> And all she said, that she ever did say,
> Was young man, I think you're dyin'!

Rose thought of a life Flo seemed to have had beyond that, earlier than that, crowded and legendary, with Barbara Allen and Becky Tyde's father and all kinds of outrages and sorrows jumbled up together in it.

The royal beatings. What got them started?

Suppose a Saturday, in spring. Leaves not out yet but the doors open to the sunlight. Crows. Ditches full of running water. Hopeful weather. Often on Saturdays Flo left Rose in charge of the store—it's a few years now, these are the years when Rose was nine, ten, eleven, twelve—while she herself went across the bridge to Hanratty (going uptown they called it) to shop and see people, and listen to them. Among the people she listened to were Mrs. Lawyer Davies, Mrs. Anglican Rector Henley-Smith, and Mrs. Horse-Doctor McKay. She came home and imitated their flibberty voices. Monsters, she made them seem; of foolishness, and showiness, and self-approbation.

When she finished shopping she went into the coffee shop of the Queen's Hotel and had a sundae. What kind? Rose and Brian wanted to know when she got home, and they would be disappointed if it was only pineapple or butterscotch, pleased if it was a Tin Roof, or Black and White. Then she smoked a cigarette. She had some ready-rolled, that she carried with her, so that she wouldn't have to roll one in public. Smoking was the one thing she did that she would have called showing off in anybody else. It was a habit left over from her working days, from Toronto. She knew it was asking for trouble. Once the Catholic priest came over to her right in the Queen's Hotel, and flashed his lighter at her before she could get her matches out. She thanked him but did not enter into conversation, lest he should try to convert her.

Another time, on the way home, she saw at the town end of the bridge a boy in a blue jacket, apparently looking at the water. Eighteen, nineteen years old. Nobody she knew. Skinny, weakly looking, something the matter with him, she saw at once. Was he thinking of jumping? Just as she came up even with him, what does he do but turn and display himself, holding his jacket open, also his pants. What he must have suffered from the cold, on a day that had Flo holding her coat collar tight around her throat.

When she first saw what he had in his hand, Flo said, all she could think of was, what is he doing out here with a baloney sausage?

She could say that. It was offered as truth; no joke. She maintained that she despised dirty talk. She would go out and yell at the old men sitting in front of her store.

"If you want to stay where you are you better clean your mouths out!"

Saturday, then. For some reason Flo is not going uptown, has decided to stay home and scrub the kitchen floor. Perhaps this has put her in a bad mood. Perhaps she was in a bad mood anyway, due to people not paying their bills, or the stirring-up of feelings in spring. The wrangle with Rose has already commenced, has been going on forever, like a dream that goes back and back into other dreams, over hills and through doorways, maddeningly dim and populous and familiar and elusive. They are carting all the chairs out of the kitchen preparatory to the scrubbing, and they have also got to move some extra provisions for the store, some cartons of canned goods, tins of maple syrup, coal-oil cans, jars of vinegar. They take these things out to the woodshed. Brian who is five or six by this time is helping drag the tins.

"Yes," says Flo, carrying on from our lost starting point. "Yes, and that filth you taught to Brian."

"What filth?"

"And he doesn't know any better."

There is one step down from the kitchen to the woodshed, a bit of carpet on it so worn Rose can't ever remember seeing the pattern. Brian loosens it, dragging a tin.

"Two Vancouvers," she says softly.

Flo is back in the kitchen. Brian looks from Flo to Rose and Rose says again in a slightly louder voice, an encouraging sing-song, "Two Vancouvers—"

"Fried in snot!" finishes Brian, not able to control himself any longer.

"Two pickled arseholes—"

"—tied in a knot!"

There it is. The filth.

> *Two Vancouvers fried in snot!*
> *Two pickled arseholes tied in a knot!*

Rose has known that for years, learned it when she first went to school. She came home and asked Flo, what is a Vancouver?

"It's a city. It's a long ways away."

"What else besides a city?"

Flo said, what did she mean, what else? How could it be fried, Rose said, approaching the dangerous moment, the delightful moment, when she would have to come out with the whole thing.

"Two Vancouvers fried in snot!/Two pickled arseholes tied in a knot!"

"You're going to get it!" cried Flo in a predictable rage. "Say that again and you'll get a good clout!"

Rose couldn't stop herself. She hummed it tenderly, tried saying the innocent words aloud, humming through the others. It was not just the words snot and arsehole that gave her pleasure, though of course they did. It was the pickling and tying and the unimaginable Vancouvers. She saw them in her mind shaped rather like octopuses, twitching in the pan. The tumble of reason; the spark and spit of craziness.

Lately she has remembered it again and taught it to Brian, to see if it has the same effect on him, and of course it has.

"Oh, I heard you!" says Flo. "I heard that! And I'm warning you!"

So she is. Brian takes the warning. He runs away, out the woodshed door, to do as he likes. Being a boy, free to help or not, involve himself or not. Not committed to the household struggle. They don't need him anyway, except to use against each other, they hardly notice his going. They continue, can't help continuing, can't leave each other alone. When they seem to have given up they really are just waiting and building up steam.

Flo gets out the scrub pail and the brush and the rag and the pad for her knees, a dirty red rubber pad. She starts to work on the floor. Rose sits on the kitchen table, the only place left to sit, swinging her legs. She can feel the cool oilcloth, because she is wearing shorts, last summer's tight faded shorts dug out of the summer-clothes bag. They smell a bit moldy from winter storage.

Flo crawls underneath, scrubbing with the brush, wiping with the rag. Her legs are long, white and muscular, marked all over with blue veins as if somebody had been drawing rivers on them with an indelible pencil. An abnormal energy, a violent disgust, is expressed in the chewing of the brush at the linoleum, the swish of the rag.

What do they have to say to each other? It doesn't really matter. Flo speaks of Rose's smart-aleck behavior, rudeness and sloppiness and conceit. Her willingness to make work for others, her lack of gratitude. She mentions Brian's innocence, Rose's corruption. Oh, don't you think you're somebody, says Flo, and a moment later, Who do you think you are? Rose contradicts and objects with such poisonous reasonableness and mildness, displays theatrical unconcern. Flo goes beyond her ordinary scorn and self-possession and becomes amazingly theatrical herself, saying it was for Rose that she sacrificed her life. She saw her father saddled with a baby daughter and she thought, what is that man going to do? So she married him, and here she is, on her knees.

At that moment the bell rings, to announce a customer in the store. Because the fight is on, Rose is not permitted to go into the store and wait on whoever it is. Flo gets up and throws off her apron, groaning—but not communicatively, it is not a groan whose exasperation Rose is allowed to share—and goes in and serves. Rose hears her using her normal voice.

"About time! Sure is!"

She comes back and ties on her apron and is ready to resume.

"You never have a thought for anybody but your ownself! You never have a thought for what I'm doing."

"I never asked you to do anything. I wish you never had. I would have been a lot better off."

Rose says this smiling directly at Flo, who has not yet gone down on her knees. Flo sees the smile, grabs the scrub rag that is hanging on the side of the pail, and throws it at her. It may be meant to hit her in the face but instead it falls against Rose's leg and she raises her foot and catches it, swinging it negligently against her ankle.

"All right," says Flo. "You've done it this time. All right."

Rose watches her go to the woodshed door, hears her tramp through the woodshed, pause in the doorway, where the screen door hasn't yet been hung, and the storm door is standing open, propped with a brick. She calls Rose's father. She calls him in a warning, summoning voice, as if against her will preparing him for bad news. He will know what this is about.

The kitchen floor has five or six different patterns of linoleum on it. Ends, which Flo got for nothing and ingeniously trimmed and fitted together, bordering them with tin strips and tacks. While Rose sits on the table waiting, she looks at the floor, at this satisfying arrangement of rectangles, triangles, some other shape whose name she is trying to remember. She hears Flo coming back through the woodshed, on the creaky plank walk laid over the dirt floor. She is loitering, waiting, too. She and Rose can carry this no further, by themselves.

Rose hears her father come in. She stiffens, a tremor runs through her legs, she feels them shiver on the oilcloth. Called away from some peaceful, absorbing task, away from the words running in his head, called out of himself, her father has to say something. He says, "Well? What's wrong?"

Now comes another voice of Flo's. Enriched, hurt, apologetic, it seems to have been manufactured on the spot. She is sorry to have called him from his work. Would never have done it, if Rose was not driving her to distraction. How to distraction? With her back talk and impudence and her terrible tongue. The things Rose has said to Flo are such that, if Flo had said them to her mother, she knows her father would have thrashed her into the ground.

Rose tries to butt in, to say this isn't true.

What isn't true?

Her father raises a hand, doesn't look at her, says, "Be quiet."

When she says it isn't true, Rose means that she herself didn't start this, only responded, that she was goaded by Flo, who is now, she believes, telling the grossest sort of lies, twisting everything to suit herself. Rose puts aside her other knowledge that whatever Flo has said or done, whatever she herself has said or done, does not really matter at all. It is the struggle itself that counts, and that can't be stopped, can never be stopped, short of where it has got to, now.

Flo's knees are dirty, in spite of the pad. The scrub rag is still hanging over Rose's foot.

Her father wipes his hands, listening to Flo. He takes his time. He is slow at getting into the spirit of things, tired in advance, maybe, on the verge of rejecting the role he has to play. He won't look at Rose, but at any sound or stirring from Rose, he holds up his hand.

"Well we don't need the public in on this, that's for sure," Flo says, and she goes to lock the door of the store, putting in the store window the sign that says BACK SOON, a sign Rose made for her with a great deal of fancy curving and shading of letters in black and red crayon. When she comes back she shuts the door to the store, then the door to the stairs, then the door to the woodshed.

Her shoes have left marks on the clean wet part of the floor.

"Oh, I don't know," she says now, in a voice worn down from its emotional peak. "I don't know what to do about her." She looks down and sees her dirty knees (following Rose's eyes) and rubs at them viciously with her bare hands, smearing the dirt around.

"She humiliates me," she says, straightening up. There it is, the explanation. "She humiliates me," she repeats with satisfaction. "She has no respect."

"I do not!"

"Quiet, you!" says her father.

"If I hadn't called your father you'd still be sitting there with that grin on your face! What other way is there to manage you?"

Rose detects in her father some objections to Flo's rhetoric, some embarrassment and reluctance. She is wrong, and ought to know she is wrong, in thinking that she can count on this. The fact that she knows about it, and he knows she knows, will not make things any better. He is beginning to warm up. He gives her a look. This look is at first cold and challenging. It informs her of his judgment, of the hopelessness of her position. Then it clears, it begins to fill up with something else, the way a spring fills up when you clear the leaves away. It fills with hatred and pleasure. Rose sees that and knows it. Is that just a description of anger, should she see his eyes filling up with anger? No. Hatred is right. Pleasure is right. His face loosens and changes and grows younger, and he holds up his hand this time to silence Flo.

"All right," he says, meaning that's enough, more than enough, this part is over, things can proceed. He starts to loosen his belt.

Flo has stopped anyway. She has the same difficulty Rose does, a difficulty in believing that what you know must happen really will happen, that there comes a time when you can't draw back.

"Oh, I don't know, don't be too hard on her." She is moving around nervously as if she has thoughts of opening some escape route. "Oh, you don't have to use the belt on her. Do you have to use the belt?"

He doesn't answer. The belt is coming off, not hastily. It is being grasped at the necessary point. *All right you.* He is coming over to Rose. He pushes her off the table. His face, like his voice, is quite out of character. He is like a bad actor, who turns a part grotesque. As if he must savor and insist on just what is shameful and terrible about this. That is not to say he is pretending, that he is acting, and does not mean it. He is acting, and he means it. Rose knows that, she knows everything about him.

She has since wondered about murders, and murderers. Does the thing have to be carried through, in the end, partly for the effect, to prove to the audience of one—who won't be able to report, only register, the lesson—that such a thing can happen, that there is nothing that can't happen, that the most dreadful antic is justified, feelings can be found to match it?

She tries again looking at the kitchen floor, that clever and comforting geometrical arrangement, instead of looking at him or his belt. How can this go on in front of such daily witnesses—the linoleum, the calendar with the mill and creek and autumn trees, the old accommodating pots and pans?

Hold out your hand!

Those things aren't going to help her, none of them can rescue her. They turn bland and useless, even unfriendly. Pots can show malice, the patterns of linoleum can leer up at you, treachery is the other side of dailiness.

At the first, or maybe the second, crack of pain, she draws back. She will not accept it. She runs around the room, she tries to get to the doors. Her father blocks her off. Not an ounce of courage or of stoicism in her, it would seem. She runs, she screams, she implores. Her father is after her, cracking the belt at her when he can, then abandoning it and using his hands. Bang over the ear, then bang over the other ear. Back and forth, her head ringing. Bang in the face. Up against the wall and bang in the face again. He shakes her and hits her against the wall, he kicks her legs. She is incoherent, insane, shrieking. *Forgive me! Oh please, forgive me!*

Flo is shrieking too. *Stop, stop!*

Not yet. He throws Rose down. Or perhaps she throws herself down. He kicks her legs again. She has given up on words but is letting out a noise, the sort of noise that makes Flo cry, *Oh, what if people can hear her?* The very last-ditch willing sound of humiliation and defeat it is, for it seems Rose must play her part in this with the same grossness, the same exaggeration, that her father displays, playing his. She plays his victim with a self-indulgence that arouses, and maybe hopes to arouse, his final, sickened contempt.

They will give this anything that is necessary, it seems, they will go to any lengths.

Not quite. He has never managed really to injure her, though there are times, of course, when she prays that he will. He hits her with an open hand, there is some restraint in his kicks.

Now he stops, he is out of breath. He allows Flo to move in, he grabs Rose up and gives her a push in Flo's direction, making a sound of disgust. Flo retrieves her, opens the stair door, shoves her up the stairs.

"Go on up to your room now! Hurry!"

Rose goes up the stairs, stumbling, letting herself stumble, letting herself fall against the steps. She doesn't bang her door because a gesture like that could still bring him after her, and anyway, she is weak. She lies on the bed. She can hear through the stovepipe hole Flo snuffling and remonstrating, her father saying angrily that Flo should have kept quiet then, if she did not want Rose punished she should not have recommended it. Flo says she never recommended a hiding like that.

They argue back and forth on this. Flo's frightened voice is growing stronger, getting its confidence back. By stages, by arguing, they are being drawn back into themselves. Soon it's only Flo talking; he will not talk anymore. Rose has had to fight down her noisy sobbing, so as to listen to them, and when she loses interest in listening, and wants to sob some more, she finds she can't work herself up to it. She has passed into a state of calm, in which outrage is perceived as complete and final. In this state events and possibilities take on a lovely simplicity. Choices are mercifully clear. The words that come to mind are not the quibbling, seldom the conditional. Never is a word to which the right is suddenly established. She will never speak to them, she will never look at them with anything but loathing, she will never forgive them. She will punish them; she will finish them. Encased in these finalities, and in her bodily pain, she floats in curious comfort, beyond herself, beyond responsibility.

Suppose she dies now? Suppose she commits suicide? Suppose she runs away? Any of these things would be appropriate. It is only a matter of choosing, of figuring out the way. She floats in her pure superior state as if kindly drugged.

And just as there is a moment, when you are drugged, in which you feel perfectly safe, sure, unreachable, and then without warning and right next to it a moment in which you know the whole protection has fatally cracked, though it is still pretending to hold soundly together, so there is a moment now—the moment, in fact, when Rose hears Flo step on the stairs—that contains for her both present peace and freedom and a sure knowledge of the whole down-spiraling course of events from now on.

Flo comes into the room without knocking, but with a hesitation that shows it might have occurred to her. She brings a jar of cold cream. Rose is hanging on to advantage as long as she can, lying face down on the bed, refusing to acknowledge or answer.

"Oh come on," Flo says uneasily. "You aren't so bad off, are you? You put some of this on and you'll feel better."

She is bluffing. She doesn't know for sure what damage has been done. She has the lid off the cold cream. Rose can smell it. The intimate, babyish, humiliating smell. She won't allow it near her. But in order to avoid it, the big ready clot of it in Flo's hand, she has to move. She scuffles, resists, loses dignity, and lets Flo see there is not really much the matter.

"All right," Flo says. "You win. I'll leave it here and you can put it on when you like."

Later still a tray will appear. Flo will put it down without a word and go away. A large glass of chocolate milk on it, made with Vita-Malt from the store. Some rich streaks of Vita-Malt around the bottom of the glass. Little sandwiches, neat and appetizing. Canned salmon of the first quality and reddest color, plenty of mayonnaise. A couple of butter tarts from a bakery package, chocolate biscuits with a peppermint filling. Rose's favorites, in the sandwich, tart, and cookie line. She will turn away, refuse to look, but left alone with these eatables will be miserably tempted, roused and troubled and drawn back from thoughts of suicide or flight by the smell of salmon, the anticipation of crisp chocolate, she will reach out a finger, just to run it around the edge of one of the sandwiches (crusts cut off!) to get the overflow, get a taste. Then she will decide to eat one, for strength to refuse the rest. One will not be noticed. Soon, in helpless corruption, she will eat them all. She will drink the chocolate milk, eat the tarts, eat the cookies. She will get the malty syrup out of the bottom of the glass with her finger, though she sniffles with shame. Too late.

Flo will come up and get the tray. She may say, "I see you got your appetite still," or, "Did you like the chocolate milk, was it enough syrup in it?" depending on how chastened she is feeling, herself. At any rate, all advantage will be lost. Rose will understand that life has started up again, that they will all sit around the table eating again, listening to the radio news. Tomorrow morning, maybe even tonight. Unseemly and unlikely as that may be. They will be embarrassed, but rather less than you might expect considering how they have behaved. They will feel a queer lassitude, a convalescent indolence, not far off satisfaction.

One night after a scene like this they were all in the kitchen. It must have been summer, or at least warm weather, because her father spoke of the old men who sat on the bench in front of the store.

"Do you know what they're talking about now?" he said, and nodded his head toward the store to show who he meant, though of course they were not there now, they went home at dark.

"Those old coots," said Flo. "What?"

There was about them both a geniality not exactly false but a bit more emphatic than was normal, without company.

Rose's father told them then that the old men had picked up the idea somewhere that what looked like a star in the western sky, the first star that came out after sunset, the evening star, was in reality an airship hovering over Bay City, Michigan, on the other side of Lake Huron. An American invention, sent up to rival the heavenly bodies. They were all in agreement about this, the idea was congenial to them. They believed it to be lit by ten thousand electric light bulbs. Her father had ruthlessly disagreed with them, pointing out that it was the planet Venus they saw, which had appeared in the sky long before the invention of an electric light bulb. They had never heard of the planet Venus.

"Ignoramuses," said Flo. At which Rose knew, and knew her father knew, that Flo had never heard of the planet Venus either. To distract them from this, or even apologize for it, Flo put down her teacup, stretched out with her head resting on the chair she had been sitting on and her feet on another chair (somehow she managed to tuck her dress modestly between her legs at the same time), and lay stiff as a board, so that Brian cried out in delight, "Do that! Do that!"

Flo was double-jointed and very strong. In moments of celebration or emergency she would do tricks.

They were silent while she turned herself around, not using her arms at all but just her strong legs and feet. Then they all cried out in triumph, though they had seen it before.

Just as Flo turned herself Rose got a picture in her mind of that airship, an elongated transparent bubble, with its strings of diamond lights, floating in the miraculous American sky.

"The planet Venus!" her father said, applauding Flo. "Ten thousand electric lights!"

There was a feeling of permission, relaxation, even a current of happiness, in the room.

Years later, many years later, on a Sunday morning, Rose turned on the radio. This was when she was living by herself in Toronto.

Well sir.

It was a different kind of place in our day. Yes it was.

It was all horses then. Horses and buggies. Buggy races up and down the main street on the Saturday nights.

"Just like the chariot races," says the announcer's, or interviewer's, smooth encouraging voice.

I never seen a one of them.

"No sir, that was the old Roman chariot races I was referring to. That was before your time."

Musta been before my time. I'm a hunerd and two years old.

"That's a wonderful age, sir."

It is so.

She left it on, as she went around the apartment kitchen, making coffee for herself. It seemed to her that this must be a staged interview, a scene from some play, and she wanted to find out what it was. The old man's voice was so vain and belligerent, the interviewer's quite hopeless and alarmed, under its practiced gentleness and ease. You were surely meant to see him holding the microphone up to some toothless, reckless, preening centenarian, wondering what in God's name he was doing here, and what would he say next?

"They must have been fairly dangerous."

What was dangerous?

"Those buggy races."

They was. Dangerous. Used to be the runaway horses. Used to be a-plenty of accidents. Fellows was dragged along on the gravel and cut their face open. Wouldna matter so much if they was dead. Heh.

Some of them horses was the high-steppers. Some, they had to have the mustard under their tail. Some wouldn step out for nothin. That's the thing it is with the horses. Some'll work and pull till they drop down dead and some wouldn pull your cock out of a pail of lard. Hehe.

It must be a real interview after all. Otherwise they wouldn't have put that in, wouldn't have risked it. It's all right if the old man says it. Local color. Anything rendered harmless and delightful by his hundred years.

Accidents all the time then. In the mill. Foundry. Wasn't the precautions.

"You didn't have so many strikes then, I don't suppose? You didn't have so many unions?"

Everybody taking it easy nowadays. We worked and we was glad to get it. Worked and was glad to get it.

"You didn't have television."

Didn't have no TV. Didn't have no radio. No picture show.

"You made your own entertainment."

That's the way we did.

"You had a lot of experiences young men growing up today will never have."

Experiences.

"Can you recall any of them for us?"

I eaten groundhog meat one time. One winter. You wouldna cared for it. Heh.

There was a pause, of appreciation, it would seem, then the announcer's voice saying that the foregoing had been an interview with Mr. Wilfred Nettleton of Hanratty, Ontario, made on his hundred and second birthday, two weeks before his death, last spring. A living link with our past. Mr. Nettleton had been interviewed in the Wawanash County Home for the Aged.

Hat Nettleton.

Horsewhipper into centenarian. Photographed on his birthday, fussed over by nurses, kissed no doubt by a girl reporter. Flash bulbs popping at him. Tape recorder drinking in the sound of his voice. Oldest resident. Oldest horsewhipper. Living link with our past.

Looking out from her kitchen window at the cold lake, Rose was longing to tell somebody. It was Flo who would enjoy hearing. She thought of her saying *Imagine!* in a way that meant she was having her worst suspicions gorgeously confirmed. But Flo was in the same place Hat Nettleton had died in, and there wasn't any way Rose could reach her. She had been there even when that interview was recorded, though she would not have heard it, would not have known about it. After Rose put her in the Home, a couple of years earlier, she had stopped talking. She had removed herself, and spent most of her time sitting in a corner of her crib, looking crafty and disagreeable, not answering anybody, though she occasionally showed her feelings by biting a nurse.

Jayne Ann Phillips

SOUVENIR

～≈～

Kate always sent her mother a card on Valentine's Day. She timed the mails from wherever she was so that the cards arrived on February 14th. Her parents had celebrated the day in some small fashion, and since her father's death six years before, Kate made a gesture of compensatory remembrance. At first, she made the cards herself: collage and pressed grasses on construction paper sewn in fabric. Now she settled for art reproductions, glossy cards with blank insides. Kate wrote in them with colored inks, "You have always been my Valentine," or simply "Hey, take care of yourself." She might enclose a present as well, something small enough to fit into an envelope;

a sachet, a perfumed soap, a funny tintype of a prune-faced man in a bowler hat.

This time, she forgot. Despite the garish displays of paper cupids and heart-shaped boxes in drugstore windows, she let the day nearly approach before remembering. It was too late to send anything in the mail. She called her mother long-distance at night when the rates were low.

"Mom? How are you?"

"It's you! How are *you?*" Her mother's voice grew suddenly brighter; Kate recognized a tone reserved for welcome company. Sometimes it took a while to warm up.

"I'm fine," answered Kate. "What have you been doing?"

"Well, actually I was trying to sleep."

"Sleep? You should be out setting the old hometown on fire."

"The old hometown can burn up without me tonight."

"Really? What's going on?"

"I'm running in-service training sessions for the primary teachers." Kate's mother was a school superintendent. "They're driving me batty. You'd think their brains were rubber."

"They are," Kate said. "Or you wouldn't have to train them. Think of them as a salvation, they create a need for your job."

"Some salvation. Besides, your logic is ridiculous. Just because someone needs training doesn't mean they're stupid."

"I'm just kidding. But *I'm* stupid. I forgot to send you a Valentine's card."

"You did? That's bad. I'm trained to receive one. They bring me luck."

"You're receiving a phone call instead," Kate said. "Won't that do?"

"Of course," said her mother, "but this is costing you money. Tell me quick, how are you?"

"Oh, you know. Doctoral pursuits. Doing my student trip, grooving with the professors."

"The professors? You'd better watch yourself."

"It's a joke, Mom, a joke. But what about you? Any men on the horizon?"

"No, not really. A married salesman or two asking me to dinner when they come through the office. Thank heavens I never let those things get started."

"You should do what you want to," Kate said.

"Sure," said her mother. "And where would I be then?"

"I don't know. Maybe Venezuela."

"They don't even have plumbing in Venezuela."

"Yes, but their sunsets are perfect, and the villages are full of dark passionate men in blousy shirts."

"That's your department, not mine."

"Ha," Kate said, "I wish it were my department. Sounds a lot more exciting than teaching undergraduates."

Her mother laughed. "Be careful," she said. "You'll get what you want. End up sweeping a dirt floor with a squawling baby around your neck."

"A dark baby," Kate said, "to stir up the family blood."

"Nothing would surprise me," her mother said as the line went fuzzy. Her voice was submerged in static, then surfaced. "Listen," she was saying. "Write to me. You seem so far away."

They hung up and Kate sat watching the windows of the neighboring house. The curtains were transparent and flowered and none of them matched. Silhouettes of the window frames spread across them like single dark bars. Her mother's curtains were all the same, white cotton hemmed with a ruffle, tiebacks blousing the cloth into identical shapes. From the street it looked as if the house was always in order.

Kate made a cup of strong Chinese tea, turned the lights off, and sat holding the warm cup in the dark. Her mother kept no real tea in the house, just packets of instant diabetic mixture which tasted of chemical sweetener and had a bitter aftertaste. The packets sat on the shelf next to her mother's miniature scales. The scales were white. Kate saw clearly the face of the metal dial on the front, its markings and trembling needle. Her mother weighed portions of food for meals: frozen broccoli, slices of plastic-wrapped Kraft cheese, careful chunks of roast beef. A dog-eared copy of *The Diabetic Diet* had remained propped against the salt shaker for the last two years.

Kate rubbed her forehead. Often at night she had headaches.

Sometimes she wondered if there were an agent in her body, a secret in her blood making ready to work against her.

The phone blared repeatedly, careening into her sleep. Kate scrambled out of bed, naked and cold, stumbling, before she recognized the striped wallpaper of her bedroom and realized the phone was right there on the bedside table, as always. She picked up the receiver.

"Kate?" said her brother's voice. "It's Robert. Mom is in the hospital. They don't know what's wrong but she's in for tests."

"Tests? What's happened? I just talked to her last night."

"I'm not sure. She called the neighbors and they took her to the emergency room around dawn." Robert's voice still had that slight twang Kate knew was disappearing from her own. He would be calling from his insurance office, nine o'clock their time, in his thick glasses and wide, perfectly knotted tie. He was a member of the million-dollar club and his picture, tiny, the size of a postage stamp, appeared in the Mutual of Omaha magazine. His voice seemed small, too, over the distance. Kate felt heavy and dulled. She would never make much money, and recently she had begun wearing make-up again, waking in smeared mascara as she had in high school.

"Is Mom all right?" she managed now. "How serious is it?"

"They're not sure," Robert said. "Her doctor thinks it could have been any of several things, but they're doing X-rays."

"Her doctor *thinks?* Doesn't he know? Get her to someone else. There aren't any doctors in that one-horse town."

"I don't know about that," Robert said defensively. "Anyway, I can't force her. You know how she is about money."

"Money? She could have a stroke and drop dead while her doctor wonders what's wrong."

"Doesn't matter. You know you can't tell her what to do."

"Could I call her somehow?"

"No, not yet. And don't get her all worried. She's been scared enough as it is. I'll tell her what you said about getting another opinion, and I'll call you back in a few hours when I have some news. Meanwhile, she's all right, do you hear?"

The line went dead with a click and Kate walked to the bathroom to wash her face. She splashed her eyes and felt guilty about the Valentine's card. Slogans danced in her head like reprimands. *For A Special One. Dearest Mother. My Best Friend.* Despite Robert, after breakfast she would call the hospital.

She sat a long time with her coffee, waiting for minutes to pass, considering how many meals she and her mother ate alone. Similar times of day, hundreds of miles apart. Women by themselves. The last person Kate had eaten breakfast with had been someone she'd met in a bar. He was passing through town. He liked his fried eggs gelatinized in the center, only slightly runny, and Kate had studiously looked away as he ate. The night before he'd looked down from above her as he finished and she still moved under him. "You're still wanting," he'd said. "That's nice." Mornings now, Kate saw her own face in the mirror and was glad she'd forgotten his name. When she looked at her reflection from the side, she saw a faint etching of lines beside her mouth. She hadn't slept with anyone for five weeks, and the skin beneath her eyes had taken on a creamy darkness.

She reached for the phone but drew back. It seemed bad luck to ask for news, to push toward whatever was coming as though she had no respect for it.

Standing in the kitchen last summer, her mother had stirred gravy and argued with her.

"I'm thinking of your own good, not mine," she'd said. "Think of what you put yourself through. And how can you feel right about it? You were born here, I don't care what you say." Her voice broke and she looked, perplexed, at the broth in the pan.

"But, hypothetically," Kate continued, her own voice unaccountably shaking, "If I'm willing to endure whatever I have to, do you have a right to object? You're my mother. You're supposed to defend my choices."

"You'll have enough trouble without choosing more for yourself. Using birth control that'll ruin your insides, moving from one place to another. I can't defend your choices. I can't even defend myself against you." She wiped her eyes on a napkin.

"Why do you have to make me feel so guilty?" Kate said, fighting tears of frustration. "I'm not attacking you."

"You're not? Then who are you talking to?"

"Oh Mom, give me a break."

"I've tried to give you more than that," her mother said. "I know what your choices are saying to me." She set the steaming gravy off the stove. "You may feel very differently later on. It's just a shame I won't be around to see it."

"Oh? Where will you be?"

"Floating around on a fleecy cloud."

Kate got up to set the table before she realized her mother had already done it.

The days went by. They'd gone shopping before Kate left. Standing at the cash register in an antique shop on Main Street, they bought each other pewter candle holders. "A souvenir," her mother said. "A reminder to always be nice to yourself. If you live alone you should eat by candlelight."

"Listen," Kate said, "I eat in a heart-shaped tub with bubbles to my chin. I sleep on satin sheets and my mattress has a built-in massage engine. My overnight guests are impressed. You don't have to tell me about the solitary pleasures."

They laughed and touched hands.

"Well," her mother said. "If you like yourself, I must have done something right."

Robert didn't phone until evening. His voice was fatigued and thin. "I've moved her to the university hospital," he said. "They can't deal with it at home."

Kate waited, saying nothing. She concentrated on the toes of her shoes. They needed shining. *You never take care of anything,* her mother would say.

"She has a tumor in her head." He said it firmly, as though Kate might challenge him.

"I'll take a plane tomorrow morning," Kate answered, "I'll be there by noon."

Robert exhaled. "Look," he said, "don't even come back here unless you can keep your mouth shut and do it my way."

"Get to the point."

"The point is they believe she has a malignancy and we're not going to tell her. I almost didn't tell you." His voice faltered. "They're going to operate but if they find what they're expecting, they don't think they can stop it."

For a moment there was no sound except an oceanic vibration of distance on the wire. Even that sound grew still. Robert breathed. Kate could almost see him, in a booth at the hospital, staring straight ahead at the plastic instructions screwed to the narrow rectangular body of the telephone. It seemed to her that she was hurtling toward him.

"I'll do it your way," she said.

The hospital cafeteria was a large room full of orange Formica tables. Its southern wall was glass. Across the highway, Kate saw a small park modestly dotted with amusement rides and bordered by a narrow band of river. How odd, to build a children's park across from a medical center. The sight was pleasant in a cruel way. The rolling lawn of the little park was perfectly, relentlessly green.

Robert sat down. Their mother was to have surgery in two days.

"After it's over," he said, "they're not certain what will happen. The tumor is in a bad place. There may be some paralysis."

"What kind of paralysis?" Kate said. She watched him twist the green-edged coffee cup around and around on its saucer.

"Facial. And maybe worse."

"You've told her this?"

He didn't answer.

"Robert, what is she going to think if she wakes up and—"

He leaned forward, grasping the cup and speaking through clenched teeth. "Don't you think I thought of that?" He gripped the sides of the table and the cup rolled onto the carpeted floor with a dull thud. He seemed ready to throw the table after it, then grabbed Kate's wrists and squeezed them hard.

"You didn't drive her here," he said. "She was so scared she couldn't talk. How much do you want to hand her at once?"

Kate watched the cup sitting solidly on the nubby carpet.

"We've told her it's benign," Robert said, "that the surgery will cause complications, but she can learn back whatever is lost."

Kate looked at him. "Is that true?"

"They hope so."

"We're lying to her, all of us, more and more." Kate pulled her hands away and Robert touched her shoulder.

"What do *you* want to tell her, Kate? 'You're fifty-five and you're done for'?"

She stiffened. "Why put her through the operation at all?"

He sat back and dropped his arms, lowering his head. "Because without it she'd be in bad pain. Soon." They were silent, then he looked up. "And anyway," he said softly, "we don't *know*, do we? She may have a better chance than they think."

Kate put her hands on her face. Behind her closed eyes she saw a succession of blocks tumbling over.

They took the elevator up to the hospital room. They were alone and they stood close together. Above the door red numerals lit up, flashing. Behind the illuminated shapes droned an impersonal hum of machinery.

Then the doors opened with a sucking sound. Three nurses stood waiting with a lunch cart, identical covered trays stacked in tiers. There was a hot bland smell, like warm cardboard. One of the women caught the thick steel door with her arm and smiled. Kate looked quickly at their rubber-soled shoes. White polish, the kind that rubs off. And their legs seemed only white shapes, boneless and two-dimensional, stepping silently into the metal cage.

She looked smaller in the white bed. The chrome side rails were pulled up and she seemed powerless behind them, her dark hair pushed back from her face and her forearms delicate in the baggy hospital gown. Her eyes were different in some nearly imperceptible way; she held them wider, they were shiny with a veiled wetness. For a moment the room seemed empty of all else; there were only her eyes and the dark blossoms of the flowers on the table beside her. Red roses with pine. Everyone had sent the same thing.

Robert walked close to the bed with his hands clasped behind his back, as though afraid to touch. "Where did all the flowers come from?" he asked.

"From school, and the neighbors. And Katie." She smiled.

"FTD," Kate said. "Before I left home. I felt so bad for not being here all along."

"That's silly," said their mother. "You can hardly sit at home and wait for some problem to arise."

"Speaking of problems," Robert said, "the doctor tells me you're not eating. Do I have to urge you a little?" He sat down on the edge of the bed and shook the silverware from its paper sleeve.

Kate touched the plastic tray. "Jell-O and canned cream of chicken soup. Looks great. We should have brought you something."

"They don't *want* us to bring her anything," Robert said. "This is a hospital. And I'm sure your comments make her lunch seem even more appetizing."

"I'll eat it!" said their mother in mock dismay. "Admit they sent you in here to stage a battle until I gave in."

"I'm sorry," Kate said. "He's right."

Robert grinned. "Did you hear that? She says I'm right. I don't believe it." He pushed the tray closer to his mother's chest and made a show of tucking a napkin under her chin.

"Of course you're right, dear." She smiled and gave Kate an obvious wink.

"Yeah," Robert said, "I know you two. But seriously, you eat this. I have to go make some business calls from the motel room."

Their mother frowned. "That motel must be costing you a fortune."

"No, it's reasonable," he said. "Kate can stay for a week or two and I'll drive back and forth from home. If you think this food is bad, you should see the meals in that motel restaurant." He got up to go, flashing Kate a glance of collusion. "I'll be back after supper."

His footsteps echoed down the hallway. Kate and her mother looked wordlessly at each other, relieved. Kate looked away guiltily. Then her mother spoke, apologetic. "He's so tired," she said. "He's been with me since yesterday."

She looked at Kate, then into the air of the room. "I'm in a fix," she said. "Except for when the pain comes, it's all a show that goes on without me. I'm like an invalid, or a lunatic."

Kate moved close and touched her mother's arms. "That's all right, we're going to get you through it. Someone's covering for you at work?"

"I had to take a leave of absence. It's going to take a while afterward—"

"I know. But it's the last thing to worry about, it can't be helped."

"Like spilt milk. Isn't that what they say?"

"I don't know what they say. But why didn't you tell me? Didn't you know something was wrong?"

"Yes . . . bad headaches. Migraines, I thought, or the diabetes getting worse. I was afraid they'd start me on insulin." She tightened the corner of her mouth. "Little did I know . . ."

They heard the shuffle of slippers. An old woman stood at the open door of the room, looking in confusedly. She seemed about to speak, then moved on.

"Oh," said Kate's mother in exasperation, "shut that door, please? They let these old women wander around like refugees." She sat up, reaching for a robe. "And let's get me out of this bed."

They sat near the window while she finished eating. Bars of moted yellow banded the floor of the room. The light held a tinge of spring which seemed painful because it might vanish. They heard the rattle of the meal cart outside the closed door, and the clunk-slide of patients with aluminum walkers. Kate's mother sighed and pushed away the half-empty soup bowl.

"They'll be here after me any minute. More tests. I just want to stay with you." Her face was warm and smooth in the slanted light, lines in her skin delicate, unreal; as though a face behind her face was now apparent after many years. She sat looking at Kate and smiled.

"One day when you were about four you were dragging a broom around the kitchen. I asked what you were doing and you told me that when you got old you were going to be an angel and sweep the rotten rain off the clouds."

"What did you say to that?"

"I said that when you were old I was sure God would see to it." Her mother laughed. "I'm glad you weren't such a smart aleck then," she said. "You would have told me my view of God was paternalistic."

"Ah yes," sighed Kate. "God, that famous dude. Here I am, getting old, facing unemployment, alone, and where is He?"

"You're not alone," her mother said, "I'm right here."

Kate didn't answer. She sat motionless and felt her heart begin to open like a box with a hinged lid. The fullness had no edges.

Her mother stood. She rubbed her hands slowly, twisting her wedding rings. "My hands are so dry in the winter," she said softly, "I brought some hand cream with me but I can't find it anywhere, my suitcase is so jumbled. Thank heavens spring is early this year. . . . They told me that little park over there doesn't usually open till the end of March . . ."

She's helping me, thought Kate, I'm not supposed to let her down.

". . . but they're already running it on weekends. Even past dusk. We'll see the lights tonight. You can't see the shapes this far away, just the motion . . ."

A nurse came in with a wheelchair. Kate's mother pulled a wry face. "This wheelchair is a bit much," she said.

"We don't want to tire you out," said the nurse.

The chair took her weight quietly. At the door she put out her hand to stop, turned, and said anxiously, "Kate, see if you can find that hand cream?"

It was the blue suitcase from years ago, still almost new. She'd brought things she never used for everyday; a cashmere sweater, lace slips, silk underpants wrapped in tissue. Folded beneath was a stack of postmarked envelopes, slightly ragged, tied with twine. Kate opened one and realized that all the cards were there, beginning with the first of the marriage. There were a few photographs of her and Robert, baby pictures almost indistinguishable from each other, and then Kate's homemade Valentines, fastened together with rubber bands. Kate stared. *What will I do with these things?* She wanted air; she needed to breathe. She walked to the window and put the bundled papers on the sill. She'd raised the glass and pushed back the screen when suddenly, her mother's clock radio went off with a flat buzz. Kate moved to switch it off and brushed the cards with her arm. Envelopes shifted and slid, scattering on the floor of the room. A few snapshots wafted silently out the window. They dipped and turned, twirling. Kate didn't try to reach them. They seemed only scraps, buoyant and yellowed, blown away, the faces small as pennies. Somewhere far-off there were sirens, almost musical, drawn out and carefully approaching.

The nurse came in with evening medication. Kate's mother lay in bed. "I hope this is strong enough," she said. "Last night I couldn't sleep at all. So many sounds in a hospital . . ."

"You'll sleep tonight," the nurse assured her.

Kate winked at her mother. "That's right," she said, "I'll help you out if I have to."

They stayed up for an hour, watching the moving lights outside and the stationary glows of houses across the distant river. The halls grew darker, were lit with night lights, and the hospital dimmed. Kate waited. Her mother's eyes fluttered and finally she slept. Her breathing was low and regular.

Kate didn't move. Robert had said he'd be back; where was he? She felt a sunken anger and shook her head. She'd been on the point of telling her mother everything. The secrets were a travesty. What if there were things her mother wanted done, people she needed to see? Kate wanted to wake her before these hours passed in the dark and confess that she had lied. Between them, through the tension, there had always been a trusted clarity. Now it was twisted. Kate sat leaning forward, nearly touching the hospital bed.

Suddenly her mother sat bolt upright, her eyes open and her face transfixed. She looked blindly toward Kate but seemed to see nothing. "Who are you?" she whispered. Kate stood, at first unable to move. The woman in the bed opened and closed her mouth several times, as though she were gasping. Then she said loudly, "Stop moving the table. Stop it this instant!" Her eyes were wide with fright and her body was vibrating.

Kate reached her. "Mama, wake up, you're dreaming." Her mother jerked, flinging her arms out. Kate held her tightly.

"I can hear the wheels," she moaned.

"No, no," Kate said. "You're here with me."

"It's not so?"

"No," Kate said. "It's not so."

She went limp. Kate felt for her pulse and found it rapid, then regular. She sat rocking her mother. In a few minutes she lay her back on the pillows and smoothed the damp hair at her temples, smoothed the sheets of the bed. Later she slept fitfully in a chair, waking repeatedly to assure herself that her mother was breathing.

Near dawn she got up, exhausted, and left the room to walk in the corridor. In front of the window at the end of the hallway she saw a man slumped on a couch; the man slowly stood and wavered before her like a specter. It was Robert.

"Kate?" he said.

Years ago he had flunked out of a small junior college and their mother sat in her bedroom rocker, crying hard for over an hour while Kate tried in vain to comfort her. Kate went to the university the next fall, so anxious that she studied frantically, outlining whole textbooks in yellow ink. She sat in the front rows of large classrooms to take voluminous notes, writing quickly in her thick notebook. Robert had gone home, held a job in a plant that manufactured business forms and worked his way through the hometown college. By that time their father was dead, and Robert became, always and forever, the man of the house.

"Robert," Kate said, "I'll stay. Go home."

After breakfast they sat waiting for Robert, who had called and said he'd arrive soon. Kate's fatigue had given way to an intense awareness of every sound, every gesture. How would they get through the day? Her mother had awakened from the drugged sleep still groggy, unable to eat. The meal was sent away untouched and she watched the window as though she feared the walls of the room.

"I'm glad your father isn't here to see this," she said. There was a silence and Kate opened her mouth to speak. "I mean," said her mother quickly, "I'm going to look horrible for a few weeks, with my head all shaved." She pulled an afghan up around her lap and straightened the magazines on the table beside her chair.

"Mom," Kate said, "your hair will grow back."

Her mother pulled the afghan closer. "I've been thinking of your father," she said. "It's not that I'd have wanted him to suffer. But if he had to die, sometimes I wish he'd done it more gently. That heart attack, so finished; never a warning. I wish I'd had some time to nurse him. In a way, it's a chance to settle things."

"Did things need settling?"

"They always do, don't they?" She sat looking out the window, then said softly, "I wonder where I'm headed."

"You're not headed anywhere," Kate said. "I want you right here to see me settle down into normal American womanhood."

Her mother smiled reassuringly. "Where are my grandchildren?" she said. "That's what I'd like to know."

"You stick around," said Kate, "and I promise to start working on it." She moved her chair closer, so that their knees were touching and they could both see out the window. Below them cars moved on the highway and the Ferris wheel in the little park was turning.

"I remember when you were one of the little girls in the parade at the county fair. You weren't even in school yet; you were beautiful in that white organdy dress and pinafore. You wore those shiny black patent shoes and a crown of real apple blossoms. Do you remember?"

"Yes," Kate said. "That long parade. They told me not to move and I sat so still my legs went to sleep. When they lifted me off the float I couldn't stand up. They put me under a tree to wait for you, and you came, in a full white skirt and white sandals, your hair tied back in a red scarf. I can see you yet."

Her mother laughed. "Sounds like a pretty exaggerated picture."

Kate nodded. "I was little. You were big."

"You loved the county fair. You were wild about the carnivals." They looked down at the little park. "Magic, isn't it?" her mother said.

"Maybe we could go see it," said Kate. "I'll ask the doctor."

They walked across a pedestrian footbridge spanning the highway. Kate had bundled her mother into a winter coat and gloves despite the sunny weather. The day was sharp, nearly still, holding its bright air like illusion. Kate tasted the brittle water of her breath, felt for the cool handrail and thin steel of the webbed fencing. Cars moved steadily under the bridge. Beyond a muted roar of motors the park spread green and wooded, its limits clearly visible.

Kate's mother had combed her hair and put on lipstick. Her mouth was defined and brilliant; she linked arms with Kate like an escort. "I was afraid they'd tell us no," she said. "I was ready to run away!"

"I promised I wouldn't let you. And we only have ten minutes, long enough for the Ferris wheel." Kate grinned.

"I haven't ridden one in years. I wonder if I still know how."

"Of course you do. Ferris wheels are genetic knowledge."

"All right, whatever you say." She smiled. "We'll just hold on."

They drew closer and walked quickly through the sounds of the highway. When they reached the grass it was ankle-high and thick, longer and more ragged than it appeared from a distance. The Ferris wheel sat squarely near a grove of swaying elms, squat and laboring, taller than trees. Its neon lights still burned, pale in the sun, spiraling from inside like an imagined bloom. The naked elms surrounded it, their topmost branches tapping. Steel ribs of the machine were graceful and slightly rusted, squeaking faintly above a tinkling music. Only a few people were riding.

"Looks a little rickety," Kate said.

"Oh, don't worry," said her mother.

Kate tried to buy tickets but the ride was free. The old man running the motor wore an engineer's cap and patched overalls. He stopped the wheel and led them on a short ramp to an open car. It dipped gently, padded with black cushions. An orderly and his children rode in the car above. Kate saw their dangling feet, the girls' dusty sandals and gray socks beside their father's shoes and the hem of his white pants. The youngest one swung her feet absently, so it seemed the breeze blew her legs like fabric hung on a line.

Kate looked at her mother. "Are you ready for the big sky?" They laughed. Beyond them the river moved lazily. Houses on the opposite bank seemed empty, but a few rowboats bobbed at the docks. The surface of the water lapped and reflected clouds, and as

Kate watched, searching for a definition of line, the Ferris wheel jerked into motion. The car rocked. They looked into the distance and Kate caught her mother's hand as they ascended.

Far away the hospital rose up white and glistening, its windows catching the glint of the sun. Directly below, the park was nearly deserted. There were a few cars in the parking lot and several dogs chasing each other across the grass. Two or three lone women held children on the teeter-totters and a wind was coming up. The forlorn swings moved on their chains. Kate had a vision of the park at night, totally empty, wind weaving heavily through the trees and children's playthings like a great black fish about to surface. She felt a chill on her arms. The light had gone darker, quietly, like a minor chord.

"Mom," Kate said, "it's going to storm." Her own voice seemed distant, the sound strained through layers of screen or gauze.

"No," said her mother, "it's going to pass over." She moved her hand to Kate's knee and touched the cloth of her daughter's skirt.

Kate gripped the metal bar at their waists and looked straight ahead. They were rising again and she felt she would scream. She tried to breathe rhythmically, steadily. She felt the immense weight of the air as they moved through it.

They came almost to the top and stopped. The little car swayed back and forth.

"You're sick, aren't you," her mother said.

Kate shook her head. Below them the grass seemed to glitter coldly, like a sea. Kate sat wordless, feeling the touch of her mother's hand. The hand moved away and Kate felt the absence of the warmth.

They looked at each other levelly.

"I know all about it," her mother said, "I know what you haven't told me."

The sky circled around them, a sure gray movement. Kate swallowed calmly and let their gaze grow endless. She saw herself in her mother's wide brown eyes and felt she was falling slowly into them.

Maxine Hong Kingston

ON
DISCOVERY

〜〜〜

Once upon a time, a man, named Tang Ao, looking for the Gold Mountain, crossed an ocean, and came upon the Land of Women. The women immediately captured him, not on guard against ladies. When they asked Tang Ao to come along, he followed; if he had had male companions, he would've winked over his shoulder.

"We have to prepare you to meet the queen," the women said. They locked him in a canopied apartment equipped with pots of makeup, mirrors, and a woman's clothes. "Let us help you off with your armor and boots," said the women. They slipped his coat off his shoulders, pulled it down his arms, and shackled his wrists behind him. The women who kneeled to take off his shoes chained his ankles together.

A door opened, and he expected to meet his match, but it was only two old women with sewing boxes in their hands. "The less you struggle, the less it'll hurt," one said, squinting a bright eye as she threaded her needle. Two captors sat on him while another held his head. He felt an old woman's dry fingers trace his ear; the long nail on her little finger scraped his neck. "What are you doing?" he asked. "Sewing your lips together," she joked, blackening needles in a candle flame. The ones who sat on him bounced with laughter. But the old women did not sew his lips together. They pulled his earlobes taut and jabbed a needle through each of them. They had to poke and probe before puncturing the layers of skin correctly, the hole in the front of the lobe in line with the one in back, the layers of skin sliding about so. They worked the needle through—a last jerk for the needle's wide eye ("needle's nose" in Chinese). They strung his raw flesh with silk threads; he could feel the fibers.

The women who sat on him turned to direct their attention to his feet. They bent his toes so far backward that his arched foot cracked. The old ladies squeezed each foot and broke many tiny bones along the sides. They gathered his toes, toes over and under one another like a knot of ginger root. Tang Ao wept with pain. As they wound the bandages tight and tighter around his feet, the women sang footbinding songs to distract him: "Use aloe for binding feet and not for scholars."

During the months of a season, they fed him on women's food: the tea was thick with white chrysanthemums and stirred the cool female winds inside his body; chicken wings made his hair shine; vinegar soup improved his womb. They drew the loops of thread through the scabs that grew daily over the holes in his earlobes. One day they inserted gold hoops. Every night they unbound his feet, but his veins had shrunk, and the blood pumping through them hurt so much, he begged to have his feet rewrapped tight. They forced him to wash his used bandages, which were embroidered with flowers and smelled of rot and cheese. He hung the bandages up to dry, streamers that drooped and draped wall to wall. He felt embarrassed; the wrappings were like underwear, and they were his.

One day his attendants changed his gold hoops to jade studs and strapped his feet to shoes that curved like bridges. They plucked out each hair on his face, powdered him white, painted his eyebrows like a moth's wings, painted his cheeks and lips red. He served a meal at the queen's court. His hips swayed and his shoulders swiveled because of his shaped feet. "She's pretty, don't you agree?" the diners said, smacking their lips at his dainty feet as he bent to put dishes before them.

In the Women's Land there are no taxes and no wars. Some scholars say that that country was discovered during the reign of Empress Wu (A.D. 694–705), and some say earlier than that, A.D. 441, and it was in North America.

Alice Walker

THE
ABORTION

～～～

They had discussed it, but not deeply, whether they wanted the baby she was now carrying. "I don't *know* if I want it," she said, eyes filling with tears. She cried at anything now, and was often nauseous. That pregnant women cried easily and were nauseous seemed banal to her, and she resented banality.

"Well, think about it," he said, with his smooth reassuring voice (but with an edge of impatience she now felt) that used to soothe her.

It was all she *did* think about, all she apparently *could*; that he could dream otherwise enraged her. But she always lost, when they argued. Her temper would flare up, he would become instantly reasonable, mature, responsible, if not responsive precisely, to her mood, and she would swallow down her tears and hate herself. It was because she believed him "good." The best human being she had ever met.

"It isn't as if we don't already have a child," she said in a calmer tone, carelessly wiping at the tear that slid from one eye.

"We have a perfect child," he said with relish, "thank the Good Lord!"

Had she ever dreamed she'd marry someone humble enough to go around thanking the Good Lord? She had not.

Now they left the bedroom, where she had been lying down on their massive king-size bed with the forbidding ridge in the middle, and went down the hall—hung with bright prints—to the cheerful, spotlessly clean kitchen. He put water on for tea in a bright yellow pot.

She wanted him to want the baby so much he would try to save its life. On the other hand, she did not permit such presumptuousness. As he praised the child they already had, a daughter of sunny disposition and winning smile, Imani sensed subterfuge, and hardened her heart.

"What am I talking about," she said, as if she'd been talking about it. "Another child would kill me. I can't imagine life with two children. Having a child is a good experience *to have had*, like graduate school. But if you've had one, you've had the experience and that's enough."

He placed the tea before her and rested a heavy hand on her hair. She felt the heat and pressure of his hand as she touched the cup and felt the odor and steam rise up from it. Her throat contracted.

"I can't drink that," she said through gritted teeth. "Take it away."

There were days of this.

Clarice, their daughter, was barely two years old. A miscarriage brought on by grief (Imani had lost her fervidly environmentalist mother to lung cancer shortly after Clarice's birth; the asbestos ceiling in the classroom where she taught first graders had leaked for twenty years) separated Clarice's birth from the new pregnancy. Imani felt her body had been assaulted by these events and was, in fact, considerably weakened, and was also, in any case, chronically anaemic and run down. Still, if she had wanted the baby more than she did not want it, she would not have planned to abort it.

They lived in a small town in the South. Her husband, Clarence, was, among other things, legal adviser and defender of the new black mayor of the town. The mayor was much in their lives because of the difficulties being the first black mayor of a small town assured, and because, next to the major leaders of black struggles in the South, Clarence respected and admired him most.

Imani reserved absolute judgment, but she did point out that Mayor Carswell would never look at her directly when she made a comment or posed a question, even sitting at her own dinner table, and would instead talk to Clarence as if she were not there. He assumed that as a woman she would not be interested in, or even understand, politics. (He would comment occasionally on her cooking or her clothes. He noticed when she cut her hair.) But Imani understood every shade and variation of politics: she understood, for example, why she fed the mouth that did not speak to her; because for the present she must believe in Mayor Carswell, even as he could not believe in her. Even understanding this, however, she found dinners with Carswell hard to swallow.

But Clarence was dedicated to the mayor, and believed his success would ultimately mean security and advancement for them all.

On the morning she left to have the abortion, the mayor and Clarence were to have a working lunch, and they drove her to the airport deep in conversation about municipal funds, racist cops, and the facilities for teaching at the chaotic, newly integrated schools. Clarence had time for the briefest kiss and hug at the airport ramp.

"Take care of yourself," he whispered lovingly as she walked away. He was needed, while she was gone, to draft the city's new charter. She had agreed this was important; the mayor was already being called incompetent by local businessmen and the chamber of commerce, and one inferred from television that no black person alive even knew what a city charter was.

"Take care of myself." Yes, she thought. I see that is what I have to do. But she thought this self-pityingly, which invalidated it. She had expected *him* to take care of her, and she blamed him for not doing so now.

Well, she was a fraud, anyway. She had known after a year of marriage that it bored her. "The Experience of Having a Child" was to distract her from this fact. Still, she expected him to "take care of her." She was lucky he didn't pack up and leave. But he seemed to know, as she did, that if anyone packed and left, it would be her. Precisely *because* she was a fraud and because in the end he would settle for fraud and she could not.

On the plane to New York her teeth ached and she vomited bile—bitter, yellowish stuff she hadn't even been aware her body produced. She resented and appreciated the crisp help of the stewardess, who asked if she needed anything, then stood chatting with the cigarette-smoking white man next to her, whose fat hairy wrist, like a large worm, was all Imani could bear to see out of the corner of her eye.

Her first abortion, when she was still in college, she frequently remembered as wonderful, bearing as it had all the marks of a supreme coming of age and a seizing of the direction of her own life, as well as a comprehension of existence that never left her: that life—what one saw about one and called Life—was not a facade. There was nothing behind it which used "Life" as its manifestation. Life was itself. Period. At the time, and afterwards, and even now, this seemed a marvelous thing to know.

The abortionist had been a delightful Italian doctor on the Upper East Side in New York, and before he put her under he told her about his own daughter who was just her age, and a junior at Vassar. He babbled on and on until she was out, but not before Imani had thought how her thousand dollars, for which she would be in debt for years, would go to keep her there.

When she woke up it was all over. She lay on a brown Naugahyde sofa in the doctor's outer office. And she heard, over her somewhere in the air, the sound of a woman's voice. It was a Saturday, no nurses in attendance, and she presumed it was the doctor's wife. She was pulled gently to her feet by this voice and encouraged to walk.

"And when you leave, be sure to walk as if nothing is wrong," the voice said.

Imani did not feel any pain. This surprised her. Perhaps he didn't do anything, she thought. Perhaps he took my thousand dollars and put me to sleep with two dollars' worth of ether. Perhaps this is a racket.

But he was so kind, and he was smiling benignly, almost fatherly, at her (and Imani realized how desperately she needed this "fatherly" look, this "fatherly" smile). "Thank you," she murmured sincerely: she was thanking him for her life.

Some of Italy was still in his voice. "It's nothing, nothing," he said. "A nice, pretty girl like you; in school like my own daughter, you didn't need this trouble."

"He's nice," she said to herself, walking to the subway on her way back to school. She lay down gingerly across a vacant seat, and passed out.

She hemorrhaged steadily for six weeks, and was not well again for a year.

But this was seven years later. An abortion law now made it possible to make an appointment at a clinic, and for seventy-five dollars a safe, quick, painless abortion was yours.

Imani had once lived in New York, in the Village, not five blocks from where the abortion clinic was. It was also near the Margaret Sanger clinic, where she had received her very first diaphragm, with utter gratitude and amazement that someone apparently understood and actually cared about young women as alone and ignorant as she. In fact, as she walked up the block, with its modern office buildings side by side with older, more elegant brownstones, she felt how close she was still to that earlier self. Still not in control of her sensuality, and only through violence and with money (for the flight, for the operation itself) in control of her body.

She found that abortion had entered the age of the assembly line. Grateful for the lack of distinction between herself and the other women—all colors, ages, states of misery or nervousness—she was less happy to notice, once the doctor started to insert the catheter, that the anesthesia she had been given was insufficient. But assembly lines don't stop because the product on them has a complaint. Her doctor whistled, and assured her she was all right, and carried the procedure through to the horrific end. Imani fainted some seconds before that.

They laid her out in a peaceful room full of cheerful colors. Primary colors: yellow, red, blue. When she revived she had the feeling of being in a nursery. She had a pressing need to urinate.

A nurse, kindly, white-haired and with firm hands, helped her to the toilet. Imani saw herself in the mirror over the sink and was alarmed. She was literally gray, as if all her blood had leaked out.

"Don't worry about how you look," said the nurse. "Rest a bit here and take it easy when you get back home. You'll be fine in a week or so."

She could not imagine being fine again. Somewhere her child—she never dodged into the language of "fetuses" and "amorphous growths"—was being flushed down a sewer. Gone all her or his chances to see the sunlight, savor a fig.

"Well," she said to this child, "it was you or me, Kiddo, and I chose me."

There were people who thought she had no right to choose herself, but Imani knew better than to think of those people now.

It was a bright, hot Saturday when she returned.

Clarence and Clarice picked her up at the airport. They had brought flowers from Imani's garden, and Clarice presented them with a stout-hearted hug. Once in her mother's lap she rested content all the way home, sucking her thumb, stroking her nose with the forefinger of the same hand, and kneading a corner of her blanket with the three fingers that were left.

"How did it go?" asked Clarence.

"It went," said Imani.

There was no way to explain abortion to a man. She thought castration might be an apt analogy, but most men, perhaps all, would insist this could not possibly be true.

"The anesthesia failed," she said. "I thought I'd never faint in time to keep from screaming and leaping off the table."

Clarence paled. He hated the thought of pain, any kind of violence. He could not endure it; it made him physically ill. This was one of the reasons he was a pacifist, another reason she admired him.

She knew he wanted her to stop talking. But she continued in a flat, deliberate voice.

"All the blood seemed to run out of me. The tendons in my legs felt cut. I was gray."

He reached for her hand. Held it. Squeezed.

"But," she said, "at least I know what I don't want. And I intend never to go through any of this again."

They were in the living room of their peaceful, quiet and colorful house. Imani was in her rocker, Clarice dozing on her lap. Clarence sank to the floor and rested his head against her knees. She felt he was asking for nurture when she needed it herself. She felt the two of them, Clarence and Clarice, clinging to her, using her. And that the only way she could claim herself, feel herself distinct from them, was by doing something painful, self-defining but self-destructive.

She suffered the pressure of his head as long as she could.

"Have a vasectomy," she said, "or stay in the guest room. Nothing is going to touch me anymore that isn't harmless."

He smoothed her thick hair with his hand. "We'll talk about it," he said, as if that was not what they were doing. "We'll see. Don't worry. We'll take care of things."

She had forgotten that the third Sunday in June, the following day, was the fifth memorial observance for Holly Monroe, who had been shot down on her way home from her high-school graduation ceremony five years before. Imani *always* went to these memorials. She liked the reassurance that her people had long memories, and that those people who fell in struggle or innocence were not forgotten. She was, of course, too weak to go. She was dizzy and still losing blood. The white lawgivers attempted to get around assassination—which Imani considered extreme abortion—by saying the victim provoked it (there had been some difficulty saying this about Holly Monroe, but they had tried) but were antiabortionist to a man. Imani thought of this as she resolutely showered and washed her hair.

Clarence had installed central air conditioning their second year in the house. Imani had at first objected. "I want to smell the trees, the flowers, the natural air!" she cried. But the first summer of 110-degree heat had cured her of giving a damn about any of that. Now she wanted to be cool. As much as she loved trees, on a hot day she would have sawed through a forest to get to an air conditioner.

In fairness to him, she had to admit he asked her if she thought she was well enough to go. But even to be asked annoyed her. She was not one to let her own troubles prevent her from showing proper respect and remembrance toward the dead, although she understood perfectly well that once dead, the dead do not exist. So respect, remembrance was for herself, and today herself needed rest. There was something mad about her refusal to rest, and she felt it as she tottered about getting Clarice dressed. But she did not stop. She ran a bath, plopped the child in it, scrubbed her plump body on her knees, arms straining over the tub awkwardly in a way that made her stomach hurt—but not yet her uterus—dried her hair, lifted her out and dried the rest of her on the kitchen table.

"You are going to remember as long as you live what kind of people they are," she said to the child, who, gurgling and cooing, looked into her mother's stern face with light-hearted fixation.

"You are going to hear the music," Imani said. "The music they've tried to kill. The music they try to steal." She felt feverish and was aware she was muttering. She didn't care.

"They think they can kill a continent—people, trees, buffalo—and then fly off to the moon and just forget about it. But you and me we're going to remember the people, the trees, and the fucking buffalo. Goddammit."

"Buffwoe," said the child, hitting at her mother's face with a spoon.

She placed the baby on a blanket in the living room and turned to see her husband's eyes, full of pity, on her. She wore pert green velvet slippers and a lovely sea green robe. Her body was bent within it. A reluctant tear formed beneath his gaze.

"Sometimes I look at you and I wonder 'What is this man doing in my house?' "

This had started as a joke between them. Her aim had been never to marry, but to take in lovers who could be sent home at dawn, freeing her to work and ramble.

"I'm here because you love me," was the traditional answer. But Clarence faltered, meeting her eyes, and Imani turned away.

It was a hundred degrees by ten o'clock. By eleven, when the memorial service began, it would be ten degrees hotter. Imani staggered from the heat. When she sat in the car she had to clench her teeth against the dizziness until the motor prodded the air conditioning to envelop them in coolness. A dull ache started in her uterus.

The church was not of course air conditioned. It was authentic Primitive Baptist in every sense.

Like the four previous memorials this one was designed by Holly Monroe's classmates. All twenty-five of whom—fat and thin—managed to look like the dead girl. Imani had never seen Holly Monroe, though there were always photographs of her dominating the pulpit of this church where she had been baptized and where she had sung in the choir—and to her, every black girl of a certain vulnerable age *was* Holly Monroe. And an even deeper truth was that Holly Monroe was herself. Herself shot down, aborted on the eve of becoming herself.

She was prepared to cry and to do so with abandon. But she did not. She clenched her teeth against the steadily increasing pain and her tears were instantly blotted by the heat.

Mayor Carswell had been waiting for Clarence in the vestibule of the church, mopping his plumply jowled face with a voluminous handkerchief and holding court among half a dozen young men and women who listened to him with awe. Imani exchanged greetings with the mayor, he ritualistically kissed her on the cheek, and kissed Clarice on the cheek, but his rather heat-glazed eye was already fastened on her husband. The two men huddled in a corner away from the awed young group. Away from Imani and Clarice, who passed hesitantly, waiting to be joined or to be called back, into the church.

There was a quarter hour's worth of music.

"Holly Monroe was five feet, three inches tall, and weighed one hundred and eleven pounds," her best friend said, not reading from notes, but talking to each person in the audience. "She was a stubborn, loyal Aries, the best kind of friend to have. She had black kinky hair that she experimented with a lot. She was exactly the color of this oak church pew in the summer; in the winter she was the color [pointing up] of this heart pine ceiling. She loved green. She did not like lavender because she said she also didn't like pink. She had brown eyes and wore glasses, except when she was meeting someone for the first time. She had a sort of rounded nose. She had beautiful large teeth, but her lips were always chapped so she didn't smile as much as she might have if she'd ever gotten used to carrying Chap Stick. She had elegant feet.

"Her favorite church song was 'Leaning on the Everlasting Arms.' Her favorite other kind of song was 'I Can't Help Myself— I Love You and Nobody Else.' She was often late for choir rehearsal though she loved to sing. She made the dress she wore to her graduation in Home Ec. She *hated* Home Ec . . ."

Imani was aware that the sound of low, murmurous voices had been the background for this statement all along. Everything was quiet around her, even Clarice sat up straight, absorbed by the simple friendliness of the young woman's voice. All of Holly Monroe's classmates and friends in the choir wore vivid green. Imani imagined Clarice entranced by the brilliant, swaying color as by a field of swaying corn.

Lifting the child, her uterus burning, and perspiration already a stream down her back, Imani tiptoed to the door. Clarence and the mayor were still deep in conversation. She heard "board meeting . . . aldermen . . . city council." She beckoned to Clarence.

"Your voices are carrying!" she hissed.

She meant: How dare you not come inside.

They did not. Clarence raised his head, looked at her, and shrugged his shoulders helplessly. Then, turning, with the abstracted air of priests, the two men moved slowly toward the outer door, and into the churchyard, coming to stand some distance from the church beneath a large oak tree. There they remained throughout the service.

Two years later, Clarence was furious with her: What is the matter with you? he asked. You never want me to touch you. You told me to sleep in the guest room and I did. You told me to have a vasectomy I didn't want and *I did*. (Here, there was a sob of hatred for her somewhere in the anger, the humiliation: he thought of himself as a eunuch, and blamed her.)

She was not merely frigid, she was remote.

She had been amazed after they left the church that the anger she'd felt watching Clarence and the mayor turn away from the Holly Monroe memorial did not prevent her accepting a ride home with him. A month later it did not prevent her smiling on him fondly. Did not prevent a trip to Bermuda, a few blissful days of very good sex on a deserted beach screened by trees. Did not prevent her listening to his mother's stories of Clarence's youth as though she would treasure them forever.

And yet. From that moment in the heat at the church door, she had uncoupled herself from him, in a separation that made him, except occasionally, little more than a stranger.

And he had not felt it, had not known.

"What have I done?" he asked, all the tenderness in his voice breaking over her. She smiled a nervous smile at him, which he interpreted as derision—so far apart had they drifted.

They had discussed the episode at the church many times. Mayor Carswell—whom they never saw anymore—was now a model mayor, with wide biracial support in his campaign for the legislature. Neither could easily recall him, though television frequently brought him into the house.

"It was so important that I help the mayor!" said Clarence. "He was our *first!*"

Imani understood this perfectly well, but it sounded humorous to her. When she smiled, he was offended.

She had known the moment she left the marriage, the exact second. But apparently that moment had left no perceptible mark.

They argued, she smiled, they scowled, blamed and cried—as she packed.

Each of them almost recalled out loud that about this time of the year their aborted child would have been a troublesome, "terrible" two-year-old, a great burden on its mother, whose health was by now in excellent shape, each wanted to think aloud that the marriage would have deteriorated anyway, because of that.

Bobbie Ann Mason

SHILOH

L eroy Moffitt's wife, Norma Jean, is working on her pectorals. She lifts three-pound dumbbells to warm up, then progresses to a twenty-pound barbell. Standing with her legs apart, she reminds Leroy of Wonder Woman.

"I'd give anything if I could just get these muscles to where they're real hard," says Norma Jean. "Feel this arm. It's not as hard as the other one."

"That's 'cause you're right-handed," says Leroy, dodging as she swings the barbell in an arc.

"Do you think so?"

"Sure."

Leroy is a truckdriver. He injured his leg in a highway accident four months ago, and his physical therapy, which involved weights and a pulley, prompted Norma Jean to try building herself up. Now she is attending a bodybuilding class. Leroy has been collecting temporary disability since his tractor-trailer jackknifed in Missouri, badly twisting his left leg in its socket. He has a steel pin in his hip. He will probably not be able to drive his rig again. It sits in the backyard, like a gigantic bird that has flown home to roost. Leroy has been home in Kentucky for three months, and his leg is almost healed, but the accident frightened him and he does not want to drive any more long hauls. He is not sure what to do next. In the meantime, he makes things from craft kits. He started by building a miniature log cabin from notched Popsicle sticks. He varnished it and placed it on the TV set, where it remains. It reminds him of a rustic Nativity scene. Then he tried string art (sailing ships on black velvet), a macramé owl kit, a snap-together B-17 Flying Fortress, and a lamp made out of a model truck, with a light fixture screwed in the top of the cab. At first the kits were diversions, something to kill time, but now he is thinking about building a full-scale log house from a kit. It would be considerably cheaper than building a regular house, and besides, Leroy has grown to appreciate how things are put together. He has begun to realize that in all the years he was on the road he never took time to examine anything. He was always flying past scenery.

"They won't let you build a log cabin in any of the new subdivisions," Norma Jean tells him.

"They will if I tell them it's for you," he says, teasing her. Ever since they were married, he has promised Norma Jean he would build her a new home one day. They have always rented, and the house they live in is small and nondescript. It does not even feel like a home, Leroy realizes now.

Norma Jean works at the Rexall drugstore, and she has acquired an amazing amount of information about cosmetics. When she explains to Leroy the three stages of complexion care, involving creams, toners, and moisturizers, he thinks happily of other petro-

leum products—axle grease, diesel fuel. This is a connection between him and Norma Jean. Since he has been home, he has felt
unusually tender about his wife and guilty over his long absences.
But he can't tell what she feels about him. Norma Jean has never
complained about his traveling; she has never made hurt remarks,
like calling his truck a "widow-maker." He is reasonably certain
she has been faithful to him, but he wishes she would celebrate his
permanent homecoming more happily. Norma Jean is often startled
to find Leroy at home, and he thinks she seems a little disappointed
about it. Perhaps he reminds her too much of the early days of
their marriage, before he went on the road. They had a child who
died as an infant, years ago. They never speak about their memories
of Randy, which have almost faded, but now that Leroy is home
all the time, they sometimes feel awkward around each other, and
Leroy wonders if one of them should mention the child. He has
the feeling that they are waking up out of a dream together—that
they must create a new marriage, start afresh. They are lucky they
are still married. Leroy has read that for most people losing a child
destroys the marriage—or else he heard this on *Donahue*. He can't
always remember where he learns things anymore.

At Christmas, Leroy bought an electric organ for Norma Jean.
She used to play the piano when she was in high school. "It don't
leave you," she told him once. "It's like riding a bicycle."

The new instrument had so many keys and buttons that she was
bewildered by it at first. She touched the keys tentatively, pushed
some buttons, then pecked out "Chopsticks." It came out in an
amplified fox-trot rhythm, with marimba sounds.

"It's an orchestra!" she cried.

The organ had a pecan-look finish and eighteen preset chords,
with optional flute, violin, trumpet, clarinet, and banjo accompa-
niments. Norma Jean mastered the organ almost immediately. At
first she played Christmas songs. Then she bought *The Sixties
Songbook* and learned every tune in it, adding variations to each
with the rows of brightly colored buttons.

"I didn't like these old songs back then," she said. "But I have
this crazy feeling I missed something."

"You didn't miss a thing," said Leroy.

Leroy likes to lie on the couch and smoke a joint and listen to

Norma Jean play "Can't Take My Eyes Off You" and "I'll Be Back." He is back again. After fifteen years on the road, he is finally settling down with the woman he loves. She is still pretty. Her skin is flawless. Her frosted curls resemble pencil trimmings.

Now that Leroy has come home to stay, he notices how much the town has changed. Subdivisions are spreading across western Kentucky like an oil slick. The sign at the edge of town says "Pop: 11,500"—only seven hundred more than it said twenty years before. Leroy can't figure out who is living in all the new houses. The farmers who used to gather around the courthouse square on Saturday afternoons to play checkers and spit tobacco juice have gone. It has been years since Leroy has thought about the farmers, and they have disappeared without his noticing.

Leroy meets a kid named Stevie Hamilton in the parking lot at the new shopping center. While they pretend to be strangers meeting over a stalled car, Stevie tosses an ounce of marijuana under the front seat of Leroy's car. Stevie is wearing orange jogging shoes and a T-shirt that says CHATTAHOOCHEE SUPER-RAT. His father is a prominent doctor who lives in one of the expensive subdivisions in a new white-columned brick house that looks like a funeral parlor. In the phone book under his name there is a separate number, with the listing "Teenagers."

"Where do you get this stuff?" asks Leroy. "From your pappy?"

"That's for me to know and you to find out," Stevie says. He is slit-eyed and skinny.

"What else you got?"

"What you interested in?"

"Nothing special. Just wondered."

Leroy used to take speed on the road. Now he has to go slowly. He needs to be mellow. He leans back against the car and says, "I'm aiming to build me a log house, soon as I get time. My wife, though, I don't think she likes the idea."

"Well, let me know when you want me again," Stevie says. He has a cigarette in his cupped palm, as though sheltering it from the wind. He takes a long drag, then stomps it on the asphalt and slouches away.

Stevie's father was two years ahead of Leroy in high school.

Leroy is thirty-four. He married Norma Jean when they were both eighteen, and their child Randy was born a few months later, but he died at the age of four months and three days. He would be about Stevie's age now. Norma Jean and Leroy were at the drive-in, watching a double feature (*Dr. Strangelove* and *Lover Come Back*), and the baby was sleeping in the back seat. When the first movie ended, the baby was dead. It was the sudden infant death syndrome. Leroy remembers handing Randy to a nurse at the emergency room, as though he were offering her a large doll as a present. A dead baby feels like a sack of flour. "It just happens sometimes," said the doctor, in what Leroy always recalls as a nonchalant tone. Leroy can hardly remember the child anymore, but he still sees vividly a scene from *Dr. Strangelove* in which the President of the United States was talking in a folksy voice on the hot line to the Soviet premier about the bomber accidentally headed toward Russia. He was in the War Room, and the world map was lit up. Leroy remembers Norma Jean standing catatonically beside him in the hospital and himself thinking: Who is this strange girl? He had forgotten who she was. Now scientists are saying that crib death is caused by a virus. Nobody knows anything, Leroy thinks. The answers are always changing.

When Leroy gets home from the shopping center, Norma Jean's mother, Mabel Beasley, is there. Until this year, Leroy has not realized how much time she spends with Norma Jean. When she visits, she inspects the closets and then the plants, informing Norma Jean when a plant is droopy or yellow. Mabel calls the plants "flowers," although there are never any blooms. She always notices if Norma Jean's laundry is piling up. Mabel is a short, overweight woman whose tight, brown-dyed curls look more like a wig than the actual wig she sometimes wears. Today she has brought Norma Jean an off-white dust ruffle she made for the bed; Mabel works in a custom-upholstery shop.

"This is the tenth one I made this year," Mabel says. "I got started and couldn't stop."

"It's real pretty," says Norma Jean.

"Now we can hide things under the bed," says Leroy, who gets along with his mother-in-law primarily by joking with her. Mabel has never really forgiven him for disgracing her by getting Norma Jean pregnant. When the baby died, she said that fate was mocking her.

"What's that thing?" Mabel says to Leroy in a loud voice, pointing to a tangle of yarn on a piece of canvas.

Leroy holds it up for Mabel to see. "It's my needlepoint," he explains. "This is a *Star Trek* pillow cover."

"That's what a woman would do," says Mabel. "Great day in the morning!"

"All the big football players on TV do it," he says.

"Why, Leroy, you're always trying to fool me. I don't believe you for one minute. You don't know what to do with yourself—that's the whole trouble. Sewing!"

"I'm aiming to build us a log house," says Leroy. "Soon as my plans come."

"Like *heck* you are," says Norma Jean. She takes Leroy's needlepoint and shoves it into a drawer. "You have to find a job first. Nobody can afford to build now anyway."

Mabel straightens her girdle and says, "I still think before you get tied down y'all ought to take a little run to Shiloh."

"One of these days, Mama," Norma Jean says impatiently.

Mabel is talking about Shiloh, Tennessee. For the past few years, she has been urging Leroy and Norma Jean to visit the Civil War battleground there. Mabel went there on her honeymoon—the only real trip she ever took. Her husband died of a perforated ulcer when Norma Jean was ten, but Mabel, who was accepted into the United Daughters of the Confederacy in 1975, is still preoccupied with going back to Shiloh.

"I've been to kingdom come and back in that truck out yonder," Leroy says to Mabel, "but we never yet set foot in that battleground. Ain't that something? How did I miss it?"

"It's not even that far," Mabel says.

After Mabel leaves, Norma Jean reads to Leroy from a list she has made. "Things you could do," she announces. "You could get a job as a guard at Union Carbide, where they'd let you set on a stool. You could get on at the lumberyard. You could do a little carpenter work, if you want to build so bad. You could—"

"I can't do something where I'd have to stand up all day."

"You ought to try standing up all day behind a cosmetics counter. It's amazing that I have strong feet, coming from two parents that never had strong feet at all." At the moment Norma Jean is holding on to the kitchen counter, raising her knees one at a time as she talks. She is wearing two-pound ankle weights.

"Don't worry," says Leroy. "I'll do something."

"You could truck calves to slaughter for somebody. You wouldn't have to drive any big old truck for that."

"I'm going to build you this house," says Leroy. "I want to make you a real home."

"I don't want to live in any log cabin."

"It's not a cabin. It's a house."

"I don't care. It looks like a cabin."

"You and me together could lift those logs. It's just like lifting weights."

Norma Jean doesn't answer. Under her breath, she is counting. Now she is marching through the kitchen. She is doing goose steps.

Before his accident, when Leroy came home he used to stay in the house with Norma Jean, watching TV in bed and playing cards. She would cook fried chicken, picnic ham, chocolate pie—all his favorites. Now he is home alone much of the time. In the mornings, Norma Jean disappears, leaving a cooling place in the bed. She eats a cereal called Body Buddies, and she leaves the bowl on the table, with the soggy tan balls floating in a milk puddle. He sees things about Norma Jean that he never realized before. When she chops onions, she stares off into a corner, as if she can't bear to look. She puts on her house slippers almost precisely at nine o'clock every evening and nudges her jogging shoes under the couch. She saves bread heels for the birds. Leroy watches the birds at the feeder. He notices the peculiar way goldfinches fly past the window. They close their wings, then fall, then spread their wings to catch and lift themselves. He wonders if they close their eyes when they fall. Norma Jean closes her eyes when they are in bed. She wants the lights turned out. Even then, he is sure she closes her eyes.

He goes for long drives around town. He tends to drive a car rather carelessly. Power steering and an automatic shift make a car feel so small and inconsequential that his body is hardly involved in the driving process. His injured leg stretches out comfortably. Once or twice he has almost hit something, but even the prospect of an accident seems minor in a car. He cruises the new subdivisions, feeling like a criminal rehearsing for a robbery. Norma Jean is probably right about a log house being inappropriate here in the new subdivisions. All the houses look grand and complicated. They depress him.

One day when Leroy comes home from a drive he finds Norma Jean in tears. She is in the kitchen making a potato and mushroom-soup casserole, with grated-cheese topping. She is crying because her mother caught her smoking.

"I didn't hear her coming. I was standing here puffing away pretty as you please," Norma Jean says, wiping her eyes.

"I knew it would happen sooner or later," says Leroy, putting his arm around her.

"She don't know the meaning of the word 'knock,' " says Norma Jean. "It's a wonder she hadn't caught me years ago."

"Think of it this way," Leroy says. "What if she caught me with a joint?"

"You better not let her!" Norma Jean shrieks. "I'm warning you, Leroy Moffitt!"

"I'm just kidding. Here, play me a tune. That'll help you relax."

Norma Jean puts the casserole in the oven and sets the timer. Then she plays a ragtime tune, with horns and banjo, as Leroy lights up a joint and lies on the couch, laughing to himself about Mabel's catching him at it. He thinks of Stevie Hamilton—a doctor's son pushing grass. Everything is funny. The whole town seems crazy and small. He is reminded of Virgil Mathis, a boastful policeman Leroy used to shoot pool with. Virgil recently led a drug bust in a back room at a bowling alley, where he seized ten thousand dollars' worth of marijuana. The newspaper had a picture of him holding up the bags of grass and grinning widely. Right now, Leroy can imagine Virgil breaking down the door and arresting him with a lungful of smoke. Virgil would probably have been alerted to the scene because of all the racket Norma Jean is making. Now she sounds like a hard-rock band. Norma Jean is terrific. When she switches to a Latin-rhythm version of "Sunshine Superman," Leroy hums along. Norma Jean's foot goes up and down, up and down.

"Well, what do you think?" Leroy says, when Norma Jean pauses to search through her music.

"What do I think about what?"

His mind has gone blank. Then he says, "I'll sell my rig and build us a house." That wasn't what he wanted to say. He wanted to know what she thought—what she *really* thought—about them.

"Don't start in on that again," says Norma Jean. She begins playing "Who'll Be the Next in Line?"

Leroy used to tell hitchhikers his whole life story—about his travels, his hometown, the baby. He would end with a question: "Well, what do you think?" It was just a rhetorical question. In time, he had the feeling that he'd been telling the same story over and over to the same hitchhikers. He quit talking to hitchhikers when he realized how his voice sounded—whining and self-pitying, like some teenage-tragedy song. Now Leroy has the sudden impulse to tell Norma Jean about himself, as if he had just met her. They have known each other so long they have forgotten a lot about each other. They could become reacquainted. But when the oven timer goes off and she runs to the kitchen, he forgets why he wants to do this.

The next day, Mabel drops by. It is Saturday and Norma Jean is cleaning. Leroy is studying the plans of his log house, which have finally come in the mail. He has them spread out on the table— big sheets of stiff blue paper, with diagrams and numbers printed in white. While Norma Jean runs the vacuum, Mabel drinks coffee. She sets her coffee cup on a blueprint.

"I'm just waiting for time to pass," she says to Leroy, drumming her fingers on the table.

As soon as Norma Jean switches off the vacuum, Mabel says in a loud voice, "Did you hear about the datsun dog that killed the baby?"

Norma Jean says, "The word is 'dachshund.' "

"They put the dog on trial. It chewed the baby's legs off. The mother was in the next room all the time." She raises her voice. "They thought it was neglect."

Norma Jean is holding her ears. Leroy manages to open the refrigerator and get some Diet Pepsi to offer Mabel. Mabel still has some coffee and she waves away the Pepsi.

"Datsuns are like that," Mabel says. "They're jealous dogs. They'll tear a place to pieces if you don't keep an eye on them."

"You better watch out what you're saying, Mabel," says Leroy.

"Well, facts is facts."

Leroy looks out the window at his rig. It is like a huge piece of furniture gathering dust in the backyard. Pretty soon it will be an antique. He hears the vacuum cleaner. Norma Jean seems to be cleaning the living room rug again.

Later, she says to Leroy, "She just said that about the baby because she caught me smoking. She's trying to pay me back."

"What are you talking about?" Leroy says, nervously shuffling blueprints.

"You know good and well," Norma Jean says. She is sitting in a kitchen chair with her feet up and her arms wrapped around her knees. She looks small and helpless. She says, "The very idea, her bringing up a subject like that! Saying it was neglect."

"She didn't mean that," Leroy says.

"She might not have *thought* she meant it. She always says things like that. You don't know how she goes on."

"But she didn't really mean it. She was just talking."

Leroy opens a king-sized bottle of beer and pours it into two glasses, dividing it carefully. He hands a glass to Norma Jean and she takes it from him mechanically. For a long time, they sit by the kitchen window watching the birds at the feeder.

Something is happening. Norma Jean is going to night school. She has graduated from her six-week body-building course and now she is taking an adult-education course in composition at Paducah Community College. She spends her evenings outlining paragraphs.

"First you have a topic sentence," she explains to Leroy. "Then you divide it up. Your secondary topic has to be connected to your primary topic."

To Leroy, this sounds intimidating. "I never was any good in English," he says.

"It makes a lot of sense."

"What are you doing this for, anyhow?"

She shrugs. "It's something to do." She stands up and lifts her dumbbells a few times.

"Driving a rig, nobody cared about my English."

"I'm not criticizing your English."

Norma Jean used to say, "If I lose ten minutes' sleep, I just drag all day." Now she stays up late, writing compositions. She got a B on her first paper—a how-to theme on soup-based casseroles. Recently Norma Jean has been cooking unusual foods—tacos, lasagna, Bombay chicken. She doesn't play the organ anymore, though her second paper was called "Why Music Is Important to Me." She sits at the kitchen table, concentrating on her outlines, while Leroy plays with his log house plans, practicing with a set of Lincoln Logs. The thought of getting a truckload of notched, numbered logs scares him, and he wants to be prepared. As he and Norma Jean work together at the kitchen table, Leroy has the hopeful thought that they are sharing something, but he knows he is a fool to think this. Norma Jean is miles away. He knows he is going to lose her. Like Mabel, he is just waiting for time to pass.

One day, Mabel is there before Norma Jean gets home from work, and Leroy finds himself confiding in her. Mabel, he realizes, must know Norma Jean better than he does.

"I don't know what's got into that girl," Mabel says. "She used to go to bed with the chickens. Now you say she's up all hours. Plus her a-smoking. I like to died."

"I want to make her this beautiful home," Leroy says, indicating the Lincoln Logs. "I don't think she even wants it. Maybe she was happier with me gone."

"She don't know what to make of you, coming home like this."

"Is that it?"

Mabel takes the roof off his Lincoln Log cabin. "You couldn't get *me* in a log cabin," she says. "I was raised in one. It's no picnic, let me tell you."

"They're different now," says Leroy.

"I tell you what," Mabel says, smiling oddly at Leroy.

"What?"

"Take her on down to Shiloh. Y'all need to get out together, stir a little. Her brain's all balled up over them books."

Leroy can see traces of Norma Jean's features in her mother's face. Mabel's worn face has the texture of crinkled cotton, but suddenly she looks pretty. It occurs to Leroy that Mabel has been hinting all along that she wants them to take her with them to Shiloh.

"Let's all go to Shiloh," he says. "You and me and her. Come Sunday."

Mabel throws up her hands in protest. "Oh, no, not me. Young folks want to be by theirselves."

When Norma Jean comes in with groceries, Leroy says excitedly, "Your mama here's been dying to go to Shiloh for thirty-five years. It's about time we went, don't you think?"

"I'm not going to butt in on anybody's second honeymoon," Mabel says.

"Who's going on a honeymoon, for Christ's sake?" Norma Jean says loudly.

"I never raised no daughter of mine to talk that-a-way," Mabel says.

"You ain't seen nothing yet," says Norma Jean. She starts putting away boxes and cans, slamming cabinet doors.

"There's a log cabin at Shiloh," Mabel says. "It was there during the battle. There's bullet holes in it."

"When are you going to *shut up* about Shiloh, Mama?" asks Norma Jean.

"I always thought Shiloh was the prettiest place, so full of history," Mabel goes on. "I just hoped y'all could see it once before I die, so you could tell me about it." Later, she whispers to Leroy, "You do what I said. A little change is what she needs."

"Your name means 'the king,' " Norma Jean says to Leroy that evening. He is trying to get her to go to Shiloh, and she is reading a book about another century.

"Well, I reckon I ought to be right proud."

"I guess so."

"Am I still king around here?"

Norma Jean flexes her biceps and feels them for hardness. "I'm not fooling around with anybody, if that's what you mean," she says.

"Would you tell me if you were?"

"I don't know."

"What does *your* name mean?"

"It was Marilyn Monroe's real name."

"No kidding!"

"Norma comes from the Normans. They were invaders," she says. She closes her book and looks hard at Leroy. "I'll go to Shiloh with you if you'll stop staring at me."

On Sunday, Norma Jean packs a picnic and they go to Shiloh. To Leroy's relief, Mabel says she does not want to come with them. Norma Jean drives, and Leroy, sitting beside her, feels like some boring hitchhiker she has picked up. He tries some conversation, but she answers him in monosyllables. At Shiloh, she drives aimlessly through the park, past bluffs and trails and steep ravines. Shiloh is an immense place, and Leroy cannot see it as a battleground. It is not what he expected. He thought it would look like a golf course. Monuments are everywhere, showing through the thick clusters of trees. Norma Jean passes the log cabin Mabel mentioned. It is surrounded by tourists looking for bullet holes.

"That's not the kind of log house I've got in mind," says Leroy apologetically.

"I know *that*."

"This is a pretty place. Your mama was right."

"It's O.K.," says Norma Jean. "Well, we've seen it. I hope she's satisfied."

They burst out laughing together.

At the park museum, a movie on Shiloh is shown every half hour, but they decide that they don't want to see it. They buy a souvenir Confederate flag for Mabel, and then they find a picnic spot near the cemetery. Norma Jean has brought a picnic cooler, with pimiento sandwiches, soft drinks, and Yodels. Leroy eats a sandwich and then smokes a joint, hiding it behind the picnic cooler. Norma Jean has quit smoking altogether. She is picking cake crumbs from the cellophane wrapper, like a fussy bird.

Leroy says, "So the boys in gray ended up in Corinth. The Union soldiers zapped 'em finally. April 7, 1862."

They both know that he doesn't know any history. He is just talking about some of the historical plaques they have read. He feels awkward, like a boy on a date with an older girl. They are still just making conversation.

"Corinth is where Mama eloped to," says Norma Jean.

They sit in silence and stare at the cemetery for the Union dead and, beyond, at a tall cluster of trees. Campers are parked nearby, bumper to bumper, and small children in bright clothing are cavorting and squealing. Norma Jean wads up the cake wrapper and squeezes it tightly in her hand. Without looking at Leroy, she says, "I want to leave you."

Leroy takes a bottle of Coke out of the cooler and flips off the cap. He holds the bottle poised near his mouth but cannot remember to take a drink. Finally he says, "No, you don't."

"Yes, I do."

"I won't let you."

"You can't stop me."

"Don't do me that way."

Leroy knows Norma Jean will have her own way. "Didn't I promise to be home from now on?" he says.

"In some ways, a woman prefers a man who wanders," says Norma Jean. "That sounds crazy, I know."

"You're not crazy."

Leroy remembers to drink from his Coke. Then he says, "Yes, you *are* crazy. You and me could start all over again. Right back at the beginning."

"We *have* started all over again," says Norma Jean. "And this is how it turned out."

"What did I do wrong?"

"Nothing."

"Is this one of those women's lib things?" Leroy asks.

"Don't be funny."

The cemetery, a green slope dotted with white markers, looks like a subdivision site. Leroy is trying to comprehend that his marriage is breaking up, but for some reason he is wondering about white slabs in a graveyard.

"Everything was fine till Mama caught me smoking," says Norma Jean, standing up. "That set something off."

"What are you talking about?"

"She won't leave me alone—*you* won't leave me alone." Norma Jean seems to be crying, but she is looking away from him. "I feel eighteen again. I can't face that all over again." She starts walking away. "No, it *wasn't* fine. I don't know what I'm saying. Forget it."

Leroy takes a lungful of smoke and closes his eyes as Norma Jean's words sink in. He tries to focus on the fact that thirty-five hundred soldiers died on the grounds around him. He can only think of that war as a board game with plastic soldiers. Leroy almost smiles, as he compares the Confederates' daring attack on the Union camps and Virgil Mathis's raid on the bowling alley. General Grant, drunk and furious, shoved the Southerners back to Corinth, where Mabel and Jet Beasley were married years later, when Mabel was still thin and good-looking. The next day, Mabel and Jet visited the battleground, and then Norma Jean was born, and then she married Leroy and they had a baby, which they lost, and now Leroy and Norma Jean are here at the same battleground. Leroy knows he is leaving out a lot. He is leaving out the insides of history. History was always just names and dates to him. It occurs to him that building a house out of logs is similarly empty—too simple. And the real inner workings of a marriage, like most of history, have escaped him. Now he sees that building a log house is the dumbest idea he could have had. It was clumsy of him to think Norma Jean would want a log house. It was a crazy idea. He'll have to think of something else, quickly. He will wad the blueprints into tight balls and fling them into the lake. Then he'll get moving again. He opens his eyes. Norma Jean has moved away and is walking through the cemetery, following a serpentine brick path.

Leroy gets up to follow his wife, but his good leg is asleep and his bad leg still hurts him. Norma Jean is far away, walking rapidly toward the bluff by the river, and he tries to hobble toward her. Some children run past him, screaming noisily. Norma Jean has reached the bluff, and she is looking out over the Tennessee River. Now she turns toward Leroy and waves her arms. Is she beckoning to him? She seems to be doing an exercise for her chest muscles. The sky is unusually pale—the color of the dust ruffle Mabel made for their bed.

Tama Janowitz

THE SLAVES
IN
NEW YORK

∾

There was a joke that my cousin told my brother Roland when he was five years old. The joke went, "Fat and Fat Fat and Pinch Me were in a boat. Fat and Fat Fat fell out. Who was left?" And my brother said, "Pinch Me," and my cousin pinched him. So when my brother got home he told my mother he was going to tell her a joke, and he said, "Fat and Fat Fat were in a boat. Fat and Fat Fat fell out. Who was left?" My mother said, "Nobody." My brother repeated the joke, and when my mother said "Nobody" a second time, my brother kicked her.

Twenty years went by, I was always older than my brother, and my mother still talks about my brother's fury at her incorrect response. All he wanted was to do to her what had been done to him. So now I'm living in New York, the city, and what it is, it's the apartment situation. I had a little apartment in an old brownstone on the upper West Side, but it was too expensive, and there were absolutely no inexpensive apartments to be found. Besides, things weren't going all that smoothly for me, I mean, I wasn't exactly earning money. I thought I'd just move to New York and sell my jewelry—I worked in rubber, shellacked sea horses, plastic James Bond-doll earrings—but it turned out a lot of other girls had already beaten me to it. So it was during this period that I gave up and told Stashua I was going home to live with my mother. Stash and I had been dating for six months. That was when Stash said we could try living together.

We've been living together in his place in the Village about a year now. One room, it's big, but he has a lot of stuff here—boxes, closetfuls of papers. Well, he's been here for ten years, and after his divorce he hadn't lived with anyone in six years or so.

I'm getting used to it. In the morning I clean up some, I walk his Dalmatian, Andrew, then I come back and cook Stash two poached eggs, raisin tea biscuits, coffee with three spoons sugar. Usually around this time of day, the doorman buzzes on the intercom and I have to go down to pick up a package, or run to the store for some more cigarettes, whatever. Then Stash goes off to work. He's a graffiti artist, he works for himself, so he doesn't have to go in until late, except recently he's been out of the house by ten, since he's nervous about getting ready for his show coming up soon at his gallery on Fifty-seventh Street.

I watch a few soap operas and have a second cup. Then usually I start to plan the evening dinner. I'll make, let's say, Cornish game hen with orange glaze, curried rice, asparagus, or it could be fettuccine Alfredo with garlic bread and arugula salad. Nothing too fancy. I take Andrew to the Key Food and tie him up outside, return the empty bottles. Stash likes Coca-Cola, Cracker Jack, eats marshmallows out of the bag.

Well, I'm getting used to it. He still complains a lot if I leave makeup on the back of the toilet. He kept saying, "Eleanor, look at this sin," until I pointed out to him he was regressing to his Catholic childhood. I forget what else bugs him. If I do the dishes and there's, let's say, a little spot of grease on the floor from where I carried the roasting pan over to the garbage pail—this just drives him crazy. Clothes—if I leave any clothes out, or if after I wash them I put them away where he can't find them. If I buy the wrong kind of deodorant—why, he has to take fifteen minutes to explain to me why he only uses deodorant and not antiperspirant. Antiperspirant clogs up the pores and prevents you from perspiring, it's unhealthy, whereas deodorant just masks the odor. Well, it's his apartment, and if we have a fight or something I sometimes get this panicky feeling: Where the hell am I going to go?

I have a couple of girlfriends in the city. One is renting out her second bedroom for six hundred and fifty dollars a month. The other has a three-year-old baby, and I'm sure she'd be glad if I slept on her couch in the living room in return for day-care services or whatever, but would I be better off? Anyway, I'm trying to learn how to get along with a man.

So what happens is, I went out to this party without Stash. He wasn't feeling too well, and once in a while I really make an attempt to go out without him. It's one of the most difficult things in the world for me to do. I'd much rather go out with him, and when he's saying hello to all his friends I can kind of lurk behind him and smile every once in a while, but I don't actually have to come up with anything to *say*. For instance, at a night club some guy comes over—well, he isn't talking to me, he's talking to Stash, about business or the softball team they both play on. What do I have to say? I don't have anything to say.

Anyway, this party was a housewarming for this couple, Mona and Phil. I didn't know them too well. They had just found a new apartment on Fourteenth Street, fifteen hundred dollars a month— Mona had some money from her parents—a real find, a sixth-floor walkup. Phil was a carpenter, and so he could install the toilet and fixtures himself. Most of their boxes and stuff hadn't yet been unpacked. For a while I sat on the couch drinking a Margarita that had been mixed up in a blender and listening to Mona's mother and father talk about their trip to China. They had deluxe accommodations at some hotel in Peking, and there was a lottery among the members of their tour group, and Mona's mother and father won and got to stay in the Grand Suite, which had a fully stocked liquor bar.

When I finished listening to them, I turned around and there was a totally stunning man sitting on a chair next to me eating some Kentucky Fried Chicken. Mona and her husband, Phil, had made their own dipping sauce, but since they were in the middle of moving they went out and got the chicken at Kentucky and arranged it in a linen-covered basket. I wasn't eating anything. I had already made dinner for myself and Stash, and because he wasn't feeling well I kept the meal simple and just served homemade black bean soup with macaroni-and-cheese and a small salad. I felt sort of annoyed at first when I saw this guy eating fried chicken and staring at me, because it occurred to me that (a) he was far too gorgeous, with his green eyes and curly black hair, and (b) he was probably an actor, because he seemed to be reënacting the dinner scene from "Tom Jones," that old movie with Albert Finney. Stash always tells me I have "buggywhip" arms, and it made me uncomfortable the way this guy was eating a scrawny chicken wing and looking at me. You know, I just wanted to tell him to knock it off and be a person.

He introduced himself and we started talking. It was the first time in ages I had talked to a man, other than Stash. Stash is half Polish and half Italian, so conversation between the sexes doesn't go over so good with him.

This guy's name was Mikell and he was from South Africa and wrote novels, political-type novels, so he had been thrown out of the country some time back. They didn't actually throw him out, they just confiscated a work in progress. I asked him if he knew Jimmy Gwynne, who is from Cape Town, and naturally Mikell knew Jimmy—in fact, he had shared a flat with him in London about six years ago. He had come to the party with Millie, who I had always wanted to meet—Millie was one of the few successful women painters in New York. So I said hello to Millie, and it turned out we had gone to the same college but at different times and she had graduated some eight years before me. I never thought Mikell and Millie were actually together, I thought they just came to the party at the same time. Whatever. Millie excused herself, and Mikell went back to talking to me.

As it happened, I gave Mikell my address and phone number without bothering to mention that I lived with someone. Let me tell you, at this point there was nothing devious going on in my head. Stash was always encouraging me to develop a life of my own. This Mikell had eyes that were truly sickening—green pools like you never see and never want to see: when he looked at you, it made you weak in the knees, which in actual fact made me mad. So I didn't respond—I mean, come on already, I didn't let my knees get weak, I just talked to Mikell like he was one of my girlfriends. Come to think of it, that was the only way I knew how to talk to anyone anymore.

A few days later, after Stash had gone off to work, Mikell called, and I agreed to meet him for a cup of coffee. It turned out he lived only a few blocks away. I sat in the back corner of the White Horse Tavern, hoping no one would be able to see me if they walked past the window and report me to Stash or anything.

Mikell showed up. Such white teeth, like you wouldn't believe (they must have something in the water over there in South Africa), and those eyes—brilliant green (maybe he wore contact lenses). I couldn't even believe it. He had a copy of his novel for me. It had been published in England, and he was looking for an American publisher. It was called "Registered Alien." After a while, I had to explain that I lived with a person, and Mikell asked me how it was going. I said O.K., but that my dream was that someday I would get some bucks and then maybe I could move out. I said I got along all right with Stash, but he never wanted to have anyone over, we had no couch, just a bed, all his stuff was all over the place, it hadn't been painted in ten years, and my dream was to have a real apartment, maybe with a little terrace, geraniums, and then I'd have dinner parties for eight or ten every once in a while.

Well, it turned out that Mikell lived with Millie. They had met in L.A. Millie went out there for a show and Mikell was living there reading screenplays for some production company. So Mikell invited Millie to South Africa, she met his mother, and they got along really well. Mikell took Millie to meet some Zulus and she danced with them, they stayed up all night drinking some local concoction, and Millie had a great time. When Millie went back to New York, she invited Mikell to move in with her—New York was where the publishing was. Mikell said yes, they got along great, there was only one problem, which was that they fought all the time.

What the situation was, Millie owned her own co-op, and her former boyfriend, during the time they were engaged to be married, had purchased the co-op next to hers, and they had torn down the walls between the two apartments. So now Millie's former boyfriend rented out his half of the space to Mikell at a very, very tiny rent, a rent so small that even though Mikell was absolutely broke he was able to afford living in New York, which was where he wanted to be. The reason the former boyfriend rented out his half of the co-op to Mikell at such a reduced rate was that it would have cost a fortune to rebuild the walls between the two apartments, and Millie absolutely refused to live with a complete stranger. But it was lucky for Mikell that Millie didn't consider him a complete stranger, otherwise he would have had to go back to Los Angeles and his job, when that was something he had nothing for but contempt.

We both just sat there. Mikell put his hand over mine. It wasn't a sexual thing, not really, it was just the two of us sitting there at a wooden table in the White Horse Tavern, looking at each other and sitting there. We were both in the same position. Things might have been different if one of us had our own apartment. It wasn't that Mikell wasn't very fond of Millie—he was. But they had a lot of fights, and he wasn't allowed to go out by himself at night, and Millie didn't feel like going out all that often, and Mikell would have liked to be able to see some of the New York scene now that he was finally here.

When we got up to leave, I let Mikell pay for my espresso. He said he would call me in a couple of days. I asked him only to call between the hours of eleven and one, when I could be certain that

Stash would be out. I asked him to sign his novel. He wrote, "To Eleanor by the River, with love from Mikell." So I said, "Listen, why don't you write down your number, in case I have to give you a call?"

It was all totally out in the open. I just wanted to keep him like a girlfriend, and that was why I told Stash about meeting Mikell. I figured that things could never work out between me and Mikell because we were both in the same position, but maybe as a foursome I could be friends with Millie and Stash could go shoot pool with Mikell. It was important to bring new people into a relationship, to make new friends, and if you're part of a couple, well, then it's easier to have new friends who are also a couple.

Stash almost had a nervous breakdown. For two days he wouldn't speak to me, then he started screaming. He told me to go move out so I could start sleeping with this guy, and said how dare I bring home little love notes from some cretin.

I said, "Well, Stash, I wouldn't have told you about it if there was anything going on. All I did was tell Mikell about you and how great you are, and he talked about Millie."

Stash said, "Don't give me that, that's how it begins—you go out and talk to each other about your relationships and then jump into bed with each other. Maybe we should just end this," he said. "You're beginning to bore me."

This went on all day. I started crying. I said, "If you want me to leave, then I won't stay here any longer. You know how much I love you, and I can't understand your reaction." I said, "I thought you'd really like this guy—he's interested in seeing your paintings, and I thought I could be friends with her."

"Who?" Stash said.

"The girlfriend," I said.

Stash said, "You want me to call her up and go out with her? Is that what you want? Fine. You're doing this out of insecurity. What is it about you I hate the most?"

"My messiness?" I said.

"No."

"My personality?"

"No," he said. "Your insecurity. That's what I hate about you the most. You are so damn insecure. Why don't you stop?"

I couldn't figure it out. I mean, I'm insecure, but I couldn't see how this related. My having coffee with a man didn't seem to illustrate this character defect. I cried all day Sunday, and Stash went out with his friends and played softball.

Mikell called at twelve-thirty. I tried to sound bright and happy. He really was intelligent, and it was beyond me how Millie could ever think of anything to argue with him about. I wanted to see him for coffee, except my eyes were all swollen up. I just broke down and told him how things had been hell around here for three days, how Stash went insane because I told him I had gone out for coffee with a man.

Mikell said, "Actually, that's what's been going on around here. She's gone totally out of her mind."

There was a silence. I said, "Well, let's meet for coffee to-morrow."

He said, "I can't. How about Wednesday?"

I said, "Let me call you in the morning, since I'm not sure if I can make it."

There was a silence. He said it would be better if I didn't call him.

We did get to meet one other time. It was really sad. After that, I bumped into him once at the bank. He was with Millie, and she gave me a strange smile. I had no makeup on, and I was wearing my glasses, which were pointy and had little rhinestones at the corners, and maybe she only half recognized me. I mean, at the party, the one other time she had seen me, I had been wearing my contact lenses and had on a lot of my original jewelry, things like my James Bond/Oddjob necklace-and-earring set. When Millie went to use the cash machine, Mikell came over to me and asked if I was going home after the bank.

Luckily, when I got home Stash wasn't there, and Mikell called a few minutes later. We spoke briefly. Mikell said things would be best if we didn't speak for a while. He was talking in a whisper. I said, "But Mikell, I must meet you to continue our mad, passionate affair."

There was a moment of silence.

"Just kidding," I said.

After that, whenever Stash was home in the afternoons I just prayed the phone wouldn't ring.

I tried to keep the apartment clean. My mother lived upstate in a one-bedroom apartment. I couldn't escape to her. I got up at seven-thirty to walk Andrew. Things went O.K. Stash bought me a coat, Day-Glo orange wool with a green velvet collar. It wasn't the one I would have chosen—I guess I would have selected something a little more conservative. But it was nice to have a new winter coat.

My friend Abby called me up from Boston. She was all hysterical. It's like this: She's been living with this guy for a few years. He was an art director for an advertising agency, and she has a good job teaching at Simmons, tenure. But it's Roger's house, an old Back Bay brownstone that he's fixed up, and now he's lost his job and he wants her to start making some financial contribution, but he still doesn't want to marry her. Just at this time Abby's old flame reappears. He wants her to move to New York and live with him.

"What are you going to do?" I said.

Abby said that even though this old flame, Bruce, was a jerk, she was bored with Boston and Roger. "I could live in New York with Bruce," she said, "and fly up to Boston to teach one day a week, and maybe I'll meet someone I like better than Bruce in New York."

I said, "Abby, don't do it. In the old days, marriages were arranged by the parents, and maybe you ended up with a jerk but at least you had the security of marriage, no one could dump you out on the street. In today's world, it's the slave system. If you live with this guy in New York, you'll be the slave."

"Well," she said, "I'm used to Roger cooking for me. Would I have to cook for Bruce?"

She already knew all about my dinner menus, the frantic daily preparations. "Yes," I said. "You'd have to cook for Bruce. What are you going to do if you two have a fight and he tells you to leave? With your salary, you'll never be able to find an apartment."

"I know Bruce is a creep," she said. "But I thought I'd be with him while I looked for someone else."

I said, "Abby, forget it. You think you'll be making an improvement, but that's not the case." I didn't want to tell her this before, because I didn't know the situation with Roger, but quite frankly it didn't sound so bad. I said, "If you live with Bruce, you'll be the slave. It's not the same in other cities, the rents aren't so high. Roger doesn't have the same power over you, because you could always threaten to move out and get your own place in Boston."

"I didn't know," she said. "I'm going to reconsider. Are you sure there're no available men in New York?"

"There're women," I said. "There're hundreds of women. They are out on the prowl. And all the men are gay or are in the slave class themselves. Your only solution is to get rich, so you can get an apartment and then you can have your own slave. He would be poor but amenable."

"Are these women, the ones that are prowling—are they attractive?" Abby said.

I could tell she hadn't been listening. "Abby," I said. "It's New York. They have seventy-dollar haircuts and wear black leather belts with sterling-silver buckles."

"Oh," she said. "How are things otherwise?"

"Stash and I are getting along very well," I said. "He just bought me a new winter coat. I should probably go. Andrew needs his walkies."

After I hung up, I thought about what I should have told Abby: See, Fat and Fat Fat fell out, and in New York all that's left is Pinch Me. But I'm not sure she would have understood. I remembered when my brother Roland was five he wore these little boots with metal toe caps and after my cousin told him the joke and pinched him my brother kicked him. My cousin was really enraged at Roland's behavior and called up my mother to complain. He had a black-and-blue mark. My mother was ashamed: obviously she was doing something all wrong in her child-rearing practices. Now Roland is a first-year resident in obstetrics/gynecology down in Texas.

Susan Minot

LUST

~~~

L eo was from a long time ago, the first one I ever saw nude. In the spring before the Hellmans filled their pool, we'd go down there in the deep end, with baby oil, and like that. I met him the first month away at boarding school. He had a halo from the campus light behind him. I flipped.

Roger was fast. In his illegal car, we drove to the reservoir, the radio blaring, talking fast, fast, fast. He was always going for my zipper. He got kicked out sophomore year.

◇   ◇   ◇

By the time the band got around to playing "Wild Horses," I had tasted Bruce's tongue. We were clicking in the shadows on the other side of the amplifier, out of Mrs. Donovan's line of vision. It tasted like salt, with my neck bent back, because we had been dancing so hard before.

Tim's line: "I'd like to see you in a bathing suit." I knew it was his line when he said the exact same thing to Annie Hines.

You'd go on walks to get off campus. It was raining like hell, my sweater as sopped as a wet sheep. Tim pinned me to a tree, the woods light brown and dark brown, a white house half-hidden with the lights already on. The water was as loud as a crowd hissing. He made certain comments about my forehead, about my cheeks.

We started off sitting at one end of the couch and then our feet were squished against the armrest and then he went over to turn off the TV and came back after he had taken off his shirt and then we slid onto the floor and he got up again to close the door, then came back to me, a body waiting on the rug.

You'd try to wipe off the table or to do the dishes and Willie would untuck your shirt and get his hands up under in front, standing behind you, making puffy noises in your ear.

He likes it when I wash my hair. He covers his face with it and if I start to say something, he goes, "Shush."

For a long time, I had Philip on the brain. The less they noticed you, the more you got them on the brain.

My parents had no idea. Parents never really know what's going on, especially when you're away at school most of the time. If she met them, my mother might say, "Oliver seems nice" or "I like that one" without much of an opinion. If she didn't like them, "He's a funny fellow, isn't he?" or "Johnny's perfectly nice but a drink of water." My father was too shy to talk to them at all, unless they played sports and he'd ask them about that.

The sand was almost cold underneath because the sun was long gone. Eben piled a mound over my feet, patting around my ankles, the ghostly surf rumbling behind him in the dark. He was the first person I ever knew who died, later that summer, in a car crash. I thought about it for a long time.

"Come here," he says on the porch.
I go over to the hammock and he takes my wrist with two fingers.
"What?"
He kisses my palm then directs my hand to his fly.

Songs went with whichever boy it was. "Sugar Magnolia" was Tim, with the line "Rolling in the rushes/down by the riverside." With "Darkness Darkness," I'd picture Philip with his long hair. Hearing "Under my Thumb" there'd be the smell of Jamie's suede jacket.

We hid in the listening rooms during study hall. With a record cover over the door's window, the teacher on duty couldn't look in. I came out flushed and heady and back at the dorm was surprised how red my lips were in the mirror.

One weekend at Simon's brother's, we stayed inside all day with the shades down, in bed, then went out to Store 24 to get some ice cream. He stood at the magazine rack and read through *MAD* while I got butterscotch sauce, craving something sweet.

I could do some things well. Some things I was good at, like math or painting or even sports, but the second a boy put his arm around me, I forgot about wanting to do anything else, which felt like a relief at first until it became like sinking into a muck.

It was different for a girl.

◇   ◇   ◇

When we were little, the brothers next door tied up our ankles. They held the door of the goat house and wouldn't let us out till we showed them our underpants. Then they'd forget about being after us and when we played whiffle ball, I'd be just as good as them.

Then it got to be different. Just because you have on a short skirt, they yell from the cars, slowing down for a while and if you don't look, they screech off and call you a bitch.

"What's the matter with me?" they say, point-blank.
Or else, "Why won't you go out with me? I'm not asking you to get married," about to get mad.
Or it'd be, trying to be reasonable, in a regular voice, "Listen, I just want to have a good time."
So I'd go because I couldn't think of something to say back that wouldn't be obvious, and if you go out with them, you sort of have to do something.

I sat between Mack and Eddie in the front seat of the pickup. They were having a fight about something. I've a feeling about me.

Certain nights you'd feel a certain surrender, maybe if you'd had wine. The surrender would be forgetting yourself and you'd put your nose to his neck and feel like a squirrel, safe, at rest, in a restful dream. But then you'd start to slip from that and the dark would come in and there'd be a cave. You make out the dim shape of the windows and feel yourself become a cave, filled absolutely with air, or with a sadness that wouldn't stop.

Teenage years. You know just what you're doing and don't see the things that start to get in the way.

Lots of boys, but never two at the same time. One was plenty to keep you in a state. You'd start to see a boy and something would rush over you like a fast storm cloud and you couldn't possibly think of anyone else. Boys took it differently. Their eyes perked up at any little number that walked by. You'd act like you weren't noticing.

The joke was that the school doctor gave out the pill like aspirin. He didn't ask you anything. I was fifteen. We had a picture of him in assembly, holding up an IUD shaped like a T. Most girls were on the pill, if anything, because they couldn't handle a diaphragm. I kept the dial in my top drawer like my mother and thought of her each time I tipped out the yellow tablets in the morning before chapel.

If they were too shy, I'd be more so. Andrew was nervous. We stayed up with his family album, sharing a pack of Old Golds. Before it got light, we turned on the TV. A man was explaining how to plant seedlings. His mouth jerked to the side in a tic. Andrew thought it was a riot and kept imitating him. I laughed to be polite. When we finally dozed off, he dared to put his arm around me but that was it.

You wait till they come to you. With half fright, half swagger, they stand one step down. They dare to touch the button on your coat then lose their nerve and quickly drop their hand so you— you'd do anything for them. You touch their cheek.

The girls sit around in the common room and talk about boys, smoking their heads off.
"What are you complaining about?" says Jill to me when we talk about problems.
"Yeah," says Giddy. "You always have a boyfriend."
I look at them and think, As if.

I thought the worst thing anyone could call you was a cock-teaser. So, if you flirted, you had to be prepared to go through with it. Sleeping with someone was perfectly normal once you had done it. You didn't really worry about it. But there were other problems. The problems had to do with something else entirely.

◊   ◊   ◊

Mack was during the hottest summer ever recorded. We were renting a house on an island with all sorts of other people. No one slept during the heat wave, walking around the house with nothing on which we were used to because of the nude beach. In the living room, Eddie lay on top of a coffee table to cool off. Mack and I, with the bedroom door open for air, sweated and sweated all night. "I can't take this," he said at 3 A.M. "I'm going for a swim." He and some guys down the hall went to the beach. The heat put me on edge. I sat on a cracked chest by the open window and smoked and smoked till I felt even worse, waiting for something—I guess for him to get back.

One was on a camping trip in Colorado. We zipped our sleeping bags together, the coyotes' hysterical chatter far away. Other couples murmured in other tents. Paul was up before sunrise, starting a fire for breakfast. He wasn't much of a talker in the daytime. At night, his hand leafed about in the hair at my neck.

There'd be times when you overdid it. You'd get carried away. All the next day, you'd be in a total fog, delirious, absent-minded, crossing the street and nearly getting run over.

The more girls a boy has, the better. He has a bright look, having reaped fruits, blooming. He stalks around, sure-shouldered, and you have the feeling he's got more in him, a fatter heart, more stories to tell. For a girl, with each boy it's like a petal gets plucked each time.

Then you start to get tired. You begin to feel diluted, like watered-down stew.

Oliver came skiing with us. We lolled by the fire after everyone had gone to bed. Each creak you'd think was someone coming downstairs. The silver-loop bracelet he gave me had been a present from his girlfriend before.

◊   ◊   ◊

On vacations, we went skiing, or you'd go south if someone invited you. Some people had apartments in New York that their families hardly ever used. Or summer houses, or older sisters. We always managed to find some place to go.

We made the plan at coffee hour. Simon snuck out and met me at Main Gate after lights-out. We crept to the chapel and spent the night in the balcony. He tasted like onions from a submarine sandwich.

The boys are one of two ways: either they can't sit still or they don't move. In front of the TV, they won't budge. On weekends they play touch football while we sit on the sidelines, picking blades of grass to chew on, and watch. We're always watching them run around. We shiver in the stands, knocking our boots together to keep our toes warm and they whizz across the ice, chopping their sticks around the puck. When they're in the rink, they refuse to look at you, only eyeing each other beneath low helmets. You cheer for them but they don't look up, even if it's a face-off when nothing's happening, even if they're doing drills before any game has started at all.

Dancing under the pink tent, he bent down and whispered in my ear. We slipped away to the lawn on the other side of the hedge. Much later, as he was leaving the buffet with two plates of eggs and sausage, I saw the grass stains on the knees of his white pants.

Tim's was shaped like a banana, with a graceful curve to it. They're all different. Willie's like a bunch of walnuts when nothing was happening, another's as thin as a thin hot dog. But it's like faces; you're never really surprised.

Still, you're not sure what to expect.

I look into his face and he looks back. I look into his eyes and they look back at mine. Then they look down at my mouth so I look at his mouth, then back to his eyes then, backing up, at his

whole face. I think, Who? Who are you? His head tilts to one side.
I say, "Who are you?"
"What do you mean?"
"Nothing."
I look at his eyes again, deeper. Can't tell who he is, what he
thinks.
"What?" he says. I look at his mouth.
"I'm just wondering," I say and go wandering across his face.
Study the chin line. It's shaped like a persimmon.
"Who are you? What are you thinking?"
He says, "What the hell are you talking about?"

Then they get mad after when you say enough is enough. After,
when it's easier to explain that you don't want to. You wouldn't
dream of saying that maybe you weren't really ready to in the first
place.

Gentle Eddie. We waded into the sea, the waves round and plow-
ing in, buffalo-headed, slapping our thighs. I put my arms around
his freckled shoulders and he held me up, buoyed by the water,
and rocked me like a sea shell.

I had no idea whose party it was, the apartment jam-packed,
stepping over people in the hallway. The room with the music was
practically empty, the bare floor, me in red shoes. This fellow slides
onto one knee and takes me around the waist and we rock to jazzy
tunes, with my toes pointing heavenward, and waltz and spin and
dip to "Smoke Gets in Your Eyes" or "I'll Love You Just for Now."
He puts his head to my chest, runs a sweeping hand down my
inside thigh and we go loose-limbed and sultry and as smooth as
silk and I stamp my red heels and he takes me into a swoon. I never
saw him again after that but I thought, I could have loved that one.

You wonder how long you can keep it up. You begin to feel
like you're showing through, like a bathroom window that only
lets in grey light, the kind you can't see out of.

◊   ◊   ◊

They keep coming around. Johnny drives up at Easter vacation from Baltimore and I let him in the kitchen with everyone sound asleep. He has friends waiting in the car.

"What are you crazy? It's pouring out there," I say.

"It's okay," he says. "They understand."

So he gets some long kisses from me, against the refrigerator, before he goes because I hate those girls who push away a boy's face as if she were made out of Ivory soap, as if she's that much greater than he is.

The note on my cubby told me to see the headmaster. I had no idea for what. He had received complaints about my amorous displays on the town green. It was Willie that spring. The headmaster told me he didn't care what I did but that Casey Academy had a reputation to uphold in the town. He lowered his glasses on his nose. "We've got twenty acres of woods on this campus," he said. "If you want to smooch with your boyfriend, there are twenty acres for you to do it out of the public eye. You read me?"

Everybody'd get weekend permissions for different places then we'd all go to someone's house whose parents were away. Usually there'd be more boys than girls. We raided the liquor closet and smoked pot at the kitchen table and you'd never know who would end up where, or with whom. There were always disasters. Ceci got bombed and cracked her head open on the bannister and needed stitches. Then there was the time Wendel Blair walked through the picture window at the Lowe's and got slashed to ribbons.

He scared me. In bed, I didn't dare look at him. I lay back with my eyes closed, luxuriating because he knew all sorts of expert angles, his hands never fumbling, going over my whole body, pressing the hair up and off the back of my head, giving an extra hip shove, as if to say *There*. I parted my eyes slightly, keeping the screen of my lashes low because it was too much to look at him, his mouth loose and pink and parted, his eyes looking through my forehead, or kneeling up, looking through my throat. I was ashamed but couldn't look him in the eye.

◇   ◇   ◇

You wonder about things feeling a little off-kilter. You begin to feel like a piece of pounded veal.

At boarding school, everyone gets depressed. We go in and see the housemother, Mrs. Gunther. She got married when she was eighteen. Mr. Gunther was her high-school sweetheart, the only boyfriend she ever had.

"And you knew you wanted to marry him right off?" we ask her.

She smiles and says, "Yes."

"They always want something from you," says Jill, complaining about her boyfriend.

"Yeah," says Giddy. "You always feel like you have to deliver something."

"You do," say Mrs. Gunther. "Babies."

After sex, you curl up like a shrimp, something deep inside you ruined, slammed in a place that sickens at slamming, and slowly you fill up with an overwhelming sadness, an elusive gaping worry. You don't try to explain it, filled with the knowledge that it's nothing after all, everything filling up finally and absolutely with death. After the briskness of loving, loving stops. And you roll over with death stretched out alongside you like a feather boa, or a snake, light as air, and you . . . you don't even ask for anything or try to say something to him because it's obviously your own damn fault. You haven't been able to—to what? To open your heart. You open your legs but can't, or don't dare anymore, to open your heart.

It starts this way:

You stare into their eyes. They flash like all the stars are out. They look at you seriously, their eyes at a low burn and their hands no matter what starting off shy and with such a gentle touch that the only thing you can do is take that tenderness and let yourself be swept away. When, with one attentive finger they tuck the hair behind your ear, you—

You do everything they want.

Then comes after. After when they don't look at you. They scratch their balls, stare at the ceiling. Or if they do turn, their gaze is altogether changed. They are surprised. They turn casually to look at you, distracted, and get a mild distracted surprise. You're gone. Their blank look tells you that the girl they were fucking is not there anymore. You seem to have disappeared.

Sandra Cisneros

HAIRS

~~~

Everybody in our family has different hair. My Papa's hair is like a broom, all up in the air. And me, my hair is lazy. It never obeys barrettes or bands. Carlos' hair is thick and straight. He doesn't need to comb it. Nenny's hair is slippery—slides out of your hand. And Kiki, who is the youngest, has hair like fur.

But my mother's hair, my mother's hair, like little rosettes, like little candy circles all curly and pretty because she pinned it in little pincurls all day, sweet to put your nose into when she is holding you, holding you and you feel safe, is the warm smell of bread before you bake it, is the smell when she makes a little room for you on her side of the bed still warm with her skin, and you sleep near her, the rain outside falling and Papa snoring. The snoring, the rain, and Mama's hair that smells like bread.

A Rice
Sandwich

∼∾∽∿

The special kids, the ones who wear keys around their necks, get to eat in the canteen. The canteen! Even the name sounds important. And these kids at lunch time go there because their mothers aren't home or home is too far away to get to.

My home isn't far but it's not close either, and somehow I got it in my head one day to ask my mother to make me a sandwich and write a note to the principal so I could eat in the canteen too.

Oh no, she says pointing the butter knife at me as if I'm starting trouble, no sir. Next thing you know everybody will be wanting a bag lunch—I'll be up all night cutting bread into little triangles, this one with mayonnaise, this one with mustard, no pickles on mine, but mustard on one side please. You kids just like to invent more work for me.

But Nenny says she doesn't want to eat at school—ever—because she likes to go home with her best friend Gloria who lives across the schoolyard. Gloria's mama has a big color T.V. and all they do is watch cartoons. Kiki and Carlos, on the other hand, are patrol boys. They don't want to eat at school either. They like to stand out in the cold especially if it's raining. They think suffering is good for you ever since they saw that movie "300 Spartans."

I'm no Spartan and hold up an anemic wrist to prove it. I can't even blow up a balloon without getting dizzy. And besides, I know how to make my own lunch. If I ate at school there'd be less dishes to wash. You would see me less and less and like me better. Everyday at noon my chair would be empty. Where is my favorite daughter you would cry, and when I came home finally at 3 p.m. you would appreciate me.

Okay, okay, my mother says after three days of this. And the following morning I get to go to school with my mother's letter and a rice sandwich because we don't have lunch meat.

Mondays or Fridays, it doesn't matter, mornings always go by slow and this day especially. But lunch time came finally and I got to get in line with the stay-at-school kids. Everything is fine until the nun who knows all the canteen kids by heart looks at me and says: you, who sent you here? And since I am shy, I don't say anything, just hold out my hand with the letter. This is no good, she says, till Sister Superior gives the okay. Go upstairs and see her. And so I went.

I had to wait for two kids in front of me to get hollered at, one because he did something in class, the other because he didn't. My turn came and I stood in front of the big desk with holy pictures under the glass while the Sister Superior read my letter. It went like this:

Dear Sister Superior, Please let Esperanza eat in the lunch room because she lives too far away and she gets tired. As you can see she is very skinny. I hope to God she does not faint. Thanking you, Mrs. E. Cordero.

You don't live far, she says. You live across the boulevard. That's only four blocks. Not even. Three maybe. Three long blocks away from here. I bet I can see your house from my window. Which one? Come here. Which one is your house?

And then she made me stand up on a box of books and point. That one? she said pointing to a row of ugly 3-flats, the ones even the raggedy men are ashamed to go into. Yes, I nodded even though I knew that wasn't my house and started to cry. I always cry when nuns yell at me, even if they're not yelling.

Then she was sorry and said I could stay—just for today, not tomorrow or the day after—you go home. And I said yes and could I please have a Kleenex—I had to blow my nose.

In the canteen, which was nothing special, lots of boys and girls watched while I cried and ate my sandwich, the bread already greasy and the rice cold.

HIPS

~~~

I like coffee. I like tea.
I like the boys and the boys like me.
Yes, no, maybe so. Yes, no, maybe so . . .

One day you wake up and they are there. Ready and waiting like a new Buick with the keys in the ignition. Ready to take you where?

They're good for holding a baby when you're cooking, Rachel says turning the jump rope a little quicker. She has no imagination.

You need them to dance, says Lucy.

If you don't get them you may turn into a man. Nenny says this and she believes it. She is this way because of her age.

That's right, I add before Lucy or Rachel can make fun of her. She is stupid alright, but she *is* my sister.

But most important, hips are scientific, I say repeating what Alicia already told me. It's the bones that let you know which skeleton was a man's when it was a man and which a woman's.

They bloom like roses, I continue because it's obvious I'm the only one that can speak with any authority; I have science on my side. The bones just one day open. Just like that. One day you might decide to have kids, and then where are you going to put them? Got to have room. Bones got to give.

But don't have too many or your behind will spread. That's how it is, says Rachel whose mama is as wide as a boat. And we just laugh.

What I'm saying is who here is ready? You gotta be able to know what to do with hips when you get them, I say making it up as I go. You gotta know how to walk with hips, practice you know— like if half of you wanted to go one way and the other half the other.

That's to lullaby it, Nenny says, that's to rock the baby asleep inside you. And then she begins singing seashells, copper bells, eevy, ivy, o-ver.

I'm about to tell her that's the dumbest thing I've ever heard, but the more I think about it . . .

You gotta get the rhythm, and Lucy begins to dance. She has the idea that she's having trouble keeping her end of the double dutch steady.

It's gotta be just so, I say. Not too fast and not too slow. Not too fast and not too slow.

We slow the double circles down to a certain speed so Rachel who has just jumped in can practice shaking it.

I want to shake like hoochi-coochie, Lucy says. She is crazy.

I want to move like heebie-jeebie, I say picking up on the cue.

I want to be Tahiti. Or *merengue*. Or electricity.

Or *tembleque!*

Yes, *tembleque.* That's a good one.

And then it's Rachel who starts it:

> *Skip, skip,*
> *snake in your hips.*
> *Wiggle around*
> *and break your lip.*

Lucy waits a minute before her turn. She is thinking. Then she begins:

> *The waitress with the big fat hips*
> *who pays the rent with taxi tips . . .*
> *says nobody in town will kiss her on the lips*
> *because . . .*
> *because she looks like Christopher Columbus!*
> *Yes, no, maybe so. Yes, no, maybe so.*

She misses on maybe so. I take a little while before my turn, take a breath, and dive in:

> *Some are skinny like chicken lips.*
> *Some are baggy like soggy band-aids*
> *after you get out of the bathtub.*
> *I don't care what kind I get.*
> *Just as long as I get hips.*

Everybody getting into it now except Nenny who is still humming not a girl, not a boy, just a little baby. She's like that.

When the two arcs open wide like jaws Nenny jumps in across from me, the rope tick-ticking, the little gold earrings our mama gave her for her First Holy Communion bouncing. She is the color of a bar of naphtha laundry soap, she is like the little brown piece left at the end of the wash, the hard little bone, my sister. Her mouth opens. She begins:

> *My mother and your mother were washing*
> *clothes.*
> *My mother punched your mother right in the*
> *nose.*
> *What color blood came out?*

Not that old song, I say. You gotta use your own song. Make it up, you know? But she doesn't get it or won't listen. It's hard to say which. The rope turning, turning, turning.

Engine, engine number nine,
running down Chicago line.
If the train runs off the track
do you want your money back?
Do you want your MONEY back?
Yes, no, maybe so. Yes, no, maybe so . . .

I can tell Lucy and Rachel are disgusted, but they don't say anything because she's *my* sister.

Yes, no, maybe so. Yes, no, maybe so . . .

Nenny, I say, but she doesn't hear me. She is too many light years away. She is in a world we don't belong to anymore. Nenny. Going. Going.

Y-E-S spells yes and out you go!

Ann Beattie

JANUS

༄

The bowl was perfect. Perhaps it was not what you'd select if you faced a shelf of bowls, and not the sort of thing that would inevitably attract a lot of attention at a crafts fair, yet it had real presence. It was as predictably admired as a mutt who has no reason to suspect he might be funny. Just such a dog, in fact, was often brought out (and in) along with the bowl.

Andrea was a real-estate agent, and when she thought that some prospective buyers might be dog-lovers, she would drop off her dog at the same time she placed the bowl in the house that was up for sale. She would put a dish of water in the kitchen for Mondo, take his squeaking plastic frog out of her purse and drop it on the floor. He would pounce delightedly, just as he did every day at home, batting around his favorite toy. The bowl usually sat on a coffee table, though recently she had displayed it on top of a pine blanket chest and on a lacquered table. It was once placed on a cherry table beneath a Bonnard still-life, where it held its own.

Everyone who has purchased a house or who has wanted to sell a house must be familiar with some of the tricks used to convince a buyer that the house is quite special: a fire in the fireplace in early evening; jonquils in a pitcher on the kitchen counter, where no one ordinarily has space to put flowers; perhaps the slight aroma of spring, made by a single drop of scent vaporizing from a lamp bulb.

The wonderful thing about the bowl, Andrea thought, was that it was both subtle and noticeable—a paradox of a bowl. Its glaze was the color of cream and seemed to glow no matter what light it was placed in. There were a few bits of color in it—tiny geometric flashes—and some of these were tinged with flecks of silver. They were as mysterious as cells seen under a microscope; it was difficult not to study them, because they shimmered, flashing for a split second, and then resumed their shape. Something about the colors and their random placement suggested motion. People who liked country furniture always commented on the bowl, but then it turned out that people who felt comfortable with Biedermeier loved it just as much. But the bowl was not at all ostentatious, or even so noticeable that anyone would suspect that it had been put in place deliberately. They might notice the height of the ceiling on first entering a room, and only when their eye moved down from that, or away from the refraction of sunlight on a pale wall, would they see the bowl. Then they would go immediately to it and comment. Yet they always faltered when they tried to say something. Perhaps it was because they were in the house for a serious reason, not to notice some object.

Once, Andrea got a call from a woman who had not put in an offer on a house she had shown her. That bowl, she said—would it be possible to find out where the owners had bought that beautiful bowl? Andrea pretended that she did not know what the woman was referring to. A bowl, somewhere in the house? Oh, on a table under the window. Yes, she would ask, of course. She let a couple of days pass, then called back to say that the bowl had been a present and the people did not know where it had been purchased.

When the bowl was not being taken from house to house, it sat on Andrea's coffee table at home. She didn't keep it carefully wrapped (although she transported it that way, in a box); she kept it on the table, because she liked to see it. It was large enough so that it didn't seem fragile, or particularly vulnerable if anyone si-deswiped the table or Mondo blundered into it at play. She had asked her husband to please not drop his house key in it. It was meant to be empty.

When her husband first noticed the bowl, he had peered into it and smiled briefly. He always urged her to buy things she liked. In recent years, both of them had acquired many things to make up for all the lean years when they were graduate students, but now that they had been comfortable for quite a while, the pleasure of new possessions dwindled. Her husband had pronounced the bowl "pretty," and he had turned away without picking it up to examine it. He had no more interest in the bowl than she had in his new Leica.

She was sure that the bowl brought her luck. Bids were often put in on houses where she had displayed the bowl. Sometimes the owners, who were always asked to be away or to step outside when the house was being shown, didn't even know that the bowl had been in their house. Once—she could not imagine how—she left it behind, and then she was so afraid that something might have happened to it that she rushed back to the house and sighed with relief when the woman owner opened the door. The bowl, Andrea explained—she had purchased a bowl and set it on the chest for safekeeping while she toured the house with the prospective buyers, and she . . . She felt like rushing past the frowning woman and seizing her bowl. The owner stepped aside, and it was only when Andrea ran to the chest that the lady glanced at her a little strangely. In the few seconds before Andrea picked up the bowl, she realized that the owner must have just seen that it had been perfectly placed, that the sunlight struck the bluer part of it. Her pitcher had been

moved to the far side of the chest, and the bowl predominated. All
the way home, Andrea wondered how she could have left the bowl
behind. It was like leaving a friend at an outing—just walking off.
Sometimes there were stories in the paper about families forgetting
a child somewhere and driving to the next city. Andrea had only
gone a mile down the road before she remembered.

In time, she dreamed of the bowl. Twice, in a waking dream—
early in the morning, between sleep and a last nap before rising—
she had a clear vision of it. It came into sharp focus and startled
her for a moment—the same bowl she looked at every day.

She had a very profitable year selling real estate. Word spread,
and she had more clients than she felt comfortable with. She had
the foolish thought that if only the bowl were an animate object
she could thank it. There were times when she wanted to talk to
her husband about the bowl. He was a stockbroker, and sometimes
told people that he was fortunate to be married to a woman who
had such a fine aesthetic sense and yet could also function in the
real world. They were a lot alike, really—they had agreed on that.
They were both quiet people—reflective, slow to make value judg-
ments, but almost intractable once they had come to a conclusion.
They both liked details, but while ironies attracted her, he was
more impatient and dismissive when matters became many-sided
or unclear. But they both knew this; it was the kind of thing they
could talk about when they were alone in the car together, coming
home from a party or after a weekend with friends. But she never
talked to him about the bowl. When they were at dinner, exchang-
ing their news of the day, or while they lay in bed at night listening
to the stereo and murmuring sleepy disconnections, she was often
tempted to come right out and say that she thought that the bowl
in the living room, the cream-colored bowl, was responsible for
her success. But she didn't say it. She couldn't begin to explain it.
Sometimes in the morning, she would look at him and feel guilty
that she had such a constant secret.

Could it be that she had some deeper connection with the bowl—
a relationship of some kind? She corrected her thinking: how could
she imagine such a thing, when she was a human being and it was

a bowl? It was ridiculous. Just think of how people lived together and loved each other . . . But was that always so clear, always a relationship? She was confused by these thoughts, but they remained in her mind. There was something within her now, something real, that she never talked about.

The bowl was a mystery, even to her. It was frustrating, because her involvement with the bowl contained a steady sense of unrequited good fortune; it would have been easier to respond if some sort of demand were made in return. But that only happened in fairy tales. The bowl was just a bowl. She did not believe that for one second. What she believed was that it was something she loved.

In the past, she had sometimes talked to her husband about a new property she was about to buy or sell—confiding some clever strategy she had devised to persuade owners who seemed ready to sell. Now she stopped doing that, for all her strategies involved the bowl. She became more deliberate with the bowl, and more possessive. She put it in houses only when no one was there, and removed it when she left the house. Instead of just moving a pitcher or a dish, she would remove all the other objects from a table. She had to force herself to handle them carefully, because she didn't really care about them. She just wanted them out of sight.

She wondered how the situation would end. As with a lover, there was no exact scenario of how matters would come to a close. Anxiety became the operative force. It would be irrelevant if the lover rushed into someone else's arms, or wrote her a note and departed to another city. The horror was the possibility of the disappearance. That was what mattered.

She would get up at night and look at the bowl. It never occurred to her that she might break it. She washed and dried it without anxiety, and she moved it often, from coffee table to mahogany corner table or wherever, without fearing an accident. It was clear that she would not be the one who would do anything to the bowl. The bowl was only handled by her, set safely on one surface or another; it was not very likely that anyone would break it. A bowl was a poor conductor of electricity: it would not be hit by lightning. Yet the idea of damage persisted. She did not think beyond that— to what her life would be without the bowl. She only continued to fear that some accident would happen. Why not, in a world where people set plants where they did not belong, so that visitors touring a house would be fooled into thinking that dark corners got sunlight—a world full of tricks?

She had first seen the bowl several years earlier, at a crafts fair she had visited half in secret, with her lover. He had urged her to buy the bowl. She didn't *need* any more things, she told him. But she had been drawn to the bowl, and they had lingered near it. Then she went on to the next booth, and he came up behind her, tapping the rim against her shoulder as she ran her fingers over a wood carving. "You're still insisting that I buy that?" she said. "No," he said. "I bought it for you." He had bought her other things before this—things she liked more, at first—the child's ebony-and-turquoise ring that fitted her little finger; the wooden box, long and thin, beautifully dovetailed, that she used to hold paper clips; the soft gray sweater with a pouch pocket. It was his idea that when he could not be there to hold her hand she could hold her own—clasp her hands inside the lone pocket that stretched across the front. But in time she became more attached to the bowl than to any of his other presents. She tried to talk herself out of it. She owned other things that were more striking or valuable. It wasn't an object whose beauty jumped out at you; a lot of people must have passed it by before the two of them saw it that day.

Her lover had said that she was always too slow to know what she really loved. Why continue with her life the way it was? Why be two-faced, he asked her. He had made the first move toward her. When she would not decide in his favor, would not change her life and come to him, he asked her what made her think she could have it both ways. And then he made the last move and left. It was a decision meant to break her will, to shatter her intransigent ideas about honoring previous commitments.

Time passed. Alone in the living room at night, she often looked at the bowl sitting on the table, still and safe, unilluminated. In its way, it was perfect: the world cut in half, deep and smoothly empty. Near the rim, even in dim light, the eye moved toward one small flash of blue, a vanishing point on the horizon.

Ursula K. LeGuin

SHE UNNAMES
THEM

~~~

Most of them accepted name-
lessness with the perfect indifference with which they
had so long accepted and ignored their names. Whales and dolphins,
seals and sea otters consented with particular grace and alacrity,
sliding into anonymity as into their element. A faction of yaks,
however, protested. They said that "yak" sounded right, and that
almost everyone who knew they existed called them that. Unlike
the ubiquitous creatures such as rats and fleas, who had been called
by hundreds or thousands of different names since Babel, the yaks
could truly say, they said, that they had a *name*. They discussed
the matter all summer. The councils of the elderly females finally

agreed that though the name might be useful to others it was so redundant from the yak point of view that they never spoke it themselves and hence might as well dispense with it. After they presented the argument in this light to their bulls, a full consensus was delayed only by the onset of severe early blizzards. Soon after the beginning of the thaw, their agreement was reached and the designation "yak" was returned to the donor.

Among the domestic animals, few horses had cared what anybody called them since the failure of Dean Swift's attempt to name them from their own vocabulary. Cattle, sheep, swine, asses, mules, and goats, along with chickens, geese, and turkeys, all agreed enthusiastically to give their names back to the people to whom—as they put it—they belonged.

A couple of problems did come up with pets. The cats, of course, steadfastly denied ever having had any name other than those self-given, unspoken, ineffably personal names which, as the poet named Eliot said, they spend long hours daily contemplating— though none of the contemplators has ever admitted that what they contemplate is their names and some onlookers have wondered if the object of that meditative gaze might not in fact be the Perfect, or Platonic, Mouse. In any case, it is a moot point now. It was with the dogs, and with some parrots, lovebirds, ravens, and mynahs, that the trouble arose. These verbally talented individuals insisted that their names were important to them, and flatly refused to part with them. But as soon as they understood that the issue was precisely one of individual choice, and that anybody who wanted to be called Rover, or Froufrou, or Polly, or even Birdie in the personal sense, was perfectly free to do so, not one of them had the least objection to parting with the lowercase (or, as regards German creatures, uppercase) generic appellations "poodle," "parrot," "dog," or "bird," and all the Linnaean qualifiers that had trailed along behind them for two hundred years like tin cans tied to a tail.

The insects parted with their names in vast clouds and swarms of ephemeral syllables buzzing and stinging and humming and flitting and crawling and tunnelling away.

As for the fish of the sea, their names dispersed from them in silence throughout the oceans like faint, dark blurs of cuttlefish ink, and drifted off on the currents without a trace.

None were left now to unname, and yet how close I felt to them when I saw one of them swim or fly or trot or crawl across my way or over my skin, or stalk me in the night, or go along beside me for a while in the day. They seemed far closer than when their names had stood between myself and them like a clear barrier: so close that my fear of them and their fear of me became one same fear. And the attraction that many of us felt, the desire to smell one another's smells, feel or rub or caress one another's scales or skin or feathers or fur, taste one another's blood or flesh, keep one another warm—that attraction was now all one with the fear, and the hunter could not be told from the hunted, nor the eater from the food.

This was more or less the effect I had been after. It was somewhat more powerful than I had anticipated, but I could not now, in all conscience, make an exception for myself. I resolutely put anxiety away, went to Adam, and said, "You and your father lent me this—gave it to me, actually. It's been really useful, but it doesn't exactly seem to fit very well lately. But thanks very much! It's really been very useful."

It is hard to give back a gift without sounding peevish or ungrateful, and I did not want to leave him with that impression of me. He was not paying much attention, as it happened, and said only, "Put it down over there, O.K.?" and went on with what he was doing.

One of my reasons for doing what I did was that talk was getting us nowhere, but all the same I felt a little let down. I had been prepared to defend my decision. And I thought that perhaps when he did notice he might be upset and want to talk. I put some things away and fiddled around a little, but he continued to do what he was doing and to take no notice of anything else. At last I said, "Well, goodbye, dear. I hope the garden key turns up."

He was fitting parts together, and said, without looking around, "O.K., fine, dear. When's dinner?"

"I'm not sure," I said. "I'm going now. With the—" I hesitated, and finally said, "With them, you know," and went on out. In fact, I had only just then realized how hard it would have been to explain myself. I could not chatter away as I used to do, taking it all for granted. My words now must be as slow, as new, as single, as tentative as the steps I took going down the path away from the house, between the dark-branched, tall dancers motionless against the winter shining.

Francine Prose

OTHER
LIVES

‹≈≈≈›

Climbing up with a handful of star decals to paste on the bathroom ceiling, Claire sees a suspect-looking shampoo bottle on the cluttered top shelf. When she opens it, the whole room smells like a subway corridor where bums have been pissing for generations. She thinks back a few days to when Miranda and Poppy were playing in here with the door shut. She puts down the stars and yells for the girls with such urgency they come running before she's finished emptying it into the sink.

From the doorway, Poppy and her best friend Miranda look at Claire, then at each other. "Mom," says Poppy, "you threw it *out*?"

Claire wants to ask why they're saving their urine in bottles. But sitting on the edge of the tub has lowered her eye level and she's struck speechless by the beauty of their kneecaps, their long suntanned legs. How strong and shaky and elegant they are. Like newborn giraffes. By now she can't bring herself to ask, so she tells them not to do it again and is left with the rest of the morning to wonder what they had in mind.

She thinks it has something to do with alchemy and with faith, with those moments when children are playing with such pure concentration that anything is possible and the rest of the world drops away and becomes no more real than one of their 3-D Viewmaster slides. She remembers when she was Poppy's age, playing with her own best friend Evelyn. Evelyn's father had been dead several years, but his medical office in a separate wing of their house was untouched, as if office hours might begin any minute. In his chilly consulting room, smelling of carpet dust and furniture polish and, more faintly, of gauze and sterilizing pans, Claire and Evelyn played their peculiar version of doctor. Claire would come in, and from behind the desk Evelyn would give her some imaginary pills. Then Claire would fall down dead and Evelyn would kneel and listen to her heart and say, "I'm sorry, it's too late."

But what Claire remembers best is the framed engraving on Evelyn's father's desk. It was one of those trompe l'oeil pieces you see sometimes in cheap art stores. From one angle, it looked like two Gibson girls at a table sipping ice cream sodas through straws. From another, it looked like a skull. Years later, when Claire learned that Evelyn's father had actually died in jail where he'd been sent for performing illegal abortions, she'd thought: What an odd picture to have on an abortionist's desk. But at the time, it had just seemed marvelous. She used to unfocus her eyes and tilt her head so that it flipped back and forth. Skull, ladies. Skull, ladies. Skull.

Dottie's new hairdo, a wide corolla of pale blond curls, makes her look even more like a sunflower—spindly, graceful, rather precariously balanced. At one, when Dottie comes to pick up Miranda, Claire decides not to tell her about the shampoo bottle.

Lately, Dottie's had her mind on higher things. For the past few months, she's been driving down to the New Consciousness Academy in Bennington where she takes courses with titles like "Listening to the Inner Silence" and "Weeds for Your Needs." Claire blames this on one of Dottie's friends, an electrician named Jeanette. Once at a party, Claire overheard Jeanette telling someone how she and her boyfriend practice birth control based on lunar astrology and massive doses of wintergreen tea.

"Coffee?" says Claire tentatively. It's hard to keep track of what substances Dottie's given up. Sometimes, most often in winter, when Joey and Raymond are working and the girls are at school, Dottie and Claire get together for lunch. Walking into Dottie's house and smelling woodsmoke and wine and fresh-baked bread, seeing the table set with blue bowls and hothouse anemones and a soup thick with sausage, potatoes, tomatoes put up from the fall, Claire used to feel that she must be living her whole life right. All summer she's been praying that Dottie won't give up meat.

Dottie says, "Have you got any herbal tea?" and Claire says, "Are you kidding?" "All right, coffee," says Dottie. "Just this once."

As Claire pours the coffee, Dottie fishes around in her enormous parachute-silk purse. Recently Dottie's been bringing Claire reading material. She'd started off with Krishnamurti, Rajneesh, the songs of Milarepa. Claire tried, but she just couldn't; she'd returned them unread. A few weeks back, she'd brought something by Dashiell Hammett about a man named Flitcraft who's walking to lunch one day and a beam falls down from a construction site and just misses him, and he just keeps walking and never goes to his job or back to his wife and family again.

When Claire read that, she wanted to call Dottie up and make her promise not to do something similar. But she didn't. The last time she and Dottie discussed the Academy, Dottie described a technique she'd learned for closing her eyes and pressing on her eyelids just hard enough to see thousands of pinpricks of light. Each one of those dots represents a past life, and if you know how to look, you can see it. In this way, Dottie learned that she'd spent a former life as a footsoldier in Napoleon's army on the killing march to Moscow. That's why she so hates the cold. Somehow Claire

hadn't known that Dottie hated the winter, but really, it follows:
a half-starved, half-frozen soldier cooking inspired sausage soup
three lives later.

"I meant to bring you a book," says Dottie. Then she says, "A
crazy thing happened this morning. I was working in front of the
house, digging up those irises by the side of the road so I could
divide them. I didn't hear anything but I must have had a sense
because I turned around and there was this old lady—coiffed, poly-
estered, dressed for church, it looked like. She told me she'd come
over from Montpelier with some friends for a picnic and got separated. Now she was lost and so upset.

"I said, 'Well, okay, I'll drive you back to Montpelier.' We got
as far as Barre when suddenly her whole story started coming apart,
and I realized: She hadn't been in Montpelier for twenty years. She
was from the Good Shepherd House, that old folks' home up the
road from us. I drove her back to the Good Shepherd—what else
could I do? The manager thanked me, he was very embarrassed
she'd escaped. Then just as I was pulling out, the old lady pointed
up at the sky and gave me the most hateful triumphant smile, and
I looked up through the windshield and there was this flock of geese
heading south." Dottie catches her breath, then says, "You know
what? It's August. I'd forgotten."

What Claire can't quite forget is that years ago, the first time she
and Joey met Dottie and Raymond, afterward Joey said, "They
don't call her 'dotty' for nothing." It took them both a while to
see that what looked at first like dottiness was really an overflow
of the same generosity which makes Dottie cook elegant, warming
meals and drive senile old ladies fifty miles out of her way to
Montpelier. On Tuesdays and Thursdays, when Dottie goes down
to the Academy, she's a volunteer chauffeur service, picking up
classmates—including Jeanette the electrician—from all over central
Vermont. Even Joey's come around to liking her, though Claire's
noticed that he's usually someplace else when Dottie's around.

Now he's in the garden, tying up some tomatoes that fell last
night in the wind. Finding them this morning—perfect red tomatoes smashed on top of each other—had sent her straight to the
bathroom with her handful of star decals. That's the difference

between me and Joey, Claire thinks. Thank God there's someone to save what's left of the vines.

Joey doesn't see Claire watching him but Dottie does and starts to flutter, as if she's overstayed. She calls up to Miranda, and just when it begins to seem as if they might not have heard, the girls drag themselves downstairs.

"Why does Miranda have to go?" says Poppy.

"Because it's fifteen miles and Miranda's mom isn't driving fifteen miles back and forth all day," says Claire.

"But I don't want to go," says Miranda.

They stand there, deadlocked, until Poppy says, "I've got an idea. I'll go home with Miranda and tonight her mom and dad can come to dinner and bring us both back and then Miranda can sleep over."

"That's fine with me," says Claire.

"Are you sure?" says Dottie.

Claire's sure. As Dottie leans down to kiss her goodbye, Claire thinks once more of sunflowers, specifically of the ones she and Joey and Poppy plant every summer on a steep slope so you can stand underneath and look up and the sunflowers look forty feet tall.

Washing his hands at the sink, Joey says, "One day she's going to show up in saffron robes with a begging bowl and her hair shaved down to one skanky topknot and then what?"

Claire thinks: Well, then we'll cook up some gluey brown rice and put a big glob in Dottie's bowl. But this sounds like something they'd say at the New Consciousness Academy, some dreadful homily about adaptation and making do. All she can think of is, "I cried because I had no shoes until I met a man who had no feet," and that's not it.

One night, not long after Dottie started attending the Academy, they were all sitting outside and Dottie looked up and said, "Sometimes I feel as if my whole life is that last minute of the planetarium show when they start showing off—that is, showing off what their projector can do—and the moon and planets and stars and even those distant galaxies begin spinning like crazy while they tell you

the coming attractions and what time the next show begins. I just
want to find someplace where it's not rushing past me so fast. Or
where, if it is, I don't care."

"I hope you find it," Joey said. "I really do." Later that night,
he told Claire that he knew what Dottie meant. "Still," he said,
"it was creepy. The whole conversation was like talking to someone
who still thinks *El Topo* is the greatest movie ever made."

Joey had gone through his own spiritual phase: acid, Castaneda,
long Sunday afternoons in front of the tankas in the Staten Island
Tibetan museum. All this was before he met Claire. He feels that
his having grown out of it fifteen years ago gives him the right to
criticize. Though actually, he's not mocking Dottie so much as
protecting her husband Raymond, his best friend. Remote as the
possibility seems, no one wants Dottie to follow in Flitcraft's
footsteps.

Now Claire says, "I don't think she'd get her hair permed if she
was planning to shave it." Then she steels herself, and in the tone
of someone expecting bad news asks if any tomatoes are left. Joey
says, "We'll be up to our ears in tomatoes," and Claire thinks: He'd
say that no matter what.

One thing she loves about Joey is his optimism. If he's ever
discontent, she doesn't know it. Once he'd wanted to be on stage,
then he'd worked for a while as a landscaper, now he's a junior-
high science teacher—a job which he says requires the combined
talents of an actor and a gardener. His real passion is for the names
of things: trees, animals, stars. But he's not one of those people
who use such knowledge to make you feel small. It's why he's a
popular teacher and why Poppy so loves to take walks with him,
naming the wildflowers in the fields. Claire knows how rare it is
for children to want to learn anything from their parents.

When Claire met Joey, she'd just moved up to Vermont with a
semi-alcoholic, independently wealthy photographer named Dell.
Dell hired Joey to clear a half acre around their cabin so they could
have a garden and lawn. Upstairs there's a photo Dell took of them
at the time and later sent as a wedding present to prove there were
no hard feelings. It shows Claire and Joey leaning against Joey's
rented backhoe; an uprooted acacia tree is spilling out of the bucket.

Joey and Claire look cocky and hard in the face, like teenage killers, Charlie Starkweather and his girl. Claire can hardly remember Dell's face. He always had something in front of it—a can of beer, a camera. If he had only put it down and looked, he'd have seen what was going on. Anyone would have. In the photo, it's early spring, the woods are full of musical names: trillium, marsh marigold, jack-in-the-pulpit.

On the day they learned Claire was pregnant and went straight from the doctor's to the marriage license bureau in Burlington, Joey pulled off the road on the way home and took Claire's face in his hands and told her which animals mated for life. Whooping cranes, snow geese, macaws, she's forgotten the rest. Now they no longer talk this way, or maybe it goes without saying. Claire's stopped imagining other lives; if she could, she'd live this one forever. Though she knows it's supposed to be dangerous to get too comfortable, she feels it would take a catastrophe to tear the weave of their daily routine. They've weathered arguments, and those treacherous, tense, dull periods when they sneak past each other as if they're in constant danger of sneezing in each other's faces. Claire knows to hold on and wait for the day when what interests her most is what Joey will have to say about it.

Some things get better. Claire used to hate thinking about the lovers they'd had before; now all that seems as indistinct as Dell's face. Though they've had eight years to get used to the fact of Poppy's existence, they're still susceptible to attacks of amazement that they've created a new human being. And often when they're doing something together—cooking, gardening, making love—Claire comes as close as she ever has to those moments of pure alchemy, that communion Poppy and Miranda must share if they're storing their pee in bottles.

Soon they'll get up and mix some marinade for the chickens they'll grill outside later for Dottie and Raymond. But now Joey pours himself some coffee and they sit at the table, not talking. It is precisely the silence they used to dream of when Poppy was little and just having her around was like always having the bath water running or something about to boil over on the stove.

◇　◇　◇

First the back doors fly open and the girls jump out of the car and run up to Poppy's room. Then Dottie gets out, then Raymond. From the beginning, Raymond's reminded Claire of the tin woodsman in *The Wizard of Oz*, and often he'll stop in the middle of things as if waiting for someone to come along with the oil can. He goes around to the trunk and takes out a tripod and something wrapped in a blanket which looks at first like a rifle and turns out to be a telescope.

"Guess what!" When Raymond shouts like that, you can see how snaggletoothed he is. "There's a meteor shower tonight. The largest concentration of shooting stars all year."

The telescope is one of the toys Raymond's bought since his paintings started selling. Raymond's success surprises them all, including Raymond. His last two shows were large paintings of garden vegetables with skinny legs and big feet in familiar dance situations. It still surprises Claire that the New York art world would open its heart—would have a heart to open—to work bordering on the cartoonish and sentimental. But there's something undeniably mysterious and moving about those black daikon radishes doing the tango, those little cauliflowers in pink tutus on point before an audience of sleek and rather parental-looking green peppers. And there's no arguing with Raymond's draftmanship or the luminosity of his color; it's as if Memling lived through the sixties and took too many drugs. What's less surprising is that there are so many rich people who for one reason or another want to eat breakfast beneath a painting of dancing vegetables.

Claire has a crush on Raymond; at least that's what she thinks it is. It's not especially intense or very troublesome; it's been going on a long time and she doesn't expect it to change. If anything did change, it would probably disappear. She doesn't want to live with Raymond, and now, as always when he hugs her hello, their bones grate; it's not particularly sexual.

She just likes him, that's all. When it's Raymond coming to dinner, she cooks and dresses with a little more care than she otherwise might, and spends the day remembering things to tell him which she promptly forgets. Of course, she's excited when Dottie, or anyone, is coming over. The difference is, with Dottie, Claire enjoys her food. With Raymond, she often forgets to eat.

Barbecued chicken, tomatoes with basil and mozzarella, pasta with chanterelles Joey's found in the woods—it all goes right by her. Luckily, everyone else is eating, the girls trekking back and forth from the table to the TV. The television noise makes it hard to talk. It's like family dinner, they can just eat. Anyway, conversation's been strained since Dottie started at the Academy. Claire fears that Joey might make some semi-sarcastic remark which will hurt Raymond more than Dottie. Raymond's protective of her; they seem mated for life. It's occurred to them all that Dottie is the original dancing vegetable.

What does get said is that the meteor shower isn't supposed to pick up till around midnight. But they'll set up the telescope earlier so the girls can have a look before they're too tired to see.

Joey and Raymond and the girls go outside while Dottie and Claire put the dishes in the sink. Claire asks if Poppy was any trouble that afternoon and Dottie says, "Oh, no. They played in the bathroom so quiet, I had to keep yelling up to make sure they were breathing. Later they told me they'd been making vanishing cream from that liquidy soap at the bottom of the soap dish. I said, you're eight years old, what do you need with vanishing cream? They said, to vanish. I told them they'd better not use it till they had something to bring them back from wherever they vanished to, and they said, yeah, they'd already thought of that."

"Where did they *hear* about vanishing cream?" says Claire. She feels she ought to tell Dottie—feels disloyal for not telling her—to watch for suspicious-looking shampoo bottles on the upper shelves. But she doesn't. It's almost as if she's saving it for something.

"Speaking of vanishing," says Dottie. She hands Claire the book she'd forgotten that afternoon. It's Calvino's *The Baron in the Trees*. Claire's read it before, and it seems like the right moment to ask, so she says, "Does this mean that you're going to get up from the table one night and climb up in the trees and never come down again?"

Dottie just looks at her. "Me in the trees?" she says. "With *my* allergies?"

They're amazed by how dark it is when they go outside. "I told you," says Dottie. "It's August."

The grass is damp and cool against their ankles as they walk across the lawn to where Miranda and Poppy are taking turns at the telescope. "Daddy," Claire hears Poppy say, "what's that?"

Joey crouches down and looks over her shoulder. Claire wonders what they see. Scorpio? Andromeda? Orion? Joey's told her a thousand times but she can never remember what's in the sky when.

Before Joey can answer, Raymond pulls Poppy away from the telescope and kneels and puts one arm around her and the other around Miranda. "That one?" he says, pointing. "That one's the Bad Baby. And it's lying in the Big Bassinet."

"Where?" cry the girls, and then they say, "Yes, I see!"

"And that one there's the Celestial Dog Dish. And that"—he traces his finger in a wavy circle—"is the Silver Dollar Pancake."

"What's that one?" says Miranda.

"Remember *Superman II*?" Raymond's the one who takes the girls to movies no one else wants to see. "That's what's left of the villains after they get turned to glass and smashed to smithereens."

"Oh, no," say the girls, and hide their faces against Raymond's long legs.

Claire's tensed, as if Raymond's infringed on Joey's right to name things, or worse, is making fun of him. But Joey's laughing, he likes Raymond's names as much as the real ones. Claire steps up to the telescope and aims it at the thin crescent moon, at that landscape of chalk mountains and craters like just-burst bubbles. But all she sees is the same flat white she can see with her naked eye. Something's wrong with the telescope, or with her. The feeling she gets reminds her of waking up knowing the day's already gone wrong but not yet why, of mornings when Poppy's been sick in the night, or last summer when Joey's mother was dying.

By now the others are all lying on the hillside looking for shooting stars. There aren't any, not yet. Claire wonders if Dottie is listening to the inner silence, or thinking of past lives; if Raymond is inventing more constellations. She can't imagine what Joey's thinking. She herself can't get her mind off Jeanette the electrician and her boyfriend, drinking wintergreen tea and checking that sliver of moon to see if this is a safe night for love.

On the way in, Joey says, "Lying out there, I remembered this magazine article I read years ago, about Jean Genet at the '68 Democratic convention in Chicago. The whole time, he kept staring at the dashboard of the car they were driving him in. And afterwards, when they asked him what he thought about the riots, the beatings and so forth, he just shrugged and said, 'What can you expect from a country that would make a car named Galaxy?' "

Over coffee, the conversation degenerates into stories they've told before, tales of how the children tyrannize and abuse them, have kept them prisoner in their own homes for years at a time. The reason they can talk like this is that they all know: the children are the light of their lives. A good part of why they stay here is that Vermont seems like an easy place to raise kids. Even their children have visionary names: Poppy, Miranda. O brave new world!

When Claire first moved here with Dell, she commuted to New York, where she was working as a freelance costume designer. She likes to tell people that the high point of her career was making a holster and fringed vest and chaps for a chicken to wear on *Hee Haw*. Later she got to see it on TV, the chicken panicky and humiliated in its cowboy suit, flapping in circles while Grandpa Jones fired blanks at its feet and yelled, "Dance!" Soon it will be Halloween and Claire will sew Poppy a costume. So far she's been a jar of peanut butter, an anteater with pockets full of velveteen ants, Rapunzel. Last fall Claire made her a caterpillar suit with a back that unzipped and reversed out into butterfly wings. Poppy's already told her that this year she wants to be new wave, so all Claire will have to do is rip up a T-shirt and buy tights and wraparound shades and blue spray-on washable hair dye.

Dottie is telling about the girls making vanishing cream when Joey pretends to hear something in the garden and excuses himself and goes out. Dottie says she wants to stay up for the meteor shower but is feeling tired so she'll lie down awhile on the living-room couch.

Claire and Raymond are left alone at the table. It takes them so long to start talking, Claire's glad her crush on Raymond will never be anything more; if they had to spend a day in each other's company, they'd run out of things to say. Still, it's exciting. Raymond seems nervous, too.

Finally he asks how her day was, and Claire's surprised to hear herself say, "Pretty awful." She hadn't meant to complain, nor had she thought her day was so awful. Now she thinks maybe it was. "Nothing really," she says. "One little thing after another. Have you ever had days when you pick up a pen and the phone rings and when you get off, you can't find the pen?"

"Me?" says Raymond. "I've had decades like that."

Claire says, "I woke up thinking I'd be nice and cook Poppy some French toast. So I open the egg carton and poke my finger through one of those stuck-on leaky eggs. When I got through cleaning the egg off the refrigerator, the milk turned out to be sour. I figured: Well, I'll make her scrambled eggs with coriander, she likes that. I went out to the garden for coriander and all the tomatoes were lying on the ground. The awful part was that most of them looked fine from on top, you had to turn them over to see they were smashed. You know, first you think it's all right, and then it isn't all right."

"I almost never think it's all right," says Raymond. "That's how I take care of that."

"Know how *I* took care of it?" says Claire. "I went crying to Joey. Then I went upstairs and got out these star decals I'd been saving. I thought it would make me feel better. I'd been planning to paste them on the ceiling over the tub so I could take a shower with all the lights out and the stars glowing up above, and even in winter it would be like taking a shower outside." Suddenly Claire is embarrassed by this vision of herself naked in the warm steamy blackness under the faint stars. She wonders if Dottie is listening from the other room and is almost glad the next part is about finding the shampoo bottle.

"That's life," says Raymond. "Reach for the stars and wind up with a bottle of piss."

"That's what I thought," says Claire. "But listen." She tells him about calling the girls in, and when she says "like newborn giraffes," she really does feel awful, as if she's serving her daughter up so Raymond will see her as a complicated person with a daily life rich in similes and astonishing spiritual reverses. Now she understands why she hadn't mentioned the incident to Dottie or Joey. She was saving it for Raymond so it wouldn't be just a story she'd told before. But Raymond's already saying, "I know. Sometimes one second can turn the whole thing around.

"One winter," he says, "Miranda was around two, she was sick all the time. We were living in Roxbury, freezing to death. We decided it was all or nothing. We sold everything, got rid of the apartment, bought tickets to some dinky Caribbean island where somebody told us you could live on fish and mangoes and coconuts off the trees. I thought, I'll paint shells, sell them to the tourists. But when we got there, it wasn't mango season, the fish weren't running, and the capital city was one giant cinderblock motel. There was a housing shortage, a food shortage, an everything shortage.

"So we took a bus across the island, thinking we'd get off at the first tropical paradise, but no place seemed very friendly, and by then Miranda was running another fever. We wound up in the second-biggest city, which looked pretty much like a bad neighborhood in L.A. We were supposed to be glad that our hotel room had a balcony facing main street. Dottie put Miranda to bed, then crawled in and pulled the covers over her head and said she wasn't coming out except to fly back to Boston.

"At that moment, we heard a brass band, some drums. By the time I wrestled the balcony shutters open, a parade was coming by. It was the tail end of Carnival, I think. The whole island was there, painted and feathered and glittered to the teeth, marching formations of guys in ruffly Carmen Miranda shirts with marimbas, little girls done up like bumblebees with antennae bobbing on their heads. Fever or no fever, we lifted Miranda up to see. And maybe it was what she'd needed all along. Because by the time the last marcher went by, her fever was gone.

"Miranda fell asleep, then Dottie. I went for a walk. On the corner, a guy was selling telescopes. Japanese-made, not like the one out there, but good. They must have been stolen off some boat—they were selling for practically nothing. So I bought one and went down to the beach. The beach was deserted. I stayed there I don't know how long. It was the first time I ever looked through a telescope. It was something."

For the second time that day, Claire's struck speechless. Only this time, what's astonishing is, she's in pain. She feels she's led her whole life wrong. What did she think she was doing? If only she could have been on that beach with Raymond looking through a telescope for the first time, or even at the hotel when he came back. Suddenly her own memories seem two-dimensional, like photographs, like worn-out duplicate baseball cards she'd trade all at once for that one of Raymond's. She tells herself that if she'd married Raymond, she might be like Dottie now, confused and restless and wanting only to believe that somewhere there is a weed for her need. She remembers the end of the Hammett story: after Flitcraft's brush with death, he goes to Seattle and marries a woman exactly like the wife he left on the other side of that beam. There's no guarantee that another life will be better or even different from your own, and Claire knows that. But it doesn't help at all.

There's a silence. Claire can't look at Raymond. At last he says, "If I could paint what I saw through that telescope that night, do you think I'd ever paint another dancing vegetable in my whole fucking life?"

For all Raymond's intensity, it's kind of a funny question, and Claire laughs, mostly from relief that the moment is over. Then she notices that Dottie has come in. Dottie looks a little travel-worn, as if she might actually have crossed the steppes from Moscow to Paris. She seems happy to be back. As it turns out, she's been closer than that. Because what she says is, "Suppose I'd believed that old lady and dropped her off in the middle of Montpelier? What would have happened then?"

Claire wants to say something fast before Raymond starts inventing adventures for a crazy old lady alone in Montpelier. Just then, Joey reappears. Apparently, he's come back in and gone upstairs without their hearing; he's got the girls ready for bed, scrubbed and shiny, dressed in long white cotton nightgowns like slender Edwardian angels. Claire looks at the children and the two sets of parents and thinks a stranger walking in would have trouble telling: Which one paints dancing vegetables? Which one's lived before as a Napoleonic soldier? Which ones have mated for life? She thinks they are like constellations, or like that engraving on Evelyn's father's desk, or like sunflowers seen from below. Depending on how you look, they could be anything.

Then Raymond says, "It's almost midnight," and they all troop outside. On the way out, Raymond hangs back, and when Claire catches up with him, he leans down so his lips are grazing her ear and says, "I hope this doesn't turn out to be another Comet Kohoutek."

Outside, Claire loses sight of them, except for the girls, whose white nightgowns glow in the dark like phosphorescent stars. She lies down on the grass. She's thinking about Kohoutek and about that first winter she and Joey lived together. How excited he was at the prospect of seeing a comet; and later, how disappointed! She remembers that the Museum of Natural History set up a dial-in Comet News Hotline which was supposed to announce new sightings and wound up just giving data about Kohoutek's history and origins. Still, Joey kept calling long distance and letting the message run through several times. Mostly he did it when Claire was out of the house, but not always. Now, as Claire tries not to blink, to stretch her field of vision wide enough for even the most peripheral shooting star, she keeps seeing how Joey looked in those days when she'd come home and stamp the snow off her boots and see him— his back to her, his ear to the phone, listening. And now, as always, it's just when she's thinking of something else that she spots it— that ribbon of light streaking by her so fast she can never be sure if she's really seen it or not.

Louise Erdrich

FLEUR

~~~

The first time she drowned in the cold and glassy waters of Lake Turcot, Fleur Pillager was only a girl. Two men saw the boat tip, saw her struggle in the waves. They rowed over to the place she went down, and jumped in. When they dragged her over the gunwales, she was cold to the touch and stiff, so they slapped her face, shook her by the heels, worked her arms back and forth, and pounded her back until she coughed up lake water. She shivered all over like a dog, then took a breath. But it wasn't long afterward that those two men disappeared. The first wandered off, and the other, Jean Hat, got himself run over by a cart.

It went to show, my grandma said. It figured to her, all right. By saving Fleur Pillager, those two men had lost themselves.

The next time she fell in the lake, Fleur Pillager was twenty years old and no one touched her. She washed onshore, her skin a dull dead gray, but when George Many Women bent to look closer, he saw her chest move. Then her eyes spun open, sharp black riprock, and she looked at him. "You'll take my place," she hissed. Everybody scattered and left her there, so no one knows how she dragged herself home. Soon after that we noticed Many Women changed, grew afraid, wouldn't leave his house, and would not be forced to go near water. For his caution, he lived until the day that his sons brought him a new tin bathtub. Then the first time he used the tub he slipped, got knocked out, and breathed water while his wife stood in the other room frying breakfast.

Men stayed clear of Fleur Pillager after the second drowning. Even though she was good-looking, nobody dared to court her because it was clear that Misshepeshu, the waterman, the monster, wanted her for himself. He's a devil, that one, love-hungry with desire and maddened for the touch of young girls, the strong and daring especially, the ones like Fleur.

Our mothers warn us that we'll think he's handsome, for he appears with green eyes, copper skin, a mouth tender as a child's. But if you fall into his arms, he sprouts horns, fangs, claws, fins. His feet are joined as one and his skin, brass scales, rings to the touch. You're fascinated, cannot move. He casts a shell necklace at your feet, weeps gleaming chips that harden into mica on your breasts. He holds you under. Then he takes the body of a lion or a fat brown worm. He's made of gold. He's made of beach moss. He's a thing of dry foam, a thing of death by drowning, the death a Chippewa cannot survive.

Unless you are Fleur Pillager. We all knew she couldn't swim. After the first time, we thought she'd never go back to Lake Turcot. We thought she'd keep to herself, live quiet, stop killing men off by drowning in the lake. After the first time, we thought she'd keep the good ways. But then, after the second drowning, we knew that we were dealing with something much more serious. She was haywire, out of control. She messed with evil, laughed at the old women's advice, and dressed like a man. She got herself into some half-forgotten medicine, studied ways we shouldn't talk about. Some say she kept the finger of a child in her pocket and a powder of unborn rabbits in a leather thong around her neck. She laid the heart of an owl on her tongue so she could see at night, and went out, hunting, not even in her own body. We know for sure because the next morning, in the snow or dust, we followed the tracks of her bare feet and saw where they changed, where the claws sprang out, the pad broadened and pressed into the dirt. By night we heard her chuffing cough, the bear cough. By day her silence and the wide grin she threw to bring down our guard made us frightened. Some thought that Fleur Pillager should be driven off the reservation, but not a single person who spoke like this had the nerve. And finally, when people were just about to get together and throw her out, she left on her own and didn't come back all summer. That's what this story is about.

During that summer, when she lived a few miles south in Argus, things happened. She almost destroyed that town.

When she got down to Argus in the year of 1920, it was just a small grid of six streets on either side of the railroad depot. There were two elevators, one central, the other a few miles west. Two stores competed for the trade of the three hundred citizens, and three churches quarreled with one another for their souls. There was a frame building for Lutherans, a heavy brick one for Episcopalians, and a long narrow shingled Catholic church. This last had a tall slender steeple, twice as high as any building or tree.

No doubt, across the low, flat wheat, watching from the road as she came near Argus on foot, Fleur saw that steeple rise, a shadow thin as a needle. Maybe in that raw space it drew her the way a lone tree draws lightning. Maybe, in the end, the Catholics are to blame. For if she hadn't seen that sign of pride, that slim prayer, that marker, maybe she would have kept walking.

But Fleur Pillager turned, and the first place she went once she came into town was to the back door of the priest's residence attached to the landmark church. She didn't go there for a handout, although she got that, but to ask for work. She got that too, or the town got her. It's hard to tell which came out worse, her or the men or the town, although the upshot of it all was that Fleur lived.

The four men who worked at the butcher's had carved up about a thousand carcasses between them, maybe half of that steers and the other half pigs, sheep, and game animals like deer, elk, and bear. That's not even mentioning the chickens, which were beyond counting. Pete Kozka owned the place, and employed Lily Veddar, Tor Grunewald, and my stepfather, Dutch James, who had brought my mother down from the reservation the year before she disappointed him by dying. Dutch took me out of school to take her place. I kept house half the time and worked the other in the butcher shop, sweeping floors, putting sawdust down, running a hambone across the street to a customer's bean pot or a package of sausage to the corner. I was a good one to have around because until they needed me, I was invisible. I blended into the stained brown walls, a skinny, big-nosed girl with staring eyes. Because I could fade into a corner or squeeze beneath a shelf, I knew everything, what the men said when no one was around, and what they did to Fleur.

Kozka's Meats served farmers for a fifty-mile area, both to slaughter, for it had a stock pen and chute, and to cure the meat by smoking it or spicing it in sausage. The storage locker was a marvel, made of many thicknesses of brick, earth insulation, and Minnesota timber, lined inside with sawdust and vast blocks of ice cut from Lake Turcot, hauled down from home each winter by horse and sledge.

A ramshackle board building, part slaughterhouse, part store, was fixed to the low, thick square of the lockers. That's where Fleur worked. Kozka hired her for her strength. She could lift a haunch or carry a pole of sausages without stumbling, and she soon learned cutting from Pete's wife, a string-thin blonde who chain-smoked and handled the razor-sharp knives with nerveless precision, slicing close to her stained fingers. Fleur and Fritzie Kozka worked afternoons, wrapping their cuts in paper, and Fleur hauled the packages to the lockers. The meat was left outside the heavy oak doors that were only opened at 5:00 each afternoon, before the men ate supper.

Sometimes Dutch, Tor, and Lily ate at the lockers, and when they did I stayed too, cleaned floors, restoked the fires in the front smokehouses, while the men sat around the squat cast-iron stove spearing slats of herring onto hardtack bread. They played long games of poker or cribbage on a board made from the planed end of a salt crate. They talked and I listened, although there wasn't much to hear since almost nothing ever happened in Argus. Tor was married, Dutch had lost my mother, and Lily read circulars. They mainly discussed about the auctions to come, equipment, or women.

Every so often, Pete Kozka came out front to make a whist, leaving Fritzie to smoke cigarettes and fry raised doughnuts in the back room. He sat and played a few rounds but kept his thoughts to himself. Fritzie did not tolerate him talking behind her back, and the one book he read was the New Testament. If he said something, it concerned weather or a surplus of sheep stomachs, a ham that smoked green or the markets for corn and wheat. He had a good-luck talisman, the opal-white lens of a cow's eye. Playing cards, he rubbed it between his fingers. That soft sound and the slap of cards was about the only conversation.

Fleur finally gave them a subject.

Her cheeks were wide and flat, her hands large, chapped, muscular. Fleur's shoulders were broad as beams, her hips fishlike, slippery, narrow. An old green dress clung to her waist, worn thin where she sat. Her braids were thick like the tails of animals, and swung against her when she moved, deliberately, slowly in her work, held in and half-tamed, but only half. I could tell, but the others never saw. They never looked into her sly brown eyes or noticed her teeth, strong and curved and very white. Her legs were bare, and since she padded around in beadwork moccasins they never saw that her fifth toes were missing. They never knew she'd drowned. They were blinded, they were stupid, they only saw her in the flesh.

And yet it wasn't just that she was a Chippewa, or even that she was a woman, it wasn't that she was good-looking or even that she was alone that made their brains hum. It was how she played cards.

Women didn't usually play with men, so the evening that Fleur drew a chair up to the men's table without being so much as asked, there was a shock of surprise.

"What's this," said Lily. He was fat, with a snake's cold pale eyes and precious skin, smooth and lily-white, which is how he got his name. Lily had a dog, a stumpy mean little bull of a thing with a belly drum-tight from eating pork rinds. The dog liked to play cards just like Lily, and straddled his barrel thighs through games of stud, rum poker, vingt-un. The dog snapped at Fleur's arm that first night, but cringed back, its snarl frozen, when she took her place.

"I thought," she said, her voice soft and stroking, "you might deal me in."

There was a space between the heavy bin of spiced flour and the wall where I just fit. I hunkered down there, kept my eyes open, saw her black hair swing over the chair, her feet solid on the wood floor. I couldn't see up on the table where the cards slapped down, so after they were deep in their game I raised myself up in the shadows, and crouched on a sill of wood.

I watched Fleur's hands stack and ruffle, divide the cards, spill them to each player in a blur, rake them up and shuffle again. Tor, short and scrappy, shut one eye and squinted the other at Fleur. Dutch screwed his lips around a wet cigar.

"Gotta see a man," he mumbled, getting up to go out back to the privy. The others broke, put their cards down, and Fleur sat alone in the lamplight that glowed in a sheen across the push of her breasts. I watched her closely, then she paid me a beam of notice for the first time. She turned, looked straight at me, and grinned the white wolf grin a Pillager turns on its victims, except that she wasn't after me.

"Pauline there," she said, "how much money you got?"

We'd all been paid for the week that day. Eight cents was in my pocket.

"Stake me," she said, holding out her long fingers. I put the coins in her palm and then I melted back to nothing, part of the walls and tables. It was a long time before I understood that the men would not have seen me no matter what I did, how I moved.

I wasn't anything like Fleur. My dress hung loose and my back was already curved, an old woman's. Work had roughened me, reading made my eyes sore, caring for my mother before she died had hardened my face. I was not much to look at, so they never saw me.

When the men came back and sat around the table, they had drawn together. They shot each other small glances, stuck their tongues in their cheeks, burst out laughing at odd moments, to rattle Fleur. But she never minded. They played their vingt-un, staying even as Fleur slowly gained. Those pennies I had given her drew nickels and attracted dimes until there was a small pile in front of her.

Then she hooked them with five-card draw, nothing wild. She dealt, discarded, drew, and then she sighed and her cards gave a little shiver. Tor's eye gleamed, and Dutch straightened in his seat.

"I'll pay to see that hand," said Lily Veddar.

Fleur showed, and she had nothing there, nothing at all.

Tor's thin smile cracked open, and he threw his hand in too.

"Well, we know one thing," he said, leaning back in his chair, "the squaw can't bluff."

With that I lowered myself into a mound of swept sawdust and slept. I woke up during the night, but none of them had moved yet, so I couldn't either. Still later, the men must have gone out again, or Fritzie come out to break the game, because I was lifted, soothed, cradled in a woman's arms and rocked so quiet that I kept my eyes shut while Fleur rolled me into a closet of grimy ledgers, oiled paper, balls of string, and thick files that fit beneath me like a mattress.

The game went on after work the next evening. I got my eight cents back five times over, and Fleur kept the rest of the dollar she'd won for a stake. This time they didn't play so late, but they played regular, and then kept going at it night after night. They played poker now, or variations, for one week straight, and each time Fleur won exactly one dollar, no more and no less, too consistent for luck.

By this time, Lily and the other men were so lit with suspense that they got Pete to join the game with them. They concentrated, the fat dog sitting tense in Lily Veddar's lap, Tor suspicious, Dutch stroking his huge square brow, Pete steady. It wasn't that Fleur won that hooked them in so, because she lost hands too. It was rather that she never had a freak hand or even anything above a straight. She only took on her low cards, which didn't sit right. By chance, Fleur should have gotten a full or flush by now. The irritating thing was she beat with pairs and never bluffed, because she couldn't, and still she ended up each night with exactly one dollar. Lily couldn't believe, first of all, that a woman could be smart enough to play cards, but even if she was, that she would then be stupid enough to cheat for a dollar a night. By day I watched him turn the problem over, his hard white face dull, small fingers probing at his knuckles, until he finally thought he had Fleur figured out as a bit-time player, caution her game. Raising the stakes would throw her.

More than anything now, he wanted Fleur to come away with something but a dollar. Two bits less or ten more, the sum didn't matter, just so he broke her streak.

Night after night she played, won her dollar, and left to stay in a place that just Fritzie and I knew about. Fleur bathed in the slaughtering tub, then slept in the unused brick smokehouse behind the lockers, a windowless place tarred on the inside with scorched fats. When I brushed against her skin I noticed that she smelled of the walls, rich and woody, slightly burnt. Since that night she put me in the closet I was no longer afraid of her, but followed her close, stayed with her, became her moving shadow that the men never noticed, the shadow that could have saved her.

August, the month that bears fruit, closed around the shop, and Pete and Fritzie left for Minnesota to escape the heat. Night by night, running, Fleur had won thirty dollars, and only Pete's presence had kept Lily at bay. But Pete was gone now, and one payday, with the heat so bad no one could move but Fleur, the men sat and played and waited while she finished work. The cards sweat, limp in their fingers, the table was slick with grease, and even the walls were warm to the touch. The air was motionless. Fleur was in the next room boiling heads.

Her green dress, drenched, wrapped her like a transparent sheet. A skin of lakeweed. Black snarls of veining clung to her arms. Her braids were loose, half-unraveled, tied behind her neck in a thick loop. She stood in steam, turning skulls through a vat with a wooden paddle. When scraps boiled to the surface, she bent with a round tin sieve and scooped them out. She'd filled two dishpans.

"Ain't that enough now?" called Lily. "We're waiting." The stump of a dog trembled in his lap, alive with rage. It never smelled me or noticed me above Fleur's smoky skin. The air was heavy in my corner, and pressed me down. Fleur sat with them.

"Now what do you say?" Lily asked the dog. It barked. That was the signal for the real game to start.

"Let's up the ante," said Lily, who had been stalking this night all month. He had a roll of money in his pocket. Fleur had five bills in her dress. The men had each saved their full pay.

"Ante a dollar then," said Fleur, and pitched hers in. She lost, but they let her scrape along, cent by cent. And then she won some. She played unevenly, as if chance was all she had. She reeled them in. The game went on. The dog was stiff now, poised on Lily's knees, a ball of vicious muscle with its yellow eyes slit in concentration. It gave advice, seemed to sniff the lay of Fleur's cards, twitched and nudged. Fleur was up, then down, saved by a scratch. Tor dealt seven cards, three down. The pot grew, round by round, until it held all the money. Nobody folded. Then it all rode on one last card and they went silent. Fleur picked hers up and blew a long breath. The heat lowered like a bell. Her card shook, but she stayed in.

Lily smiled and took the dog's head tenderly between his palms.

"Say, Fatso," he said, crooning the words, "you reckon that girl's bluffing?"

The dog whined and Lily laughed. "Me too," he said, "let's show." He swept his bills and coins into the pot and then they turned their cards over.

Lily looked once, looked again, then he squeezed the dog up like a fist of dough and slammed it on the table.

Fleur threw her arms out and drew the money over, grinning that same wolf grin that she'd used on me, the grin that had them.

She jammed the bills in her dress, scooped the coins up in waxed white paper that she tied with string.

"Let's go another round," said Lily, his voice choked with burrs. But Fleur opened her mouth and yawned, then walked out back to gather slops for the one big hog that was waiting in the stock pen to be killed.

The men sat still as rocks, their hands spread on the oiled wood table. Dutch had chewed his cigar to damp shreds, Tor's eye was dull. Lily's gaze was the only one to follow Fleur. I didn't move. I felt them gathering, saw my stepfather's veins, the ones in his forehead that stood out in anger. The dog had rolled off the table and curled in a knot below the counter, where none of the men could touch it.

Lily rose and stepped out back to the closet of ledgers where Pete kept his private stock. He brought back a bottle, uncorked and tipped it between his fingers. The lump in his throat moved, then he passed it on. They drank, quickly felt the whiskey's fire, and planned with their eyes things they couldn't say out loud.

When they left, I followed. I hid out back in the clutter of broken boards and chicken crates beside the stock pen, where they waited. Fleur could not be seen at first, and then the moon broke and showed her, slipping cautiously along the rough board chute with a bucket in her hand. Her hair fell, wild and coarse, to her waist, and her dress was a floating patch in the dark. She made a pig-calling sound, rang the tin pail lightly against the wood, froze suspiciously. But too late. In the sound of the ring Lily moved, fat and nimble, stepped right behind Fleur and put out his creamy hands. At his first touch, she whirled and doused him with the bucket of sour slops. He pushed her against the big fence and the package of coins split, went clinking and jumping, winked against the wood. Fleur rolled over once and vanished in the yard.

The moon fell behind a curtain of ragged clouds, and Lily followed into the dark muck. But he tripped, pitched over the huge flank of the pig, who lay mired to the snout, heavily snoring. I sprang out of the weeds and climbed the side of the pen, stuck like glue. I saw the sow rise to her neat, knobby knees, gain her balance, and sway, curious, as Lily stumbled forward. Fleur had backed into the angle of rough wood just beyond, and when Lily tried to jostle past, the sow tipped up on her hind legs and struck, quick and hard as a snake. She plunged her head into Lily's thick side and snatched a mouthful of his shirt. She lunged again, caught him lower, so that he grunted in pained surprise. He seemed to ponder, breathing deep. Then he launched his huge body in a swimmer's dive.

The sow screamed as his body smacked over hers. She rolled, striking out with her knife-sharp hooves, and Lily gathered himself upon her, took her foot-long face by the ears and scraped her snout and cheeks against the trestles of the pen. He hurled the sow's tight skull against an iron post, but instead of knocking her dead, he merely woke her from her dream.

She reared, shrieked, drew him with her so that they posed standing upright. They bowed jerkily to each other, as if to begin. Then his arms swung and flailed. She sank her black fangs into his shoulder, clasping him, dancing him forward and backward through the pen. Their steps picked up pace, went wild. The two dipped as one, box-stepped, tripped each other. She ran her split foot though his hair. He grabbed her kinked tail. They went down and came up, the same shape and then the same color, until the men couldn't tell one from the other in that light and Fleur was able to launch herself over the gates, swing down, hit gravel.

The men saw, yelled, and chased her at a dead run to the smoke-house. And Lily too, once the sow gave up in disgust and freed him. That is where I should have gone to Fleur, saved her, thrown myself on Dutch. But I went stiff with fear and couldn't unlatch myself from the trestles or move at all. I closed my eyes and put my head in my arms, tried to hide, so there is nothing to describe but what I couldn't block out, Fleur's hoarse breath, so loud it filled me, her cry in the old language, and my name repeated over and over among the words.

The heat was still dense the next morning when I came back to work. Fleur was gone but the men were there, slack-faced, hung over. Lily was paler and softer than ever, as if his flesh had steamed on his bones. They smoked, took pulls off a bottle. It wasn't noon yet. I worked awhile, waiting shop and sharpening steel. But I was sick, I was smothered, I was sweating so hard that my hands slipped on the knives, and I wiped my fingers clean of the greasy touch of the customers' coins. Lily opened his mouth and roared once, not in anger. There was no meaning to the sound. His boxer dog, sprawled limp beside his foot, never lifted its head. Nor did the other men.

They didn't notice when I stepped outside, hoping for a clear breath. And then I forgot them because I knew that we were all balanced, ready to tip, to fly, to be crushed as soon as the weather broke. The sky was so low that I felt the weight of it like a yoke. Clouds hung down, witch teats, a tornado's green-brown cones, and as I watched one flicked out and became a delicate probing thumb. Even as I picked up my heels and ran back inside, the wind blew suddenly, cold, and then came rain.

Inside, the men had disappeared already and the whole place was trembling as if a huge hand was pinched at the rafters, shaking it. I ran straight through, screaming for Dutch or for any of them, and then I stopped at the heavy doors of the lockers, where they had surely taken shelter. I stood there a moment. Everything went still. Then I heard a cry building in the wind, faint at first, a whistle and then a shrill scream that tore through the walls and gathered around me, spoke plain so I understood that I should move, put my arms out, and slam down the great iron bar that fit across the hasp and lock.

Outside, the wind was stronger, like a hand held against me. I struggled forward. The bushes tossed, the awnings flapped off storefronts, the rails of porches rattled. The odd cloud became a fat snout that nosed along the earth and sniffled, jabbed, picked at things, sucked them up, blew them apart, rooted around as if it was following a certain scent, then stopped behind me at the butcher shop and bored down like a drill.

I went flying, landed somewhere in a ball. When I opened my eyes and looked, stranger things were happening.

A herd of cattle flew through the air like giant birds, dropping dung, their mouths opened in stunned bellows. A candle, still lighted, blew past, and tables, napkins, garden tools, a whole school of drifting eyeglasses, jackets on hangers, hams, a checkerboard, a lampshade, and at last the sow from behind the lockers, on the run, her hooves a blur, set free, swooping, diving, screaming as everything in Argus fell apart and got turned upside down, smashed, and thoroughly wrecked.

Days passed before the town went looking for the men. They were bachelors, after all, except for Tor, whose wife had suffered a blow to the head that made her forgetful. Everyone was occupied with digging out, in high relief because even though the Catholic steeple had been torn off like a peaked cap and sent across five fields, those huddled in the cellar were unhurt. Walls had fallen, windows were demolished, but the stores were intact and so were the bankers and shop owners who had taken refuge in their safes or beneath their cash registers. It was a fair-minded disaster, no one could be said to have suffered much more than the next, at least not until Fritzie and Pete came home.

Of all the businesses in Argus, Kozka's Meats had suffered worst. The boards of the front building had been split to kindling, piled in a huge pyramid, and the shop equipment was blasted far and wide. Pete paced off the distance the iron bathtub had been flung— a hundred feet. The glass candy case went fifty, and landed without so much as a cracked pane. There were other surprises as well, for the back rooms where Fritzie and Pete lived were undisturbed. Fritzie said the dust still coated her china figures, and upon her kitchen table, in the ashtray, perched the last cigarette she'd put out in haste. She lit it up and finished it, looking through the window. From there, she could see that the old smokehouse Fleur had slept in was crushed to a reddish sand and the stockpens were completely torn apart, the rails stacked helter-skelter. Fritzie asked for Fleur. People shrugged. Then she asked about the others and, suddenly, the town understood that three men were missing.

There was a rally of help, a gathering of shovels and volunteers. We passed boards from hand to hand, stacked them, uncovered what lay beneath the pile of jagged splinters. The lockers, full of the meat that was Pete and Fritzie's investment, slowly came into sight, still intact. When enough room was made for a man to stand on the roof, there were calls, a general urge to hack through and see what lay below. But Fritzie shouted that she wouldn't allow it because the meat would spoil. And so the work continued, board by board, until at last the heavy oak doors of the freezer were revealed and people pressed to the entry. Everyone wanted to be the first, but since it was my stepfather lost, I was let go in when Pete and Fritzie wedged through into the sudden icy air.

Pete scraped a match on his boot, lit the lamp Fritzie held, and then the three of us stood still in its circle. Light glared off the skinned and hanging carcasses, the crates of wrapped sausages, the bright and cloudy blocks of lake ice, pure as winter. The cold bit into us, pleasant at first, then numbing. We must have stood there a couple of minutes before we saw the men, or more rightly, the humps of fur, the iced and shaggy hides they wore, the bearskins they had taken down and wrapped around themselves. We stepped closer and tilted the lantern beneath the flaps of fur into their faces. The dog was there, perched among them, heavy as a doorstop. The three had hunched around a barrel where the game was still laid out, and a dead lantern and an empty bottle, too. But they had thrown down their last hands and hunkered tight, clutching one another, knuckles raw from beating at the door they had also attacked with hooks. Frost stars gleamed off their eyelashes and the stubble of their beards. Their faces were set in concentration, mouths open as if to speak some careful thought, some agreement they'd come to in each other's arms.

Power travels in the bloodlines, handed out before birth. It comes down through the hands, which in the Pillagers were strong and knotted, big, spidery, and rough, with sensitive fingertips good at dealing cards. It comes through the eyes, too, belligerent, darkest brown, the eyes of those in the bear clan, impolite as they gaze directly at a person.

In my dreams, I look straight back at Fleur, at the men. I am no longer the watcher on the dark sill, the skinny girl.

The blood draws us back, as if it runs through a vein of earth. I've come home and, except for talking to my cousins, live a quiet life. Fleur lives quiet too, down on Lake Turcot with her boat. Some say she's married to the waterman, Misshepeshu, or that she's living in shame with white men or windigos, or that she's killed them all. I'm about the only one here who ever goes to visit her. Last winter, I went to help out in her cabin when she bore the child, whose green eyes and skin the color of an old penny made more talk, as no one could decide if the child was mixed blood or what, fathered in a smokehouse, or by a man with brass scales, or by the lake. The girl is bold, smiling in her sleep, as if she knows what people wonder, as if she hears the old men talk, turning the story over. It comes up different every time and has no ending, no beginning. They get the middle wrong too. They only know that they don't know anything.

Mary Gordon

THE
DANCING
PARTY

❧

I know why you're in this mood," says the angry wife, "I just wish you'd admit it."

They drive in darkness on the sandy road; she has no confidence that he will find the house, which they have only seen in daylight. And she half wishes he would get a wheel stuck in the sand. She would be pleased to see him foolish.

"I'm in a bad mood for one reason," says the husband. "Because you said to me: Shape up. No one should say that to someone: Shape up."

"I could tell by your face how you were planning to be. That way that makes the other people at a party want to cut their throats."

"Must I sparkle to be allowed among my kind?"

"And I know why you're like that. Don't think I don't. It's because you watched the children while I swam. For once."

"Yes, it's true, the day was shaped by your desires. But I'm not resentful. Not at all. You must believe me."

"But I don't believe you."

"Then where do we go?"

"We go, now, to the party. But I beg you: Please don't go in with your face like that. It's such a wonderful idea, a dancing party."

The house is built atop the largest dune. In daylight you can see the ocean clearly from the screened-in porch. The married couple climb the dune, not looking at each other, walking far apart. When they come to the door, they see the hostess dancing with her brother.

How I love my brother, thinks the hostess. There are no men in the world like him.

The hostess's brother has just been divorced. His sister's house is where he comes, the house right on the ocean, the house she was given when her husband left her for someone else. Her brother comes here for consolation, for she has called it "my consolation prize." And it *has* been a consolation, and still is, though she is now, at forty-five, successful. She can leave her store to her assistants, take a month off in the summer, and come here. She earns more money than her ex-husband, who feels, by this alone, betrayed. She comes, each morning, to the screened-in porch and catches in the distance the blue glimpse of sea, the barest hint, out in the distance, longed for, but in reach. She'd brought her daughters here for the long, exhausting summers of the single mother. Watched their feuds, exclusions, the shore life of children on long holiday, so brimming and so cruel. But they are grown now, and remarkably, they both have jobs, working in the city. One is here, now, for the weekend only. Sunday night, tomorrow, like the other grownups, she will leave. The daughter will be in her car, stuck in the line of traffic, that reptilian creature that will take her in its coils. Exhausted, she will arrive in her apartment in Long Island City. She will wait till morning to return her rented car.

I will not be like my mother, thinks the daughter of the hostess.

I will not live as she lives. How beautiful she is, and how I love her. But I will not live like that.

She lifts an angry shoulder at the poor young man, her partner, who does not know why. She is saying: I will not serve you or your kind. I will not be susceptible.

She sees her mother, dancing, not with her brother any longer, but with another man. She sees her mother's shoulder curving toward him. Sees her mother's head bent back. Susceptible. Will this be one more error of susceptibility? Oh, no, my mother, beautiful and still so young, do not. Shore up and guard yourself. As I have. Do not fall once more into those arms that seem strong but will leave you. Do not fall.

The daughter leaves the young man now to dance with the best friend of her mother. This woman has no husband and a child of two. The mother with no husband and a child of two dreams of her lover as she dances with the daughter of the hostess. She thinks: I have known this girl since she was five. How can it be? I have a child of two; my best friend has a daughter who lifts her angry shoulder and will drive away on Sunday to the working world. Do not be angry at your mother, the mother with no husband wants to say. She is young, she is beautiful, she needs a man in her bed. The mother with no husband thinks of her own lover, who is someone else's husband, and the father of the two-year-old child. Someday, she thinks, it is just possible that we will live together, raise together, this boy of ours, now only mine. She longs for her lover; she spends, she thinks in anger, too much life on longing. But she chose that. Now she thinks about his hair, his ribcage, the feel of his bones when she runs her fingers up his back, the shape of his ear when she can see him in the distance. She thinks: He is torn, always. When the child was conceived she said, being nearly forty: I will have it. There is nothing you need do. He said: I will stand with you. He came on the first day of their son's life and visits weekly—uncle? friend?—and puts, each month, three hundred dollars in a small account and in a trust fund for college. Says: I cannot leave my wife. The mother with no husband longs sometimes to be with her lover in a public place, dancing, simply, like the married couple, without fear among the others of their kind.

The scientist has come without her lover. He has said: Oh, go alone. You know I hate to dance. She phoned her friend, a man in love with other men. Come dancing with me. Yes, of course, he says. He is glad to be with her; he too is a scientist. They work together; they study the habits of night birds. They are great friends. The lover of the scientist is brilliant, difficult. In ten years she has left him twice. She thinks now she will never leave him.

The daughter of the hostess puts on music that the angry wife, the mother with no husband and the scientist don't like. So they sit down. Three friends, they sit together on the bench that rests against the wall. They look out the large window; they can see the moon and a newly lit square white patch of sea. They like each other; they are fortyish; they are successful. For a month each summer they live here by the ocean, a mile apart. The angry wife is a bassoonist of renown. The mother with no husband writes studies of women in the ancient world. These women, all of them, have said to each other: What a pleasure we are, good at what we do. And people know it. The angry wife has said: You know you are successful when you realize how many people hope that you will fail.

And how are you? they ask each other. Tired say the two, the angry wife, the mother with no husband, who have young children. I would like to have a child, the scientist says. Of course you must, say the two who are mothers. Now they think with pleasure of the soft flesh of their children, of their faces when they sleep. Oh, have a child, they tell the scientist. Nothing is better in the world.

Yes, have a child, the hostess says. Look at my daughter. See how wonderful. The daughter of the hostess has forgotten, for a time, her anger and is laughing with the young man. Asks him: Are you going back on Sunday? Would you like a ride? The hostess thinks: Good, good. My daughter will not drive alone. And maybe he will love her.

I am afraid of being tired, says the scientist to her three friends.

You will be tired if you have a child, they say to her. There is no getting round it. You will be tired all the time.

And what about my work?

You will do far less work. We must tell you the truth.

I am afraid, then, says the scientist.

The widow sits beside them. And they say to her, for she is old now: What do you think our friend should do?

The widow says: Two things in the world you never regret: a swim in the ocean, the birth of a child.

She says things like this; it is why they come to her, these four women near the age of forty. She has Russian blood; it makes her feel free to be aphoristic. She can say: To cross a field is not to live a life. To drink tea is not to hew wood. Often she is wrong. They know that, and it doesn't matter. She sits before them, shining, like a bowl of water colored, just for pleasure, blue. They would sit at her feet forever; they would listen to her all night long. She says: I think that I have made mistakes.

But they do not believe her.

She says: In my day we served men. We did not divorce. I do not think then we knew how to be good to our children and love men at the same time. We had wonderful affairs. Affairs are fine, but you must never fall in love. You must be in love only with your husband.

But only one of them has a husband. He is sitting, drinking, talking to another man. His wife would like to say: Look at the moon, don't turn your back to it. But she is tired of her voice tonight, the voice that speaks to him so cruelly, more cruelly than he deserves. She would like to say: Let's dance now. But she doesn't want to dance with him. Will I get over being angry, she wonders, before the party ends? She hopes she will and fears that she will not.

The widow greets her friend across the room. They have both understood the history of clothes. And so they watched, in the late 1960s, the sensitive and decorative march of vivid-colored trousers and light, large-sleeved printed shirts, of dresses made of Indian material, of flat, bright, cotton shoes. So, in their seventies, they greet each other wearing purple and magenta. As they kiss, the gauzy full sleeves of their blouses touch. Tonight to be absurd, the widow's friend has worn a feather boa. Her husband, her fifth husband, stands beside her, gallant and solicitous for her and for her friend.

The widow says to her old friend, pointing to the four women sitting on the bench: I think they've got it right. Their lovely work.

The friend says: But look, they are so tired, and so angry.

The widow says: But we were tired at that age, and angry. They will have something to show.

Who knows, the widow's friend says, turning to her husband. Dance with me, she says, I think this one's a waltz.

He kisses her, for she has made him laugh. They dance, they are the only ones now dancing with the hostess's daughter and her friends. The music has gone angular and mean, it seems to the four women on the bench. The hostess's daughter thinks: Perhaps, then, I should marry a rich man. I am not ambitious, but I like nice things.

The mother without a husband thinks about her lover. Of his mouth, his forearms, his way of standing with his knees always a little bent, the black hairs on the backs of his small hands.

The hostess thinks: Perhaps I will ask this new man to stay.

The scientist thinks: I will live forever with a man who hates to dance.

The daughter of the hostess thinks: I love my mother, but I will not live like her.

The widow thinks: How wonderful their lives are. I must tell them so that they will know.

Her friend thinks: If this man dies I will be once more alone.

The angry wife wishes she were not angry.

Suddenly a funny song comes on. It has a name that makes them laugh, "Girls Just Want to Have Fun." The daughter of the hostess claps her hands and says: No men. The women, all of them: the hostess and her daughter, the scientist, the mother with no husband, the angry wife, the widow and her friend, stand in a circle, kick their legs in unison and laugh. And they can see outside the circle all the men, ironical or bored looking, the kindly ones amused. They all look shiftless there, and unreliable, like vagabonds. The two old women cannot bear it, that the men should be unhappy as the women dance. The widow's friend is first to break the circle. She takes her husband's hand and leads him to the center of the room. The widow dances with the handsomest young man. The daughter of the hostess walks away. But the four women near to forty sit down on the bench. The angry wife can see her husband's back. His back is turned against her; he is looking at the moon.

Becky Birtha

IN THE
LIFE

~~~

Grace come to me in my sleep last night. I feel somebody presence, in the room with me, then I catch the scent of Posner's Bergamot Pressing Oil, and that cocoa butter grease she use on her skin. I know she standing at the bedside, right over me, and then she call my name.

"Pearl."

My Christian name Pearl Irene Jenkins, but don't nobody ever call me that no more. I been Jinx to the world for longer than I care to specify. Since my mother passed away, Grace the only one ever use my given name.

"Pearl," she say again. "I'm just gone down to the garden awhile. I be back."

I'm so deep asleep I have to fight my way awake, and when I do be fully woke, Grace is gone. I ease my tired bones up and drag em down the stairs, cross the kitchen in the dark, and out the back screen door onto the porch. I guess I'm half expecting Gracie to be there waiting for me, but there ain't another soul stirring tonight. Not a sound but singing crickets, and nothing staring back at me but that old weather-beaten fence I ought to painted this summer, and still ain't made time for. I lower myself down into the porch swing, where Gracie and I have sat so many still summer nights and watched the moon rising up over Old Mister Thompson's field.

I never had time to paint that fence back then, neither. But it didn't matter none, cause Gracie had it all covered up with her flowers. She used to sit right here on this swing at night, when a little breeze be blowing, and say she could tell all the different flowers apart, just by they smell. The wind pick up a scent, and Gracie say, "Smell that jasmine, Pearl?" Then a breeze come up from another direction, and she turn her head like somebody calling her and say, "Now that's my honeysuckle, now."

It used to tickle me, cause she knowed I couldn't tell all them flowers of hers apart when I was looking square at em in broad daylight. So how I'm gonna do it by smell in the middle of the night? I just laugh and rock the swing a little, and watch her enjoying herself in the soft moonlight.

I could never get enough of watching her. I always did think that Grace Simmons was the prettiest woman north of the Mason-Dixon line. Now I've lived enough years to know it's true. There's been other women in my life besides Grace, and I guess I loved them all, one way or another, but she was something special— Gracie was something else again.

She was a dark brownskin woman—the color of fresh gingerbread hot out the oven. In fact, I used to call her that—my gingerbread girl. She had plenty enough of that pretty brownskin flesh to fill your arms up with something substantial when you hugging her, and to make a nice background for them dimples in her cheeks and other places I won't go into detail about.

Gracie could be one elegant good looker when she set her mind to it. I'll never forget the picture she made, that time the New Year's Eve party was down at the Star Harbor Ballroom. That was the first year we was in the Club, and we was going to every event they had. Dressed to kill. Gracie had on that white silk dress that set off her complexion so perfect, with her hair done up in all them little curls. A single strand of pearls that could have fooled anybody. Long gloves. And a little fur stole. We was serious about our partying back then! I didn't look too bad myself, with that black velvet jacket I used to have, and the pleats in my slacks pressed so sharp you could cut yourself on em. I weighed quite a bit less than I do now, too. Right when you come in the door of the ballroom, they have a great big floor to ceiling gold frame mirror, and if I remember rightly, we didn't get past that for quite some time.

Everybody want to dance with Gracie that night. And that's fine with me. Along about the middle of the evening, the band is playing a real hot number, and here come Louie and Max over to me, all long-face serious, wanting to know how I can let my woman be out there shaking her behind with any stranger that wander in the door. Now they know good and well ain't no strangers here. The Cinnamon & Spice Club is a private club, and all events is by invitation only.

Of course, there's some thinks friends is more dangerous than strangers. But I never could be the jealous, overprotective type. And the fact is, I just love to watch the woman. I don't care if she out there shaking it with the Virgin Mary, long as she having a good time. And that's just what I told Max and Lou. I could lean up against that bar and watch her for hours.

You wouldn't know, to look at her, she done it all herself. Made all her own dresses and hats, and even took apart a old ratty fur coat that used to belong to my great aunt Malinda to make that cute little stole. She always did her own hair—every week or two. She used to do mine, too. Always be teasing me about let her make me some curls this time. I'd get right aggravated. Cause you can't have a proper argument with somebody when they standing over your head with a hot comb in they hand. You kinda at they mercy. I'm sitting fuming and cursing under them towels and stuff, with the sweat dripping all in my eyes in the steamy kitchen—and she just laughing. "Girl," I'm telling her, "you know won't no curls fit under my uniform cap. Less you want me to stay home this week and you gonna go work my job and your job too."

Both of us had to work, always, and we still ain't had much. Everybody always think Jinx and Grace doing all right, but we was scrimping and saving all along. Making stuff over and making do. Half of what we had to eat grew right here in this garden. Still and all, I guess we *was* doing all right. We had each other.

Now I finally got the damn house paid off, and she ain't even here to appreciate it with me. And Gracie's poor bedraggled garden is just struggling along on its last legs—kinda like me. I ain't the kind to complain about my lot, but truth to tell, I can't be down crawling around on my hands and knees no more—this body I got put up such a fuss and holler. Can't enjoy the garden at night proper nowadays, nohow. Since Mister Thompson's land was took over by the city and they built them housing projects where the field used to be, you can't even see the moon from here, till it get up past the fourteenth floor. Don't no moonlight come in my yard no more. And I guess I might as well pick my old self up and go on back to bed.

Sometimes I still ain't used to the fact that Grace is passed on. Not even after these thirteen years without her. She the only woman I ever lived with—and I lived with her more than half my life. This house her house, too, and she oughta be here in it with me.

I rise up by six o'clock most every day, same as I done all them years I worked driving for the C.T.C. If the weather ain't too bad, I take me a walk—and if I ain't careful, I'm liable to end up down at the Twelfth Street Depot, waiting to see what trolley they gonna give me this morning. There ain't a soul working in that office still remember me. And they don't even run a trolley on the Broadway line no more. They been running a bus for the past five years.

I forgets a lot of things these days. Last week, I had just took in the clean laundry off the line, and I'm up in the spare room fixing to iron my shirts, when I hear somebody pass through that squeaky side gate and go on around to the back yard. I ain't paid it no mind at all, cause that's the way Gracie most often do when she come home. Go see about her garden fore she even come in the house. I always be teasing her she care more about them collards and string beans than she do about me. I hear her moving around out there while I'm sprinkling the last shirt and plugging in the iron—hear leaves rustling, and a crate scraping along the walk.

While I'm waiting for the iron to heat up, I take a look out the window, and come to see it ain't Gracie at all, but two a them sassy little scoundrels from over the projects—one of em standing on a apple crate and holding up the other one, who is picking my ripe peaches off my tree, just as brazen as you please. Don't even blink a eyelash when I holler out the window. I have to go running down all them stairs and out on the back porch, waving the cord I done jerked out the iron—when Doctor Matthews has told me a hundred times I ain't supposed to be running or getting excited about nothing, with my pressure like it is. And I ain't even supposed to be *walking* up and down no stairs.

When they seen the ironing cord in my hand, them two little sneaks had a reaction all right. The one on the bottom drop the other one right on his padded quarters and lit out for the gate, hollering, "Look out, Timmy! Here come Old Lady Jenkins!"

When I think about it now, it was right funny, but at the time I was so mad it musta took me a whole half hour to cool off. I sat there on that apple crate just boiling.

Eventually, I begun to see how it wasn't even them two kids I was so mad at. I was mad at time. For playing tricks on me the way it done. So I don't even remember that Grace Simmons has been dead now for the past thirteen years. And mad at time just for passing—so fast. If I had my life to live over, I wouldn't trade in none of them years for nothing. I'd just slow em down.

The church sisters around here is always trying to get me to be thinking about dying, myself. They must figure, when you my age, that's the only excitement you got left to look forward to. Gladys Hawkins stopped out front this morning, while I was mending a patch in the top screen of the front door. She was grinning from ear to ear like she just spent the night with Jesus himself.

"Morning, Sister Jenkins. Right pretty day the good Lord seen fit to send us, ain't it?"

I ain't never known how to answer nobody who manages to bring the good Lord into every conversation. If I nod and say yes, she'll think I finally got religion. But if I disagree, she'll think I'm crazy, cause it truly is one pretty August morning. Fortunately, it don't matter to her whether I agree or not, cause she gone right on talking according to her own agenda anyway.

"You know, this Sunday is Women's Day over at Blessed Endurance. Reverend Solomon Moody is gonna be visiting, speaking on 'A Woman's Place in the Church.' Why don't you come and join us for worship? You'd be most welcome."

I'm tempted to tell her exactly what come to my mind—that I ain't never heard of no woman name Solomon. However, I'm polite enough to hold my tongue, which is more than I can say for Gladys.

She ain't waiting for no answer from me, just going right on. "I don't spose you need me to point it out to you, Sister Jenkins, but you know you ain't as young as you used to be." As if both of our ages wasn't common knowledge to each other, seeing as we been knowing one another since we was girls. "You reaching that time of life when you might wanna be giving a little more attention to the spiritual side of things than you been doing. . . ."

She referring, politely as she capable of, to the fact that I ain't been seen inside a church for thirty-five years.

". . . And you know what the good Lord say. 'Watch therefore, for ye know neither the day nor the hour . . .' But, 'He that believeth on the Son hath everlasting life . . .' "

It ain't no use to argue with her kind. The Lord is on they side in every little disagreement, and he don't never give up. So when she finally wind down and ask me again will she see me in church this Sunday, I just say I'll think about it.

Funny thing, I been thinking about it all day. But not the kinda thoughts she want me to think, I'm sure. Last time I went to church was on a Easter Sunday. We decided to go on accounta Gracie's old meddling cousin, who was always nagging us about how we unnatural and sinful and a disgrace to her family. Seem like she seen it as her one mission in life to get us two sinners inside a church. I guess she figure, once she get us in there, God gonna take over the job. So Grace and me finally conspires that the way to get her off our backs is to give her what she think she want.

Course, I ain't had on a skirt since before the war, and I ain't aiming to change my lifelong habits just to please Cousin Hattie. But I did take a lotta pains over my appearance that day. I'd had my best tailor-made suit pressed fresh, and slept in my stocking cap the night before so I'd have every hair in place. Even had one a Gracie's flowers stuck in my buttonhole. And a brand new narrow-brim dove gray Stetson hat. Gracie take one look at me when I'm ready and shake her head. "The good sisters is gonna have a hard time concentrating on the preacher today!"

We arrive at her cousin's church nice and early, but of course it's a big crowd inside already on accounta it being Easter Sunday. The organ music is wailing away, and the congregation is dazzling—decked out in nothing but the finest and doused with enough perfume to outsmell even the flowers up on the altar.

But as soon as we get in the door, this kinda sedate commotion break out—all them good Christian folks whispering and nudging each other and trying to turn around and get a good look. Well, Grace and me, we used to that. We just find us a nice seat in one of the empty pews near the back. But this busy buzzing keep up, even after we seated and more blended in with the crowd. And finally it come out that the point of contention ain't even the bottom half of my suit, but my new dove gray Stetson.

This old gentleman with a grizzled head, wearing glasses about a inch thick is turning around and leaning way over the back of the seat, whispering to Grace in a voice plenty loud enough for me to hear, "You better tell your beau to remove that hat, entering in Jesus' Holy Chapel."

Soon as I get my hat off, some old lady behind me is grumbling. "I declare, some of these children haven't got no respect at all. Oughta know you sposed to keep your head covered, setting in the house of the Lord."

Seem like the congregation just can't make up its mind whether I'm supposed to wear my hat or I ain't.

I couldn't hardly keep a straight face all through the service. Every time I catch Gracie eye, or one or the other of us catch a sight of my hat, we off again. I couldn't wait to get outa that place. But it was worth it. Gracie and me was entertaining the gang with that story for weeks to come. And we ain't had no more problems with Cousin Hattie.

Far as life everlasting is concerned, I imagine I'll cross that bridge when I reach it. I don't see no reason to rush into things. Sure, I know Old Man Death is gonna be coming after me one of these days, same as he come for my mother and dad, and Gracie and, just last year, my old buddy Louie. But I ain't about to start nothing that might make him feel welcome. It might be different for Gladys Hawkins and the rest of them church sisters, but I got a whole lot left to live for. Including a mind fulla good time memories. When you in the life, one thing your days don't never be, and that's dull. Your nights neither. All these years I been in the life, I loved it. And you know Jinx ain't about to go off with no Old *Man* without no struggle, nohow.

To tell the truth, though, sometime I do get a funny feeling bout Old Death. Sometime I feel like he here already—been here. Waiting on me and watching me and biding his time. Paying attention when I have to stop on the landing of the stairs to catch my breath. Paying attention if I don't wake up till half past seven some morning, and my back is hurting me so bad it take me another half hour to pull myself together and get out the bed.

The same night after I been talking to Gladys in the morning, it take me a long time to fall asleep. I'm lying up in bed waiting for the aching in my back and my joints to ease off some, and I can swear I hear somebody else in the house. Seem like I hear em downstairs, maybe opening and shutting the icebox door, or switching off a light. Just when I finally manage to doze off, I hear somebody footsteps right here in the bedroom with me. Somebody tippy-toeing real quiet, creaking the floor boards between the bed and the dresser . . . over to the closet . . . back to the dresser again.

I'm almost scared to open my eyes. But it's only Gracie—in her old raggedy bathrobe and a silk handkerchief wrapped up around all them little braids in her head—putting her finger up to her lips to try and shush me so I won't wake up.

I can't help chuckling. "Hey Gingerbread Girl. Where you think you going in your house coat and bandana and it ain't even light out yet. Come on get back in this bed."

"You go on to sleep," she say. "I'm just going out back a spell."

It ain't no use me trying to make my voice sound angry, cause she so contrary when it come to that little piece of ground down there I can't help laughing. "What you think you gonna complish down there in the middle of the night? It ain't even no moon to watch tonight. The sky been filling up with clouds all evening, and the weather forecast say rain tomorrow."

"Just don't pay me no mind and go on back to sleep. It ain't the middle of the night. It's almost daybreak." She grinning like she up to something, and sure enough, she say, "This the best time to pick off them black and yellow beetles been making mildew outa my cucumber vines. So I'm just fixing to turn the tables around a little bit. You gonna read in the papers tomorrow morning bout how the entire black and yellow beetle population of number Twenty-seven Bank Street been wiped off the face of the earth—while you was up here sleeping."

Both of us is laughing like we partners in a crime, and then she off down the hall, calling out, "I be back before you even know I'm gone."

But the full light of day is coming in the window, and she ain't back yet.

I'm over to the window with a mind to holler down to Grace to get her behind back in this house, when the sight of them housing projects hits me right in the face: stacks of dirt-colored bricks and little caged-in porches, heaped up into the sky blocking out what poor skimpy light this cloudy morning brung.

It's a awful funny feeling start to come over me. I mean to get my housecoat, and go down there anyway, just see what's what. But in the closet I can see it ain't but my own clothes hanging on the pole. All the shoes on the floor is mine. And I know I better go ahead and get washed, cause it's a whole lot I want to get done fore it rain, and that storm is coming in for sure. Better pick the rest of them ripe peaches and tomatoes. Maybe put in some peas for fall picking, if my knees'll allow me to get that close to the ground.

The rain finally catch up around noon time and slow me down a bit. I never could stand to be cooped up in no house in the rain.

Always make me itchy. That's one reason I used to like driving a trolley for the C.T.C. Cause you get to be out every day, no matter what kinda weather coming down—get to see people and watch the world go by. And it ain't as if you exactly out in the weather, neither. You get to watch it all from behind that big picture window.

Not that I woulda minded being out in it. I used to want to get me a job with the post office, delivering mail. Black folks could make good money with the post office, even way back then. But they wouldn't out you on no mail route. Always stick em off in a back room someplace, where nobody can't see em and get upset cause some little colored girl making as much money as the white boy working next to her. So I stuck with the C.T.C. all them years, and got my pension to prove it.

The rain still coming down steady along about three o'clock, when Max call me up say do I want to come over to her and Yvonne's for dinner. Say they fried more chicken that they can eat, and anyway Yvonne all involved in some new project she want to talk to me about. And I'm glad for the chance to get out the house. Max and Yvonne got the place all picked up for company. I can smell that fried chicken soon as I get in the door.

Yvonne don't never miss a opportunity to dress up a bit. She got the front of her hair braided up, with beads hanging all in her eyes, and a kinda loose robe-like thing, in colors look like the fruit salad at a Independence Day picnic. Max her same old self in her slacks and loafers. She ain't changed in all the years I known her—cept we both got more wrinkles and gray hairs. Yvonne a whole lot younger than us two, but she hanging in there. Her and Max been together going on three years now.

Right away, Yvonne start to explain about this project she doing with her women's club. When I first heard about this club she in, I was kinda interested. But I come to find out it ain't no social club, like the Cinnamon & Spice Club used to be. It's more like a or-ganization. Yvonne call it a collective. They never has no outings or parties or picnics or nothing—just meetings. And projects.

The project they working on right now, they all got tape re-corders. And they going around tape-recording people story. Talk-ing to people who been in the life for years and years, and asking

em what it was like, back in the old days. I been in the life since
before Yvonne born. But the second she stick that microphone in
my face, I can't think of a blessed thing to say.

"Come on, Jinx, you always telling us all them funny old time
stories."

Them little wheels is rolling round and round, and all that
smooth, shiny brown tape is slipping off one reel and sliding onto
the other, and I can't think of not one thing I remember.

"Tell how the Cinnamon & Spice Club got started," she say.

"I already told you about that before."

"Well tell how it ended, then. You never told me that."

"Ain't nothing to tell. Skip and Peaches broke up." Yvonne
waiting, and the reels is rolling, but for the life of me I can't think
of another word to say about it. And Max is sitting there grinning,
like I'm the only one over thirty in the room and she don't remember a thing.

Yvonne finally give up and turn the thing off, and we go on and
stuff ourselves on the chicken they fried and the greens I brung
over from the garden. By the time we start in on the sweet potato
pie, I have finally got to remembering. Telling Yvonne about when
Skip and Peaches had they last big falling out, and they was both
determine they was gonna stay in the Club—and couldn't be in the
same room with one another for fifteen minutes. Both of em keep
waiting on the other one to drop out, and both of em keep showing
up, every time the gang get together. And none of the rest of us
couldn't be in the same room with the two a them for even as long
as they could stand each other. We'd be sneaking around, trying
to hold a meeting without them finding out. But Peaches was the
president and Skip was the treasurer, so you might say our hands
was tied. Wouldn't neither one of em resign. They was both convince the Club couldn't go on without em, and by the time they
was finished carrying on, they had done made sure it wouldn't.

Max is chiming in correcting all the details, every other breath
come outa my mouth. And then when we all get up to go sit in
the parlor again, it come out that Yvonne has sneaked that tape
recording machine in here under that African poncho she got on,
and has got down every word I said.

When time come to say good night, I'm thankful, for once, that

Yvonne insist on driving me home—though it ain't even a whole mile. The rain ain't let up all evening, and is coming down in bucketfuls while we in the car. I'm half soaked just running from the car to the front door.

Yvonne is drove off down the street, and I'm halfway through the front door, when it hit me all of a sudden that the door ain't been locked. Now my mind may be getting a little threadbare in spots, but it ain't wore out yet. I know it's easy for me to slip back into doing things the way I done em twenty or thirty years ago, but I could swear I distinctly remember locking this door and hooking the key ring back on my belt loop, just fore Yvonne drove up in front. And now here's the door been open all this time.

Not a sign a nobody been here. Everything in its place, just like I left it. The slipcovers on the couch is smooth and neat. The candy dishes and ash trays and photographs is sitting just where they belong, on the end tables. Not even so much as a throw rug been moved a inch. I can feel my heart start to thumping like a blowout tire.

Must be, whoever come in here ain't left yet.

The idea of somebody got a nerve like that make me more mad than scared, and I know I'm gonna find out who it is broke in my house, even if it don't turn out to be nobody but them little peach-thieving rascals from round the block. Which I wouldn't be surprised if it ain't. I'm scooting from room to room, snatching open closet doors and whipping back curtains—tiptoeing down the hall and then flicking on the lights real sudden.

When I been in every room, I go back through everywhere I been, real slow, looking in all the drawers, and under the old glass doorstop in the hall, and in the back of the recipe box in the kitchen—and other places where I keep things. But it ain't nothing missing. No money—nothing.

In the end, ain't nothing left for me to do but go to bed. But I'm still feeling real uneasy. I know somebody or something done got in here while I was gone. And ain't left yet. I lay wake in the bed a long time, cause I ain't too particular about falling asleep tonight. Anyway, all this rain just make my joints swell up worse, and the pains in my knees just don't let up.

The next thing I know Gracie waking me up. She lying next to me and kissing me all over my face. I wake up laughing, and she say, "I never could see no use in shaking somebody I rather be kissing." I can feel the laughing running all through her body and mine, holding her up against my chest in the dark—knowing there must be a reason why she woke me up in the middle of the night, and pretty sure I can guess what it is. She kissing under my chin now, and starting to undo my buttons.

It seem like so long since we done this. My whole body is all a shimmer with this sweet, sweet craving. My blood is racing, singing, and her fingers is sliding inside my nightshirt. "Take it easy," I say in her ear. Cause I want this to take us a long, long time.

Outside, the sky is still wide open—the storm is throbbing and beating down on the roof over our heads, and pressing its wet self up against the window. I catch ahold of her fingers and bring em to my lips. Then I roll us both over so I can see her face. She smiling up at me through the dark, and her eyes is wide and shiny. And I run my fingers down along her breast, underneath her own nightgown. . . .

I wake up in the bed alone. It's still night. Like a flash I'm across the room, knowing I'm going after her, this time. The carpet treads is nubby and rough, flying past underneath my bare feet, and the kitchen linoleum cold and smooth. The back door standing wide open, and I push through the screen.

The storm is moved on. That fresh air feel good on my skin through the cotton nightshirt. Smell good, too, rising up outa the wet earth, and I can see the water sparkling on the leaves of the collards and kale, twinkling in the vines on the bean poles. The moon is riding high up over Thompson's field, spilling moonlight all over the yard, and setting all them blossoms on the fence to shining pure white.

There ain't a leaf twitching and there ain't a sound. I ain't moving either. I'm just gonna stay right here on this back porch. And hold still. And listen close. Cause I know Gracie somewhere in this garden. And she waiting for me.

The Authors

MARGARET ATWOOD was born in 1939 and raised in Ottawa, Ontario. She published her first book of poems, *Double Persephone*, in 1962, the same year she graduated from the University of Toronto. After she received her master's degree from Radcliffe, she took a series of positions in English departments at various Canadian universities. In the fall of 1972, she achieved prominence with both *Surfacing*, which became almost a cult novel with teachers of women's studies, and *Survival*, a thematic study of Canadian literature which helped disengage Canada's cultural identity from both English and American influences. Internationally one of the best-known Canadian writers, Atwood is the author of more than twenty books, including poetry, fiction, and nonfiction. Her works of fiction include *The Edible Woman* (1969), *Surfacing* (1972), *Lady Oracle* (1976), *Dancing Girls and Other Stories* (1977), *Life Before Man* (1978), *Bodily Harm* (1982), *Bluebeard's Egg* (1983) and *Murder in the Dark* (1983), both collections of short stories, *The Handmaid's Tale* (1986), and *Cat's Eye* (1988).

TONI CADE BAMBARA was born in 1939 and grew up in Harlem and Bedford-Stuyvestant, New York. In 1959 she graduated from Queens College with a B.A. in theater arts and literature; she received an M.A. in American literature from City College of New York in 1963. Trained as a dancer and actress, she has worked with

Katherine Dunham and the Etienne Decroux School of Mime in New York and Paris. She is a founding member of the Southern Collective of African-American Writers and the author of a novel, *The Salt Eaters* (1980), which won the American Book Award. Her two collections of short stories, *Gorilla, My Love* (1972) and *The Seabirds Are Still Alive and Other Stories* (1977), have received acclaim for their critique of stereotypes of black women. She has also edited the anthologies *The Black Woman* (1970) and *Tales and Short Stories for Black Folks* (1971). A former assistant professor at Rutgers University and a visiting professor at Duke University, Bambara frequently conducts writers' workshops. The name *Bambara* she took from a signature she found in her great-grandmother's trunk.

ANN BEATTIE was born in Washington, D.C. in 1947. She graduated from American University in Washington, D.C. with a B.A. in English in 1969. During her graduate school days at the University of Connecticut, she began to take her writing seriously. She published her first short story, "A Rose for Judy Garland's Casket," in 1972. The recipient of a Guggenheim grant (1977) and an Excellence Award from the National Academy and Institute of Arts and Letters (1980), Beattie has taught briefly at the University of Virginia, and at Harvard as the Briggs Copeland Lecturer in English. Her short story collections are *Distortions* (1976), *Secrets and Surprises* (1979), *Jacklighting* (1981), and *The Burning House* (1982), and her novels are *Chilly Scenes of Winter* (1976), *Falling in Place* (1980), and *Love Always* (1985).

BECKY BIRTHA was born in Hampton, Virginia, in 1948. She graduated with a B.A. in children's studies from State University of New York, Buffalo, in 1973. For ten years she was employed as a preschool teacher. Her first collection of short stories, *For Nights Like This One: Stories of Loving Women*, was published in 1983. After receiving an M.A. in fine arts from Vermont College in 1984, she was awarded a fellowship from the Pennsylvania Council of the Arts. She completed a second volume of short stories, *Lover's Choice*, in 1987. Central to Becky Birtha's fiction is the lesbian experience, where relationships between women are depicted as part of a "normal, familiar, and comfortable reality." Recently, she was awarded an NEA fellowship. She has just completed a volume of poetry and is presently at work on a novel.

SANDRA CISNEROS is a poet and prose writer who was born in 1954. As an undergraduate she studied at Loyola University of Chicago, receiving a B.A. in English in 1976, and she received an M.F.A. in creative writing from the University of Iowa Writers' Workshop in 1978. Her published works include *The House on Mango Street* (1984), a book of linked stories, and the poetry collections *Bad Boys* (1980) and *My Wicked Wicked Ways* (1987). She is the recipient of two National Endowment for the Arts Fellowships for poetry and fiction (1982, 1988), and in Fall 1988 she was awarded the Roberta Holloway Lectureship at the University of California, Berkeley. She has taught creative writing at practically every level, and currently she is Associate Editor for *Third Woman* literary journal.

LOUISE ERDRICH, the eldest of seven children, was born in 1954 in Little Falls, Minnesota. She spent her childhood in Wahpeton, North Dakota, where her German father and Chippewa mother both taught for the Bureau of Indian Affairs. She received her B.A. from Dartmouth in 1976 and went on to study creative writing at Johns Hopkins University, where she received her M.F.A. in 1978. In 1981, Erdrich was named Writer-in-Residence at Dartmouth's Native American Studies Program. Her close collaboration with her husband, anthropologist and novelist Michael Dorris, is an unusual aspect of Erdrich's writing. They read every page of manuscript aloud to each other until "we agree on every word." Erdrich finds that this support facilitates the creative process: "you write the draft by yourself, but the other person is always there emotionally and mentally." *Love Medicine* (1984), the first novel of a projected quartet, won the Sue Kaufman Prize for Best First Novel from the American Academy and Institute of Arts and Letters. The next two books in the quartet are *The Beet Queen* (1986) and *Tracks* (1988). Her short stories have appeared in *The Atlantic Monthly*, *Ms.*, *Mother Jones*, *Chicago*, and *The Paris Review*.

MARY GORDON was born in 1949 in Long Island, New York. From the time she was three, her father, a writer and publisher, taught her to read and instructed her in French and then Latin. He died when Gordon was eight, and her mother, crippled since the age of three by polio, supported the family as a legal secretary. Gordon received her B.A. from Barnard College in 1971, her M.A. from Syracuse University in 1973, and then began work on a dissertation on Virginia Woolf, whom she credits with teaching her about prose rhythms. Her first novel, the highly successful *Final Payments* (1978), was followed by *The Company of Women* (1981), and *Men and Angels* (1985). Her most recent work is a collection of short stories entitled *Temporary Shelter* (1987).

TAMA JANOWITZ was born in 1957 in San Francisco, California. Her father is the head of the mental health department at the University of Massachusetts and her mother is a poet and professor of poetry at Cornell. Janowitz received her B.A. from Barnard College in 1977, her M.A. from Hollins College in 1979, and did some post-graduate work at Yale in 1980–81. Janowitz's consciously flamboyant public persona was strongly influenced by her friend, Andy Warhol. Her editor aptly calls Janowitz "mediagenic." In 1981, she published her first novel, *American Dad*. Her second work, *Slaves of New York* (1986), a collection of short stories, confirmed Janowitz's popularity as a humorous, chic satirist of Manhattan life. Her most recent work is the novel *A Cannibal in Manhattan* (1987). Her honors include an award from the National Endowment for the Arts in 1982.

MAXINE HONG KINGSTON was born in 1940, in Stockton, California, to Chinese immigrant parents. She attended the University of California at Berkeley, receiving her B.A. in 1962 and her teaching certificate in 1964. She has taught high school English in California and taught at both the secondary and university levels in Hawaii. Kingston's two published memoirs of her girlhood in Stockton, *The Woman Warrior: Memoirs of a Girlhood among Ghosts* (1977) and *China Men* (1980), have both received enthusiastic critical praise. *The Woman Warrior* was awarded the National Book Critics Circle Award for general nonfiction in 1976, and in 1979 it was named one of the top ten nonfiction works of the decade by *Time* magazine. *China Men* was included in the American Library Association Notable Books List in 1980 and received the American Book Award for general nonfiction in 1981. Kingston's first novel, *Tripmaster Monkey—His Fake Book*, appeared in 1989. She has also contributed stories and articles to periodicals including the *New York Times Magazine*, *Ms.*, the *New Yorker*, *American Heritage*, *Redbook*, and the *Washington Post*.

URSULA K. LE GUIN was born in Berkeley, California, in 1929. She received her B.A. in 1951 from Radcliffe and her M.A. in 1952 from Columbia University. *The Left Hand of Darkness* (winner of the Nebula and Hugo Awards for best novel in 1969) was Le Guin's way of defining for herself the "meaning of gender in [her] life and in our society." During her career as novelist, essayist, and short story writer, Ursula Le Guin has created an impressive body of work including The Earthsea Trilogy, which contains the novels, *A Wizard of Earthsea* (1968), *The Tombs of Atuan* (1971), and the National Book Award winner *The Farthest Shore* (1972). She is also the author of the novels *The Dispossessed: An Ambiguous Utopia* (1974), which won the Nebula, Hugo and Jupiter Awards, *The Beginning Place* (1980), and *Always Coming Home* (1985).

MARY MCCARTHY was born in 1912, the eldest child of parents who were killed in an influenza epidemic in 1918. She was raised in Minneapolis and Seattle by a series of relatives. In *Memories of a Catholic Girlhood* (1957), she explores her early years and her development into a "lapsed Catholic." After graduating from Vassar in 1933, she became a drama critic of the *Partisan Review*. The author of over twenty-two volumes of essays, social analysis, cultural commentary, and fiction, McCarthy received many honors, including two Guggenheim fellowships (1949, 1959), the National Medal for Literature (1984), and membership in the National Institute of Arts and Letters. Her short story collections are *Cast a Cold Eye* (1952) and *The Hounds of Summer and Other Stories* (1981).

Her novels include *The Company She Keeps* (1942), *The Oasis* (1949), *The Groves of Academe* (1952), *A Charmed Life* (1955), *The Group* (1963), *Winter Visitors* (1970), *Birds of America* (1971), and *Cannibals and Missionaries* (1979). She contributed to distinguished periodicals in the United States and abroad. She died in 1989.

PAULE MARSHALL was born in 1929 in Brooklyn, New York, to immigrant parents from Barbados. Graduating from Brooklyn College in 1955 with a B.A., Marshall continued her education at Hunter College. In addition to working as a librarian and an editor, Marshall began lecturing on creative writing at Yale in 1970. Her fiction reflects a strong interest in matriarchy and is very much influenced by her West Indian background, as are her essays and lectures on Black literature. She has lectured at Oxford, Columbia, Michigan State University, and Cornell. Her writings include two novels, *Brown Girl, Brownstones* (1959), and *Praisesong for the Widow* (1983), and several collections of short stories, *Soul Clap Hands and Sing* (1961), *The Chosen Place, the Timeless People* (1969), and *Reena and Other Stories* (1983). She has been awarded a Guggenheim fellowship (1960), a National Endowment for the Arts grant (1967–68), and the Before Columbus Foundation American Book Award (1984), among others.

BOBBIE ANN MASON was born in 1940 in rural Mayfield, Kentucky, into a family of dairy farmers. She received her B.A. in 1962 from the University of Kentucky and her M.A. in 1966 from the State University of New York at Binghamton, and in 1972 received her Ph.D. from the University of Connecticut. Mason has written extensively for magazines and taught English as an assistant professor at Mansfield State College in Pennsylvania. Her writings include *Nabokov's Garden: A Nature Guide to Ada* (1974), *The Girl Sleuth: A Feminist Guide to the Bobbsey Twins, Nancy Drew, and Their Sisters* (1975), and *Shiloh and Other Stories* (1982), for which she was nominated for a P.E.N. Faulkner Award for fiction and was given the Ernest Hemingway Foundation Award, as well as the novels *In Country* (1985) and *Spence and Lila* (1988).

SUSAN MINOT, one of seven children, was born in 1957 to an established Boston family. She attended Concord Academy, an exclusive college preparatory school for girls outside Boston, went on to Brown University for a B.A., and finished her M.F.A. at Columbia's writing program. Minot's stories have appeared in *The Paris Review, The New Yorker*, and *Grand Street*. Her first novel, *Monkeys*, a composite of seven previously published stories and four new chapters, was published in 1986. *Lust and Other Stories* appeared in 1989. She now lives in Brooklyn and, in addition to writing fiction, works as an editor for *The Paris Review*.

ALICE MUNRO was born in 1931 in Wingham, Ontario, in the environs of Lake Huron, an area which serves as the setting for most of her fiction. She began writing stories when she was fifteen, creating romantic tales that she recalls featured rape, abortion, and the occult with a gothic twist. She attended the University of Western Ontario from 1949 until 1951. *Dance of the Happy Shades* appeared in 1968 and won the Governor General's Award for fiction. Published in 1971, her novel *Lives of Girls and Women* won the 1971–72 Canadian Booksellers' Award. Her other novels include *Something I've Been Meaning to Tell You* (1974), *Who Do You Think You Are?* (1978), and *The Moons of Jupiter* (1983). She has recently published stories in *Grand Street, Canadian Forum, The New Yorker*, and *Mademoiselle*.

JOYCE CAROL OATES was born in Lockport, New York, a small town on the Erie Canal, in 1938. While attending college at Syracuse University, she wrote a novel every semester. Her story "In the Old World" won *Mademoiselle*'s college fiction award in 1959, becoming her first published piece. She received her B.A. from Syracuse in 1960 and completed an M.A. in English Literature at the University of Wisconsin in 1961. She now teaches creative writing at Princeton University. Among her many novels are *By the North Gate* (1963), *Expensive People* (1968), *them* (1969), for which she won the National Book Award, *The Assassins* (1975), *You Must Remember This* (1987), and *American Appetites* (1989). Continuing accolades for Oates' prolific achievement in fiction include the Rosenthal Foundation Award of the National Institute of Arts and Letters, and the O. Henry Award (1963, 1967).

MARY FLANNERY O'CONNOR was born in Savannah, Georgia, in 1925, the only child of Roman Catholic parents. Despite the debilitating lupus that governed her adult life, she published two novels and thirty-two short stories before her death at thirty-nine in 1964. She completed a B.A. at Women's College of Georgia in 1945, where she was both the literary and art editor of the newspaper, literary quarterly, and the yearbook. She was awarded a Rinehart Fellowship at the University of Iowa's Writers' Workshop, and in 1946 her first story was published in *Accent*. In 1947 O'Connor received her M.F.A. from Iowa and moved first to Yaddo where she began *Wise Blood* and then to New York City where chapters of the novel were published in *Sewanee Review*, *Partisan Review*, and *Mademoiselle*. In late 1950, when she was diagnosed as suffering from disseminated lupus, she left New York City and moved to Andalusia, a dairy farm in Milledgeville, Georgia, where her mother managed the farm and O'Connor wrote in a ground-floor room. She received many accolades, among them a Kenyon Review Fellowship in Fiction and O. Henry Award first prizes in 1957, 1963 and 1964. A collection of stories, *A Good Man Is Hard to Find*, appeared in 1955, and a second novel, *The Violent Bear It Away*, in 1960. Another collection of stories, *Everything that Rises Must Converge*, was published posthumously in 1965.

GRACE PALEY was born in 1922 and raised in the Bronx, New York. She attended Hunter College, the New School for Social Research, and New York University, though she never completed a college degree. Experience and family history proved to be more influential teachers: the exile of her father, Isaac Goodside, to Siberia as a young man, and of her mother, Mary Ridnyik, to Germany, gave Paley a legacy of political activism which surfaced in her own life in the fifties and continues to the present day. In 1959 eleven stories, only three of which had been published previously, were collected as *The Little Disturbances of Man*. *Enormous Changes at the*

Last Minute appeared in 1974, consisting of 17 stories which had taken 15 years to write. During the same period Paley remained politically active, shifting from civil defense projects in the fifties to non-violent, anti-war protests in the sixties, and later to efforts to free American POW's and interned Soviet dissidents. She continues to write and to teach creative writing at Sarah Lawrence College.

JAYNE ANNE PHILLIPS was born in 1952 in Buckhannon, West Virginia. She graduated from West Virginia University in 1974 and in 1978 completed a master's degree in fine arts at the University of Iowa's Writers' Workshop. Her poetry has appeared in *Paris Review* and *New Letters*, among other publications. In 1979 she published *Black Tickets*, a collection of stories set in the rural South which present grotesque vignettes from city street life and the ordinary tragedies of family life. *How Mickey Made It*, another story collection, appeared in 1981, followed by *Machine Dreams*, Phillips's first novel, in 1984. Among her many awards are the Fels Award in fiction, two National Endowment for the Arts Fellowships (1978, 1985), a St. Lawrence Award for fiction (1979), the Sue Kaufman Award for first fiction, and an O. Henry Award.

FRANCINE PROSE was born in 1947 in Brooklyn, New York. She received her B.A. from Radcliffe College in 1968 and an M.A. from Harvard University in 1969. She won immediate recognition with her first novel, *Judah the Pious* (1973). In each successive novel, Prose continued to balance her metaphysical themes with a lucid narrative style. Her range of characters varies from seventeenth-century *commedia dell'arte* actors to the nineteenth-century mystic of New Orleans, Marie Laveau. In addition to *Judah the Pious*, Francine Prose's novels include *The Glorious Ones* (1974), *Marie Laveau* (1977), *Animal Magnetism* (1978), *Household Saints* (1981), *Hungry Hearts* (1983), and *Bigfoot Dreams* (1986). She is also a contributor of short fiction to various periodicals including *Mademoiselle, The Atlantic Monthly, The Village Voice, The New Yorker*, and *Commentary*, and is the author of the short story collection *Women and Children First* (1988).

LESLIE MARMON SILKO was born in Albuquerque, New Mexico in 1948. In 1969 she received a B.A. from the University of New Mexico, where she is now an assistant professor. Her work draws on the oral traditions and folklore of the Pueblo Indians. Her novel *Ceremony* emphasizes communal participation in traditional storytelling as a means of achieving personal freedom. Publications by Leslie Marmon Silko include *Laguna Woman: Poems* (1974), *Ceremony* (1977), *Storyteller* (poems and short stories) (1981), and *With the Delicacy and Strength of Lace: Letters Between Leslie Marmon Silko and James Wright* (1985). Silko's work in progress is tentatively titled *The Almanac of the Dead*. The author was awarded the Pushcart prize for poetry in 1977, and in 1983 she was a recipient of a MacArthur Foundation grant.

ANNE TYLER was born in 1941 in Minneapolis, Minnesota. She received a B.A. in Russian in 1961 from Duke University and did graduate work at Columbia University in 1961–62. Thematically, Anne Tyler concentrates on the past and its relationship to the present as a means of delving into family history. An intensely private person, she avoids the lecture circuit and grants few interviews. Her priority is to devote herself consistently to the craft of writing. Her novels include *If Morning Ever Comes* (1964), *The Tin Can Tree* (1965), *A Slipping Down Life* (1970), *The Clock Winder* (1972), *Celestial Navigation* (1974), *Searching for Caleb* (1976), *Earthly Possessions* (1977), *Morgan's Passing* (1980), which won the Janet Heideiger Kafka Prize, *Dinner at the Homesick Restaurant* (1982), which won the P.E.N.-Faulkner Award and was nominated for the Pulitzer Prize, *The Accidental Tourist* (1984), and her latest novel, *Breathing Lessons* (1988).

ALICE WALKER was born in Eatonton, Georgia, in 1944. She attended Spelman College from 1961–63 and received her B.A. in 1965 from Sarah Lawrence College. Committed to an active involvement in the civil rights movement, she returned to the south in the late 1960s and there assisted in black voter registration and worked for welfare rights. Her second novel, *Meridian* (1976), is considered one of the best studies of the civil rights movement.

Her works include her first novel, *The Third Life of Grange Copeland* (1970), *Revolutionary Petunias and Other Poems* (1973), which won the Lillian Smith Award, *A Zora Neale Hurston Reader* (1979), which she edited, the novel *The Color Purple* (1983), which won the Pulitzer Prize and the American Book Award, a non-fiction book called *In Search of Our Mother's Gardens* (1983), and her latest novel, *The Temple of My Familiar* (1989).

EUDORA WELTY was born in Jackson, Mississippi, in 1909. She attended Mississippi State College for Women in 1926–27, then received her B.A. from the University of Wisconsin in 1929. Her first novel, *The Robber Bridegroom*, was published in 1942, followed by *Delta Wedding* in 1946. Her success as a writer was confirmed with a Pulitzer Prize for *The Optimist's Daughter* (1972). In addition to her many novels, she has written numerous short stories, among them "Why I Live at the P.O." (1941) and "Bride of the Innisfallen" (1955). The most comprehensive edition of works by the author may be found in *The Collected Stories of Eudora Welty* (1980); autobiographical commentary is available in *One Writer's Beginnings* (1984). One of her strengths as a writer is her ability to balance the "mixed form": in the midst of the tragic or in exploring the darkest elements of the human spirit, Welty transforms the moment into the light-hearted or the comic. In 1987 Eudora Welty was honored by the University of Akron, which convened a conference dedicated solely to her prose. Ruth M. Vande Kieft precisely summarizes Welty's contribution to literature, calling her a "lyricist in prose fiction."

The Editor

WENDY MARTIN, the editor of this collection, is Chair of the Department of English at the Claremont Graduate School and has taught American literature and American studies at Queens College, CUNY, since 1968. She has been a visiting professor at Stanford University, the University of North Carolina, and the University of California at Los Angeles. The author of numerous articles and reviews on American women writers and early American literature and culture, she was a founder of *Women's Studies: An Interdisciplinary Journal*, where she has been the editor since 1972. Her most recent book is *An American Triptych: The Lives and Work of Anne Bradstreet, Emily Dickinson, and Adrienne Rich*. She was also the editor of *The American Sisterhood: Feminist Writing from Colonial Times to the Present* (1972), and is an editor of the forthcoming *Heath Anthology of American Literature*.